TIME
AND
TIDE

Also by J. M. Frey

(Back)

Triptych

City by Night

<u>The Accidental Turn Series</u>

The Untold Tale

The Forgotten Tale

The Silenced Tale

The Accidental Tales, more stories from the Accidental Turn series

<u>The Skylark's Saga</u>

The Skylark's Song

The Skylark's Sacrifice

<u>For Children</u>

The Dark Lord and the Seamstress

<u>Written as Peggy Barnett</u>

Lips Like Ice

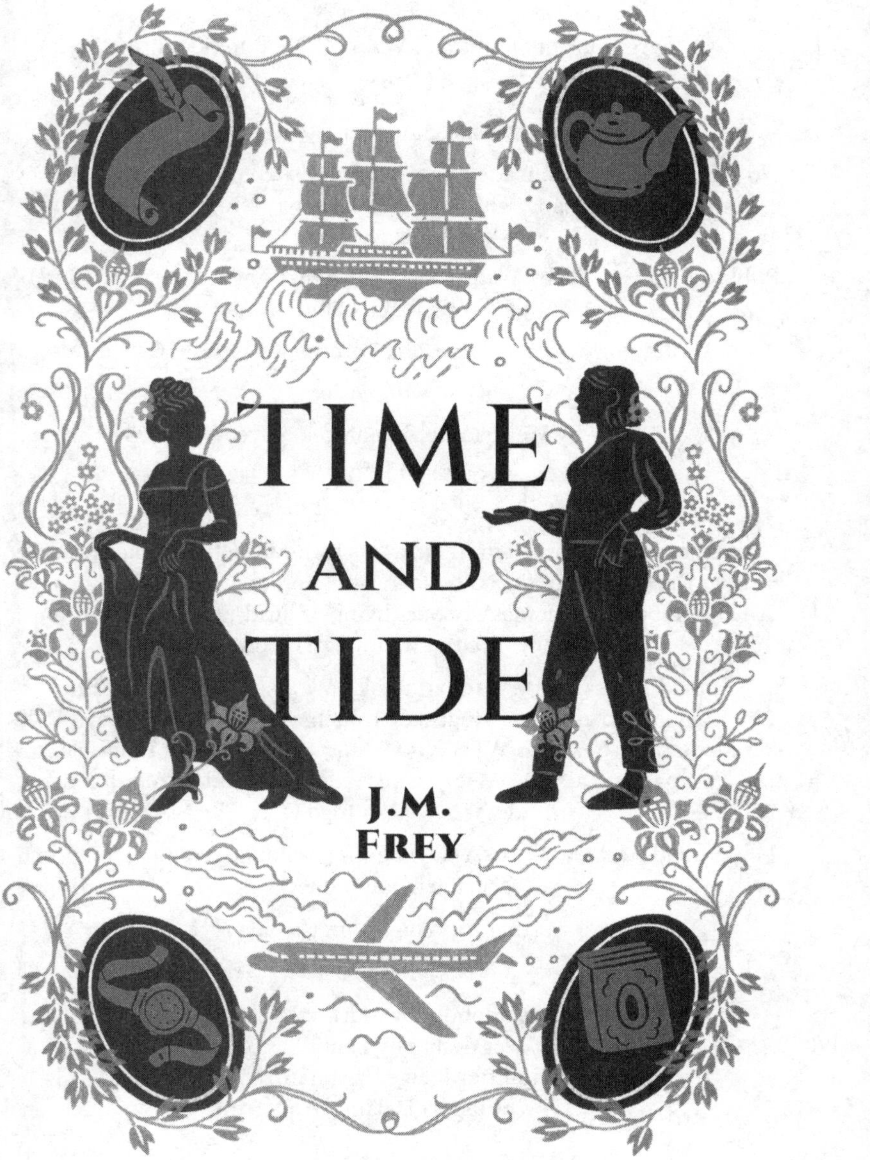

TIME AND TIDE

J.M. FREY

by wattpad books

W by wattpad books

An imprint of Wattpad WEBTOON Book Group

Published in Canada by Wattpad WEBTOON Book Group, a division of Wattpad WEBTOON Studios, Inc.

36 Wellington Street E., Suite 200, Toronto, ON M5E 1C7 Canada

www.wattpad.com

First W by Wattpad Books edition: November 2024

ISBN 978-1-99885-455-4 (Trade Paper original)
ISBN 978-1-99885-457-8 (eBook edition)

Library and Archives Canada Cataloguing in Publication information is available upon request.

Printed and bound in Canada

1 3 5 7 9 10 8 6 4 2

Author photo by Marion Voysey
Cover design by Laura Eckes
Interior image by Skliarova
Typesetting by Delaney Anderson

For all the women I've ever had crushes on, who will never know how much they meant to me in those longing, lonely moments.

"Men have had every advantage of us in telling their own story.
Education has been theirs in so much higher a degree; the pen
has been in their hands.
I will not allow books to prove anything."

—Jane Austin, *Persuassion*

Chapter One

IN WHICH SAM FALLS

If adventures will not befall a young lady in her own village, she must seek them abroad.

—Jane Austen, *Northanger Abbey*

Dahlia got out of the taxi without a suitcase.

I knew we were on the rocks. I wasn't *that* emotionally constipated. But this trip was supposed to *fix* things. To show Dahl how freeing it could be to hold hands in public, how nice it could be to cuddle as we watched the sun set over the Sagrada Familia, and how romantic it could be to kiss in dark corners of cheap Spanish tapas restos. To give her the chance to get comfortable with being *out*. More importantly, to being out *with me*, before she told her mother.

"The fuck?" was all I said, standing outside Toronto Pearson Airport like the victim of a TV prank show. That had to be the reason Dahl only had a purse. Because the alternative was . . .

She wouldn't, I thought. But it was more like a prayer. To whom, I didn't know. Virginia Woolf, maybe. Marsha P. Johnson, definitely. Sheela Lambert, of course.

Dahlia wasn't dressed to travel either. Despite the warm October day, she wore a cute knit dress with leggings, with those strappy shoes I liked. The ones with the impractical heel and the ribbons that crisscrossed over her dusky ankles. The ones I liked to undo with my teeth.

The absolute *bitch*.

I was dressed for the air-conditioned plane, the most perfect stereotype of a bi girl imaginable—cuffed jeans, wavy bob, button-down collared shirt patterned with oranges and teal feathers, denim jacket with enamel pin–encrusted lapels. I was wearing a soft, purple Basque hat, because *Barcelona.* I'd bought Dahlia a matcha green one as a surprise.

She's really doing this to me. Shame prickled hot along my nape.

From her purse, Dahlia withdrew a wrapped gift.

It was book shaped, wrapped in white and pink gingham fabric and held together with a sweet blue ribbon, because Dahlia didn't believe in single-use papers.

I'd told her I had trouble sleeping on planes. That I usually read. She'd bought me a book. It was terribly thoughtful.

A peace offering. Or a desperate plea to absolve her cowardice.

I wanted neither.

Instead I crossed my arms over my backpack straps and scowled.

"I can't do it," she said.

"Clearly. What am I supposed to do about the hotels?"

"I won't cancel the reservations that are on my card. Just pay me back when you can."

"Are you kidding me? Dahl, we're doing this for *you.*"

She rolled her eyes. "For *you*, Sam."

It felt like a punch to the gut. It drove the air out of my body the same way. "I—wha—no . . . *Dhal.*"

Dahlia's dark hair billowed in the stinking breeze of car and airplane exhaust, with notes of rotting coffee and melting gum from the sun-warmed Toronto concrete. If I put my nose against it, I knew her hair would smell of strawberry and matcha shampoo.

I wanted to dig my fingers into it, to kiss her, beg her, tell her that it wasn't too late. She could get back in the cab, go get her suitcase. I could go inside, pay to switch our tickets to a later flight. We could make it work. It *had* to work. Or what had two years of sneaking around, lying and hiding, been *for*?

"I know you'll be happier if you just—"

"You'll be happier, you mean!" She stomped her pretty little foot, adorably petulant.

"That's not fair."

"*This* isn't fair. This is about you dragging me from the closet whether I'm ready or not."

"Baby—"

Her dark cheeks flushed an ugly mottled red, nothing at all like the sweet blush she got when I laid her back against my pillows and teased my hand up her frilly skirts. "Just because you've known exactly who you were since fourth grade, just because *your* culture and your family don't care, doesn't mean—"

"Dahlia, you know my folks love you, too, you can—"

Like she'd been rehearsing it in the cab the whole way to the airport, Dahlia said, "I'm not going just so you can live your fantasy of playing house."

"Hey, fuck you," I sneered.

"And that's my cue." She jiggled the book, where it still hung in the air between us. "You're going to miss your flight."

"Yeah," I snapped back. "Wouldn't want that. How terrible, to miss going to Barcelona with my girlfriend for *her* dream vacation."

"Hey, fuck *you*." There was no heat in her riposte. "You're the one who wanted to drink all the wine."

"Don't need you to do that." I laughed flatly, throwing my arms wide. "Don't need you to do *any* of it, do I? Maybe I'll find some girls there to kiss instead of you. Or boys, I'm not picky."

"Christ, can't you have one conversation without mentioning how obnoxiously bi you are?"

"Not when there are still people terrified to be out. Oh, wait, hey look." It was cruel, but I cut a gesture directly at her.

Her face flickered with hurt. The tiniest dart of regret stung me. "Oh, now we're doing the thing where you have to get the last word. Awesome."

I clamped my mouth shut, jutting out my chin spitefully.

She waggled the book again.

I did not reach for it.

"Just take the goddamn book, Sam!" It wasn't the volume at which she yelled but the tears suddenly spilling over her lashes in rivulets of mascara that shocked me into finally reaching for it.

The second it was in my hands Dahlia turned on her heel and marched down the curb to the taxi stand. She was gone before I had the chance to call after her.

My phone pinged.

Fishing it from the inner pocket of my jacket, I thumbed it on. Besides the text messages from my mother admonishing me to remember my passport and my father offering up an amusing fact about the statistical safety of air travel, there was just one from Dahlia: *I'm sorry.*

~

"No rush," the counter agent said with the kind of saccharine patience that meant the opposite.

"Sorry." I bent double to dig through my backpack for the beat-up leather travel folder that was a hand-me-down from my mother.

I could have sworn I put it in last. Or maybe I put it in first, so I wouldn't forget it?

My headphone wires were tangled with the Velcro strap of my sandals. I didn't even *remember* putting my headphones in that pocket. I should have invested in those packing cubes that Dahlia was obsessed with, it would have—*stop it.* At the very top of the bag was the matcha-green hat I'd picked specifically because it matched Dahl's favorite scarf.

"A-ha!" I crowed, straightening. "It *was* at the bottom."

"What joy," the agent drawled.

Once my boarding pass was in hand, I made a detour to the nearest trash can. Throwing in the hat would have been far more satisfying if it had made a breaking noise. But leaving the felted wool there to soak up the garbage juice from sad, wet coffee cups felt close enough.

Ten minutes later, my day got even better when I discovered that the metal detector hated the pins on my jacket, that I'd forgotten to take my boarding pass and ID out of the pocket of my coat, and that I somehow ended up leaving my shoes in the scanning tray. I got ten steps away before it occurred to me that I was still in my socks, and I had to dash back for my purple Chucks. I sat sheepishly by security to slip them on, then slumped to my gate. I was already exhausted and I hadn't *done* anything yet. My ache for Dahl was like a screaming hamster in my brain, not just because my heart hadn't caught up with what had happened yet, but because of how *organized* she always was. How organized she always made me.

Yeah, and how much of that is emotional labor you've dumped on her? I thought glumly, pretending the gift jammed into the side pocket of my backpack wasn't glaring at me.

I didn't call my parents. If I called my parents, I would start crying in the middle of the airport. I was mortified enough without having strangers staring at me. Or worse, trying to comfort me.

I'd call them from Barcelona.

Then it would be too late to be talked out of going on the trip. I would be in Spain, and there would be nothing to do but have my stupid little adventure without my stupid little girlfriend.

Ex-girlfriend.

Shit.

I yanked my tablet out of my backpack. Dahlia had never moved into my crappy student bachelor, no matter how many times I had invited her, so there wasn't any furniture to divvy up. Dahl had never even filled the dresser drawer I'd emptied for her. The strawberry-matcha shampoo in my shower was a duplicate of her favorite, which I'd bought. Our lives were already completely separate.

We had talked about getting a place together while we worked a final season at the part-time jobs that had gotten us through school. Me at the cell phone kiosk at the mall, her as an usher at the cinema, figuring out how to twine our lives together as we both searched for the perfect first step into our chosen careers. I hadn't been planning to job hunt so soon after graduation.

I had no reason to wait now.

My plans for the rest of the autumn—the rest of my *life*—were shot to hell.

Shot through the heart, my stupid traitorous brain sang.

Shut up, stupid traitorous brain, I told it.

Work in public policy seemed a good place to wriggle my way into some good old-fashioned queer activist organizations down the road, so I distracted myself by filling out tedious, fiddly job application after tedious, fiddly job application. After which I uploaded a résumé with the exact same information. Because welcome to the hellscape that is late-stage capitalism.

When the gate agent called for my row to start boarding, I scrambled to collect all my stuff, which had somehow spread onto the chairs on either side of me.

I gave half a thought to leaving Dahl's gift behind. While I was hurt and feeling terribly petty, I wasn't *that* petty. This book was the last thing Dahlia had ever given me. Sentimental future-me would *hate* present-me if I purposefully abandoned it.

I waited until I was buckled in and the airplane was taxiing away from the Jetway before opening the gift. The ribbon slid away smoothly and I forced myself not to think about how, just yesterday, I would have braided it into Dahl's hair. The gingham fluttered open. The book was an emerald-green, cloth-bound hardback with deeply embossed gold lettering—one of those collector's editions made to look antique.

The Welshman's Daughters by Margaret Goodenough.

Dahlia's favorite.

I could damn near recite the television adaptation, because of how often Dahl comfort-watched it and therefore I, as a kind and giving girlfriend, had watched it with her. (How on *earth* did her mother still think Dahl was straight when she'd spent her teenage years rewatching that kiss?)

I wasn't sure what Dahl's message with this gift was supposed to be, but it felt pointed all the same. I balled up the square of fabric and jammed it into my pocket, annoyed at my failure to *understand*.

The flight crew went through the safety demonstration. We took off. Snacks and wine were delivered. I asked for two glasses. The cabin lights dimmed. I turned on the reading light and flipped open the cover. There was an introduction written by the screenwriter of Dahl's beloved adaptation.

> *The kiss heard 'round the world. The kiss that changed the landscape of historical fiction and queer representation. The kiss that, in the way drag queens have adopted Cher for their own, and gay men are friends of Dorothy, created of its authoress the Patron Saint of Lesbians.*
>
> *In its context upon publication by Pickering & Sons in 1807, in the years leading up to the Regency era, the kiss shared by Mariana and Jane is as platonic as a handshake. By the admission of Goodenough's own pen, the participants in "the kiss" had only been "very firm, very bosom companions." They had kissed one another on the pretense of practicing for their respective fiancés, soon to be returning home from war with France. It is only in later generations, with later readings, do we see the relationship transform from one of perfectly normal physical intimacy between female friends into something romantic, even sexual.*

Once the repressed Victorian era arrived, people started paying attention to "that kiss." And in the ensuing decades, while corsets and morals loosened, queer folks of all stripes were shipping off to the Great War. They sent their left-behind lovers "practice kisses" from hospital beds and trenches. Among the Bright Young Things of the '20s and '30s, "pulling practice" became covert slang for necking in places where homosexuality was illegal. Then the academics, for the first time, gave credence to a book previously thought of as just cult-classic high-gothic romance schlock.

By the time I took my turn with adapting the novel in 1993, Margaret Goodenough's legacy had solidified as the writer who had snuck an extremely queer book under the noses of her publishers, and the authoress of the first sapphic kiss in British literature. While perhaps not as influential on the form and prevalence of the modern novel as her contemporary Jane Austen, Goodenough's oeuvre nonetheless echoes in the work and the hearts of thousands of writers who have taken their own turn with a quill since.

And yet, the greatest achievement of Goodenough's eight novels wasn't her ability to pack so much emotional resonance into every phrase, or her witty, cutting understanding of the perils and pleasures of Regency-era upper-middle class Britain, or even "that kiss." It's that, in an age where marriage and motherhood stripped would-be artists of their ability to focus on their craft, Margaret Goodenough somehow managed to carve out the hours and physical space to put pencil to paper.

And so when speaking of Goodenough, we must always remember the Wealthy Widow, who was instrumental in midwifing Goodenough's work. History knows so little about her, and yet it is to her that the queer community of today owes so much. Without her support, patronage, and (ahem) company, Margaret Goodenough would have likely been forced into a financial arrangement of a marriage, thus robbing herself of the time to write and the world of her eight beautiful novels. And an assortment of covert idioms with which we have been able to communicate with one another about our desires when it historically has not been safe to do so.

For example, "greening a gown," the famous phrase from Goodenough's final, posthumously published novel, for those not in the know, has nothing to do with picnicking. It refers to the kind of stains a woman could achieve while lying back in the verge for a different kind of feast.

For those of us who desperately wish to believe in them, Goodenough and the Widow's companionship was a wonderful happily ever after, especially when so much of queer history is filled with tragic endings and separated lovers. Oscar Wilde was romantic, fine, but as a young reader who slid around the Kinsey Scale, his story didn't fill me with hope for my own chances of finding safe relationships.

It is no wonder, then, that the overriding theme of Goodenough's canon is this: devotion to one's own heart, the loyalty of true friendship, the kindness of unwavering determination, and the slow patience of revelation lead to the most satisfying and fulfilling loves. She was a woman who refused to do what society expected of her, who refused marriage in order to keep a pen in her hand, and who not only loved where she wanted, but, by all accounts, loved well.

Margaret Goodenough was not, by modern standards, what we would consider "out." The labels we'd use for her today—sapphic, lesbian, queer—weren't in widespread use, if they even existed within the context of women loving women at all. And yet she and her lifelong companion were unashamedly

I snapped the cover closed. When the flight attendant arrived with a garbage bag to collect the split pretzel packets, wine-dotted napkins, and empty plastic cups, I tipped *The Welshman's Daughters* in with them.

~

For the first time in my life I managed to fall asleep on an airplane, and it had everything to do with the two additional glasses of wine and the Gravol I'd popped as soon as dinner had been cleared away. So of course, the minute I began to doze, everything went wrong.

First, the cabin shook. It was a bone-deep rumble. The drugs and the booze tried to drag me back down into slumber. But then it happened again. When I sat up, I wasn't the only one meerkating.

"Seat belts!" the flight attendant snarled at some big yikes on legs who was all up in her face a few rows away. "Now!"

Fun fact, my dad had once told me at dinner. (He was a big fan of bar trivia and useless facts, and had a stockpile of them for any situation.) *Airlines install seat belts on planes not to protect people while in the air, but to keep corpses attached to their seats so they can identify who's who in the event of a tragedy.*

"This is your captain speaking," the pilot said over the speaker. Though it was meant to be reassuring, her shivering voice was anything but. I screwed my eyes shut, felt my heart rise against the back of my throat, and tasted fear—tangy and coppery, bile sour. She had been so warm and reassuring when we'd taken off. Now I could barely understand what she was saying—oh, it was clear enough, but my brain didn't want to register it.

I caught the words *turbulence* and *unexpected* and just off *Gibraltar*.

For a moment everything stopped.

The shaking vanished.

The shouting quieted.

There was a soft, gentle *whoosh*, like an anticipatory inhale.

Fun fact, Dad had also once said, *in moments of extreme emergency, humans can experience time in slow motion. It's a neurological trick our ancestors developed to help in times of disaster.*

From the kitchenette up ahead, a streak of intense light flared between the curtains.

It was emerald green.

And gold.

No, yellow.

No, *gold*, shimmering like glitter and—

Christ, no, just yellow and orange, flames crawling up the curtains toward the cabin ceiling. The fire alarm shrilled, masks dropped from the overheads, and I had just one thought as I scrambled into mine: *Thank god Dahl's not here.*

The plane lurched, driving my seat belt hard enough against my lower ribs that one of them popped.

The flames reached the bulkhead.

There was the bright blue flare of an oxygen tank bursting open.

That was when people started screaming.

Another bone-rattling shake. I bit my lip between my teeth and prayed to taste blood. It would be a distraction, at least.

The plane heaved, snapping us into the air like damp dishrags. The seat belt dug into my hips.

I just wanted to live, to experience Spain, to let myself mourn Dahl, and to celebrate the next chapter of my life. I just wanted to *live*.

Please. Just let me live.

The plane snapped hard against the sky.

I finally tasted blood.

It wasn't half the distraction I'd hoped for.

~

Coldness in my mouth. Too salty. I coughed, tried to suck in air, and got seawater instead.

Crashed!

I pawed at my waist but I wasn't strapped to my seat; it wasn't dragging me down. Had I already released myself? Didn't remember. Thankful, anyway. Groped next for the pull cord of my life vest. Gone. Not wearing it.

No!

I flailed. My fingers brushed dry air, but maybe it was my feet. Maybe it was a trick. Which way was up? I hung suspended in the water; ballooned out my cheeks. I used to do this as a kid: front flip into the community swimming pool, crash through the chlorinated glory of summertime relief, topsy-turvy, let myself float near the bottom until the oxygen in my lungs bubbled upward, telling me which way the surface was. A light kick, and I would be in the air.

But it wasn't working.

Crushing.

I panicked, unable to stay still for fear of wasting precious surface-reaching seconds. I opened my eyes. The salt stung. Shadows loomed around me, and I couldn't tell in my oxygen-deprived haze if they were pieces of airplane, or fish, or corpses.

I refuse! I thought. *Anything but this!*

A swirling blot of darkness passed so near my face that I swatted at it. It was a strange and stupid reflex to give into while slowly dying, but the human body is a bizarre machine. The thing was slick and moving fast. My fingers curled into the cord trailing from it.

Jellyfish! I won't drown, I'll get stung! How's that for irony?

But the sharpish tug wasn't the jolting burn of a sting. It was more painful than that, my whole arm wrenching sideways. My shoulder cracked.

The only thing I could hear was white noise—leftover static from the hissing shriek of tearing metal, or the throbbing call of the bottom of the ocean?

The world blurred. I zipped past the shadows now, up, up to where the water shaded from still black to churning frothy gray, heaving with whitecaps.

The shadow I held on to resolved into something desperately yellow.

Dark shapes blocked out the sun on the surface. Oval, backlit by crackling flashes of bright green, the shadow of lacework rope swaying in whatever wind was blowing up there in the, air, air, *air*, *air*—

That can't be right.

I spluttered as my fingers, then my hand, then my nose, my cheeks, my face, my whole head broke the surface. I sucked, but there was no space in my lungs around the saltwater, and it *burned.*

That ship is weird, I thought, and then was pushed under the waves again. I thrashed but my legs wouldn't obey. *No, no! Kick, you stupid bitch, kick! Anything but this, c'mon!*

I tugged hard on the string of the yellow thing and punched up into the air a second time. I couldn't breathe but I could *scream*. The sound was half lost in thunder, the pounding of rain on the surface. I screamed, and screamed, and screamed.

Something beside me, a boat, an oar, a voice: "Overboard! Ahoy!"

A hand on my collar, pulling, and it *choked*, but my head was above water.

"Back to the ship! Go!"

I was hauled up, still going up, ever up, up, up. My head spun and the horizon slipped sideways to the tune of the clack of a rope ladder against a wooden hull. I came back to the world when my head hit planking.

"Careful, lads!" someone snarled.

I coughed, gagged, coughed. *Air!* My lungs burned. Cold, *fuck*, cold. I turned my head and puked; seawater and fear and lousy in-flight wine.

"Here now," someone said. "Sit up."

I let out the air so hard-won in another hacking gag and puked again, vile and slimy. I coughed until I tasted only stomach acid and blood, then sucked in great hungry lungfuls in reedy gasps. It was like breathing through a straw.

I was making a high keening sound, which bubbled out of me as surely as any empty life jacket, careening out of the depths. Somebody hadn't secured their life vest properly, had slipped out the bottom, falling down, down, down, and the vest had gone up, up, up, and me, lucky, *stupid* me, had grabbed it.

Somebody was dead.

And I was not.

We were under a shelter of some kind; the rain had stopped pounding on my back. Instead, something warm and dry scrubbed at my hair. The friction caused agonizing, delicious warmth against my scalp. Sensations chased each other down my spine but I couldn't tell if they were pleasure, or pain, or just *feeling*.

Alive!

I said it out loud, around the blood, the puke, the acid, the salt, the terror: "I'm alive."

"You most definitely are," said a voice by my ear.

I turned into it, hot and breathing, and *here*. Human. A hand down my back. I folded against a warm chest, and sobbed, and shook. So fucking *cold*.

Then the darkness rose up, crushing and cold as the bottom of the sea, and I fell headfirst again, topsy-turvy, and let fate decide when it was time to bubble back to the surface.

Chapter Two

IN WHICH SAM LANGUISHES

Let other pens dwell on guilt and misery.

—Jane Austen, *Mansfield Park*

The return to consciousness was slow. I wanted out of the darkness, quickly now, and at the same time I wanted to stay in it forever.

Why? Are you feeling guilty? You got out of the water and someone else, some poor bastard—No. *Shut up.*

The room creaked and bobbed. I found myself staring up at a ceiling of wooden beams and smooth planking. I sucked in an experimental breath, shallow and cautious. It tasted of stale tobacco. Of furniture polish. Of too many men in one place, like the change room of the community hockey rink after the teenaged boys' practices. My tongue was tender, a cut from my teeth blazing across the middle. My chapped lips stung.

My hair was wet. The rest of me was dry, swaddled naked in cool, slightly scratchy sheets that did not glimmer in the semidarkness like I thought emergency blankets would. These were cloth, roughly the texture of burlap, but with a softer, finer sheet between my skin and the warm outer blanket. The mattress was a sack, vaguely lumpy.

Surely this had to be a hospital. But then why wasn't I hooked up to a morphine drip? A saline IV? Where was the buzzer to call for a nurse?

None of this was *right*.

I sat up gently, tugging the sheets high for decency. Only my stud earrings and watch remained on me. It was a cheap analog, supposedly water resistant, but the inside of the face was beaded with condensation. The hands jerked unnervingly, lurching forward then pausing. Functioning, but no longer at the comforting, steady pace of a heartbeat. The strap was salt crusted, fraying a little at the edges, but otherwise intact.

The world under me continued to sway and bob, and I choked back another desperate whimper as it shifted my stiff and burning torso.

Why won't you stop moving?

The room pitched slightly; I bit off a mewl of pain. My shoulder was wrenched, my throat was tight and the bottom of my ribs ached from the puking, from the pressure of the seat belt, and from the burn of holding my breath so long.

"Miss?" a voice called from the other side of what must be a door. I couldn't see said door, couldn't see much farther than my own hands and the low ceiling, but the sound wasn't coming from inside the room.

"Yeah?" I croaked, mouth sour.

I was parched.

I had nearly drowned and I was *thirsty*.

Ha.

The other person took my response as an invitation to push into the darkness. Harsh sunlight cut into my eyes. I raised my hand to block it before I could think, and whined again when every muscle above my knees protested. I twisted away, squinting, feeling small and stupid.

"Please, miss, do not move," the voice said gently. Sharp clip of heeled boots across a wooden floor. The door swung closed, blocking out the light again.

A few clacks of what sounded like metal and stone, and a spark leaped out of the darkness and onto the oil-soaked safety of a lamp wick. For a moment it flared too bright, too orange—*recycled oxygen catching fire*—before it was shaded by a milky globe of glass dropped into position by nimble fingers. The glow deepened the shadows, insulating us in a haven of liminal warmth. I was able to shut out, just for a second, the memory of what had happened, trapping it in the darkness with the rest of the ignorable world.

The face revealed in the new light was youngish, more or less thirty, and handsome in a sharp-nosed, doughy-chinned way. His dark hair was rakishly tousled. His eyes were remarkably round, deep and brown like a deer's, and filled with more concern than I could digest just yet.

"How do you feel?" the man said, and dropped carefully onto a chair a respectable distance away. He held the shaded lamp by its base, perching it expertly on one knee.

"Disoriented," I admitted.

"Your accent—" he said, but cut himself off. What I had mistaken for water in my ears was actually his own British lilt. "Where are you from? Moreover, how on earth did you make it all the way out here?"

I pressed my fingers against my eyelids, pushing my eyeballs back into their sockets until they ached. It distracted me from the pain everywhere else. "Didn't you see the crash?"

"We've quite missed the battle." His thick eyebrows pulled down into a frowning vee. "I'll admit that we have arrived too late to join Lord Nelson in giving Napoleon a taste of good British cannon. But just in the nick, it seems, to save a foreigner from a watery grave. Which ship did you fall from?"

"Napoleon? *Ship?*" My brain felt too big for my skull, like a sponge that had soaked up too much seawater, in danger of cracking bone and oozing out my skull. "Where are we?"

"Off the coast of Spain, nearing Cape Trafalgar."

Fun fact, Dad's voice in my head said, *the Battle of Trafalgar was the first time the British Navy had formed a fleet. It changed the course of the Napoleonic Wars.*

A war that had ended in 1815.

"That can't be right," I gasped, sucking hard on the air. Hard enough that I gagged, and choked up some lingering seawater. The man hastily set the lamp on a nearby table and shoved a handkerchief at me. I clapped it over my mouth to catch the bile and disbelief. My lungs burned from the strain, from the confusion, from the fear, from the *panic*. "That can't be *right*."

"Miss, are you quite well?"

"No! Of course not! This isn't—" *Real*, I was going to say, but I could feel it. I could see it, smell it, and taste it. "This isn't possible."

The man was obviously concerned about my erratic answer.

He tried a different tack. "By what name shall I address you?"

"Sam. Samantha Franklin."

"American?"

"Canadian."

"Captain Fenton Goodenough, at your service." He dipped his head formally at me and before I could decide if I should dip mine back, he added: "You are aboard my ship, the HMS *Salacia*."

When I said "anything but this," I thought, staring into his earnest face, *I was really expecting . . . uh, anything but this.*

~

As my clothes were soaked, Captain Goodenough sent for a spare pair of a cabin boy's britches and a shirt. Apparently, my chubby figure in my new attire was lewd enough that the captain implored me to stay in the safety of his cabin.

But I had to be outside. I had to *see* it.

We compromised with a thick oilskin slicker over the indecent clothes, and he escorted me to the nose of the ship. I spent the next few hours on the deck of the *Salacia*. A morose figurehead, I was undoubtedly as gray in the face as the weathered carving of the ship's namesake goddess, crowned with seaweed and netting, stranding sentinel directly below me. The pounding rain had slowed to a steady drizzle, the ocean swelling only occasionally, knocking me into the rails.

This had to be a joke. It *had* to. I shoved down the desperate urge to cry. But there was enough salt water around me. I wasn't in the mood to be adding to the world's supply.

There were no planes or vapor trails in the sky. No low-slung tankers on the horizon. Only me, the gunmetal-gray vastness of the ocean, and underneath, behind, *all around me*, a nineteenth century ship with crow's nests and everything. The sodden ropes above me hung like limp spider-webs. The sails were rolled up. Even through the rain the air reeked of smoke, burning wood, and the acrid firework after-reek of black powder.

The water frothed, jumping up the hull as if to lick what was left of the future off my skin. In the distance, only darkness. Above me, only clouds. No stars. No moon. No floodlights, or city ports, or orange glow on the horizon from light pollution. I searched the rigging again, looking for LED flickers that might give away hidden technology, but even as I did, I knew it was futile.

The night was deep, and unkind.

No one could black out a whole continent's electrical infrastructure.

"Stop it," I whispered, squeezing my eyes shut, but all I saw behind them was the red orange blaze, the loose books and phones flying up to crack the plane ceiling, the sky falling away too fast through the window. Then I shouted it, screamed it from the bottom of my stomach, from my bowels, from the sour twisting place all the way down: *"Stop it!"*

The world went silent. I could not hear the rain. I could not hear the waves. I could only hear the reverberating echo of my voice, rolling back at me from across the ocean, from across the horizon, from across a time that was no longer mine.

And then a soft voice: "Miss Franklin."

There was no reproach in it, no warning, no fear. Just my name. Concern.

"I'm fine," I lied to the captain. "Sorry. Ignore me. I'm fine."

I dragged my attention back to him, to the men around us who shamelessly curved toward us to eavesdrop even as they continued their tasks.

As far as Dahlia's historic dramas had taught me, the crew that populated the ship were also impeccably dressed for the era. Some were appallingly young, hauling buckets, wrestling with wooden pegs nearly as tall as they were, coiling rope into neat piles; some were old and grizzled, beards frizzy, unwashed and uncaring, scarred and hard. In between, men of every age hustled from duty to duty, clad in blue and white striped trousers, loosely tied scarves, sweat-grayed shirts, their skin weathered dark and rough.

"What year is it?" I croaked.

The captain, who had been keeping me company, stared at me with obvious worry. "'Tis the year 1805, hand to God," he said gravely, sensing how deliberate my inquiry was. "October twenty-first, if we're to be particular about it."

There was a commotion at the rear of the ship, something to do with nets and boats, and hauling things belowdecks. Someone shouted for the captain to guide their work. I wondered who was steering the ship. Wasn't the captain supposed to steer, or was that a Hollywood trope?

"Please, remain here," the captain said, and hurried off.

I looked down.

In the churning water, scattered like a thousand tiny glimmering islets, were the remains of the airplane. Acres of debris stretched into the mist. No one was lying on it. There were no waving arms. No pleas for rescue. No screams cutting through the rain. Only yellow life vests, empty or buoying up the dead; seat cushions not quite soaked enough to sink away forever; the odd bobbing piece of overhead luggage; a laptop carrier just slipping beneath the waves; a child's doll with its plastic head filled with air, staring with emotionless painted eyes; half-filled toiletry bottles; a bath-time floating picture book; a ball cap; a cosmetics case; a piece of the wing.

Things that meant nothing to anyone but me. I, alone, among these hundreds, had survived. I alone had been rescued from horrifying death.

Sailors doffed their caps at the rail, muttering quick prayers but making no move to pick the dead out of the water. I guess there was enough grave dirt at the bottom of the ocean for all. Or empty shark stomachs.

Among my peers, the bloated blank-faced drowned, were the dead of the battle Captain Goodenough had spoken of. Red and blue uniforms alike were blackened with the weight of the water, the stain of blood and gunpowder, the char of fire. Interspersed with the plane pieces were broken planks, the ghostly billow of a sail still lashed to a bobbing mast, a crust of hull still burning, flames spluttering. The last of the battle dead began to give up the gasses that had kept them afloat.

And any proof that I was not when I belonged would soon go with them.

Then I saw it, clear as day, in my mind's eye: my parents, amid other confused and angry mourners, standing on a beach, holding a wreath with my name on the ribbon. I felt it, in a yawning pit behind my stomach: the crush of sudden loss, the lack of closure because there would be no body, the inability to hold cold clay and press a good-bye kiss to a beloved face one last time. I swallowed against the squeeze of my larynx—the ferocious resentment of ambiguous loss, unable to mark or mourn it, denied any good and final moment.

Just life, presence, and warmth.

Then *none*.

And nothing but heartbreak to fill the ragged, bleeding gap left behind.

A few sailors tried to start conversations with me but I couldn't unstick my tongue from the roof of my mouth enough to speak. And at the same time, I also couldn't bear the thought of drinking anything to make the task easier.

Water and I were quite at odds for the moment.

Just a small tiff. A fair-weather breakup. Understandable.

They each drifted off when I proved to be unsociable. They smelled like unwashed hair and unwashed clothes and too long at sea with only other men and hot hands, anyway. I had been gearing up for a run of revenge one-night stands, but I didn't want it now. Didn't think I'd ever want it ever again.

Weren't survivors of traumatic accidents supposed to feel a desperate drive to affirm life?

Right now all I wanted was to exist without each inhale being a small agony.

Why me?

Why *me*?

Why *only me*?

Would it have been better if I had drowned? Was I *meant* to have drowned? Had fate, or destiny, or whoever was responsible for airplanes that just blipped out of existence, spared me? Or had it been a mistake? The parts of the twenty-first century that were here—so anachronistically *here*, out of place, superfluous, *wrong*—would sink. They would vanish from history forever, lost to the future because they were at the bottom of the sea in the past.

And I should be with them.

Shouldn't I?

I wasn't honestly believing this, was I? No.

And yet, there were no lights on the coast.

If there was a meaning, a *reason* for my survival, I didn't know what it was. I was about as religious as any other queer who'd spent her small-town upbringing being told that people loved me as a sinner but hated my sins; that is to say, not at all. If God—whichever one of them—had saved me for a purpose, they'd forgotten the bit where they were supposed to strike me with divine inspiration and *explain why*.

I kept circling back to the idea that this had to be fiction. It was too much like the movies to be real. Like watching the footage from a public atrocity and thinking *The things they can do with CGI these days*, before realizing that the horror on the screen was really happening: shootings, vans plowing into sidewalks, buildings bombed, *airplane crashes.* The brain short-circuits and tries to yank what you're experiencing into familiar territory, and therefore right back into the realm of fiction.

People don't really survive midocean plane crashes.

They don't time travel.

And they aren't rescued by pre–Regency era naval captains.

And yet, the ship I stood on was real.

My hero was the shortish, doughy-faced Fenton Goodenough. Not exactly the chiseled Fabio that bodice rippers had promised the tumbled maidens of the world. If the captain was the person the author of this surreal adventure was trying to throw in my path, they had seriously picked the wrong heroine.

How long did I stand there, gawping in disbelief? Long enough for my hair to soak through again, wet tendrils sticking to my forehead. Long enough that my bare feet began to hurt against the planking. Long enough that the water trickled into my cocoon of warmth and denial, rolling down my spine.

A low fog crouched over the water like a shroud. The sunset faded into the smudgy strip of land that was Europe to my right—*starboard or port?*

Though the sails were furled, the ship still drifted in the currents. Eventually we passed through the field of bodies and wreckage, and the crew stopped muttering prayers for every cadaver that bumped away under the prow.

~

I woke to the sound of the night watch's hour call: "Three in the morning. All is well."

Everything would be well if he'd stop shouting every hour on the hour and waking me the fuck up. I slept fitfully after that, drowning in nightmares, both literally and in the terrible dreams themselves.

I greeted the sunrise irate.

The denial of the night before had transformed into fury at witnessing the mass graveyard that I'd been pulled from. I was angry at the sailors for fishing me out of the drink too. Angry for surviving. Angry at the uncomfortable bed the captain had given up for me. Angry at whatever that green and gold flash had been in the kitchenette, angry at Dahlia for abandoning me to go through this alone, angry that it was even happening. I was scared and confused, and my ribs ached worse after sleeping on a sack of straw. And worst of all, my fury had nowhere to go.

The little pool of darkness that had kept the real world at bay the night before dissipated in the morning light, filtered through the dirty glass of the captain's cabin. I was still wearing the borrowed breeches and shirt, and I was angry about that too. Angry that it'd taken so long for me to fall asleep last night without the familiar distraction of doomscrolling.

I wanted my own clothes. I wanted my button-down, my jeans, my phone . . . *my phone.*

If it still worked, if the water-resistant case had kept it safe, if there was enough battery left, I could put this whole ridiculous fantasy to rest and rejoin the real world.

I scrambled for my denim jacket, which had been hung over a valet stand in the corner of the cabin, hoping hard enough that it came out as a desperate sob that everything was still zipped into my pocket.

Yes!

My phone and wallet were exactly where I had left them.

But the casing of the phone was cracked, bloated with water and corroding battery acid.

Useless.

Goddamnit!

In my black billfold, the Euros I had so carefully hoarded were damp, still legible but now as obsolete as my identification and banking cards. Which I should probably, like the responsible time travelers from stories did, toss into the drink. I hoarded them instead, the last remaining proof that I was not mad. That I was not the addled heroine of *The Tempest*, or *Northanger Abbey*, or *The Welshman's Daughters*.

That I was who I thought I was.

I didn't trust anyone not to go snooping, so I tucked both phone and wallet under the mattress, between the wall and the frame. My button-down was dry but stiff with salt, and the seams and pockets of both my jeans and my jacket were still wet enough to be uncomfortable. The purple Basque hat, which I could *not* believe had stayed on my head through all of that, was a wrinkled mess. Resigned to staying in the old-fashioned clothes for now, I pulled on my socks and Converse.

Wake up, I screamed at myself. *Wake up. People don't actually time travel. Come on, put some effort into it, Sam! Wake up!*

The world crashed heavily to the side, swirled, and for a second I felt the crushing pressure of the bottom of the sea again, freezing and black. My ears rang. Water poured up my nose, down my throat, invading my lungs, cold and sharp and—

I sucked in a desperate breath of air, shouted, "No!" The world stopped swirling abruptly, and I was rooted on the solid floor so quickly that I nearly fell over.

Awake.

Here.

Not falling from a burning plane.

Not in the middle of drowning all over again.

Here.

Shit.

Shit.

Right. So. What now?

I was alone. Which meant I had the opportunity to figure out how deep this fantasy went. That I hadn't been flung into the past, because it was not possible. Surely not all of the books could be real, or complete.

The clothes in the cupboard, the maps, the ledger, something had to betray that everything around me was just an elaborate prank.

Captains had logbooks, right? I decided to start there. Perched primly on one corner of the desk blotter was a book covered in maroon leather. The log was filled with even, no-fuss handwriting made up of precise nib strokes. The most recent entry read:

22 October 1805

Fifth Bell — Morning — Fair, growing humid, light breeze.

Sails furled as we continue to navigate the detritus of the battle and, according to our new passenger, that of her crashed craft. No other survivors recovered.

And on the page before that:

21 October 1805

Fourth Bell — Morning — Clear skies, indolent breeze.

British fleet spotted. Salacia still too far out to read colors. Wind not obliging. Our protracted call at Antigua has all but guaranteed that unless the action is very extended indeed, we may not make it in time to support Nelson.

Eighth Bell —Forenoon — Slow swell. Gale likely.

Cannon fire echoes back to us across the water. Victory has run up "prepare for battle" and "England expects every man shall do his duty." Salacia still too far away to lend support. How I yearn to be there.

First Bell — Afternoon— Thunderstorm.

Freak weather has sucked the wind from our sails.

We make no further headway. Sky is black above us, clouds arcing with queer green lightning. Some of the sailors have taken to sheltering belowdecks, in fear of what they are calling fairy lights. I am too heartsore with the knowledge that we will miss the battle to offer reprimand.

Sixth Bell — Afternoon — Squall.

Gunfire in the distance ceased. Ships burn. Weather makes it difficult to make out whose.

Another ship has been late to the fight. Being on deck, I witnessed with my own eyes a great flash of green lightning leap between the thunderous clouds, and did pray to G-d that it would not strike the mast. The curve of the water and the clouds can play tricks on even the most experienced seaman's eyes, and the great explosion of fire (as if a whole ammunitions room had gone up all at once) could not possibly have happened in the air, though it appeared to fall from the sky directly above us. I can only assume that the force of the blast threw the hull of the ship upwards, to splash down around us. Thankfully none were injured among my crew as they dove for safety. From the wreckage, I cannot begin to guess what form the craft must have taken when it was together. Lookout affirms no other vessels were spotted on our approach to the fleet. Only one survivor—young woman who claims to be from the Canada colonies. Samantha Franklin. Understandably distraught by the loss of her vessel. Ship's surgeon looked her over as she slept, no injuries save severe bruising around waist, likely from some sort of harness.

And, in the margins of that entry, in spiky, irritated pencil scratches:

Too late, may G-d damn it.

I tried and failed not to feel utterly violated that some dude had "looked me over" without my consent while I was unconscious. Then again, I couldn't imagine I'd have been a very good patient last night if they'd tried to haul me in from the rain for a strip search.

"This is *too* perfect," I muttered, leaning back in the captain's chair.

But even flipping back through the book, there was no deviation from the calm, steady reporting. No *lorem ipsum* to take up space on the page, no repeated entries or gobbledygook to just make it appear to be an entry to a film camera. These were real entries, some with hilariously awful doodles of fish and birds, and they were each unique.

The captain even appeared to be using a cipher to record a secondary set of information, dot and hash marks beside some of the entries in red ink. The red was dark, too, not the vibrant shade I would expect from a modern pen.

Damn it!

And just like that, I was simmering with fury again.

This was just too *stupid* to accept at face value.

There had to be something! Maybe the maps. I knew dick all about maps, but every one I unrolled from the bin beside the desk seemed period accurate. Books next: there was a shelf with a dowel across the midpoint to keep them from tumbling. But each volume, each title page, each publisher's mark was spot-on. Thankful that twice-weekly yoga classes had left me limber enough to do so, I scrambled up the bed frame to cling to the joists and search for cables, or modern building materials, or *something*.

Each failed investigation pissed me off further.

Regrettably, I was in a perfectly executed Downward Dog, pulling at the bottom of the bookshelf to see if it had a false back, when the cabin door swung open.

"My word!" the captain spluttered from the threshold.

Chapter Three

IN WHICH SAM INVESTIGATES

I read [history] a little as a duty, but it tells me nothing that does not vex or weary me [. . .] the men all so good for nothing, and hardly any women at all.

—Jane Austen, *Northanger Abbey*

I straightened with less grace than my yoga instructor would have liked, and tried not to look too guilty. The cabin was visibly rifled, so it wasn't very effective.

Captain Goodenough was holding a wooden tray, with the kind of forced smile that made it clear that he was going to pretend I hadn't just ransacked the place. He set the tray down on top of the messy pile of papers on his desk. Wordlessly, I accepted a cup of tea still swirling with a generous daub of milk, and a hard cookie.

"I do apologize," the captain said, resuming his seat behind the desk. I perched on the edge of the bed. "Ship's biscuit is a poor breakfast for a guest, but we are a few days at slow limp from port, and our rations are otherwise depleted."

"No, it's fine," I said quickly. "I'm actually not that hungry."

Following his lead, I dipped the cookie into the tea to soften it before taking a bite.

It tasted like rancid flour.

Also, I hated milky tea.

My opinion of my first mouthful must have been extremely clear on my face, because the captain matched it with his own grimace and apologized again.

I sipped the tea anyway, because I could guess what a commodity fresh dairy must be after a voyage.

"If you are feeling more the thing, the weather has cleared," the captain offered, trying to make it seem like he wasn't judging my every bite. "It might be an opportune time for, ah, a promenade? Shall I leave you to dress? We can convene on the quarterdeck. That is"—he pointed above our heads—"up the stairs, by the wheel. I shall wait for you there."

"Works for me."

With a bemused head tilt at my turn of phrase, the captain bowed himself out, leaving me alone with the mess I'd made. Feeling like an idiot, I tidied up as best I could.

Though it was warming up in the aftermath of the storm, my button-down was too thin, and my jean jacket still too damp at the seams to be comfortable. I shrugged into one of the knit sweaters I'd found in a chest reeking of mothballs at the end of the bed.

Feeling guilty and revolted and extremely parched, I gulped the now-cold tea in one bolt. Terrible, but my tongue felt looser and my headache throbbed a bit lower. The cut on my tongue stung and my bruised ribs complained.

I wanted aspirin, morphine, codeine, *something*. Did they have pain-killers in the nineteenth century? There was a ship's surgeon, surely there had to be something he could give me.

A sudden thought occurred to me, sharpish and bright.

What if this was some reality show? What if they were filming a movie, or these were very in-character reenactors? What if this was *real*, but not *reality*?

The thought had me out the door before it finished zinging across my brain. As promised, when I craned my head back to peer up at the quarterdeck, the captain was standing by the wheel, murmuring to another officer. The timbre of his voice resonated in my marrow: *'Tis the year 1805. Hand to God.*

Instead of joining him, I went over to the rail and settled my palm against the smooth, worn lacquer. I put one foot in front of the other, heel just touching toe, and then switched. Forward I went, hand still on the rail, eyes on the water, on the joinings, on the crow's nest, in the rigging. Plastic, that was what I wanted to see: a cable, a black mesh cover, a wireless aerial, a battery pack with a flashing bulb. Microphones. Hidden cameras.

The men were doing "sailorly" things, and either ignored me or were so discreet in their regard that I didn't feel their eyes on me. I supposed I looked a sight: strange shoes, canvas-encased legs, and a knit sweater slightly too big for me swirling around my hips as I walked, the shoulder seams almost to my elbows, the cuffs rolled up in an ungainly tube of fabric. They stepped back as I passed, watching my measured steps, then returned to their work once I was out of the way. No one said a thing, indulging the wild creature among them.

I paused when I reached the rear to peer over the rail. The ship cut into the water, peeling out a white wake, no propellors visible.

Back there, I thought. *Somewhere back there, but it's gone now, the breadcrumb path. This isn't what I'm looking for.*

Any other time I would have felt a fool. But right then I yearned. It filled my belly with fire. Good for distracting me from the thirst I had no intention of quenching. I circled around the other side of the deck, step by step by step, eyes roving until I was back where I'd started.

Nothing.

Below decks. There must *be modern amenities: showers, toilets. Cameras need batteries and repair gear. Shows need a director's chair, a playback screen.*

A cabin boy went below, and I followed.

"Miss?" he said, more a question than an address when he found me descending after him. His face said *WTF?* despite a stubbornly courteous smile.

"I wanted to see . . . the chickens." I pointed to a cage against the curving wall of the hull.

But no, the chickens were not what I wanted, especially not when they looked like this. There were only a few in the fresh-swept pen. I crossed the floor, not waiting for the boy's response, eyes on the corners for power cables taped against the boards.

He followed, hovering behind my shoulder, vibrating anxiety. "S'not fit down here fer a woman like yourself."

"Like myself?" I asked, turning to the straggly birds. "There's no one like myself here. That's the problem."

The chickens would make poor eating at best, and couldn't possibly be healthy enough to be laying edible eggs, if any at all. Perhaps they had started their journey plumper, in the raucous company of their fellows. But they were quiet and sad.

I saw it in their eyes: the haunting truth of being the last ones left.

"But you're a gentlewoman, yeh?"

He was waiting for my answer, polite but eager that I should be out of here. That we both should. I turned away, repeated my careful step by step circling of the vessel, my hand skimming the wall, looking for secret passages or electrical outlets.

"No," I answered. I stopped, bit my lip, took calming breaths. No digital screen glowed in the shadows, no lights winked. "Or maybe yes. My father is a landowner. Does that count?"

Fun fact, my father's memory said, *the word gentleman originally meant "man of noble birth and means," and was often used for the otherwise untitled younger sons of minor gentry.*

I mourned Dad suddenly and fiercely, like a fist around my rib cage. I raised my eyes to the ceiling to keep from crying right then and there.

Focus. Find the truth. Find the way out.

The boy clambered back up the steep ladder, no doubt to tattle. I had to move quickly now. First, through a door in a wall that separated the coop from what appeared to be the storage for cooking implements and ingredients. There were great barrels labeled SWEET WATER, BRANDY, SALT, and TACK. Nothing behind the barrels, nothing modern in the cauldron that sat cold and congealing. Through the next door, and I peered around stacks of cannonballs, behind gunpowder and regimented rows of muskets and bayonets.

Desperation rushed me through the next door, to a wedge-shaped room at the back of the ship. There were holes cut into the floor. Under them the water rushed past, just a few feet below. I guessed the use for this room by the ripe outhouse smell.

Turning. Running now. Back past the chickens too listless to be startled as I flew by, into a room that looked like a surgery, but wrong. Everything was wood and porcelain. There were no bright lights, no stainless steel, no latex gloves. I dashed open drawers, flicked up the locking hooks and flung back cabinet doors, rifled the chest. Tinctures, bottles, books with cramped, spidery writing. No surgical masks. Nothing with computer-generated font on the labels.

Through the last door, into the nose of the vessel, a small cramped cabin with a small cramped bed, where a small cramped man startled away from a desk in the wavering candlelight. I had not caught him out of character—he was in his historical costume, writing with a quill, eyes wide and startled behind tiny spectacles.

"Miss Franklin?" he asked, stooped to avoid the low ceiling. "Is there anything I can provide?"

The driving, pulsing need to find my way behind the wizard's curtain stuttered to a shocked stop. "You know my name?"

"Of course, Miss Franklin." He wiped inky fingers on his black breeches. "I am the ship's surgeon, Dr. Begam. Do you require . . . ?"

"Painkiller," I blurted. "Oh god, an *answer*."

"Miss Franklin," he hedged, helpless in the face of my confusing desperation.

He was interrupted by shouting above deck, Captain Goodenough's distinctive voice over the fluting hysterics of the boy: "She shouldn't be down here, and you know damn well that I told you to particularly keep *everyone* away from the lower aft."

"I know, sir, it's my hide, sir, but she—"

"No!" I shouted, not sure what I was denying exactly—maybe Goodenough's approach and his inevitable calling off of my search, maybe that I couldn't find what I wanted, maybe that I was *scared* and yet I felt *nothing*, and I could not make it *stop*.

Please, please, let it make sense.

I bolted for the middle of the ship, for the hole there, for the ladder. I flew down it, feet barely touching the rungs. I hit the bottom of the boat hard, teeth clacking painfully.

"Stop her!" Captain Goodenough roared.

The ocean was loud here, sloshing in my ears again, pressing against my lungs. I couldn't breathe. I put my hands over my ears.

"No," I gasped. "No!"

I couldn't *breathe*.

I wriggled through hanging rows of hammocks and squat cots, elbowing sailors out of sleep. No anachronistic glasses or contact lenses. No hearing aids. No conspicuously modern tattoos or the bulge of a cellular phone in a pocket, or a plastic earring. No outfit that seemed like it could have been constructed and then weathered down in a costume shop.

Another door, unlocked, but only because there was someone working inside, sorting piles of detritus. The sailor froze. So did I.

"Oh." I stumbled forward, fingers splayed as if magnetized. Air filled my chest like a rush of ice. There was a stack of small cargo crates, painted black with just a small *L* chalked in a corner. I ignored those. Not important. Because in front of that . . .

The pile teetered on a piece of sheet metal. On top of it: plastic pill bottles, cushions and a few still-inflated life jackets, cell phones and clothing, hats and carry-on luggage, and the little dolly with a plastic head that had kept it above the waves while the child it used to comfort had no chance.

"No!" I said again. "We shouldn't be here."

There was a window. Sea level, half-painted shut, but I wrenched on the handle, shoved, *shoved* until the wood splintered and it thwacked open. The sailor tried to grab me. I elbowed him in the gut. First, the doll. I closed its bobble eyes then chucked it out of the porthole. The splash was lost in the rush of the waves, but salt hit my nose sharply. Then a life jacket. I pulled the air plugs and shoved it out and into the sea. Gone, gone. To drown like the rest of them.

"Miss Franklin!" someone barked, and it was familiar, but my head throbbed. My eyes burned, and I couldn't comprehend the words that followed. I picked up the pill bottles, drugs that couldn't exist, shouldn't yet, and was too into the cathartic rhythm of my wholescale decimation to check to see if any were the kind of painkillers I had begged for moments earlier.

But I did not want to read the names of the dead patients on the labels. I just opened the caps and committed the rainbow of medicines to the deep.

"Stop!" someone yelled into my ear, and then there were hands again, strong, square hands, sliding around my middle, across my collarbone to hold me secure and firm against a hard chest.

"Shhh," the voice said, soothing and grave. "Shh, shh."

I sagged, locked into his embrace, dangling. Tears dripped down my neck, soaking into my hair and my collar. I felt, finally.

I *felt*.

And it was *awful.*

"It's wrong," I sobbed, one last hitching protest. "Please. I don't understand."

"It is powerfully unfair," he said. The hand on my middle slid away, up my arm, to pet my hair, calming, steady.

"Captain?" I warbled, not even sure what I was asking for.

"I'm here," he said. He bent his legs and I could not help but go, too, sitting on the floor, his knees against the small of my back, strong and supportive. Kind. I gripped the top of his foot, fingers digging into the beat-up leather of his boot. Grounding.

Murmurs around us, men's voices low and rushed. Then something against my lips, a hot cup, the scent of a bitter tea.

"It's willow bark," the cramped little doctor said, crouching just inside my peripheral vision. His expression was strained. "For the pain. It will soothe you."

Around us, the sailors murmured *hysterical* and *brain fever*.

Nobody here had heard of post-traumatic stress disorder.

I let go of the captain reluctantly and took the tea. My hands shook so badly that I spilled half down the sweater, across his hand. He didn't jerk away. I lifted the rest to my mouth, sucked on it until there was nothing but dregs. A powerful exhaustion gripped me. The tea couldn't have worked so fast. It was just the aftermath of spent adrenaline. My limbs trembled, my joints gone to jelly.

The doctor caught the cup before I could let it fall. It was fine china, I saw. Maybe his only fine possession on board, and he had let me drink from it.

I was glad it didn't break.

"There now," the captain said. He pulled back tentatively.

The ocean pounded against the walls, against my ears.

"The sound," I whined, and even my voice sounded wrecked.

"Above decks, then," the doctor said.

The climb into the daylight was a numb haze, each action forgotten as soon as it was performed. Suddenly, I was seated on a barrel. The crew was as studiously not looking at me as much as they had been surreptitiously gawking before.

"I asked to live, but I didn't mean this," I said huskily, but knew better than to expect an answer from the universe. "Why *this*?"

That terrifying nervous laughter bubbled out of me before I could cover my mouth.

"More tea," the doctor replied.

My hands still shook and it was the captain, his doe-like eyes glittering with concern, who helped me steady the teacup toward my mouth. I drank. A blanket was thrown over my shoulders despite the blazing noon sun overhead. I shook. Was I cold? I didn't know.

Oh.

Shock again. Shame. Feeling something had been nice while it lasted.

"The hysterics are understandable," the doctor said. He sounded a thousand miles away. "She's been through the sinking of her ship, and a great loss."

I didn't like being discussed like I couldn't hear, like I was just so much furniture.

"It's . . ." My eyelids were getting heavy. Had there been more than just painkillers in that tea? "Wrong? I can't find it. Anything. How can there be nothing?"

I licked my lips. They tingled, numb. Numb. Numb, yes, I liked that word. A very good word. Numb, numb, numb.

That was just fine.

"No," I corrected myself. "It's not fine. It's October 1805."

"It is," the captain said.

"Nearly Hallowe'en."

The captain and the doctor exchanged a worried glance. Oh yes, of course. Hallowe'en wasn't a thing yet. Not the way I knew it, at least.

I was on board a sailing ship from two centuries previous and I was the ghost. I was swathed in a gray blanket staring into the gray mist collecting in the sky overhead, condensing into an angry cloud.

"Who are you really?" I asked, squinting up at the captain, reaching out to touch, to see if my hand would pass through his solidity.

It didn't.

"I am Fenton Goodenough," he answered softly. He took my hand between his, warm and reassuring. Alive. "You are Samantha Franklin."

"Am I?" I asked. "What would I have to do, to go back? To be Sammie again? Can you tell me?"

A crackle of thunder drowned out his reply. It was in my imagination, surely, that in it I heard tearing-metal-burning-air-screaming.

"Almost Hallowe'en," I said again. "Trick or treat. Helluva trick."

Chapter Four

IN WHICH SAM TRANSFORMS

. . . found themselves on the seashore; and lingering only, as all must linger and gaze on a first return to the sea, who ever deserve to look on it at all . . .

—Jane Austen, *Persuasion*

The captain no longer trusted me. I couldn't blame him, really. From the moment I opened the cabin door the next morning, I had grown a shadow. The boy from yesterday introduced himself as Worsley and herded me back inside. He obviously considered himself terribly responsible and mature to be tasked as my minder. The concern was acceptable. The condescending admonishment not to go below decks again from a kid who was half my age *at best* was not. Neither was the way he treated me as if I was as delicate as the doctor's teacup.

Worsley brought with him a tray with more revolting tea and an overly salty stew thickened with ship's biscuit he called lobscouse. I choked back both under his watchful eye. Only when they were finished did he let me outside.

I winced, shading my eyes and wishing for the sunglasses that were at the bottom of the Atlantic. In the open air, my jeans and jacket were stifling in the increasing heat, which had risen the closer we got to land. But like a knight in my armor, I wasn't ready to go without.

The ship creaked gently, shifting sideways, and ricocheted softly off of something else. I looked over the rail. We'd docked overnight. The

Salacia was now tethered at the end of a long wooden pier alongside half a dozen other similar ships in much worse shape. The one closest to us was charred and raked with holes.

Past the ships spread a picturesque town-slash-fort like any I'd ever seen in film. The land itself was lush. Palms, large leafy ferns, and voracious crawling vines were backed by pastures and rigorously tended lawns. Between us and the carpet of greenery was the port: a bustling affair of wood, yellow-white plaster, and terra-cotta. Wooden docks butted up against walkways frosted with shanties and small buildings for ships' business. The buildings leaned back against a high, solid wall bristling with squared-off openings and an intimidatingly large number of gleaming black cannons.

A conical mountain, like a miniature Mount Fuji, dominated the skyline. It was rough along the water-facing slope, as if at some point in the past it had been ripped in half by an angry god.

The small crowd around the ship was composed of sun-dark and humidity-damp folks in stripped-down versions of the garb from Dahlia's historical romances. The clothing had the look of something worn daily: trousers tucked into tall boots, printed fabric, long skirts trailing in the sand, but nothing that I could immediately pin down as modern. A pair of boys kicked a stitched-leather ball down the beach. A spare few of the people closer to the entrance to the town were dressed in their official and ostentatious best. So many *feathers*.

On the shore, workers hauled in nets and gutted fish, the smell heavy in the air.

"It stinks," I said. "Paradise shouldn't stink."

Worsley chuckled. "Don't hardly believe those stationed here would agree that this is paradise, miss. Their wives less so."

Above the shouts of the sailors on the docks I could pick out the sigh of the breeze through vegetation and the soft, plaintive cry of gulls. It sounded like a manufactured soundtrack.

But it wasn't.

This is real, I thought, the truth settling behind my heart. *There's no other explanation*.

Something deep inside me unwound, my skin finally fitting properly. It had just needed a thorough drying out before I could shrug it back on, my realization, and my acceptance, ironing it smooth again.

A brave breeze cut through the sweltering stank, ruffling the sweaty wisps of hair on my forehead. It was deliciously crisp, laden with the scent of cooking food that permeated the world beyond the fort walls. My mouth watered as I tasted olives and bread on the wind, imagining the pungent goat cheese that they must make here, the heavy beer, the bursting red tomatoes. Or no, wait, maybe not tomatoes.

I suppressed a sudden craving for the fruit; would I ever eat a tomato again? What year had tomatoes first been imported to Europe? I waited for a fun fact to jump up from my memories, but none obliged.

"Captain!" Worsley said beside me, distracting me from my attempt to remember long-lost history classes.

"Thank you, Mr. Worsley," Captain Goodenough's unmistakable voice said from the quarterdeck. "That will be all."

The captain was leaning over the railing in what appeared to be his best uniform. The frock coat was an appropriate navy blue, but he must have been *boiling*. His vest, hose, and breeches were a spotless white, hemmed with gold lace embroidery, buttons, and a single epaulet on his right shoulder. It was not at all the slightly grubby, wrinkled affair that I had seen him in these past few days. He even wore pristine white gloves. Under his arm he held a truly ludicrous hat. It was black, but folded in half like a taco, the pointy side poking out in such a way that it would rather uselessly shade only his nose. His hair was pomaded into a ridiculous bouffant of spikes and whorls.

Okay, I must still have been in shock, because I suddenly saw the appeal of a man in uniform. Well, *this* uniform, at least.

Worsley beamed at his captain's praise. He bowed so low his nose almost hit his knees before he made himself scarce.

As the captain walked down the stairs to stand beside me, he donned the taco-hat, and I couldn't hold back a small, underused laugh.

"Ah," the captain said, replying to my smile with one of his own. "There, perhaps, is the true woman behind the tragedy?"

That was enough to stifle my mirth.

"My apologies. I should not have mentioned it so cavalierly."

He toyed with the tips of his gloves for a moment, his expression suddenly vulnerable and confused. Oh. He was as thrown off by this whole bizarre occurrence as I was. Only he had better ways to deal with it than trashing the loot piles and wandering the ship like a ghost. My cheeks prickled with shame.

"On board your vessel, Miss Franklin . . . your family?" Sympathy sparkled in those doe-like eyes. He couldn't even bear to articulate the horror of the question in a full sentence. Of the loss it would have meant for me.

"No," I croaked around a lump in my throat.

"No one to support you? To miss you?" He probed tentatively, and okay, that was a strange way to ask those questions, not gonna lie. But he meant it from a good place.

"No," I croaked again.

He breathed a sigh of relief. "Excellent."

"Excellent that I have no one?" I repeated, confused and edging into hurt.

"I mean, only *excellent* that I've established that. Not that you are without—*bother*, my apologies," he said with another little bow. "I'm making a hash of . . . where is your family now, miss?"

Wait, was he trying to find out if I was *single*?

Awkward.

"I—" was all I managed to say, the world going tear blurred. "I don't know. I . . . they're . . . not here."

However the captain interpreted this confession, I couldn't guess. Perhaps he thought I feared them dead? Perhaps he thought we had been separated in such a way that I had no hope of finding them again? Whatever it was, he pulled a handkerchief out of his sleeve and urged me to use it.

"You will be taken care of," he promised soothingly.

I nodded and wiped at my nose, feeling ungainly and vulgar. And not liking that this man saw me as something that had to be taken care of instead of as a person who could take care of herself. I mean, I *couldn't*, not right now. But as soon as I had my feet on dry land and money in my pocket, I could . . . could . . . well, do something.

Although it wasn't like I could just saunter into town and buy a ticket for a time machine return trip.

The realization made the tears well harder.

There's no way home.

The thought landed inside me with the weight of the cannonballs piled next to me on the deck. I'd read about a character's stomach sinking, but for the first time actually *felt it*—the sudden, vertigo-inducing drag on my guts. I must have wobbled, because the captain's hand shot out and he steadied me with a gentlemanly grip on my elbow.

I have no idea how to get back. If this is real, I can't just swim back out to the middle of the ocean and tread water until there's another thunderstorm, or re-create that green flash, or hail a passing spaceship!

Fun fact, Dad's voice said. *The first novel to feature time travel was written by Jules Verne.*

A man who wouldn't be born for another handful of decades.

And that didn't even explain why *now*.

If I *had* to time travel, why couldn't it have been somewhere useful? Why hadn't I gone back and evacuated Pompeii, or killed Hitler, or prevented the sinking of the *Titanic*? Why couldn't I have gone back to the hospital and spoken with my grandfather the night he— I'd been too terrified that it would be the final time to actually go and *let* it be a good final time. And I regretted it to this day. Why not there?

Time travelers were supposed to change the world for the better, right?

All I'd done was lay in a cabin and delay a ship by two days. How did that help *anyone*?

Maybe it was random. Maybe people slipped through cracks in time all over the place, here one minute, gone the next, totally indiscriminate and without design. Maybe unsolved missing persons cases were actually time slips. Maybe Amelia Earhart and Theodosia Burr had been whisked away to, I dunno, the Bronze Age, never to be heard from again.

I was, the swallowed-cannonball feeling told me quite succinctly, *fucked*.

"I do believe you've lost your sea legs," the captain said, which was a very gentle way of trying to ease me away from my culminating freak-out. He threaded my arm around his kindly. "In which case, may I ask the honor of escorting you ashore, Miss Franklin?"

"Yes." *Get me off this ship. Get me out of this nightmare!* "Where are we?"

Captain Goodenough grinned, and a pair of painfully cute dimples appeared. "This is Gibraltar, merely a port of call. We must resupply, trade out some cargo, and gather news of the battle behind us."

I looked again at the impeccable dress uniform he wore, then down at my ruined sneakers, my peeling belt, my salt-crusted jeans. Under my beret, my hair was a matted tangle.

"I really, uh, don't think you should be seen with me," I confessed.

"Nonsense. Nobody can blame you for your outward appearance, not after what has happened. We will soon have you set to rights."

"But I have no money," I said weakly. Panic was building behind my tongue and I swallowed hard, but I couldn't sluice it away.

"You are in the company of an officer of King George's navy. There will be no trouble."

"But—!"

"You are lovely, Miss Franklin," he interrupted gently. "Please, do not deny me the admittedly vain pleasure of stepping onto shore with such a nereid on my arm."

I frowned. "A what?"

He dimpled again and for some reason I couldn't stop looking at them. They made him look so much more carefree.

"A woman of the sea, Miss Franklin," he said, nudging us toward the gangway. "A mermaid."

We made our way onto the pier, then down the length of it to a set of stone steps leading through the great arching entrance to the town. There, we stopped and turned to take in the whole of the HMS *Salacia*. This far from the ship, I understood how breathtakingly complicated it really was. And large—there had to be far more to the lower decks than I had managed to search in my agitated flurry. The urge to search came again, the thought that somewhere on board there had to be a camera crew, a modern toilet, a gas generator, something I had missed.

Then I took a deep, fish-guts scented breath, and dismissed it.

I just want to live, I had cried out in my heart, and the universe had answered. Who was I to tempt fate by now being picky about how the miracle had been achieved?

Instead, I forced myself to passively take in the ship. We stood to the side for a long time, watching Goodenough's men prepare for what he explained was its return to England and the colder climes. The spiderwebbing of ropes were in constant motion (what would ice do to the rigging—surely the ocean spray would crystallize?) hauling around barrels, raising and lowering for sails for repair. Cannons bobbed in and out of portholes. Sailors and officers in their cleanest clothes disembarked, saluted the captain as they passed us, and went into the town to celebrate the victory that their navy had secured.

Some of the nods were aimed at me, with a few mumbled "Miss"es. It took until the third officer gave me a queer look to figure out that they were expecting me to return the acknowledgment. The next time, I tried a head bob, which got me an even stranger look.

Shit, was I supposed to curtsy?

I watched the other women around me, stopping on the sand to smile at acquaintances or suitors, and tried to mimic them. My curtsies were deeply stiff and awkward, but soon the little knee bend came more naturally. I had to keep reminding myself not to pull out the sides of my jacket like a dress. I kept both hands firmly entwined around the captain's arm as a deterrent, and he didn't object.

Eventually Captain Goodenough patted my hand and said, "All seems well aboard the *Salacia*, Miss Franklin. May I treat you to supper?"

"I, uh," I stuttered, and wondered what I was supposed to say. Was it entirely polite for someone like me to be going alone to dinner with someone like him? I thought about what I knew of the era for about three seconds, and then viciously decided to screw it. He'd asked.

"Sure, works for me," I said.

The captain's mouth quirked, as if he couldn't quite believe my manner of speech was genuine, and led us into town. We passed through a pale stone archway, and past cramped, rough warehouses and shanties. The buildings improved the farther toward the center we went, until we were standing in a beautiful square with a fountain, surrounded by finely decorated row houses clad with cheerful flower boxes.

The scent of baking bread tickled my nose again as Captain Goodenough steered us toward a building whose swinging painted sign proclaimed it a public house and inn.

Oh, I thought. *A real bed. With a mattress! Yes, please!*

We were almost at the doors, whitewashed and fresh, when he stopped and looked at me critically.

"Perhaps before we sit to dine," he ventured, "a visit with the landlady would be advisable."

Well, what a polite way to tell me I looked like utter shit after all. And to think, just moments before he had compared me to a mermaid.

~

The sociable landlady agreed to the captain's request to "help me along." A few coins whose denominations I didn't understand were dropped in her palm, and I was whisked away to a small upstairs bedroom, presumably her own. I was steered into a seat and the jacket was pulled off my shoulders almost before I processed what was happening. I watched it anxiously, loath to be parted with any of my last connections to my real time.

The landlady only plunked it on the foot of the bed, plucked my hat off to join it, then turned to appraise me like a particularly obstinate stain that needed immediate scrubbing. I supposed I was.

She turned me to face the vanity, already gently untangling the tangles at the back of my neck with a wooden comb.

The person staring back at me from the mirror was shocking.

I knew her, but she looked like she'd aged a decade. Her reddish-brown hair was straggly, her lips pale and thin, her cheeks gaunt, her eyes surrounded by what seemed like a thousand new wrinkles.

If this was what mermaids were supposed to look like, it was only after they'd been caught in a fishing net, thrashing and screaming.

Once my hair was manageable again, the landlady gave it a scrub in a shallow wash basin with tepid water and a rough bar of straight-up soap. Then she combed it out with a flowery-scented oil that slid through the knots, and I wondered if this was the precursor to conditioner.

The whole time the landlady clucked about its absurdly short length—only to the bottom of my ears. "I suppose it's owing to the accident?" she asked, and I agreed vaguely, recognizing that I was probably going to have to lean on that excuse a lot in the coming days, weeks . . . *forever*.

She did her best to twist my hair up with pins, adding a thin white fabric headband to hold back the layers that weren't long enough. That done, I was given fresh water and more soap. She encouraged me to strip off and clean up while she went to fetch some clothing. The water was only room temperature but felt frankly *amazing*.

The landlady must have been allergic to knocking, because she bustled back in on me while I was still standing there in just my bra and undies, the former of which puzzled her greatly. She swapped them for a shift and a short corset-thing that really only went around my tits and did an awful lot more lifting and separating than WonderBra could ever achieve. And apparently for underwear, women of this era wore . . . nothing. I tried not to think too hard about what might happen in the event of a good gust of wind or if someone got their period unexpectedly.

I was persuaded to change my wrinkled shirt and jeans for a simple cream-colored, high-waisted dress with dark beige vertical stripes. I couldn't help fingering the hem of the sleeves, the small ribbon details around the scooped neckline. The stitches were just irregular enough to have not come from a machine, but so precise that I almost couldn't tell.

What incredible workmanship.

But I refused to trade in my salt-crusted sneakers for a pair of flimsy ballet flats that felt like they were going to fall off every time I took a step.

"There now, how handsome," the landlady said, standing behind me to fuss with the lacing at the back while I got an eyeful of myself in the mirror.

I had to admit, I did rock the look. I had boobs for *days* in the scooped neckline, and my plush tummy and hips had been softened from in-your-face curves into the sweetly plump voluptuousness of a Grecian fertility goddess.

As a last touch, the landlady added just a hint of a red cream from a pot on the vanity to my lips and cheeks that made them rosier.

As she bundled up my clothes in a swath of unfinished cloth, she pointed to a pin on the lapel and exclaimed, “How charming!” It was shaped like a cat curled up for a nap, dappled in the bisexual flag colors—pink, purple, and blue. “What a sweet wee pussy.”

The noise I made while trying to swallow back a sassy retort was the furthest thing from ladylike, and my grin felt a bit manic.

“Here.” I prized it off the denim. “As a thank-you.”

“I’ve been paid,” she demurred, but eyed it covetously.

“Then consider it a gift.” I pushed it into her hand.

She immediately put the pin in pride—*ha!*—of place in the center of her own ample cleavage, replacing the brooch holding a sheer shawl around her shoulders.

I might have given the pin to Captain Goodenough if I had thought he would have found any value in it, but any jeweler would know the cheap metal for what it was. It wasn’t worth selling to get pocket money. On the décolletage of the landlady, however, it was one of a kind, exotic.

Before I left the room I allowed myself one last glance in the mirror. I looked *just* like I was about to step onto the set of *Pride & Prejudice*. I looked like I blended in. Like I *belonged*.

How terrifying.

Chapter Five

IN WHICH SAM BRAWLS

> *A lady's imagination is very rapid; it jumps from admiration to love, from love to matrimony in a moment.*
>
> —Jane Austen, *Pride and Prejudice*

I made my way carefully back down the stairs to the dining room, using mincing steps so I didn't stomp on my dress. The captain was waiting at a table near an unlit fireplace filled with clay pots of fresh-cut flowers, with a small spread and a bottle of wine already at his elbow. Apparently his rank meant something, because we'd been seated at the best table in the house.

It made sense: this was an English naval port, after all, and he was an English captain. And I was his not-so-English date.

I had to remember where I was. When I was.

Without losing *who* I was.

And who is that? Outspoken queer feminist and victim of accidental time travel shenanigans? Or is what the captain said true, and I am a mermaid who's forgotten my way back to Atlantis? Or maybe I really am mad.

Maybe I really did come from a ship; maybe we were wrecked and a knock on my head had made a childhood fantasy, a well-loved daydream, become my reality. Maybe my whole life in the twenty-first century was an unexplainable delusion. But then how could I have the sneakers and the jeans, the jacket with the pins and the rectangles of plastic in my leather billfold?

Clutching the bundle of my only worldly goods, I made my way through the crowded hodgepodge of diners and furniture to Goodenough. He jumped to his feet when he caught me approaching, and hurried across the room to meet me. He bowed tersely, flushed and adorably put out, and hissed out of the side of his mouth: "*Really*, Miss Franklin. This habit you have of going about unescorted . . ." He trailed off at my frown. "A servant was to be sent up."

"Sorry," I said lamely and let him hustle me with as much elegance as I could muster to the table, where he pulled out my chair for me. Okay, that was cute. "It's just that where I'm from, I can, uh, escort myself places. If I want."

"Not here, Miss Franklin," he whispered right into my ear from behind as he helped me tuck in. "I would prefer not to provoke more talk."

"*More* talk?" I asked, but he was already making his way over to his own chair. The captain shook his head once, quick—there would be no conversation on the topic here, now.

Who was talking? And what were they saying? *We pulled a strange woman out of the water in the middle of nowhere; she dresses and talks funny; she freaked and threw our booty into the sea.* I could see how that could happen.

"Will you take wine with me?" he asked, even as he did the honors and poured. It glinted a lush ruby in the candlelight.

I wondered if it was Spanish.

He'd already started in on it, going by his half-full glass. It was comically tiny, like a thick-walled jigger on a fat stem, etched with intricate geometric motifs. They were not at all the thin glass bowls I was used to at upscale restaurants. How was a gal supposed to get drunk to toast her new life when the pours were the size of a shot?

Between us, a whole roasted fish dressed with what smelled like fennel and mint stared up at me with a ghastly cooked eyeball. There was also bread, cheese, potatoes, turnips, and some other unidentifiable wilted leaves that may have only been present as garnishes. It wasn't tapas, but despite my dinner gawking at me, the appetite I had lost on the ship returned full force.

I stowed my bundle under my chair and let the captain portion out the food, as if I was a dummy who couldn't shift for myself. It made him happy, though. It looked *proper*. Which I immediately ruined by then happily scooping up the overboiled greens he'd skipped from the serving platter.

"Miss Franklin!"

"What? You'll get scurvy if you don't eat your spinach," I admonished with a smile, trying to lighten his sullen mood. The captain pulled a face that would have been more suitable on a five-year-old. I couldn't help the bubble of surprised laughter. "No, really, the big virile captain doesn't like his greens?"

"Please, Miss Franklin," he said, the tips of his ears turning positively red. "*Virile?* I hardly think it a proper topic for a lady."

I couldn't help a cattish grin. "Not where I'm from."

Instead of rising to the bait, the captain tilted his head slightly and leaned back in his chair. "Where women wear trousers, shear off their hair, walk about unescorted, and say what they like about their gentleman companions? It must be quite a barbaric place, this colony of yours."

"Oh, it is," I said. It felt good to be smiling and teasing again, really damn good, and I wanted to *laugh*. "And the blackflies are the size of your fist. Ladies have to shear their hair or else it'll get caught in pine branches, and they must escort themselves everywhere because the men are too busy burning the Yankees' capital."

No, wait, has that happened yet? Crap, seven years too early.

He considered for a moment, sipped his wine, and then his dark eyebrows dropped into that familiar little miffed vee. "You are having a lark with me?"

"I'm having a lark with you," I agreed. The dimples made a reappearance as he sat back, satisfied with his ability to detect sarcasm. "The ladies in Canada are just like your ladies here."

"And yet," the captain persisted, "your hair is *à la victime*."

"Maybe I really am a mermaid." I shrugged. I was content and warm for the first time in days, and in a mood.

"In de Nimes trousers?"

"In blue jean trousers."

"You are a beautiful mystery, Miss Franklin."

"And I'll take that for a compliment, Captain Goodenough."

"It was meant to be."

Yeah, and that was me blushing now. Jeeze.

He smiled fondly, and tucked into his own meal. I was impressed by the delicateness with which he handled his utensils, and self-consciously attempted to mimic the same level of etiquette. It seemed there was a proper way to do *everything* around here.

I wondered if I'd ever figure out how to do it all.

I would have to.

There was no going home again.

Home. That place back on the other side of the airport security gates. That place where my parents were waiting to hear word that I had landed safely. Or would wait in the future. Or . . . whatever. That place where they never would.

The burning lump in my throat was back. I swigged my wine in an attempt to wash it back down, then covered my trembling lips with my napkin.

The captain refilled my glass with a questioning look.

"I'm fine," I said, preempting any platitudes. "Just culture shock." By the squiggle of his eyebrows, he had no idea what I was talking about. "It's . . . everything's very different and I'm—"

"Alone," he supplied softly. "And somewhere strange."

"A—" I tried to repeat, but my voice cracked dangerously, so I snapped my mouth shut and just nodded.

"You require cheering up," the captain ventured. He held out a hand, which had somehow materialized a pristine white glove. "Dinner will keep—will you dance?"

"Dance?" I asked. I had visions of strobe lights, of gyrating on an overpacked dance floor with a sweating vodka cooler clasped precariously, swinging over my head. Somehow I didn't think that was what he meant.

The captain nodded to the large double doors on the side of the room. They hadn't been visible from the bottom of the stairs. Now that I was paying attention, I heard the soft strains of a string group. I had mistaken it for common restaurant Muzak. But this was no classic rock being piped through an invisible PA system. This was the literal live thing.

"I, uh." I hesitated. "I can waltz. I learned in gym class."

The only outward indication of the captain's complete and utter horror was a straightening of his spine. "Proper gentlefolk do not *waltz*."

"Huh?" I asked, utterly confused. How many period pieces had I seen with waltzing in them? They couldn't *all* be wrong.

"I assure you that dancing of *that* sort will never occur in a civilized assembly room."

I was pretty sure that wasn't true; if nobody was waltzing now it was just because it hadn't gotten popular enough yet. Women in wide skirts with massive butt baskets and men in tight pointy trousers, *they* would waltz. I surveyed the bustle-less wardrobe of our fellow diners—*Yeah, okay, so maybe it's a few decades too early for the waltz. Huh.*

"So how *do* you dance, then?"

"The gentleman touches the lady's hand and they move in the patterns prescribed by the song."

"Oh!" I said. "The whole walking around each other in lines thing."

He was trying very hard to hold on to his scandalized bafflement, but my naivety seemed to be too amusing to allow for the heated emotion to linger. He sighed ruefully, a puffing kind of deep breath that I didn't think men in such tight waistcoats could achieve, then stood and presented his hand again.

"I never learned," I admitted, giving him mine.

"Fist-sized blackflies do not dance?"

"No." I chuckled.

"Then I must teach you," he said. And then, I shit you not, stooped over my hand and *kissed the back of it*. I did not *swoon*, absolutely not.

What I did do, shortly thereafter, was gain new respect for my female predecessors.

I might have possessed the manic coordination it took to steer a wheel and press a gas pedal while shifting the gears of a car, or to type without looking at the movement of my fingers on a keyboard, but remembering all those dance steps and in which order they came in a dance that went on for *half a frickin' hour* was just amazing. And there were dozens of these different dances—hundreds, maybe, each of them with their own choreography.

I spent way more time peering out of the corners of my eyes to copy my fellow women than I did looking at my partner. Captain Goodenough ignored the stares and glared down the worst of the gawkers at my ineptitude on my behalf.

The room was small, just big enough for a dozen officers in their blue coats with their pretty maidens. Chaperons held up the walls. A handful of men with instruments were shoved raucously into a corner, cheeks red with laughter and booze. The dance started sedate and easy to follow, but soon ladies were picking up their skirts and men were bouncing on the balls of their feet, and the swinging turns grew wide and reckless.

The captain, for all his talk of "proper" and "gentlefolk," was just as giddy as his fellow seamen. His smile was unstudied and wide. He was *handsome* like this: glowing with exertion, posture loose, laughter generous, smile unstudied, feet nimble.

You could do worse.

The thought came without warning, and I stumbled hard and careened into the captain's side. He merely slung an arm across my shoulders and steered me back into the line with good cheer.

If you're stuck here forever, there are worse people than Captain Fenton Goodenough in the world to lean on. Hell, probably in this room. I ran an appraising eye over the other gentlemen. *Less attractive too.* Then I dropped my eyes to his hands. They were gloved for the dance, but I knew he wore no wedding ring.

You could love him, I told myself. *If you tried.*

By the time we reached the end of the set my hair was falling out of its pins in sweaty tendrils, and his bangs were plastered against his forehead. The people, the dancing, the layers, and the candles made the air stifling.

"There's the smile I was hoping for," the captain said as we came together on the last chord.

It made said smile want to scurry back into hiding, but I forced it to remain where it was. To be approachable. He had done an awful lot to try to make me feel happy today—dress, dinner, and dancing. Maybe it was a bit shallow to woo contentment out of a girl by buying her things, but I decided then and there that I was going to let it work.

~

The captain proved to be a popular man, and we were kept from private conversation as soon as we returned to our table. We were visited by officers recounting the missed battle, commenting on the sudden and strange storm that had blown up directly on the eve of the fighting (*Sorry? Was that my fault?*) and the somber news that Lord Horatio Nelson, commander of the fleet, had been shot aboard the HMS *Victory*. What happened after that seemed unclear to the men docked at Gibraltar—news was still racing between ships, only as fast as semaphore, carrier pigeon, and common gossip could carry it. Some said he was overseeing the captured ships up the coast, his only injury a rakish graze. Some said he'd been wounded but leaped aboard the ship bearing the French sniper and beat the man bloody. Still others said he'd never been shot at all.

Fun fact, the memory of Dad said. *The statue at the top of Nelson's Column in London faces in the direction of Cape Trafalgar, where the man himself died.*

Yeah, I wasn't going to be the one who broke the news.

Instead, I listened, and flirted demurely every time the captain's gaze flicked my way, and made my plans. By the time the sun had set, I had made up my mind. There was just one hitch—I couldn't, I *wouldn't* spend the rest of my life pretending to be someone I wasn't. Marriage required truth, and the captain deserved mine if I was going to seduce him into it.

When we finally left the inn, the captain gallantly carrying my bundle of twenty-first century stuff, I decided to make my move.

"I have something to show you," I told him, pulling him into a nearby alley. His surprise was so great that he didn't resist as I steered him into an alcove with just enough lamplight for my purposes.

"Miss Franklin!" he gasped, scandalized all over again, and honestly, it was adorable. "This is most improper—"

"Shhh," I admonished, tugging my bundle out of his hands and working the knot open. "Someone will find us."

"They *must not*. Cease this at once, we—"

"Look." I tugged my driver's license out of my wallet. "You asked me about my family, where I come from. See? That's me in that photograph."

"What an incredible portrait," the captain whispered, all ire forgotten as he held the card close to his face to study the holographic finish. "What is this?"

"It's made of a material called plastic. It hasn't been invented yet. This is my government identification—Samantha Jayne Franklin. And this is my birthday. August second, in the year 2000."

My heart thundered in my throat. This was a precipice. Either the captain would believe me and I could back away from the brink, supported and confident. Or he'd call me mad and shove me off to fall, alone, with no way to catch myself. I was laying more than just my driver's license in his hands.

The captain's eyes snapped up to mine, shock and confusion galloping across his face. "Surely not."

"It's true," I pressed, as sincerely as I could. "Captain, *please*, you have to believe me. The green flash, the plane crash, I don't know *how*, or *why* but—"

"Hush!" He snatched my wallet from my hand, slotted the card back in, returned it to the bundle, then took the whole thing from me and tied it up tightly. He wouldn't meet my eyes. "Miss Franklin, you must stop."

"Stop what?" I asked, watching with my own helpless confusion now.

I'd screwed up. I didn't know how, but I had. The time travelers were always believed in Dahl's holiday made-for-TV movies. How had I gotten this so wrong?

"These fibs are . . . !"

I ducked low to force him to meet my eyes. "Look at me. Look. I'm not lying! I'm not!"

His face flushed. He grabbed my shoulder so hard it actually hurt. "Do not say such things! This *story* will not make you any friends here, and you are in very great need of friends."

"You're my friend—"

"No," the captain said miserably. "You cannot—I am already doing my utmost to stay the wagging tongues of my crew, you cannot spread this fiction—"

"It's not fiction!"

"It *must* be!" he snarled. I reared back, affronted. He caught himself, lowered his voice again. "For such things cannot happen. Storms, and green lightning, and strange, fairy vessels! Such madness, it is *dangerous*, do you not see? They will confine you to Bedlam or worse. You spout stranger stories than my sister!"

"But it did! And now I'm here, and I *shouldn't* be—"

"No!"

"Shhh! You're the one who was worried we'd get caught in the dark together, stop—"

"I am a good, God-fearing man, and I refuse to believe—"

"Captain—"

"No!"

I shut down his growing panic the only way I could think of. I grabbed his fancy lapels in both fists, and kissed him.

He hesitated for only a moment, surprise arresting him on the spot. Then with a groan like a parched man finally being offered relief, he dropped my bundle, sagged into my hold, and opened his mouth to mine. The prick of his late-evening stubble was strange. I'd only kissed clean-shaven guys before. I wasn't sure that I liked it. But his tongue, wow, his *tongue*. I let him walk me backward until I hit the plaster wall of the building behind us, and praised my foresight for being so diligent about doing my daily yoga when he rucked up my skirts to hoist my thigh up over his hip.

Heck *yes*, no underwear.

His strong hands squeezed my hips before sliding in opposite directions, one kneading my ass and the other palming my tits, working one free of the stays. He ducked his head and sucked my nipple into his mouth. I groaned, arching my back, and suddenly his free hand was pressing against my mouth, muffling my noises.

Goddamn, that's sexy.

I scrabbled at the unfamiliar buttons of his breeches. He let go of my ass to shove his trousers away himself one-handed. I bit the meat of his middle finger, teasing, and he cussed softly against my flesh. Surging like the tide, he threw his mouth against mine desperately, clumsily. His hip bones dug into my pelvis, the blood-hot hardness of him skittering through the moisture gathering at my entrance, and he let out a desperate, high whine, which I swallowed.

"Shh, shhh," I soothed, when he pulled back for air, petting my hands through his hair. "It's okay, no rush."

"Miss Franklin," he panted, reedy and desperate. He rested his forehead on my shoulder, chest heaving like he'd been running a marathon, breath hot on my bare nipple. His hands roamed and squeezed, up and down my ribs, dipping below the bunched fabric of the dress to clutch at my thighs, but too shy to go farther.

That's cute. Yeah, falling in love with Captain Goodenough would be easier than I thought it would be.

"Sam," I whispered, and pushed my face against his neck. He smelled of sweat, and the sea, and comfort. He smelled *alive*. He smelled like safety. "If we do this, you can call me Sam."

"Do what—?"

Before he could finish his inquiry, I wrapped my fingers around the root of his prick and guided it inside. The stretch burned in the most delicious way—it'd been a long time since I'd had a cock that wasn't silicone, and I'd forgotten the way a living one throbbed with heat. He made a punched-out sound of aroused shock, stuttering forward hard and crushing me against the wall in his startled enthusiasm. The back of my head bounced off the plaster.

"Oof!"

"Oh lord! I am so sorry—"

"Don't stop, *fuck*—"

But he did stop. He stepped in, pressing us together from nose to knees, making sure I was well supported. He wrapped one hand behind my skull to keep it from bouncing into the wall again, and I swear just the chivalry of that alone almost made me climax. *Almost*.

"Samantha," he gasped, trembling like an overeager puppy.

"Fenton," I replied with a smug smirk. His hips stuttered at his name, and I felt my own eyelids flutter. I dug my hands into his jacket, one at his nape, the other at the small of his back. "Fenton. I'm sick of hurting and I'm sick of uncertainty, and I'm sick of fucking nineteenth century manners. We wined, we dined, now let me have this."

"Samantha," he said again, like my name was a benediction, or a curse, falling from lips that hovered just over mine.

"C'mon," I said into his mouth, our hearts pressed together, thundering in harmony. "*C'mon*."

He bent his knees and snapped his hips up.

"*Fuck*, yes," I hissed.

He chuckled into the skin of my neck, hot and moist, sending goose bumps sliding down my spine. I wrapped an arm around his neck and held on, encouraging him to do it again with a filthy little hip roll and he obliged.

"Your hand," I panted into his ear, and he offered one. I pulled off his glove with my teeth and slid our fingers between our bodies. "There." I pressed his fingers to the swollen nub that was sitting up and literally begging for attention. He pressed and rubbed, and I bit down on the fabric of his collar to silence a delighted little scream. I squeezed him once with my inner muscles in gratitude, and it was his turn to muffle the scream.

"Incredible girl," he said and then we were kissing again, his fingers, then his tongue moving in sync with his thrusts.

It wasn't until I was about three seconds away from my peak that it hit me that we weren't using a condom. And I wasn't on the pill. I hadn't needed it with Dahl.

"Pull out, pull out," I hissed. He was almost too close himself to comprehend, but Fenton was a gentleman if nothing else, and withdrew just enough for me to push him back, crouch, and swallow him down.

"Lord in heaven!" he shouted. He shook through his orgasm, hands pressed against the wall behind me in tight fists. I waited until the last spurt, licked my lips clean, then stood and guided his bare hand back under my skirt.

"Now me," I said. "Put your fingers in."

He did. Clumsily, uncertain, like he'd never fingered a girl before—and maybe he hadn't, it *was* 1805, and while I had to believe he'd hired sex workers, it was possible he'd never helped them finish—either way, I was so close it didn't matter.

"Curl your finger up and . . . do you feel the little rough bit on the inside—Jesus! There! Again . . . *ung*!"

"Oh my," he said, as I shivered down from my own climax. He regarded his fingers, the glisten of them reflected in the lamplight. "I did not know women could do that."

I grinned slowly, purposefully.

"There's a lot I bet you don't know, Fenton," I said, leaning up to whisper in his ear. "Luckily, I'm a very patient teacher."

He grinned fit to match mine, cleaned up with a handkerchief, tucked himself away, and straightened his clothing. I only had to smooth down my skirt. Yup, there were some advantages to this century after all.

Fenton's hands lingered on my bundle as he fetched it up. He stared into my face for a moment, searching for . . . *something.*

"You do believe me, don't you?" I asked, desperate for confirmation. For the promise of *safety* I'd just offered myself up for.

Fenton licked his lips, still pink and glossy, but did not answer.

That was fine. It wasn't a no, and I could work with that. I could get him there.

He crooked his arm. "I believe it's time we returned to the ship. Come, Miss Franklin."

"Already did," I bandied back, but wrapped my arm around his all the same.

~

We were most of the way up the pier, and I was feeling quite smug about my ability to snag myself a man. I didn't know what all those ballroom debutants stressed about in the romances—all I'd needed was a bit of good, old-fashioned "charm." Dudes thought with their little heads in this era just as much as in mine.

I was about to suggest a repeat performance as soon as we got back to Fenton's cabin when a flash of something silver in the moonlight caught my attention.

The knife it danced along was small but edged in a wicked blade.

"So 'ere's the mermaid, then?" the wielder asked, stepping into our path from the deep shadows cast by a pile of barrels. By his clothing I guessed he was a bilge rat from the lowest part of a ship.

"Beggin' yer pardon, Cap'n," another man said, crowding up behind us. I hadn't heard him approach, and I whipped around to look at him. He was just as grimy, and flashed a similar knife. He had less hair than his compatriot, but more teeth.

"Out of my way, *sailor*," Fenton ordered. He shifted onto the balls of his feet. I slipped my hand out from around his elbow, freeing his arms for movement.

"Beggin' yer pardon, Cap'n," the second man said again, "but t'aint good luck to bring no woman on board, 'specially one that was pulled out of the water."

"I'm not a mermaid." I pulled the hem of my dress up. "See? Feet!"

"Miss Franklin, *hush*," Fenton entreated. "You are not helping matters."

Neither sailor concerned themselves with the scientific evidence of my nonfishyness.

"T'aint *right*, Cap'n," the first man insisted.

"Nor is your insistence on this foolishness," Fenton snapped. I understood, all at once, why Fenton feared "talk." His hand dropped to the pommel of his sword. He had been wearing it all day, but until now I had regarded it as simply an ornament. It occurred to me that the sword was real, and that Fenton was trained to fight with it.

"We've had enough bad luck, Cap'n!" the second man insisted. "No prizes, the salvage gone, and then Lord Nelson . . . ! It's her fault, can you not see? We stopped an' picked 'er up and *he*—"

"Enough!" Fenton roared. "Miss Franklin is a woman in distress and it is our obligation to see her delivered safely into the arms of her family."

He seemed to conveniently forget that I had twice admitted that I had no family to be delivered to. Was it that he fundamentally misunderstood, or was it a show for our assailants?

"Oh, she'll be delivered owl'ight," the thug closest to me said, his curving grin matching the angle of his blade. "Right back to where she came from."

"No!" I cried, but I was too slow, the other man too fast. Fenton lunged but the knife was coming at him already.

It was aimed at his face. Stupid blind instinct, the same one that had made me clutch the rising life jacket, made me throw out an arm to protect him.

The blade sliced through the thick, fatty flesh on the underside of it, near my armpit. The bone in my arm juddered as the knife struck, an agony like I'd never *imagined*. I'd never broken a bone before; was this what it felt like?

I screamed. Blood splattered on my face. It was more the abrupt shock of being *stabbed* than the pain itself that made me jerk backward.

The slickness of the blood spurting up the handle, or my cry, or the surprise of my movement made the sailor lose his grip on the knife. I fell back, crashing to the planking of the pier, clutching my elbow.

There was a goddamned *knife* sticking out of my arm!

Fenton launched himself into the fight. A knife doesn't have near the reach of a sword, and the man behind us let forth a pained yelp as Fenton's blade literally cut the weapon out of the second man's fingers. He clutched his hand in a gruesome mirror of my own agony.

"Cursed mermaid! Back to the devil with ye!" the man who'd stabbed me snarled. He threw his knees into my stomach, rough hands curling around my throat, driving my head back against the planking.

I gurgled, like I really was a thing from under the sea. Crushing blackness dove over my senses, and I was under the water again, drowning, kicking, drowning, fighting, *drowning* . . .

Shouting from the ship, feet on the pier, and the guy with his fingers digging into my windpipe suddenly went limp. He slumped, a floppy dead weight on top of me.

"Get him off!" I shrilled, lungs burning.

He was rolled off, faceup and sightless. More than just a dead weight. *Actually* dead.

"Oh god." I gulped.

Begam pushed through the crowd of our rescuers. Before I understood what he meant to do, he was already extracting the knife from my arm. In my agony, I wished desperately for the unconsciousness that had been so tantalizingly close just seconds earlier.

I clamped down obligingly on a roll of leather someone stuffed into my mouth; better to chomp on it than my own tongue in my frothing torment. Above me, around me, I heard angry shouts, felt the stomp of booted feet against the planks, was choked by the nauseating pain and the dizzying bob of handheld lanterns.

Fenton hovered in and out of my view, blocking out the stars far above my nose with his flushed face and furious snarls. Beside him, Worsley was plucking at his sleeve.

Fenton finally turned his glittering, furious gaze to the lad. *"Yes?"* he snarled.

"It's Lord Nelson," Worsley said, nervous now that the captain's wrath was aimed at him.

But Fenton was in no mood for hesitancy. "What *about* him?"

"We got word just now, sir," the lad whispered, voice dipping low and sodden with sorrow. "Vice-Admiral Horatio Nelson, sir . . . he's *dead*."

Chapter Six

IN WHICH SAM ARRIVES

> *Ah! My poor dear child the truth is, that in London it is always a sickly season. Nobody is healthy in London, nobody can be.*
>
> —Jane Austen, *Emma*

Pain. And a pulling at my throat that I thought was a scream that had gone on too long. Burning in the corners of my eyes where tears had dried into an irritating itch. Too damn hot. I kicked the covers with my legs, trying to get them off, off, but someone kept putting them back on, wrapped up to my ears, tight around my neck, scratchy and constricting.

". . . lucky the bone isn't broken . . ."

". . . some of the knife broke off in the flesh . . ."

". . . make her sweat it out . . ." someone said, but all I wanted was a goddamn ice pack and a few hours of sleep.

"Fever," said someone else, and I seized on the voice. I knew it. *'Tis the year 1805, my hand to God.*

"People died of fevers in 1805," I crackled, and it didn't sound like a sob, it didn't. I was parched. Didn't invalids get ice chips? "I had a flu shot."

"Shot?"

"And Hep A and B, and the new COVID variant! My arms looked like a corkboard. I'm going to *Barcelona*," I said, lips dry and numb. I wanted ChapStick, but even that small convenience was lost. "I'm going to drink Spanish wine and make love to a Spanish woman. I can't die of a fever!"

"She's delirious," the voice that was mine said, apologetically. Familiar. Comforting voice. I wanted it, turned my face toward it, seeking it. "Pay no heed, she does not mean what she says. More tea, I think, Doctor."

Something hot and wet at my lips. Astringent.

Soothing.

I swirled back down into blackness.

~

I lost the first half of November in the grip of tinctures of opium in gin with what little breakfast I could keep down, and laudanum with dinner. The world throbbed gray around the edges, boarded and measured in bouts of shivering frigidity and sweltering heat. I was lucid in spells, mostly when Begam arrived for my wound's daily bathing in boiled water and rum. I don't know how sensible I was when I moaned about antiseptic, iodine, penicillin. But he gave in to my babbling demands to run his steel through the flame, to wash his hands with carbolic soap, to use boiled rags when the wound turned inflamed and he had to cut putrid flesh away. They didn't stitch it shut, in order to actively monitor the flesh for gangrene, and the smell was so revolting that I heaved every time it was uncovered. Not because of the rot, but because of the—and I am absolutely one thousand percent serious—*the moldy Roquefort cheese* they packed it with to prevent infection.

Early penicillin, baby. They didn't know why it worked, only that it did.

It smelled like day-old baby vomit.

Luckily, bandages covered the horrid sight and most of the reek the rest of the time. But it didn't do my digestion any favors. I lived on a diet of thin tea and milk-soaked ship's biscuits. I couldn't keep anything else down.

Fun fact! Tea is a diuretic! my dad's voice warned me every time I refused water. I had already sworn never to drink water ever again. Even the fact that it was laced with lime juice to prevent scurvy wasn't enough for my PTSD to distinguish it from the gush of saltwater on my palette.

The back half of November was swallowed by depression.

I'd never been injured or severely traumatized before, but my cousin had been in a car crash when we were both in our teens. She'd been lucky and only shattered her hip, but as the reconstructive surgeries and recovery had kept her bed bound for months, she'd fallen further and further into the grip of what she called "steel wool days." Days when every thought scratched, every touch was abrasive, and every attempt to cheer her was met with resentment for needing the cheering in the first place.

Post-trauma depression was *absolutely* a real thing, but knowing so didn't help me avoid it.

Fenton hovered and fretted, and read to me at night while I lay there and tried not to relive the flash of the knife coming toward me, or remember that someone had tried very hard to kill me and had almost succeeded.

Around the beginning of December I began to spend more time awake than asleep. The wound had closed, extremely slowly, but I hadn't had the courage to look at it. It hurt enough to make my eyes water whenever I moved my arm, the internal scars pulling and burning. And the smell of my own unwashed hair drove me out of my mind. But the journey northward meant that we could no longer air out the cabin by opening the windows without freezing.

Fenton, who had long since removed himself to sleep among his officers, wrinkled his nose through our daily afternoon visit. When I mentioned the desire to be clean, he suggested perhaps I would appreciate a more thorough bath than the previous wipe downs he'd helped with up until now.

"You have a tub?"

"A small one, and enough collected rainwater to offer you a

comfortable toilette," Fenton said. "I'd have offered sooner, but your aversion to water . . ."

"You'll stay, won't you? I don't think I could do it one-handed and I'm afraid that—" I felt stupid and childish for asking, but thought it would be more childish still to suffer in silence. "You'll make sure my head doesn't go under?"

Fenton nodded solemnly. "Of course. It's a shame it's so frigid out—we could have let you hose off with the lads, if you were feeling sprightly enough."

"Now who's being vulgar?" I teased, delighted that he'd made a saucy joke.

His answering smile made it clear that he was equally delighted that I was feeling well enough for my own cheek.

I had missed him. This confident and flirty version of him, I mean.

He'd visited daily, but rarely touched me, either for fear of propriety in front of Begum or of hurting me further. We'd talked but conversation had been stilted, and mostly about either my injury or the men who had tried to kill me out of superstitious revenge for the death of Lord Nelson. He never asked me, but I could tell that my prebonking confession still bothered him. For all we'd danced around the topic when I was high off my face on painkillers, neither of us had the balls to confront the terrifying truth of it head-on.

That there *was* no explanation for it.

I had told Fenton I was from two hundred years in the future, and he had no idea what to think about that. More than once I had awoken from a drug-fueled nap to find him inspecting one of my ID cards. He never apologized that he'd taken it, but he always returned it to my wallet and tucked it back under my pillow immediately.

"Speaking of vulgar," he said with a casualness that meant whatever he was about to say was absolutely rehearsed, "what did you mean when you said you were going to Barcelona to make love to a woman?"

I batted my eyelashes at Fenton theatrically. "Why, Captain," I said huskily, pouting like a starlet. "I taught you what to do with your hand. Where did you think I learned it?"

The sight of a Georgian-era naval captain rolling his eyes like an unimpressed teenager was amazing. Instead of answering right away, he rose to relay the request for the tub to Worsley, who lingered outside the door. When he came back, he had a thoughtful look on his face.

"And this is another thing that you are permitted to do, when you are from? Wear trousers, and style your hair short, and make love to a woman as if you are a man?"

When you are from.

"Yes," I choked out, startled by his phrasing. Surprise, fear, relief, gratitude churned through me in waves. "Though, you know, I don't have to pretend to be a dude to do it. I still get to be me. I can be a woman who loves men, *and* a woman who loves women."

Fenton had no reply to that, needing the time to digest it.

I tried to give it to him, but couldn't help asking: "You believe me, then?"

"I—" he began, then hesitated. "I believe that *you* believe it."

The tidal wave of emotion solidified into a leaden lump of disappointment.

It's a start, I consoled myself. I rarely allowed myself to consider what my life might look like after I'd seduced Fenton to the altar, mortified enough by the smug self-congratulations I'd been wallowing in before we'd been attacked. One day he *would* believe me. I didn't know how I'd make it happen, but I had a lifetime to figure it out.

The arrival of the tub and a parade of sailors with buckets of steaming water prevented any further conversation. Fenton stood between the door and the bunk to hide me from view in my state, and made good on his promise to help me undress and wash. The tenderness with which he cradled my skull as he poured clean water over my soapy hair made my lungs clench with affection.

I was aware that I had probably imprinted on Fenton like a baby duckling, what with him being heroic and handsome.

Fun fact! It's called Florence Nightingale effect when a caregiver falls in love with their patient, and de Clérambault's syndrome when the patient falls in love with their caregiver.

So what if it was just transference? It felt real. And his gentle attention made it clear that I'd picked a good one.

Once the rest of me was scrubbed fresh, he unwrapped the bandages with gentle deliberation and helped me lay my right arm on the rim of the tub for support. When he noticed that I had my eyes screwed shut he said: "It's not terrible."

"I can't—"

"You cannot avoid it forever. Come now."

He sounded so *reasonable* admonishing me that I couldn't help but do as he asked. The wound had healed into a vee-shaped pucker of pitted, angry red skin about two inches south of my armpit, on the underside of my arm. The galaxy of purple-blue-green from the bone-bruise was only now clearing up.

"If the knife had not caught your arm, it very well may have gone straight into your heart," Fenton said gently, running soapy fingers around the sensitive skin around the scar. I shivered.

"Or *your* face," I added. "This is the better outcome. Only time my goddamn bat wings were good for anything." I forced out a laugh. "I'll never get angry about too-tight sleeves ever again."

Fenton disapproved of my gallows humor.

I'll need help until I'm back on my feet. Yoga will help, I just need to start up again. But it may never heal completely. Adrenaline, clear and sharp, raced down my veins. *I'll need servants. A husband. Maybe for the rest of my life. I need him. I need to make him stay.*

"Help me clean my teeth," I said urgently.

Fenton pulled back, dark eyebrows doing that adorable squiggly thing they did when he couldn't follow my conversation.

"So I can kiss you," I explained. "And then, if we go very slow, I can show you what else sleeping with women has taught me."

Fenton helped me clean my teeth.

~

The wind was bitter by the time we reached Britannia's famous white cliffs, and ice clung to the rigging like lichen. I watched the whole process from what had become, over the last week, "my spot" at the nose of the ship. I'd taken up residence as a second, silent figurehead, desperate to escape the close fetid air of my sickroom no matter how many wooly socks and sweaters I had to pilfer to do so.

I had stopped scanning for planes or long-slung tankers weeks ago. Now I just stared in the direction of England and wondered what our life would be like once we arrived.

Traversing the Thames took several days, what with the way the other naval vessels were crammed into the channel, and it was New Year's Day by the time our ship tiptoed into the Royal Navy Dockyard in London.

The other ships docked were similar in design and size, but far worse for the battle they'd suffered through. In that we were lucky.

One vessel was draped with stately swags of black cloth.

"There," Fenton murmured, indicating the black-festooned ship. He pressed closer to my side than was probably appropriate to keep our conversation private from the sailors scurrying around the deck. His right hand rested lightly on the back of my left one, where no one behind us could see it. His index finger slid along my pinkie every time he wanted to direct my attention to something he pointed out. It felt ridiculously *intimate*, especially considering what we'd done in that alleyway. "That is the HMS *Victory*, upon which Lord Nelson was returned to his people.

And there, the HMS *Pickle*, which brought the sad news of his death ahead of his arrival."

He sounded genuinely sorrowful.

Every man on the ship seemed affected, many stopping to doff their wool caps at the ships. I wondered what kind of miraculous, charismatic man this Nelson had been to inspire such unrivaled loyalty from his sailors, even down to the lowly Worsley. The lad had been openly weeping when Fenton had charged him with a rather large bundle of letters to be delivered to the dockyard's postmaster.

"I thought you guys did burials at sea," I asked, confused.

Fenton shifted a bit, slightly uncomfortable as always at my bluntness. "Lord Nelson is a national hero. He deserved to be returned home."

"Ah," I said. "But he . . . wouldn't he have gone bad?"

"His remains were transported in a cask of brandy."

Good thing the ships weren't the other way around, or he'd have been pickled on the Pickle, I thought.

I didn't say it, though. I'd already offended the deceased but greatly loved hero enough for one conversation.

The bobbing that I had become so accustomed to had ceased now that we were in port, and beyond the warehouses on the wharves, the skyline of the London I knew was absent. Big Ben wasn't there, and I couldn't quite figure out why that surprised me. Instead, there was a gaping hole where it should have been standing proudly and sticking its metaphorical tongue out at me, chiming out *nyah nyah, I exist* on every hour.

But here I was.

And here Big Ben wasn't.

I felt wild, off kilter, like a soap bubble about to pop.

"And what now, Captain Goodenough?" I asked.

"Now, we buy you a dress for a funeral," he said earnestly.

"You can't keep buying things for me." My modern sensibilities squirmed again. How on earth did Georgian-era women put up with the men having total control over their money and their lives?

Guess I would find out.

"Then you are in possession of coin that I was previously unaware of?" Fenton asked with that familiar raised eyebrow and sly smile.

I shook my head, but even that was redundant. He knew I was broke.

"I do not mind providing for you, Miss Franklin," he said with a meaningful rumble. "It is a *pleasurable* duty." The tips of his ears went red again. They'd been doing that a lot lately.

"I'm glad you said that," I bandied back. "I was afraid you were going to use a different adjective there. *Annoying, uncouth, revolting.*"

"You could never be revolting," he whispered, carefully kissing the back of my hand, lips warm in the chilly winter air. One of his fingers brushed the sensitive underside of my naked wrist.

I shivered. This time it wasn't from the cold.

There was something gratifying about this slow courtship. It was nothing like letting someone buy you a drink, giving them bedroom eyes, then going back to theirs to screw. Even if we *were* screwing. This was thoughtful, patient, and considerate. Fenton honestly and truly *cared* about my comfort, my choices, my conversation. He knew me—as well as anyone could be themselves after such trauma—and he *liked* me.

Truth was, I liked him too. Good thing, considering I planned to marry him. He looked soft and frankly kind of pretty to be a naval man, but when he was snapping orders around the deck, there was a flash and fire to him that was sexy.

I used his grip on my hand to reel him a bit closer, standing up on my toes to press a kiss to his cheek, which was as much as I dared in public. I really wanted to go for his lips, that pretty bow-shaped pout, but it was too forward.

I might have had no conceivable way home, and my ability to manage on my own was in question, but at least I had a companion other people respected, who was in turn an honorable and gentle man who respected and liked me back.

I could make this work.

As long as I didn't think hard about what I'd have to give up—independence, autonomy, the taste of a woman on my tongue ever again, any chance of having my own voice or opinion outside of our private lives . . .

"Okay," I said. "You can take me shopping."

He frowned, that endearing eyebrow vee reappearing. "O-K?" he repeated. "You say this often; I take it for an affirmative, or a confirmation of wellness, but what does it mean, exactly?"

I laughed, startled by the sudden weirdness of needing to explain something I took for granted as understood.

"Dad says that's disputed—it's either Choctaw for 'it is so,' or was invented about a decade from now by a bunch of Bostonians to stand in for 'oll korrect.' My favorite explanation is"—I circled the thumb and forefinger of my good hand and extended the other three fingers out straight—"O-K, Zero Kills. Military parlance, meaning there were no casualties on our side."

He repeated the gesture, so tentative and out of place paired with his fussy blue dress frock coat that I laughed again.

"That is the first time you've mentioned your father," Fenton pointed out, which killed my delight stone dead. "Did you much admire him?"

"I did." I clenched my teeth to keep my chin from trembling. "He was very loving, and handy, and he had the biggest store of stupid useless facts a single human brain could hold—" I snuffled hard.

Fenton offered me his handkerchief and I declined. I still had one of his other ones stuffed in my jeans pocket. He looked at it critically, and then at the rest of my ensemble.

"Perhaps I shall send *out* for a dress instead," he said as I dabbed my face dry.

"Har, har," I said, desperately missing the ability to buy clothes on my phone.

But there was no point in wishing for things I could never have.

~

The first dress that Worsley fetched back from a modiste was so fashionable as to be practically transparent. I wondered how gullible the kid had to be to let himself be talked into something so useless for any kind of activity outside of a sweltering ballroom. I sent it back, insisting that I wasn't going to be a popsicle just because it was trendy. The second dress was made of black wool, utilitarian and straight cut, with no flounces.

The next morning, my stays and chemise from my blood-ruined Gibraltar dress were put to use, and the ensemble was finished with sturdy black thigh-high socks held up by honest-to-god ribbon garters. Fenton offered to buy me new boots, but I stuck to my purple Chucks. They weren't as waterproof as leather, but with no heel I didn't have to worry about breaking an ankle on the winter-slick streets. My chest and arms were encased in a cranberry-colored wool jacket called a spencer. It ended just under my boobs, leaving my poor bottom with only a few layers of skirt to fend off the deep English winter. *Why* were these people so opposed to underwear? My hands were shoved as far as they would go into a rabbit-fur muff, dyed cranberry to match my ridiculous little coat, a sling made from the leftover material from my Gibraltar dress folded neatly inside it in case I decided I needed it later. My Basque hat rounded out the ensemble. As we made our way through the frigid cobblestone streets, I wished that I'd also had the foresight to wear my jeans under the dress.

Loath as I was to spend Fenton's money, I also wished most that the crowd wasn't so huge that we could have hired a cab. But the multitudes of people we waded through were just too prohibitive to allow any vehicle through.

I had seen the pictures of "The Queue," of the two hundred and fifty thousand people who'd waited in line to pay their respects to the late queen, Elizabeth II. Though there *had* to be fewer people crammed into the street outside of Greenwich Hospital to walk past Lord Nelson's casket, it sure didn't feel like it. I thought it was a bit morbid, to come all this way just to stare at a half-shriveled corpse. But then I didn't have the sort of connection with the man, nor the battle he had just won for them, as the people in this queue did.

The British have always admired their heroes, and preferred them dead best of all. I'd heard that in a song once, two hundred years from now.

It was still early when we arrived—the quick breakfast we'd taken on the ship was barely settled in my stomach—and the doors of the hospital were still closed. Guards in red tunics were glancing at each other and then at the growing number of lookie-loos nervously. All it would take to turn the crowd was a few impatient idiots or a handful of troublemakers. Luckily, a grim air of solemnity hovered ominously over the sea of black wool and silk flowers. Nobody seemed to have the jumping fury required for a riot.

Captain Goodenough, by privilege of his blue coat, was allowed to push to the front. I kept my hand wrapped around his elbow, letting him drag me along through the slush and mud. I did my best to keep my hem out of the mess, but it must have been splattered six inches up by the time we made it to where several more naval men with even grander epaulets, sashes, feathers, and medals stood grim faced, bracketed by tearful wives and children.

As we passed by them, Fenton shook the hands of his equals, bowed formally to his betters, saluted his superiors, and kissed the hands or cheeks of those women he knew well enough. He introduced me to no one, and though everyone's eyes followed with naked curiosity, I, too, said nothing. I was already beginning to learn the importance of keeping my mouth shut—I'd paid the price for my flapping jaw in Gibraltar.

The tight collar of my jacket felt near to choking me. Or maybe it was the way I kept biting my tongue. But I didn't fidget. See? What a good wife I'd be.

When we settled into place in the front ranks, I sighed in relief. I expected Fenton to make some soothing remark or stoop close to whisper into my ear. Instead he just looked straight ahead, his mouth a somber line. He behaved as if he didn't know me at all, as if I was but some stranger on his arm that he'd been obliged to escort, and not what we were.

More.

Was he mad at me? Was it because I hadn't wanted to be dressed as fashionably as the shivering, blue-lipped women around me? Or was I *supposed* to have introduced myself to his colleagues?

Shit.

Shit.

Something inside me twisted hard, my guts seizing. I was doing a good job at this, right? This whole "convincing Fenton that he should keep me around" thing. *Right?*

Should I make conversation? Was it my turn to fill the uncomfortable silence? Or should I follow his lead and keep my yap buttoned? I was halfway to deciding to make some stupid comment about the weather when another gentleman shoved his way forward and hailed us with a booming, too jovial: "Fen! Fen Goodenough!"

Chapter Seven

IN WHICH SAM MOURNS

I'm afraid that the pleasantness of an employment does not always evince its propriety.

—Jane Austen, *Sense and Sensibility*

The man calling to Fenton huffed toward us, three harried ladies bobbing hurriedly in his wake. They looked like nothing so much as aggrieved ducklings under their bill-like bonnets and swaddled as they were in heavy gray cloaks. They also each looked too much like Fenton for me to presume anything but a familial relationship. Mother. Two sisters. Did that make the man a brother-in-law?

"Fen!" he called again, shoving between the rank and file of the naval men, who were extremely annoyed by his impertinent line cutting—especially since he wasn't in dress blues himself.

He wore all black, save for the exertion red of his cheeks and the sharp white of his neckcloth. His hat was expensively dapper but too small for his head, and he had to keep one hand on the brim as he trotted along, paying no heed to the puddles he stepped in or the hems he trod on.

He wasn't *unattractive*, but his snubbed nose combined with his padded jowls gave him an unfortunate roundness of face that the high collar could disguise only so much, and his short-cropped hair was so light in color that it appeared as if it was thinning. He gave the impression of a soft teddy bear of a man trying too hard to disguise his physique in fashions that made him look fat, rather than leaning into the advantages of his barrel-chested frame.

As a woman who was significantly curvier than the runway sample size, I sympathized. It was hard to feel good about how you looked when everything was designed to shame you into succumbing to diet culture.

"Lewis!" Fenton said. The men shook hands and slapped shoulders. Lewis towered over both of us, and the way he squeezed Fenton's hand gave the impression of a former high-school quarterback star who hadn't quite come to terms with the fact that both his metabolism and his glories were a thing of the past. "Miss Samantha Franklin, may I introduce Judge George Lewis."

"Miss Franklin," he said jovially, giving me the kind of up-and-down look that I might have flipped him off for in another era. His gaze lingered on the way I had my arm linked through Fenton's.

"Your Honor," I replied with a curtsy.

Fenton made a stifled noise of frustration, but my apparent etiquette breach just made the judge chuckle. He had a charming, comforting smile.

"We're not in court today, Miss Franklin. Just *my lord* will do."

"Ah." Embarrassment flagged hot across my cheeks. "I don't meet many judges."

"Is that so? Good at staying out of trouble are you, little miss?"

It was supposed to be teasing. Instead it came out as condescending.

"No. It's just that no one's caught me yet," I teased back, giving him the benefit of the doubt.

Lewis seemed delighted by my sass, at least, which was more than I could say for Fenton.

By then the three ladies had caught up, and a woman I assumed was Fenton's mother bypassed the rest of us to embrace her son hard. I stepped back to give them room. She was a compact, stocky thing smothered in black lace frippery, and barely came up to his shoulder. She had on fingerless lace mittens, and the black contrasted starkly with

Fenton's tanned face when she cupped his cheeks to hold him still for a good long look.

"Hello, Mother," Fenton said warmly. "I'm very happy to see you well."

"And you, my courageous boy," Mrs. Goodenough said tearfully. "We've been reading the most *dreadful* things about the fighting in the newspapers."

"It's not as bad as all that." Fenton downplayed, but the way he flicked his eyes up at one of his sisters, the blond one, made it clear that there was at least one family member with whom he shared the real horrors of war. She rolled her eyes at him but otherwise didn't comment.

Oh, I liked her already. She was cute. I mean, not *pretty*, not in the soft round way that her brother, sister, and mother were. She was lean to the point of being androgynous, her chin stubborn, her nose strong. But her sharpness was tempered by the soft wisps of the yellow-gold hair that framed her face under her bonnet, the roses in her cheeks, and the twinkling smile in eyes the same shape as Fenton's. She was fascinating.

"My little brown-winged hawfinch," Mrs. Goodenough warbled, patting his cheek and moving aside so each of his sisters could greet him with a warm, "Welcome home, Finch."

"Finch?" I asked. "For serious?"

Lewis and I shared a glance of humor, but Fenton was gawping with no little bit of horror.

"Oh, Miss Franklin, no," he said, but it was too late.

"Finch!" I repeated. "*Captain* Finch!"

"Miss Franklin, *please*," Fenton pleaded. "It is a childhood endearment. If it got around London—"

"I promise, I won't use it. Cross my heart and hope to die." I ran a finger along my chest in an *X*, then mimed zipping my mouth shut. Neither gesture meant anything in particular to my companions, but they got the general idea.

The family reunion done, the ladies turned curious eyes to me.

"Sisters, this is Miss Franklin. Miss Franklin, my sisters, Mrs. Kempel and Miss Goodenough."

"If you're to call our brother Finch, then you must call us Marigold," the blond one added promptly, gesturing to her sister and then to herself, "and Daisy."

I stuck my hand out to shake, and when that was met with raised eyebrows, dropped it quickly to offer head bobs instead.

"Then Sam for me," I said to cover my gaffe.

"Daisy was kind enough to agree to allow me to escort her," Lewis whispered loudly enough that everyone around us could hear. "And of course, both Marigold and your mother being widowed, I couldn't let them attend alone."

Ah, he was one of the braggart Nice Guy types.

"Good of you to escort them, Lewis, thank you," Fenton said. I couldn't help but notice that he was sticking to the formal mode of addressing his friend, while the judge was splashing around given names like an overloaded paint roller.

Fenton must have caught my disapproval because he immediately looped Lewis and his mother into a conversation about how very good it was of Lewis to help his family find a place to stay in town, when the lodgings were crammed with everyone in the country come to see off Nelson.

"Our brother's rank and special permission to enter among the first being, of course, only of secondary motivation," Daisy murmured behind her scarf to her sister as soon as the men were distracted.

Marigold chuckled, then caught herself and admonished her with a low, severe "Daisy! What *will* Miss Franklin think."

I sidestepped closer, and their eyes widened as I leaned in to whisper: "She'll think it's both hilarious and accurate."

Marigold reared back, unimpressed. With her round chin, dark hair, and doe-brown eyes, she was the spitting image of Fenton at his most disapproving. But Daisy immediately curled her arm around mine and pressed against my shoulder.

It jostled my wound but I swallowed back the wince. It wasn't like she had done it on purpose. This close, Daisy smelled of violets. Her eyes were the color of a luminous, snow-laden winter sky. She must have favored her late father. I didn't see much of Daisy's statuesque facial structure in Marigold, Fenton, or their mother. Daisy was taller than me too; enough so that she had to lean down to whisper in my ear.

"I do believe we may become very good friends, Miss Franklin."

"Sam," I insisted again, maybe more flirtatiously than I should have, but my gosh, was she captivating. You couldn't blame a gal. Besides, she wouldn't know what I meant by it.

"Sam," Daisy repeated with an inscrutable narrowing of her eyes and a mischievous curl of her mouth. "How sweet."

"Funny, I was thinking the same for you three. Marigold, Daisy, Finch."

"Mother is an Iris," Daisy offered quickly.

"You're a garden of delights," I purred.

Some of the aloofness Daisy had arrived with melted away, and she pressed against my arm. Her breasts were soft and enticing against my shoulder. In a dance club, I would have turned my head and focused on her mouth so she knew exactly what I thought about that, before leaning in to try for a kiss. Instead, I laid my hand over hers on my elbow and forced myself not to think salacious things about a woman I was angling to make my sister-in-law.

Marigold looked between us sourly, irritated at being excluded from the banter. "How are you finding England, Miss Franklin?" Marigold asked, peevishly sticking to my surname.

"Cold, Mrs. Kempel," I offered, leaning back and opening my body language to make sure Marigold was included in our tête-à-tête.

"I hear the winters are harsher in the colonies."

It was a dig at what I was wearing. I let it pass. "True," I allowed. "But we dress more sensibly for the weather."

"Yes, I had noticed," Marigold said with a sniff.

Oh, two could play at that game.

"Also, my university built underground passages so we wouldn't have to go out in the snow."

"You attended university?" Daisy asked with awe.

"I did—"

"And did they not finish you?" Marigold interrupted, trying for witty but coming across as petty.

"*Tch*," Daisy clucked at her sister. "Why talk of fashion and finishing when Miss Franklin, pardon, *Sam*, has been to university. And to sea."

"Have you never?" I asked. "Been on the water, I mean."

"No, save for the little boat that the Gales have on their charming duck pond."

"Which is treacherous enough," Marigold said in a tone that made it clear that this was a threadbare argument.

Water, closing over my head, pressing against the back of my throat, salt in my lungs, hacking, burning—

"Miss Franklin?" Daisy said, but her voice seemed to come from the end of a tunnel. "Sam?"

"Mfine," I lied, clearing my throat. My heart raced so hard I thought Daisy might be able to feel it in the throb of the artery at my elbow. "But I'm with your sister on this one."

The sisters exchanged a look that made it clear that they didn't believe me, but Marigold tactfully changed the subject anyway. "It is very bold of you to take passage alone."

"How adventurous!" Daisy enthused. Fenton must have softened the telling of how I had come aboard quite a bit in his letters home. "Who are you to meet, now that you've arrived?"

I cleared my throat again. "Well. I've met you and Judge Lewis."

"Have you no relations nor friends in England?" Marigold asked in a tone that said she thought my deliberate misunderstanding of the question was tedious.

"None," I crackled, through a swell of grief like broken glass on my tongue. Daisy's hand squeezed comfortingly. "But that's part of the fun, eh? I get to . . . start over."

"Oh," Daisy said, reading the sadness behind my bravado. "You've nowhere to stay?"

"Daisy," Marigold cut in warningly. "I know we discussed taking in a lodger—"

I laughed, trying to put on a good face. "I don't think I'll need to."

"Oh?" Daisy asked, intrigued.

I sent an admiring glance at Fenton in his stupid hat. "Your brother and I have gotten close. I like him very much."

"Oh," Daisy repeated, pulling back, the peaks of her cheekbones pinkening. "Yes, of course." She almost sounded disappointed.

My BiFi pinged hard. I was good at reading the signals in a century where I was familiar with them, but she knocked me off kilter. There was no way she was throwing off enough bandwidth for me to be picking it up. Could she?

No fucking way.

Daisy?

The squirmy, tight thing in my guts creaked and tightened further. It didn't matter if Daisy *was* like that. It wasn't like there was anything she could do about it. Not now. Not here.

How tragic.

How *terrifying*.

"Miss Franklin, you should know that Finch—" Marigold began, but we were interrupted by Lewis's brash laughter.

"Be serious, Fen," Lewis howled.

"I am. Miss Franklin *is* the young lady I wrote to you about," Fenton said. Lewis's expression turned shrewd.

Without warning, Mr. Lewis seized my left arm, detaching me from Daisy. He pulled the muff off and showily pressed a kiss to my hand. I was too surprised to be embarrassed. The ladies looked away, mortified. Fenton was the only one who didn't look shocked.

"Hmm," Mr. Lewis said as he ran a finger up my sleeve. He found the knot of bandages under my arm, and pressed down.

"Ouch!" I said, more of a warning than an exclamation of pain. "What the hell?"

"It is not so bad as you had me believe in your letter," Lewis went on, as if I hadn't spoken. "Judicious use of shawls will hide the damage nicely in the warmer months. What is she?"

"Invisible, apparently," I snapped, trying to disentangle myself.

Lewis took this as his sign to instead swoop in and take both my hands between his, like a lover in a pantomime. His smile was thin. I thought: *He should be wearing a trilby instead of a top hat.* Lewis had a firm grip, and I didn't think I could shake him off without causing more of a scene than we were already producing.

"Samantha," he began, as if I was a misbehaving kindergartener who really should know better. I bristled.

"Miss Franklin, thank you," I cut in. "I don't remember giving you permission to use my first name, *my lord*."

He laughed dryly. "Apologies, Miss Franklin. I do believe I've made a very bad first impression in my eagerness to make your acquaintance. It is not every day that a man has the pleasure of meeting a mermaid."

"I'm not a mermaid. I'm a Canadian."

He laughed again, loud and performative. I turned to Fenton for a rescue. He said nothing, but his ears flushed. I couldn't make out his expression under the brim of his taco-hat. Fucker better not have been laughing.

Before I could find a way out, there was the bang of a wooden bolt being pulled back and the creak of the doors of the hospital being thrown open. The crowd surged at our backs.

“Ah, finally!” Mr. Lewis exclaimed, elbowed in between Daisy and me, and took my right arm without so much as a may-I. Pain shot up my neck from the healing wound. “O woe! The doors part and the weeping nation enters through. Let us gaze upon the fallen hero together, Miss Franklin.”

“Wait a sec—” I tried to protest as he dragged me forward, cutting in line ahead of the more deserving officers. “Aren’t you supposed to be escorting Miss Goodenough?”

“She has her brother to watch over her,” he said, but partiality over his shoulder, making it clear it was as much an admonishment for Fenton as it was an excuse for me.

Daisy and I exchanged helpless looks as we were separated by a sea of blue wool.

Lewis bowled us into a grand hall. Each tug sent new waves of pain sweeping up my nerves. I decided that there was nothing for it but to let Lewis have his way, get this over with, and get back to more sensible company. The only other option was to pitch a fit, and I wasn’t going to let that blow back on Fenton.

Lewis marched us across marble flooring to the far side of the hall. We stopped at a modest dais that was separated from the crowd by a waist-high wall.

I was afraid the body would be out in the open air. Thankfully, Lord Nelson was ensconced inside a black coffin with gilded edges and images of battle etched onto its panels. The coffin itself was draped with white fabric, sheer enough to let me appreciate the detailing on the wood beneath. A canopy of rich black swagging hung overhead. Painted cherubs and angels peered at the assembly from their aspects on the ceiling. The walls were draped with mind-bogglingly *massive* captured flags—tattered and singed from the shipboard skirmishes that had won them—medals and battle trophies, battered sails, swords, and tridents. All of it on a more epic scale than I'd expected, but then again, as my tour of the *Salacia* had proven, warships were huge.

It wasn't a funeral, it was a *spectacle*.

The coffin was flanked by two sailors, faces grim and uniforms spotless. They were probably present to keep souvenir seekers at bay, and the thought of someone making off with Lord Nelson's finger or a clipping of his hair was enough to make my stomach turn.

"There he is," Mr. Lewis hissed in a deliberate pitch that allowed him to be overheard. "Our great Lord Nelson, dead as a doornail. Blooming shame."

Around us, other mourners hissed their disapproval. I felt the back of my neck get hot, a hundred eyes on it, blaming me for the behavior of the man who had seized hold of me. But I couldn't have stoppered up his irreverence any more than I could have parted the seas.

"Push to the front, darling," Lewis said, his wide hand on the small of my back. "Get a good view." Two hundred years from now I might not have thought anything of it, but now, after months of having nobody but Fenton touch me, it felt shockingly obscene. I tried to wriggle to the side but his hand followed.

I did move, but only to get away from him.

Once there, I saw that the lid of the coffin was partially glass (pickled, still!), and Lord Nelson's face was visible through a small window. Oh god. He was pallidly bloodless. Already the skin was pulling back from his teeth, sinking against his cheekbones and deepening his eye sockets. A dip in brandy hadn't done enough to fend off natural decomposition.

I fought the urge to gag, and even though the room was clear of any scent of rot, I could recall it. It was the smell that had wafted from the ocean the day after I'd been pulled out, thick and sweet with death, moldering flesh in the creeping gloom. I clapped my hand over my mouth.

Please don't let me puke on Horatio Nelson's coffin, I thought. *That would be so uncool.*

That would be no way to honor a man who had died at the same moment I was meant to.

The twisting thing inside me wrenched so suddenly and so hard that a cracking seemed to fill the vast, echoing hall. The world swirled, black at the edges and painfully bright in the center. Voices swarmed, like air bubbles speeding past my ears.

"No," I said.

"No what, darling?" Lewis asked. His bulk was the shadow of a shark passing beside me, the brush of a sinking corpse.

"*No,*" I said again, but what I was denying I didn't know. I gripped the sides of my head, body checked Lewis to the side, shoved my way through the mass of people stinking of sweat and rosewater, sweet meats and dirt, pipe smoke and life.

I tumbled into the outside air, pushed to the edge of the great crowd still waiting to get into the hospital, and found myself knee-deep in a snowbank. The cold didn't hurt. I sucked in a great lungful of air, but it wasn't fresh, wasn't the relief I needed. It was cloying, seasoned with the grease of frying food and horse manure.

And there was no car exhaust, no aggressively sterile hospital smell, no commercial perfumes.

Horatio Nelson was dead.

And I was alive.

I was alive, here, now, when he should be. Maybe even in his place. Christ. I was in 1806. I was lost. No. Worse. I had no control. I was at the mercy of everyone around me, men who knew nothing, and believed nothing, and understood *nothing.*

I was *trapped.*

~

I don't know how Daisy found me. I don't even know how I'd gotten where I was, sitting in some half-frozen slush puddle out the back of a building reeking of piss and garbage.

Her hand on my shoulder was gentle.

"Samantha?" Daisy said, her voice the soothing softness used on startled horses and frightened children.

"Daisy." The hitch in my voice made me realize that I was sobbing. The tears clung to my cheeks, frozen, *burning*.

She tugged me upright. I leaned back against the filthy wall. I covered my face, ignoring the gritty gray wet that clung to my hands. Looking at her right now seemed like it would . . . I don't know, be the final nail in the glass, or crack in the coffin, or something like that.

"You're frozen through," she said. She stripped off her cloak and slung it over my shoulders.

"I'll get it dirty," I said, which was really a rather stupid thing to be concerned about. Hypothermia, that had to be it. My brain couldn't seem to process anything beyond the immediate.

"And we can clean it." She helped me work the muff back down my arm so I could tuck both of my filthy hands into it. "Let's get you by a fire, silly thing."

I flinched. Was I silly? Or had I gone mad?

I was fucked, that was what I was.

"I'm in the wrong place, Daisy," I blurted.

"In that, we both agree," she replied, distracted with navigating us both out of the alley without fouling our hems any further.

"I don't know what I'm doing. I don't know how to be . . . be this . . . be *you*."

"Be *me*? Whatever do you—"

"Lord, *there* you are," Fenton said from the mouth of the alley, interrupting whatever Daisy was about to say. He heaved a sigh of profound relief and irritation. "Miss Franklin, what *am* I to do with you and your queer fits."

"Ha-ha, queer." I snorted, and neither sibling was amused.

"Into the hackney with both of you, now," Fenton snapped, gesturing at a genuine horse and bloody carriage.

"Bossy," I said as he handed me up into the box, trying to smother my freak-out with humor. Fenton was in no mood for banter, though. The cab filled with his petulant, disapproving silence.

The carriage lurched into motion and after a few turns, Daisy frowned at the passing streets and said: "This is not the way to our lodgings."

Fenton's lips thinned peevishly. "Lewis is hosting us for dinner."

"All of us?" Daisy asked, startled.

"Just Miss Franklin and me," Fen said with a tone heavy with meaning I couldn't parse.

Daisy *could*, though. "He wishes to dine with Miss *Franklin*. Not me."

"No, not you," Fenton assured her.

Daisy's eyes widened with first surprise, then understanding, and I caught a flicker of relief before her expression turned carefully bland. A frisson of worry shivered up my nape.

What were they hiding? And why wasn't Fenton looking at me? What had happened to the tactile, gentle, smitten man I thought I'd managed to wrap around my finger?

He'd vanished the second we'd set foot on English soil.

Deluded, I scolded myself. *Smug. Stupid. You thought just because you were from the future you were what, smarter than everyone around you? Thought you could just swan in and manipulate everyone to do whatever you wanted? Idiot. Ask them. Ask them what they really mean. Just ask—*

The cab stopped alongside a tidy, wide row of ostentatious white-stoned townhouses. Fenton banged out of the carriage sourly and gestured impatiently for me to follow.

"What if I don't want to have dinner with his lordship either?" I asked, feeling like the ocean was closing over my head again.

"Miss Franklin, I hesitate to put so crude a point on it," Fenton growled, "but after everything that has occurred on our voyage, this is the *least* that you can do to repay me."

Goddamnit.

I pulled off Daisy's cloak and laid it over her lap, then stepped onto the curb. Fenton had the door closed and the coachman sent on his way before I could even turn to say good-bye. Daisy watched us through the back window, expression tightly shuttered, until the cab turned a corner and was out of sight.

"Come along, Miss Franklin," Fenton said, heading for the door.

"That's a lot of house to clean," I said, frowning up at the ostentatious neo-Grecian exterior. "I feel sorry for his wife."

Fenton stopped, his hand poised above the knocker, eyes going round.

"What did I say?"

Fenton cleared his throat. "Nothing. I thought perhaps . . . it's quite my own fault that I've failed to inform you. You . . . ah—" He rubbed his hand along the back of his neck, a nervous gesture that I found, god help me, cute. "Mrs. Lewis passed away last year."

"Oh. That's . . . I'm sorry."

"No need to apologize," Fenton said, softening. "You could not have known. My dear, Lewis can be uncouth, but please do try to be pleasant with him. He is my very particular acquaintance and he is quite fond of you."

"He's literally just met me," I scoffed. "He can't be *that* fond."

"His first impression of you was helped along by my letters, I'm sure," Fenton said, a bit cagey. Had I upset him? Maybe fondness was something important for first impressions?

"Okay. Only because he's your friend."

"I did not say *friend*," Fenton corrected, knocking.

I didn't have the chance to ask what he meant because the door opened. We were treated to a blast of warmth and light from within, partially blocked by a grave butler in a severely pressed suit.

"Captain Goodenough," he said, with a formal nod to Fenton. He moved aside to let us in, taking our outerwear and saying absolutely nothing about the state of my shoes and skirts.

We were shown into something he called a private parlor. Fenton and I entered, and I couldn't help the stupid, relieved grin that flitted across my face when Fenton placed his hand at the small of my back. When Lewis had done it, it'd been creepy. But from Fenton, it felt like a return to our shipboard dynamic.

Lewis was sitting in a wingback chair near a fireplace on the far wall. To the left was a bank of windows looking out over the quiet square as it grew dark with the setting sun, and to the right was a wall painted a rich dark green and dotted with what I assumed were family portraits. He held another of those comically small cut crystal glasses of something darkish brown—sherry? brandy?—and his cheeks were already flushed with it.

Was his alcohol tolerance that low or had he just been at it for a while?

"That is not Miss Goodenough," Lewis grunted as Fenton and I took our seats. I chose the end of the small sofa farthest from them both, sliding a doily from the arm under my dirty dress discreetly to preserve the upholstery.

"There's been a change," Fenton said, with such a studied air of nonchalance that even Lewis was startled into silence. It didn't last long, though.

"The announcement is drafted and set to be delivered to the papers this evening," Lewis said waspishly. "You don't truly wish for me to have to sue you for breach of promise on *top* of what you owe me for—"

"No, no, of course not," Fenton stuttered, his bluff called. His face turned ashen so quickly I feared he was about to faint. "You will have what we agreed in recompense. You need only replace the name in the announcement. It is otherwise precisely the same."

Lewis looked intrigued. "The name?"

"Miss Samantha Jayne Franklin."

"I'm sorry, what is going on?" I interrupted.

"And who are you to dispose of her thusly?" Lewis went on, as if I hadn't spoken.

"'Dispose' of me?" I repeated darkly.

Fenton flinched at my tone but steadfastly did not look at me. "I am her rescuer. She has no family to speak of, she has assured me as much. No brothers, nor father to broker with. I stand for her."

Lewis laughed, and it was an ugly, self-satisfied sound. "You mean you pulled her like flotsam from the sea and take ownership by law of salvage?"

Clearly the comparison was as distasteful to Fenton as it was to me. "Yes. Quite."

"Absolutely not!" I snapped, jumping to my feet.

Lewis's lips twisted meanly. "You seek to offload your nuisance on me."

"She is educated," Fenton said hastily. "She reads finely and writes in a tolerable hand. She dances, speaks very keenly on a great many topics, and is happy to be taught the proper ways of things when they are beyond her understanding."

"*Stop* ignoring me—"

"She has a passion for righting injustices, and as you are a judge, I cannot help but feel that she would be a better intellectual match for you than my sister."

"She is nobody."

Fenton dipped closer to him, entreating. "She is whoever you need her to be. She is a blank slate. She has no family, no one to question your affairs or methods, nor even your . . . proclivities. She's of greater social advantage to you than Daisy ever would be, and—"

I took a step toward them. "I'm gonna punch you if you don't *explain*—"

"And," Fenton added, face flushing scarlet and voice lowering even more, so I had to strain to hear, "her prowess in the married arts is unparalleled."

I froze, jaw dropping in mortification.

Lewis finally acknowledged that I was in the room, and then only with a long, lewd up-and-down stare ten times more telling than the last one. "Train her yourself on the trip home, did you, boy?"

Fenton cleared his throat, his ears going pink. "I did not have to."

"My, my," Lewis said with a salacious grin. His next words were aimed at Fenton but he turned his mean little eyes directly to me when he said them: "What *would* your fiancé say if she knew, Fen?"

Chapter Eight
IN WHICH SAM LOSES

It is a truth universally acknowledged that a single man in possession of a good fortune, must be in want of a wife.

—*Jane Austen, Pride and Prejudice*

According to Dahlia, I had a childish habit of literally physically running away from my problems. Immature? Yes. But I found that it gave me the space I needed to unpick the churning knot of my thoughts so I could come back to an argument or problem with a clean mind.

I had tried to run away to Barcelona, and look how that had turned out.

I had run away from the truth on the ship, and had caused a scene in front of Fenton's crew.

All the same, I thought this particular revelation warranted a good Rumpelstiltskin-style huff, and so suited action to thought immediately. Out the parlor doors I went, taking a sharp turn down a long hall papered with lush designs, then another, then into another room with curtains closed and no lamps lit. The light from the hallway was just enough for me to make it out as a paper-strewn office, and I slumped over to a sagging armchair beside the desk and threw myself onto it before the door swung closed behind me, plunging everything into deep darkness.

Idiot, I scolded myself. *Idiot!*

Foolish. Naïve. Ridiculous for building a fantasy about someone I didn't even know, because they were the *only* person I knew.

What had I been thinking? That I could just pick a nice man out of a lineup and *keep* him with a bit of creative fellatio, like a prize I'd won at a fair? I'd taken for granted that Fenton would just *want* me, that he'd look at me and think, *Ah, yes, that one please*, simply because I'd decided he ought to.

The same way . . .

The tears came hot and hard against the backs of my eyes, and I gulped them down, choking on the realization that I had done this exact same thing to Dahlia. I'd thought I'd known *better* than them both, thought I was the clever, enlightened one who would white knight them into a relationship with me, and instead I'd just ignored every sign, every clue that what I was dragging them into was unwelcome.

The common denominator in these disasters is you, Sammie-bear.

Fuck.

Marigold had tried to warn me. Looking back at that conversation, when I'd *bragged* about how close Fenton and I were, Marigold was going to tell me about the fiancé. The whole family knew.

So now *fucking* what?

I wasn't sure who I should be angrier at: Lewis for exposing the truth, myself for blithely throwing myself at Fenton, or Fenton himself for knowingly committing what probably amounted in this era to adultery.

Fuck adultery, he had been *courting* me.

Hadn't he?

That *was* flirting, wasn't it? The gloves, and the dancing, and the hand strokes, and the kisses on the cheek? I hadn't misread the whole thing? Or was there a cultural divide that I just didn't see—that what I'd thought was flirting was just him being pleasant and gentlemanly?

Huh! Gentlemanly! What we did in that alley was certainly *not* gentlemanly. He had felt it, too, the spiderweb-thin connection, that passion we had begun to weave into a beautiful pattern between us. And Mr. Lewis, in one swipe of a careless hand, had turned it into tattered cobwebs.

How had I let myself get turned around like this? How had I let him *do* this to me? How were we going to fix this?

No, there was no fixing. No *we*.

Fenton was getting married, and I had behaved like one of those greedy, slutty bisexual stereotypes. Because I had *needed* him. I had needed *some*body, *any*body to *want* me, to *rescue* me. But also because here I *had* to have a man to speak for me, do things for me; it was awful, but it was fact.

I bet Fenton hadn't even slept with her yet.

Jesus, had I ruined things for his future marriage? Was I going to destroy the happiness of a woman who didn't deserve it?

I was going to be sick. It felt like I was swallowing mouthful after mouthful of seawater when all I kept gulping at was the thick, dark air.

"Ah," a voice said, deep and low. "Ran all the way to the back of the house, did we, little mousie?" The door opened, letting in a crack of light that silhouetted Lewis's broad shoulders and a body cut in half, like an uncanny funhouse mirror.

"Don't call me that," I said softly into my knees, drowning in self-loathing.

"But this is where little mousies flee when they're frightened. Into the dark."

"I'm not frightened," I sneered. "And it's 'mice.'"

He chuckled, a deep, booming one with an oily veneer floating on the surface, just enough to raise goose bumps.

Shit.

We were alone.

He was between me and the only exit.

How had I let that happen?

I stood. It didn't offer a lot of an advantage, but at least I had my hands free.

"You do like to think you're clever," he said, still amused. "Could it be that you really *are* a mermaid, you strange thing?"

"Get out of the way," I said. "I'm leaving."

"Oh ho!" he boomed again. He opened the door more fully, if only to prove that his bloated shadow blocked most of the light from the bare hallway behind. "Not you, my darling."

"I am leaving," I insisted. "Captain Goodenough—"

"Fen has given you to me. And in return, I have torn up his notes of debt."

"He's . . . what?" Surprise squeezed my gullet, and the rest of what I had been going to say was choked back, sour and hard.

"Did he not explain it? I charged him with some, hmm, private shipping to do on my behalf, in payment of some bad gambling debts. His conscience got the better of him, which resulted in him then owing his wagers and the value of both the lost product and its profit. As I find myself in want of a wife, and he had several young ladies to settle, we agreed to resolve it with marriage."

"No."

"You find yourself the lucky victor."

"I won't—"

"You *will*. He's sent word to have your belongings sent to us, along with the remainder of my stock. He says he does not expect your trinkets to be worth much of anything, but I'll appraise them. They might go some way toward paying back your upkeep aboard ship, if nothing else."

"You . . . ! You can't sell my stuff!" I was torn between the urge to back myself farther into the corner or run at him full tilt with my fists up. "It's worthless here, meaningless! It's all I have *left*."

"And as such, I will in all probability allow you to keep it. I am a considerate husband that way."

The word struck me like a bucket of ice water. *"Husband?"*

"No need to be stubborn, darling," he murmured, in mockery of lover's sweet nothings. "I am rich and widowed, in need of an heir. And you are in need of a protector. I will give you a luxurious life."

"A luxurious *cage*," I spat.

"One that any woman would be thrilled to be kept in."

"Go find any woman, then. It doesn't need to be me."

"Oh, but it does," Lewis growled. The door swung shut, and my eyes couldn't adjust fast enough to track him. Had he gone out? Was he in here with me?

His hands closed around my shoulders suddenly, and I was backed into the wall, head thunking on the plaster.

"Ow!"

"Hush! I *will* have a wife. I am a great man and it is my *right*. I have decided that I want you."

"Why?"

"You will be far more satisfying to bring to heel than Fen's homely, bluestocking sister."

"Let go!"

His hands slid up over my shoulders, to the sides of my neck, pressing just tight enough against my jaw to hold my head still. It made breathing slightly difficult, and his threat clear.

"A woman who has done what you have is either a wife or a whore, darling," Lewis hissed into my face.

The insult was obvious. "I'm not a whore!"

I couldn't see it, but his smile was present enough in his tone: "No, but you are alone. You have defiled yourself in an act of seduction, and you have no dowry. Had you any sort of beauty, that would perhaps be recommendation enough, but your face is plain at best, and your manners ghastly. Be sensible, mousie. I am offering you the more delicate route."

I had a degree in social studies. I knew how impossible it would be to live my life the way I wanted to when it was so far outside of the norms and morals of the hegemony. I knew how *right* Lewis was. He nosed at the side of my face, breath sweet with wine. "You will be the wife of a respected man of the Ton. You will give me heirs to inherit my fortune and bring glory to my line."

"I will *not*!" I wriggled, but he was taller, broader, and stronger. It was like fighting a statue.

"It took fat Henry three wives to get a son." Lewis smeared the words against my cheek. *Disgusting*. "Let's see if I can do it in two."

And then he kissed me.

It was forceful, claiming, which made it revolting. His tongue pressed at my lips, and I clenched my teeth hard, keeping the barrier of bone between him and the inside of my mouth. When I wouldn't let him in, he bit my lower lip hard enough to hurt. But it freed me up to scream.

"Fento—!"

He squeezed hard around my windpipe. I gagged and clawed at his hands. He let up just enough for me to breathe.

"Shush," Lewis snarled. "Fenton will have a wife and his own children to provide for soon enough. He can't have you too."

I swallowed hard, larynx bobbing against his thumbs. "Then I'll get a job. I'll pay him back myself, you don't need to—"

"What a strange country you must come from, little mouse!" He laughed. "Women exist to be wives and mothers for their men. That is their job, and there can be no other. You will marry me."

"I was under the impression that marriage was the sort of thing that had to be done voluntarily."

He went still. He took a breath. Two. Then: "Stupid little girl."

Whatever he was planning, I wasn't about to wait for it. Fight or flight were my only options, and animal instincts had been closer to the surface lately. I shoved hard, jerking one knee up into his crotch. I hit my target, but instead of folding so I could escape, Lewis reacted by shoving me into the wall again, pinning my arms above my head with one meaty paw.

A stinging heat burst hard and sharp against the side of my face, and it took me a full five seconds to comprehend that he had *slapped* me. The pain was so intense that I saw spots. I held my hand against my cheek to stop it from smarting.

"Pain is part of the lesson, pet," he hissed. "And I will provide it as often as is necessary for you to learn it."

"Let go!"

The stinging heat was laid across my face again, and I thought it was perhaps better to shut up now than have a third slap break my nose. Or worse.

Ha! What a fucked-up reward for surviving this is! Thanks for nothing, universe!

Pulled out of the ocean, separated by centuries from my family and friends, nearly murdered for being different, and sold off in marriage to a scumbag by the man I thought was in love with me.

Lewis took my silence for surrender and eased his hold with performative gentleness. "Much better, mousie." He kissed me again, a chaste peck, and I stayed still. Allowed it. "Fast learner."

"Just one question," I said softly.

He paused, and I wondered if it was stiff anger that held him silent or surprise. Eventually he said, "Yes?" in a tone so devoid of any emotion that I had no idea what he was thinking.

"What happened to the late Mrs. Lewis?"

That oily chuckle rippled across his body and made his stomach bounce against mine, violatingly intimate.

"She did not learn her lessons quite as fast as you," he said.

~

Lewis's grip on my forearm was just short of bruising, and I wasn't sure if I was more worried about the pain or about the fact that he seemed to know how much pressure was required to avoid leaving marks. He hauled me through what felt like innumerable dark, bare, back-servant stairways before I was shoved through a door into warm, blinding light, stumbling into the back of a sofa in the same front parlor.

Fenton was still there.

He was standing by the window, glowering out of it with such intensity that he might have been trying to melt the glass.

"Sit," Lewis snarled.

I sat.

Fenton didn't turn around.

Lewis fetched a cut crystal glass and a matching decanter from a bar cart, and poured me a tipple. I hesitated, but Lewis glared, so I took it.

Booze would go a long way toward numbing my fury at this betrayal. But it could also allow Lewis to do all manner of despicable things without my being able to fight back. Or escape.

"Drink," Lewis ordered.

My thoughts and feelings were already so muddled. I figured there was no way that the booze could make it worse. It might even make it better, give me that strange desperate clarity that only the deeply drunk sometimes achieve.

If nothing, it would at least keep me warm if I bolted tonight.

I threw the liquor back like a shot, downing it in one swallow, and slapped the glass down on a spindly side table.

Ew, sherry.

Lewis's mouth curled up in a sneer at the uncouth gesture, and I dared him to do something about it.

Go on, I thought. *Give me a black eye in front of Fenton.*

Instead, he refilled my tiny glass.

"Drink," Lewis ordered.

Fenton's hands, clasped at the small of his back, balled into fists. His jaw, clenched tight, rippled.

I shot the sherry.

Lewis refilled the glass.

"Again," Lewis said, sitting forward. The red-faced anger gave way to carnal fascination.

He's getting off on this.

Gross.

I shot it back. He filled it.

What is this, half a glass of wine? Maybe less. Bro, my record is seven tequila body shots in one hour with no hangover.

"Drink."

I drank.

A knock at the door interrupted Lewis's twisted game.

Worsley had arrived at the door with a bill of lading for Lewis—"In the usual warehouse, sir,"—but more importantly, he also had the fabric bundle of my things. The lad crossed the room and handed them to me directly. Lewis gripped the arms of his chair in white-knuckled disapproval, but apparently propriety in front of a virtual stranger meant that Lewis couldn't snatch it away or order it removed.

Thank god for Worsley, then.

He then went to his captain to relay some other information, and while Lewis was distracted with eavesdropping, I wriggled my wallet and phone out of the bundle and shoved them into my stays. The moment Worsley was dismissed, Lewis ordered the footman to remove the bundle. I didn't fight him. And then Lewis did something I never expected—he left Fenton and me alone to follow it.

He was probably eager to see what I had hoarded away. Well, let him rip each pin and button off my jacket like a covetous magpie if it made him feel powerful. What did I care? I was getting *out*.

As soon as he was gone I shot across the carpet to grab Fenton's hand. He turned to face me, startled, then looked away again just as quickly. Shame? Maybe. *Good.* I sure as hell hoped it was eating him up inside.

"We have to go, now." I yanked him toward the door. "Before—"

"Absolutely not!" Fenton gasped. "Do you know what he'd do to us?"

"I don't care," I said, yanking again.

Fenton closed his hand hard around mine and pulled me to a stop with brute strength. I had once thought his growling, commanding presence sexy on the ship. But turned on me, it was belittling and frightening.

"For my part, he will sue for breach of marital contract if I steal away his bride," Fenton hissed, eyes darting between my face and the door, no doubt counting the seconds he had left before Lewis returned. "He would demand my sister instead, and I am sorry, but I *cannot*—" He cut himself off with a violent shake of his head. "He would default on his loans to me, call in my debts, expose me for a—" Again, he couldn't seem to put voice to the words. "And you, Miss Franklin. You he will treat with *much* less civility."

"You mean like he did with his first wife?"

Fenton blanched.

"Then I'll leave without you."

I tried to shake him off but he grabbed my shoulder and pushed me onto the sofa again, shocking me with his lack of gallantry.

"Are you mad?" he said. "You'll freeze to death before dawn."

"I don't care!" I hissed back.

"Lewis is wealthy and well situated, and has a tolerable temper when not *vexed*. He will make you the jewel of the Ton and the mother to the next generation of a strong legacy. What more could you want?"

"You!" I cried, before I even realized what I was saying.

Fenton reared back. "I am engaged, madam."

"Then we won't marry, I don't care. But you know you can't leave me here. That's why you stayed, isn't it?"

"I have stayed because I'm a fool, and I owe you an apology. Though I made no promises to you, Miss Franklin, I have used you ill and I should not have let you take the liberties you demanded of me," Fenton gasped, like he was running a marathon against his own feelings. "I cannot marry Miss Gale with this act blotting my conscience."

"Oh, so I'm a *blot* now?"

"I did not say—"

I stood and shoved him hard. He stumbled back a step, rocking on his heels, startled.

"You *asshole*," I spat. "I wish you'd left me to *drown*!"

"Samantha, *no*," he pleaded, wringing his hands. "You cannot ask me to regret saving you. You *cannot*, not after what we shared."

"It can't have meant that much if you're still willing to leave me with Mr. Misogynist!"

"But I must."

I grasped for my last straw. "You love me."

Fenton staggered, face widening in shock, as if I'd slapped him. I should have. I was sorely tempted.

"I am engaged to Miss Gale," he whispered, but it rose at the end, like a question.

"I don't care."

But that wasn't true.

She was his fiancé, not me. I wasn't going to claim that I loved him more than she did. Or loved him at all, really; our connection was a trembling, new thing, born from isolation and trauma. From his pity and my desperation to not be alone, a stranger in a strange land. He was my safety net, the only thing I could cling to.

For a single vicious second I wanted to be better than her. I wanted to be the better fuck, the better conversationalist, the better helpmeet. I wanted to be younger and prettier. I wanted his passion and attention. But I couldn't do it; I couldn't be that horrible, bitchy other woman.

Fine.

If I couldn't have him then at least I could convince him to do better by me.

"Okay, I do care," I amended. "Marry her, but don't leave me here."

"And take you where, for god's sake? To my mother? To Miss Gale's?" The big brown doe-like eyes that I had once thought so gentle positively burned. "I have done my duty to you, Miss Franklin! I have paid for you out of pocket, killed my own men for your protection, and was disgraced at a national funeral to chase you out into the snow. I have found a gentleman to take you with no prior references, no dowry, and no proof of your identity. You will not do me the dishonor of rejecting him."

"I sure as hell will!" I snapped. "I am *not* dying the same way his last wife did! And I think I've done pretty fucking adequately to repay your *kindness*." I had the satisfaction of watching him turn purple-red. But there wasn't enough hurt there, so I decided to twist the knife further: "Emphasis on *fucking*."

"You are *infuriating*," he hissed.

I kissed him. It was desperate and open mouthed, and for a brief moment, he crashed against me, just as desperate, just as hard. Then he yanked his head back and pushed me back onto the sofa.

"Enough, Miss Franklin. Know your place."

"Well said," Lewis crooned from behind us, and we both jumped. He was leaning against the door, his entrance having been masked by our shouting.

Fenton straightened himself like a child's toy on marionette strings pulled to attention.

"Shall I see you out, Fen?" Lewis drawled.

Fenton just barely managed to hide a revolted frown behind a carefully blank mask. "There is the matter of Miss Franklin's upkeep. I must settle my accounts before I can journey on to Whitstable."

"Yes, yes," Mr. Lewis said, as if it had just occurred to him now that he hadn't yet *paid* for the whore sitting in his parlor. "Of course."

"I pay my own debts," I said.

My fingers scrabbled against the buckle of the ruined watch strap. *This* I could part with. The mechanics were probably finer than anything they had now. The watch was still ticking, albeit jerkily, the battery insulated. Despite the beading of moisture on the inside of the glass face and the janky movement, it still functioned.

Lewis's eyes flashed with fury as I held it out. He'd thought he'd stripped me of everything worth anything.

"Take it," I said to Fenton. "I don't know what it's worth, but I'm sure the insides can be salvaged if they're repaired. Will it cover the debt?"

Fenton turned the watch over, studying its face, fascinated.

"It doesn't require winding," I pointed out.

Fenton looked up. "How is that possible?"

"There's a power source that . . . look, take it to a watchmaker, get it appraised. I'm sure it's worth far more than it looks, if only for curiosity's sake."

"That is mine," Lewis snapped, reaching to snatch it away, but Fenton was faster, and it disappeared into a coat pocket.

"Miss Franklin has not married you yet," Fenton said, his tone deceptively conversational. The skin around his eyes was tight, though, and now that I knew what to look for, his expression was filled with loathing. "Therefore what little property she has is presently *hers* to sell or keep. I will have it appraised, but I have a feeling that it will more than cover Miss Franklin's debts to me."

"Then, I can go?" I asked, hope rising tentatively.

"If you take her with you, I will sue your family into the workhouse," Lewis snarled, and the threat was no idle one based on the way the color drained from Fenton's face. "Your mother will die in squalor and your sisters will have to sell themselves on the streets. You will never step foot on a ship again, I swear to you, Goodenough!"

"You don't even know me!" I shot back. "Why do you care?"

Lewis's eyes, when he turned them on me, were lit with the narcissistic flames of a self-righteous zealot. "I keep what is *mine*."

His pronouncement was met with horror on my part, and fury on Fenton's. But neither of us said a thing. Instead we stood there, helpless in our linked impotence.

Fenton is just as trapped as I am, I thought. *Shit, there's nothing we can do. Marigold, Daisy, Iris, they'll suffer. I have to stay.*

I have to.

Lewis must have caught the moment I realized the truth, because he straightened and gave a pompous tug of his waistcoat.

"Don't bother awaiting an invitation to the wedding breakfast, Fen," Lewis pronounced with a knife-slice of a grin, smoothing his hair back. "I think it best if the future Mrs. Lewis and I celebrate our nuptials with more . . . discretion."

Scolded like a child and infuriated about it, Fen only snapped off a stiff bow to Lewis then marched out of the parlor without looking back.

Leaving me alone with a man who was probably going to end up killing me.

I used to wonder why women who were being abused never just left. I always thought that I would never let anyone treat me like that. That the moment I saw even a flicker of that first red flag, I would get out. And here I was, staring down an entire parade of the damn things, and staying right where I was. My chin trembled but I wouldn't give Lewis the satisfaction of watching me cry. I bit my lips to hold it in.

Only my lip was still tender from when Lewis had bit it, and I ended up making a pained little mewl of a noise. I quickly covered my abused mouth, but Lewis had heard it. Heard it and *liked* it, if the way he kicked the door shut was any indication.

He stalked toward me.

There was nowhere to go. None of the servants had come to investigate any of the shouting so far, so I doubted I could rely on them for help.

And it would probably get Lewis even more revved up. So I stood there, breath coming shallow and quick like the stupid fucking rabbit I was.

"Now, darling," Lewis breathed into my ear. I didn't jump, but I felt my shoulder rise without my say-so, shying away. "Let us see what you hoard so determinedly."

"I don't know what you're talking about."

"Did you think I didn't notice your petty larceny?" His fingers hooked into the drawstring at the front of my gown and *yanked*. The ribbon snapped and the bodice parted, dragged down my arms by the weight of the sleeves.

"Don't!" I jerked back, both hands covering the wallet and phone where they stuck out of the cups of my stays. I pushed them farther down, until they were pressed between the stiff layers of twill and my ribs.

"If your timepiece was so valuable, what will these fetch me, I wonder," Lewis hissed, avarice slicing through every syllable like a scalpel.

"Take the jacket," I begged, taking a stumbling step back. "Sell the jeans, and the pins, the hat, I don't care. But not these."

"But it is your very resolve to keep it from me that tells me that whatever you hide is *worth* selling."

"They're just cards. The last thing I have from my family. They were ruined in the water. But they're mine." I said nothing about the cell phone. Another step back and I stumbled against the spindly table, knocking over the empty glass.

"Oh, you poor thing," Lewis cooed, following me tightly, step for step. "Has the sherry gone to your head?"

I was on the verge of saying no, of course not, I'd partied harder than he'd ever know, but changed my mind at the last second. "It's just all so much," I whimpered, hoping I wasn't overselling it. "Please, I promise you, nothing is of any value beyond sentimental."

Lewis made a disgusted sound. "You know better than to lie to me," he hissed, his breath was revoltingly moist against my neck.

I nodded.

"Good. Keep your cards then, if they will make you agreeable. But remember that this is a favor I am granting you and I will expect a favor in return."

"What favor?" I asked, even though I already knew I wouldn't like the answer.

His lips came down on the bare spot between my neck and shoulder, leaving a slime trail. I shied away but his hand dropped heavily onto my nape, gripping tight to keep me in place. I was sure that at any moment he was going to shake me and snap my neck, like a terrier with a rat.

When he reached my ear he said, "I want you to do for me what you did for Fen."

Lewis's hand shot up and fisted hard in my hair. I was wrenched backward, curling up onto my tiptoes and thanking my yoga instructor once again that I had the core strength necessary to hold my balance. It was that or let him tip me into the table at an angle that would likely break a bone. Which was probably his aim, the sadistic fuck.

But Lewis was stronger than he looked, and with another twist, I was slammed down to my knees. I had to clutch at Lewis's thigh to keep my balance. He shifted, grinning, so that his legs were on either side of my shoulders.

"You will be my wife and you will perform your duties," Lewis said. "Do it. With your mouth."

Nausea churned in my guts. I clamped my lips shut. If he made me do this, I knew I was going to be sick all over his—

I tried to push back but he still had one hand on the back of my head. He shoved the other into my mouth when I opened it to cry out, two fingers digging against the root of my tongue, the backs of my bottom teeth. It was as effective as a ball gag. I heaved but managed to keep it down.

"No one will come," Lewis hissed. "They know better than to interrupt their master when he's at his pleasure."

I snapped my teeth down.

"Bitch!" Lewis snarled, yanking his fingers out of my mouth, only to swing them down hard against the side of my head.

Stars burst in my vision, my clapped ear ringing, and I hit the carpet so hard I felt my other cheek burn. Lewis tottered back, heading for the sideboard, and I lay where I was and waited for the world to stop reeling. When I pulled myself upright again, Lewis had one hand wrapped around the neck of a wine bottle, emptying the contents down his throat, and the other shoved down the front of his breeches.

His fingers slipped on the buttons of his flap.

I sat up.

While I may have been mildly buzzed, he was most of the way to shitfaced. I didn't know how much he'd drunk before Fenton and I had arrived, but he'd just guzzled more.

"Drink," he snarled at me, tipping forward with the bottle, and I grabbed it from his hands to prevent him from pouring it over my tits. "Drink!"

I didn't relish putting my lips where his had just been, but it was better than another backhand, so I tipped the bottle up and finished off the final third of it. It was sweet, Christ was it sweet, but it didn't taste strong.

Fun fact, my memory-dad piped up. *Alcohol is on average twice as strong in the twenty-first century than it ever was in the past.*

I could use this. I didn't know how yet, but somehow, university drinking games could be my superpower. I just had to figure out how best to deploy it.

The bottle empty, Lewis knocked it away then dug his hands into the hair behind my ears. I tried to scooch back but only managed to trap myself against the sofa. His breeches flap was down, the thin linen of his shirttail stained with old piss and tented obscenely with his excitement. I couldn't see his dick, but what I could see was enough to make my gorge rise again.

"Bite me again and I'll knock out your teeth. Now. Do. It."

I couldn't. I couldn't make my hands move, couldn't lean forward, couldn't do anything but shake and dry heave.

Wait.

This could be a superpower too.

Thinking of all of the most vile, rancid, disgusting things I'd ever seen or smelled in my life, I jammed my fingers into the back of my throat and puked.

Lewis yelped, dancing backward, away from the hot fount. "You revolting wench!"

"I'm sorry!" I caterwauled, backing away as soon as I'd emptied my stomach, though I was nothing of the sort. "I'm sorry. Please! I'm drunk." I scrambled up off the floor, wiping my lips with one of the fancy napkins on the bar cart. "You made me drink four glasses!"

So, about eight ounces. Which was a full ounce less than a standard restaurant serving.

He skirted the puddle and stomped after me, hand raised, knocking into chairs and tables as he stumbled. "I'll teach you to—"

"I can do better! I promise." I got a potted fern between us. "Let me try again, I promise, I won't disappoint you. You don't have to hit me, I've learned my lesson, I—" I clutched my stomach, clamped a hand over my mouth, and heaved again as theatrically as possible.

"Susan!" he roared, and a timid maid popped her head through the servant's door a moment later.

"Sir?"

"Take my fiancé to her room," he snapped. "Fix that ridiculous hair. And bathe her. I can still smell Fen on her. We'll do this correctly tomorrow."

Chapter Nine

IN WHICH SAM THEN WINS

Happiness in marriage is entirely a matter of chance.
—Jane Austen, *Pride and Prejudice*

The timid maid scuttled ahead of me up the grand front stairs, then down a long gallery. My high-school gym teacher would be proud of the hustle I showed following her, because she seemed just as keen to be the hell out of Lewis's sights as I was. The lamps in their sconces were turned low. They threw out just enough light along the walls to make sure no one tripped over the fancy pedestals topped by statues, flower arrangements, and other costly yet sentimentally hollow bric-a-brac that the wealthy have been decorating their houses with since the invention of disposable income.

"This is your apartment, miss," the maid said, her voice a cowed murmur.

The more I took in her mannerisms, the more I despised Lewis.

We entered an opulent private room. It was furnished with a wardrobe, vanity, washstand, and chaise.

And a bed.

A big, four-poster, curtained, frilly abomination of a bed. Everything was covered in costly textiles, and the soft furnishings were overstuffed and luxurious. It looked like something out of an immature *Playboy* fantasy. My twenty-first century clothing was discarded at the foot of the bed, apparently having been deemed worthless.

The maid was quick to light the candles on the vanity from the taper she carried, then stepped back, the perfect picture of a docile servant.

"If you'll have a seat, mistress, I can see to your toilette."

A porcelain basin and pitcher were already waiting for us, steaming gently and filling the air with damp and a faint trace of roses.

I *really* didn't like how prepared this whole thing was.

Too sore to move just yet, and still in shock from my new revelations about Fenton, I couldn't seem to make myself sit. To *submit*.

"Mistress, *please*," the girl said, eyes flicking to the closed door behind us, fearfully anticipating the damning ring of Lewis's footsteps in the hallway. She gave the impression of a girl because she was small and timid, but the silver dusted at her temples told me that she was older than me. Either that or made prematurely gray by virtue of being a veteran of Lewis's staff.

"Yes," I croaked, my throat dry and bruised. "Of course."

Immediately the maid was behind me, undoing the complicated ties that had kept my dress from falling the rest of the way off. As soon as my stays were loosened, my wallet and phone thunked to the floor with all the ominous gravitas of a guillotine blade. She bent to scoop them up, but I beat her to it.

"Ignore those," I said, not sure if this *was* the kind of order I was allowed to give. Or if she would listen to me above her master.

"Yes, mistress," she said. When I placed them on the vanity table she didn't so much as glance at them. The stays were folded into a drawer but the shift and my muddy stockings went along with the dress into a laundry basket beside the wardrobe, and I was standing there absolutely stark naked.

She handed me a folded bit of cloth, already damp with warm rose-water, and when I clearly didn't know what she wanted me to do with it, looked pointedly between my legs.

Christ. In front of the servants? What the actual hell.

I cleaned myself quickly, while she busied herself with retrieving and shaking the wrinkles out of a new shift. She tossed my used cloth in the basket. *For laundry or burning?* A second cloth appeared and she wiped the rest of me down as quickly and efficiently as currying a horse. She was gentle around the new bruises on my knees, and while curious about the stab wound under my right arm, washed around it carefully and did not ask.

The new shift went over my head, and I let the maid manipulate my arms like a doll. This garment was so thin as to be practically nonexistent, not the kind of thing I could wear to flee into the English winter. Which was probably the point.

It was invasive, and dehumanizing, and awful.

But it also wasn't her fault, and I tried to steel myself against flinching at every brisk and comfortless touch. She offered me a toothbrush and powdered chalk and charcoal to clean the foul taste off my teeth, and a spittoon for the waste.

Then the maid pulled back the vanity chair and held it toward me invitingly.

The thought of sitting in a hard-backed chair to be poked at was not appealing in the slightest. It was, however, more appealing than a black eye, so I plopped down.

The maid tipped my head back and washed the tear tracks off my face with a tender sweep of the warm washcloth. It was more soothing than I expected. She pressed a cold cloth, dipped in water from a different pitcher, to the rug burn on my cheek.

As she worked, my mind spun.

How was I going to get out of this mess?

Yes, I owed Fenton Goodenough, but I sure as hell didn't owe him *this* much.

Fuck that guy anyway. Fuck *any* guy who would see exactly what kind of a monster his bro was, then left a woman alone with him anyway.

Running away, though plausible, would certainly do no good. It wasn't like there was a Canadian embassy I could flee to, and I would bet dollars to donuts that the police, if such an establishment existed, were already in Lewis's pocket. There was no one who could protect me from the captain or the judge and his intentions. And yet the idea of life on the streets was more appealing than one as Lewis's beaten wife.

So I had to find a job. Run away, find a job, find somewhere to stay without any references or credibility, or family to recommend me, or even a personal history. In Georgian fucking England.

Jeeze, I was a miserable Canadian, I didn't even know how to make a fire without a lighter! I could drive stick in my dad's pickup truck, play with HTML coding, and I was a whiz at marketing charitable crowd-funding, but what good was any of that, here and now?

Here and *then*?

Whatever.

I was doomed.

The maid picked through the worst of my weather-wreaked tangles. Even after two months, my hair still wasn't as long as a proper woman's ought to be, and I could feel the disapproval radiating off her.

But the repetitive motion felt good, the gentle scrape of the fine-tined comb against my scalp was just as soothing as the warm cloth had been. This was probably the last moment of comfort I could expect to have any-where in the near future, so I closed my eyes and put myself at her mercy.

Funny, now that I had accepted the reality of my time slip, I was still fucked in a fun new way.

I wanted a tub of Häagen-Dazs, some stupid social media to doom-scroll, and Dahlia.

But I couldn't picture her. When I tried to recall it, her face was blurry, her strawberry-matcha scent stifled by salt and rosewater, her voice the distorted ripple of an underwater scream. It was like my mind had locked her away, protecting her from this place, and I was losing her all over again.

I was not proud to admit it, but I kicked the vanity hard in my frustration, rattling it so badly that most of the delicate glass bottles tipped over in a piercing clatter.

"Lord in heaven!" the maid shouted, springing away from me in an instant. "Mistress, are you . . . ?" The maid couldn't finish the sentence, and I didn't blame her. What could she say? *Are you well?* We both knew the answer to that one, didn't we?

"Fine," I lied. "Sorry. I won't do it again."

The maid hesitated, and I could see how little she believed me in her reflection.

"It's fine," I assured her. "I'm sorry."

Tentatively, she finished washing my hair with the now-tepid water. I didn't blame her for her being apprehensive—I'd be scared of the crazy soon-to-be wife of my abusive boss too.

I assessed her via the mirror. No bruises on her face, but her nose was slightly out of alignment in a way that didn't look genetic. There were deep pockets under her eyes, and she kept darting nervous glances at the door. Her nails, while clean, were bitten to the quick.

"What's your name?" I asked as gently, as warmly, as I could manage.

She still flinched at the unexpected sound. "Susan, mistress."

"Nice to meet you, Susan. I'm Sam."

Her crooked nose wrinkled. I wasn't sure if it was confusion or derision at the masculine diminutive. Still, she said "*Yes*, mistress," like a poppet. She started working floral-scented oil through my hair.

"Suppose we'll be getting to know one another pretty well in the next while, eh?"

"Of course, mistress."

"Gonna learn some secrets."

"Yes."

"See some things we're not gonna talk about."

She only nodded this time.

"Try to find ways to support each other."

Her eyes met mine in the mirror, confusion turning, slowly, to collusion. "Yes, mistress," she said slowly.

"Be good friends to one another?"

Her hands paused in their work.

"*Help* each other?" I ventured.

"I . . . I don't know, miss—" she said nervously.

"Are you my lady's maid?"

"Just a chambermaid, miss."

"Would you *like* to be my lady's maid?"

"I—" Her eyes went wide, mouth dropping open.

Dahl had made me sit through *Downton Abbey*. I knew what a huge step up the promotion would be. And what it would mean for her security. I turned to meet her eyes directly.

"A lady's maid *does* stay by her mistress's side, yes? All hours of the day? So she's never in places where the master may corner her alone?"

"*Yes*, miss." Susan nodded frantically.

"And as a lady's maid, it would be your job to make sure I didn't make any missteps, right? Correct me when I was being unmannerly? Drop hints when I'd made a mistake?"

"It could be."

"Then can you explain to me why I am staying here tonight? Alone, with no chaperone, in my fiancé's house? It seems rather untoward."

Susan swallowed hard. "His lordship has secured a special license," she whispered. "You're to be married straightaway, in the morning. Your inhabiting the house will be respectable before anyone of note ever learns you were even here."

My stomach dropped at the revelation. But I wasn't surprised. It seemed like exactly the kind of thing a manipulating asshole like Lewis would do: lock it down before anyone could protest.

Coward, I understood at once. *He's scared of what others will say.*

"Is that so?" I asked. I cleared my throat and turned back to the mirror. "And respectability matters to my husband-to-be?"

"Enormously," Susan confirmed.

She sectioned my hair, rolling it up in rag-knots. If she thought she was going to get lovely springy locks, she was in for a nasty surprise. The only thing that happened to my hair when it was curled was a beast Dahl called *frizzilla*.

"He's desperate to put the rumors to rest and—" She cut herself off, flushing with mortification at her slip. I waited her out, letting her decide if she wanted to add more or not. I could already guess what the rumors said, anyway. "The mamas of the Ton will not treat with him. He is barred from Almack's. Do you take my meaning?"

"The stair is broken, and no one has the power to fix it, only warn others not to step on it?"

"Precisely, mistress."

"And why hasn't the broken stair been reported to a tradesman to repair?"

"If the Bow Street Runners were to look more deeply into *that* aspect of his life," Susan said with extreme care and tact, "then there, perhaps, may be *other* aspects of his business dealings they may uncover, and that his lordship would not appreciate being meddled in." She met my gaze again with pointed meaning.

Message received.

"And so there must be a happy wife, and a happy home, and a bouncing baby boy nine months after to quell the rumors?"

"Just so, mistress. Just so." She stepped back. "Now, was there anything else you'll be wanting?"

Keep me from being dragged to a church tomorrow, I thought. There wasn't anything she could do to stop it, though. And I didn't know her well enough to trust that she wouldn't go straight to Lewis and report our whole conversation.

"No. That's all."

"Very well. Is there anything specific I can tell cook to make to break your fast tomorrow? A food from home, perhaps, that you crave?"

Greasy breakfast sandwiches from the café in the uni quad. Tim Hortons double double coffee. A steaming, cheesy bowl of poutine.

"No. But some willow bark tea, if you can swing it." I touched the rug burn on the side of my face demonstratively. "And bananas."

"Bananas?" Susan balked. "That's food for sl—plantation workers, mistress. We don't eat those *here*."

Slaves, she was going to say.

Jesus fucking Christ on a pogo stick, I'm in a world where people are still enslaved. Disgusting.

Eighteen thirty-four and abolition in the British Empire couldn't come fast enough.

I racked my brains for another luxury fruit. "How about pineapple?"

The maid shook her head. "They're far too expensive, mistress," she explained.

That piqued my interest.

"But it's possible to get one?" I couldn't help the small mischievous smile that tugged at the corner of my mouth.

"Oh, yes, mistress," she said. "But it will be at no small cost."

"S'not my money," I offered.

"Of course not, mistress," she said, her mouth stretching into a matching grin as she followed my reasoning.

"Well. See you in the morning then, Susan."

Susan scooped up the laundry basket and wash basin. "Sweet dreams, miss," she said, and bustled out of the room.

The lock clunked shut behind her.

Oh.

Sure.

Of *course* I was locked in.

Why not?

That was what made a bully: both the desire and the ability to take freedom away from people smaller and weaker than them.

Let him try, I thought as I jammed the vanity chair under the door handle. It wouldn't stop him if he really wanted in, but it would make enough noise to wake me up so I could fight back. I buried myself in the bed, pulling the covers over my head as if they would protect me from the bogeyman I was engaged to.

There was a lot I would have to get used to if I was going to manage to live any sort of comfortable life in a place where my worth was tied to my womb, and my safety to my submission. There was a lot I would have to talk myself *into* accepting, no matter how badly it clashed with my values, my upbringing, and my desires. There would be resentment I would have to soothe, frustrations I would have to let go.

But I was never going to be one of his wilting English flowers. I was a Canadian, born of resilience and resistance, a woman of the twenty-first century. I came from a time when I could vote, I could choose if and when to get pregnant, and I could decide to whom and when I got married, if ever.

Yes, I could be deprived of food and rest. Yes, I could be broken and made to bleed.

But the one thing Lewis absolutely could not achieve was to make me say "I do."

~

I woke the next morning sometime around the ass crack of dawn to the sound of the household stirring around me. I wasn't a particularly light sleeper, but I was alert to all the noises, for obvious reasons.

Clearly the sounds of servants getting ready for their own days above me wasn't stopping anytime soon, so I crawled out of bed and did my stretches. The Sun Salutations helped me to center myself in my body and my mind, the meditation of movement clearing the way for acceptance and focus.

I couldn't believe that Fenton had done this to me, but he *had*, and so I also *had* to believe it. And moreover, I had to get over it. I had to get past it. I had to get *out* of it.

There. Accepted. Dealt with.

Next.

My underarm throbbed as I forced myself flat against the floor for Chaturanga, blood flowing into the injured muscle, stretched and strained. It was a good hurt. It was a clear hurt. Groaning as my joints popped, I arched my back for Urdhva Mukha Svanasana, upward facing dog, and thought, *Okay, next step*.

Next step was to fuel up. I had no reason to suspect Lewis would poison me, so I should eat. Hydrate, even though I still hated the very idea of water. Save my energy. Make sure that when the time came, I escaped him healthy and ready to *go*.

So, breakfast.

I exhaled, felt the pain-sweat beading on my upper lip, trickling down the side of my face as I pushed my hips up and back into Adho, the downward pose, then bit back a whimper as I rolled up to standing.

The jolt of the healing muscle releasing scraped against my nerves.

"Get out of your head," I scolded myself. I grunted my way through three more rounds of salutations before my mind finally went still.

"Good. Now get dressed and sort your shit out, Sammie-bear," I said, and did just that.

I rang the bellpull for Susan, who had to be up by now, then retrieved the pink gingham square of fabric from my jeans pocket to bundle my wallet and cell phone into.

While I waited, I snooped. In the light of day, the room appeared even more garish. It was stuffed with impractical odds and ends and boxes of gewgaws and baubles that made my ears ache just imagining how heavy they must be.

I was tempted to stuff some of the shinier rings into my gingham go bag, but decided that when I left, it would be better to have nothing on me that Lewis could have me arrested for taking.

The only thing I would steal was myself.

I turned my attention to the bedside table and its stack of small, leather-covered books. I was surprised that Lewis would leave something as scandalous as a *novel* in his wife's chambers.

I scanned the spines. *Fordyce's Sermons.* That sounded dry. *Poetry, Declarations on Purity and Sin, Household Management for New Wives,* and . . . seriously? *The Singular Joys of Marriage for a Lady.*

"Absolutely not." I pulled that one off the pile to flick through it. "You can fuck all the way off with that."

~

I had been down in the breakfast parlor—different to the one I'd soiled last night, which apparently was an evening parlor—for about two hours by the time Lewis, looking the worse for drink, tromped in. I'd been dressed in what I assumed was my wedding gown. It was pale gray-green, several shades lighter than was flattering, but that might have complimented Daisy's moonstone eyes. It was also *way* too long, and tighter around the boobs and hips than was likely fashionable.

The willow bark tea had dulled the pain of my bruises. I was on to a pot of the expensive Ceylon now. I knew it was the most expensive because I had specifically asked the parlormaid to *bring* me the most expensive. I longed desperately for coffee, and wondered if Susan could procure any for me, and how much of Lewis's wealth that would eat up.

The man in question dropped into the chair opposite me. I sat as far back in my chair as it allowed.

"What in god's name has happened to your hair?" he grunted.

"Rag-curls," I answered, pushing an escaped lock of frizzilla behind my ear.

He grunted again, and reached for the teapot. He doctored his cup with a slice of lemon and a quantity of costly white sugar, sipped, and then scowled. "The fine Ceylon is for entertaining."

"Really? I had no idea."

A spiky green frond and hard peel sat on the side of my plate, the only indication that I had purposefully blown an extraordinary amount of Mr. Lewis's food allowance.

"You ate a whole pineapple?" he growled as his eyes lighted on them. *"Alone?"*

"Oh dear." I smiled. "If I'd known you liked them, I'd have saved some. Sorry."

He shoved himself away from the table hard enough that the cutlery rattled. He perused the food on the sideboard, and grunted again. "Where's the kippers, woman? Where's the *meat*."

"As your wife, it *is* my job to oversee household management, is it not? This is what I requested."

"Oh, do not say you're a follower of Dr. Chaney," Lewis sneered. "Seeds and nuts, raw vegetables and fruit!"

"There's milk soup," I pointed out, pointing to the tureen of warm broth, cream, and soggy bread.

"This is what chimps eat. Not men like me!"

"Mmm," I said, making it clear that I had opinions about his manhood.

Lewis threw his empty plate at the fireplace against the far wall, where it shattered in a glorious explosion of toxic masculinity, fragile as his ego.

He rounded on me, pulling himself up to loom furiously. Fear fluttered hard behind my ribs, tickling the air out of my lungs in a small gasp, but I steeled myself.

Bullies wanted reactions.

I wouldn't give him the pleasure.

"I can make your life miserable," he snapped, complexion puce.

"I can make yours the same," I offered back blandly, finally meeting his enraged gaze.

"You would not *dare*—" he began, but I cut him off by slamming my teacup onto its matching saucer so hard that it shattered.

The last dregs of my tea sloshed along the fine tablecloth and down the side into a tepid puddle in my lap. It wasn't my dress. What did I care if it was ruined?

"Or you'll *what*?" I asked, and couldn't keep the small laugh out of my voice. Didn't want to, anyway. "Beat me? Break my arm? Break my jaw? I can't be seen in public then, now can I? And isn't *that* what scares you the most? That people will talk? That people might worry? That someone might send the authorities around to check up on poor Mrs. Lewis, and *then* what will they disc—"

The slap came fast and hard against my rug-burned cheek.

It fucking *hurt*.

But it didn't surprise me.

The force of it had turned my head, so I just turned it back and *grinned*, daring him to keep going. To make *sure* I had something blue for my wedding day.

"You *strumpet*," he snarled.

"Sticks and stones," I tutted. I licked my lip and found a cut from the edge of my teeth. I deliberately probed it with my tongue, relishing the sting, opening the wound wider, pushing the blood out of my mouth to let it slide theatrically down my chin. "Oops."

"Cease this!"

"You want to play this game? Fine, we can play. But know that I'm not coming onto the pitch unarmed."

"Your place is to *obey*—"

"Yeah, but it's not, though," I interrupted. He puffed up, affronted by my audacity. "Just 'cause *you* think so doesn't mean I do. You don't know me, or what I'm willing to do to protect myself."

"You will not make a fool of yourself—"

"You think I give a flaming *shit* about my reputation?" I asked, standing to meet his challenge with my own. "I don't *have* one. You think I care what society thinks of me? I've been marginalized my whole life, I'm used to it. I have no maidenly shame to keep me in line. So maybe it's time to rethink this whole marriage plan, and let me go before—"

He had one hand on my neck before I could finish my threat.

Too far, I realized too late. *Sammie, you always take it too far—*

He pushed viciously, shoving me over the table. All of my weight crunched against my right arm, and the shooting agony made me cry out. Whether this was Mr. Lewis's intended result or not, he pressed my rug-burned cheek close to the hot teapot in a very clear threat to stay still. With a shove, my hips were jammed against the edge of the table, my skirts flipped up my back.

"No!" I shouted, wrenching sideways to glare over my shoulder at him.

His eyes were gimlet, pupils blown with blackout fury. He started undoing the buttons of his front fall with vicious, intent tugs.

"I told you we'd try again," he hissed, giddy with cruelty.

Bravado abandoned me. Panic swelled against my rib cage, jabbing into the places I'd secreted my wallet and phone. I shoved, tried to drive him away, good arm flailing, but he batted it aside and grabbed a fistful of my hair.

"I do not need your cooperation, Miss Franklin," he snarled. "I do not *desire* it. Scream. There is no one in this house who will come to your aid. There are none who will deny me my right to punish a misbehaving wife."

He slapped me again, but this time on my other cheeks. The spank was more humiliating than painful, but I squeezed my eyes and my lips tight. He tugged my hair again and I managed to swallow my cry, turning it into a tight squeak. His blunt fingers dug into the hinges of my jaw, but still I didn't scream, didn't give him the satisfaction of sound. It was a battle of wills. If I lost now, I would continue to lose for the rest of my life, and I *would not let that happen*.

And then, thank *fuck*, someone rang the doorbell.

Chapter Ten

IN WHICH SAM FLEES

It is always incomprehensible to a man that a woman should ever refuse an offer of marriage.

—Jane Austen, *Emma*

The coachman at the door was a loud, chatty type, and I could only silently praise him for deflating Lewis's ardor. From the hallway, we could hear him as he talked to the butler about the traffic he'd encountered bringing his lordship's town coach up from the mews, the length of time he expected the journey to the Church of St. Dunstan-in-the-West to take, how he'd overheard from the groom's assistant that the vicar was doing his lordship this special favor, squeezing in the marriage before a funeral at half ten, so he'd taken the liberty of coming to the house early to ensure his lordship arrived sharpish.

"This isn't finished," Lewis snarled in my face, before shoving himself away.

My right arm, still trapped under my body, jolted horribly. I finally cried out, unable to hold in the pain and terror.

"Is the lady in need of assistance?" the coachman called into the parlor.

Lewis rebuttoned his flies and fixed his hair in the reflection of a mirror above the sideboard.

"All is well," the butler replied smoothly, from outside the door. I imagined him standing bodily in front of the entrance, keeping the outsider from witnessing the master's terrible deeds.

Was it collusion?

Or was it fear for his own safety and position?

"She is overcome with excitement and nerves," Lewis called back, hauling me to my feet and pushing me to the mirror to have my turn to fix my appearance. As if anything could tame frizzilla. "What young lady could dream of a more wonderful morning?"

I can think of a few more things I'd definitely like more, I thought viciously, fixing the lay of my dress under his oppressive watch, hands shaking.

Suddenly, running away didn't seem like enough.

I wanted to find some way to hurt him back. To *punish* him.

Lewis helped himself to the cabinet below the breakfast spread, pulling out a liquor bottle and shoving it under his arm. The sight of the ignored breakfast gave me a brainwave.

See, I'd had something to eat. And he hadn't.

"This is as good as it gets," I said, as he straightened.

I followed him out to the street, eyes down demurely even as the coachman complimented me on my fine dress, while Susan wrapped me in a hooded velveteen cloak of darker blue for the occasion. As I predicted he would, Lewis had the cork out of the bottle and was making love to the neck before the horses had taken a dozen steps.

"My turn." I held out a hand. When he didn't immediately pass it over, I wiggled my fingers impatiently. "Couples share, don't they? Gimmie."

Lewis's eyes narrowed in disbelief, yet sparked with intrigue.

"Couples?" he husked.

"Well, it's inevitable, isn't it?" I said with put-on petulance. "You've made your point, *husband*."

"Have I?" he pushed.

"*Yes*, now give me the bottle."

He handed it over, probably worried that I intended to toss it out the window. Tempting, but no. Instead I made a point of meeting his gaze from under my lashes, putting my mouth exactly where his had been on the rim, and tossed back a swig of my own.

Woof, that burns!

Straight gin.

Classy.

I swallowed theatrically, and passed the bottle back.

He peered into its depths, as if worried that I'd dropped a poison pill in there. Spotting nothing, he swigged again. He handed the bottle back. Silently, doing my best to lull his suspicions with coy glances under my lashes, we continued until the bottle was empty. Of course, I only actually drank about one in every three passes. By the time we'd arrived at the church, his snub nose had turned bright red.

"We're here, husband," I said in a low, inviting tone. The flush made its way across his cheeks.

I wasn't confident that my ruse was totally convincing; he seemed too paranoid for that. Didn't matter, I just needed him to let down his guard enough to lose track of the time.

The coachman folded down the steps and opened the door, and I made a point of decanting myself onto the walkway as sweetly and as slowly as possible. A black and gold clock jutted out from the side of the church, floating above the sidewalk, and I maneuvered us so Lewis was facing away from it.

While Lewis stomped out on his own, I dawdled by shaking the wrinkles out of my skirts, fiddling with my buttons, and tidying my hair in the reflection of the coach windows while Lewis became increasingly impatient.

When I'd dragged out the performance as much as I thought was safe, I gasped theatrically and clutched my hands to my bosom.

"Oh dear," I simpered. "Georgie darling, we forgot my flowers! I can't possibly be married without flowers!"

"Damn the flowers," Lewis said, consonants slurring ever so slightly. The flush had traveled to his ears.

"Oh, *would* you be a dear and go back to the house to fetch my bouquet for me?" I asked the coachman, who was overjoyed at the thought of being tasked with so gallant an errand. I thought he would expire from overwrought chivalry on the spot. Of course, when he got to the house, there'd be no bouquet for him to retrieve, and he'd have to wait even longer as Susan whipped something up.

"Enough," Lewis growled, even as the coachman was pulling himself back onto the box. "Stay where you are, man."

"You can't be that cruel to me, darling," I gasped, loud enough that several passersby slowed to take in what they probably assumed was about to be a wonderful bit of street theater. "How mean you are to your new bride, George Lewis!"

My would-be husband crumbled at that, intimidated by the whispering swelling around us. "Dash it, here—" He fumbled a handful of coins out of his waistcoat pocket and practically threw them at the coachman. "Go up the street, you see that stall just there? Then get back here sharpish."

"My favorite colors are pink, purple, and blue!" I called after the coachman as he marched to the flower shop on his errand, as determined as a knight in shining armor. Then I offered a sweet "Thank you, darling," to Lewis.

"Yes, well," he blustered. "Glad you've come to your senses."

"Of course," I lied. The gin buzz was starting to hit me now, too, and I took a few deep breaths of the manure-scented London air to stave it off. "You said you could make my life miserable, and I had a good think about that, you know? It's not appealing."

"Hmph," he replied, but he sounded smug about it.

"Why fuss about it?"

"Why indeed," he said, swaying toward me with a leer.

"Save it for the altar," I teased, ducking away from his attempt at a kiss.

Aptly, considering I had given it away last night, I wished I still had my watch. I didn't want to look up and draw attention to the clock above us.

The coachman was back faster than I'd hoped. "For you, miss," he said, offering me a nosegay of dried lavender, pink and blue pansies, and fuzzy gray-green sage.

"How sweet," I told him in thanks.

"Now may we proceed?" Lewis muttered, crooking his arm with wobbling gallantry.

"We may," I allowed, and took my sweet time guiding his weaving feet up the steps.

We were met inside the door by a harried middle-aged man in the black frock and white collar of the clergy.

"My lord Lewis, there you are. This way, please." He trotted us up the aisle to where he'd left a book and a sheaf of papers on a lectern at the front. "Chop, chop."

"Our deepest apologies, Father," Lewis crooned, leaning on the stone fount. "New bride's nerves, you know. Nothing to be done to speed them along."

The vicar turned a glance to me, clocking Lewis's level of sobriety and questioning it with an eyebrow raise.

"Well, the nerves of one of us," I said cloyingly.

He huffed a chuckle, leafing through the paperwork. "I've married nervous women before. Drunk women too." His eyes twinkled mischievously, well-meaning teasing that would have been reassuring if I hadn't been here against my will. "Do not worry, my dear, his lordship will be gentle with you. He's had a wedding night before this."

Lewis arched his eyebrows at me with lewd humor. I didn't rise to the bait, and thankfully he didn't call me a slut in front of the whole church.

"I'm afraid we're rather short on time, so I'll get right into it. Have you any attendants? Family to arrive?"

"None," Lewis confirmed.

That felt pointed.

"Georgie is my family now," I agreed.

The vicar snorted at the nickname, opened a worn copy of *The Book of Common Prayer*, and began to read.

"'Dearly beloved, we are gathered together here in the sight of God, and in the face of this congregation—'" He side-eyed the coachman just behind us and the few sightseers with guide pamphlets loitering by the stained glass windows. The solemnization was wordy, and as the vicar got into the rhythm of things, he leaned into the drama of it all, taking long pauses and stopping in places where he'd marked in pencil to *looke up affctly at cpl* or *pause to praise G-d.*

Bless him for being a theater kid.

Lewis's vows went first, because of course they did. Lucky for him there was nothing to repeat or space for him to make his own speech because by the time we got there, he was listing sideways, jaw hanging open and eyes fluttering. The holy reverend had to physically poke him to get Lewis to pay attention enough to answer "I will" to the charges of estate.

Just as the vicar turned to me, the main doors behind us opened and a dozen folks in threadbare black poured in. Four men carried a simple pine coffin on their shoulders, laid with a wilting funerary arrangement.

Finally.

"Oh, just a—sorry, just a few more moments, if you don't—" the vicar called to the crowd of mourners, then caught the attention of a younger fellow who'd been resetting the candles on the altar. "Peters, can you please stall them, I haven't—your forgiveness, please, my lord, let us finish—Miss, uh…" His eyes rounded when he realized he'd never asked my name. I didn't offer it, so he plowed on: "'Wilt thou have this man to thy wedded husband, to live together after God's ordinance in the holy estate of Matrimony? Wilt thou obey him, and serve him, love, honor, and keep him in sickness and in health; and, forsaking all other, keep thee only unto him, so long as ye both shall live?'"

I made a show of thinking about it as the back of the church continued to fill.

"You know what?" I said, loud enough that my voice rang across the high stone ceiling. "Nah."

"Who giveth this woman—I'm sorry, did you say 'no'?"

"Yeah, no," I repeated at volume. Lewis swung around to glare at me and overbalanced into the side of the pew. "Changed my mind. Pretty insulting that he had to get shitfaced to marry me, you know? And that's after giving me this." I pointed at the bruising rug burn on my face. "Bye!"

With a quick, satisfying shove, I bowled Lewis into the coachman, sending them both into a heap on the floor. Lewis roared something derogatory but I was already making my way down the aisle toward the open door and freedom.

I had no idea if the gesture had any significance in 1806, but sauntering casually down the aisle with a sneer and an extended middle finger aimed at the pile of wasted flesh felt like it got the message across pretty clearly.

Fun fact, did you know that extending the middle finger was used as an insult as far back as the ancient Greeks? It's meant to represent a cock and balls.

Dad, ew, don't say cock*!*

Grief fisted around my heart, but I didn't have time to stop and mourn.

"Sorry for your loss." I ducked through the black-clad crowd and laid my bouquet on the coffin, not wanting to waste the fresh flowers.

"Samantha!" Lewis roared, and the echo of it slapped against my ears, urging my feet to move faster. "You come back here and sign the parish register this *instant*, I have *bought* you—"

The doors slammed shut behind me and I skidded to a stop and shouted, at the top of my lungs: "What a wretched beast that Judge Lewis is! I am now quite convinced that he is the last man upon whom I could ever be prevailed upon to marry!"

That sounded appropriately historical drama-y, I thought as I dashed through the now-scandalized and gossiping throng congregating at the bottom of the steps. *Thanks for that, Dahlia, babe.*

I had just made it up the block and around the corner when a hackney cab came to a rocking halt in front of me. I skidded to a stop to avoid slamming face-first into the horse.

"Samantha!" came a voice from inside. Daisy stuck her head out the window. "It *is* you. I was just coming to—please, make haste!"

She swung the door open and I scrambled aboard the two-person carriage and slammed the door behind me. I leaned into the corner and struggled to catch my breath, while Daisy gave the driver instructions. We were off in a lurching flash.

"Where? *How?*" I asked.

In answer, Daisy unfolded the newspaper that was in her lap. It was opened to the Society pages, and my own name jumped out at me at once.

> *MARRIED: The Right Honorable Sir George Henry Lewis of Russell Square to Miss Samantha Franklin, lately of the Canadas, at St. Dunstan-in-the-West in an intimate celebration by Special License. The adventurous bride wore fine Indian muslin of pale gray-blue, and the happy couple breakfasted at their coaching inn in Blackfriars before setting off to enjoy their honeymoon at Sir Lewis's country seat at Withern, Lincolnshire.*

"This makes it sound like it already happened," I said.

"The audacity of it," Daisy scoffed, picking at her bonnet ribbons in impotent frustration. "To put it in the paper the morning of the event!"

"It's arrogant as heck," I agreed.

"It is *coercion*," Daisy corrected. "Whether you are his wife in truth, you are now his wife in the eyes of the whole of London society. You will never be able to openly marry another, for you will forever be seen to be attached to him."

"Then I guess I better get out of London, eh?"

"And are you?" Daisy asked, locking me in her sights with a laser-focused gaze. "His bride in truth?"

"Hell, no." I handed back the paper.

Daisy was too refined to do something quite so obvious as sigh in relief, but she did relax back into her seat. "I find myself relieved," she confessed.

"Same," I agreed.

"His reputation—"

"I've been made aware." I pointed to my cheek.

"Oh! Your poor face," Daisy said softly, reaching one gloved hand toward the burn before hastily dropping it again, distress clear in every line of her body. "It was meant to be me."

"I know," I soothed. "This dress is too long. Damn near tripped down the stairs this morning. Is that why you were on your way to the church? To interrupt us?"

Daisy shifted, clearly uncomfortable about her own motivations. "Finch had a bad night of it," she finally said. "After Marigold and Mother went to bed, I got the whole of the story. He was terribly ashamed of his cowardice in leaving you there. I do not know what the judge holds over him—"

Gambling debts. I'd bet my britches Lewis cheated him into them in order to get power over him in the first place.

"—but he has sworn to free you both of it. He did not sleep, and as soon as the hour was reasonable he took himself off to the archbishop to have Lewis's special license revoked. He had not yet returned when the papers were delivered. I do not know what I meant to do, truly. Only that I felt a powerful kinship toward you already, and my anger at Finch was so strong, that I knew I must stop the wedding. My sister would say that this is due to my having read more than my share of terribly gothic novels, for they are always halting weddings midvows with dramatic protestations, are they not? I thought perhaps to do the same."

"I mean, that's *crazy*. But it's also very brave of you," I said. "I'm sure it would have worked if I hadn't just gotten him superdrunk and left him lying on the ground when I was supposed to be saying 'I do.'"

"No!" Daisy gasped, the tight worry on her face cracking into schadenfreude-fueled delight. Oh no. She had the same cute dimples as Fenton. Damn it. "You must furnish me with the details, immediately."

I did, and with theatrical gusto. Daisy drank it in with keen enthrallment. What conclusions she was coming to about me as I recounted the morning, softening some of the more violent moments, I couldn't guess. But the shrewd intelligence that shone in her eyes was magnetic.

"You're not . . . regretting it, are you?" I asked, as I wound down.

Daisy startled out of whatever deep contemplation my tale had inspired. "Whatever for?"

"He's rich, he's got a title and a fancy job. *You* were supposed to be his wife."

"My dear, I was grateful when Finch told me the engagement was off. I want no husband, no matter how wealthy."

No husband, eh?

Sammie, you're being ridiculous, I scolded myself. *And a complete stereotype. It doesn't matter that Daisy is a thousand percent your type—all long legs, with a sense of humor like the edge of a sword, and—stop it! What next, you're gonna get a crush on every Goodenough in London? Marigold too? Maybe Margaret the authoress, if you ever run into her? Cut it out.*

It didn't matter. As tasteless as rebounding with my ex's sister was, in 1806 it was *dangerous*. And that was even assuming Daisy *was* sapphic, and understood, or acted on those desires.

Dahlia had been afraid to come out to her mother because she'd feared being disowned. What would happen to Daisy if she was outed in a time when queer sexuality was literally illegal?

I knew from my Queer History in Western Society classes that lesbianism had never explicitly been against the law in the British Empire, in the most literal sense. Homosexuality laws were about where those with a penis were allowed to put it. But that didn't mean two women in love was accepted either.

"Miss Franklin? Are you—you've gone quite pale."

"Yeah, sorry, I'm—" I swallowed hard. "It just hit me, you know, what I've done. I don't know what to do next."

"There is no great rush to decide the entirety of your fate in this exact moment," she said warmly. "Your nerves must be trembling."

"I'm a bit shook, yeah," I confessed. "But I'm glad that you're here. I feel a powerful kinship between us too."

And that's all I'll let it be, I promised myself. For both her safety, and mine.

Chapter Eleven

IN WHICH SAM BARGAINS

Friendship is certainly the finest balm for the pangs of disappointed love.

—Jane Austen, *Northanger Abbey*

"Mistress Franklin—my lady Lewis," Susan called, then corrected herself, startling Daisy and me to a stop in the cramped hallway of the coaching inn.

"Susan?" I asked. "What are you doing here?"

"We did not expect you and his lordship just yet. The carriage is not yet packed."

Susan cut a look between Daisy and me, as confused as I was. Daisy backtracked to smile pleasantly at her.

"You recall, Finch charged your husband with finding my family lodgings so we could accompany my brother to the funeral?" Daisy asked me, eyebrows raised meaningfully so I would play along. "And so that we were here for the breakfast, to celebrate with you?"

"Yes, yes, of course," I agreed quickly. "George stayed behind to finalize some things. I've come ahead to change, you know, into my traveling clothes. For the . . . the traveling."

Susan cut another shrewd look between us, then waved for us to follow her into a small room upstairs. A private table for two was laid in anticipation of the breakfast in question.

"Remain here, my lady," Susan said urgently, throwing the bolt behind us. "I'll fetch your valise."

"You're not going to—?" I started, but wasn't sure how to finish that question, so didn't.

"Plenty of brides get cold feet," Susan said, like it was that simple. "You get your nerves about you, ma'am, and we'll have you back to the church in a jiffy." Then she slipped through a servant's door hidden in a back corner and was gone.

The room was furnished with just one window, made up of many tiny lead-mullioned diamonds of glass, which provided Daisy and me with a view of the inner coach yard. I didn't have to ask who she was really keeping an eye out for, even as we tracked Susan across the cobblestones to the grandest rig of the lot.

"Your notion of changing for travel is a wise one. This dress was described in the papers," Daisy said.

While I remained at the window to follow Susan's progress, Daisy crowded in behind me to undo the row of tiny buttons leading down from my nape. Her hands were warm and sure, her breath sweet. I wondered if she'd had drinking chocolate with her own breakfast. By the time Susan returned with a leather gladstone bag, I was down to my stockings, chemise, and stays. Daisy had noticed the two odd lumps of my wallet and phone in the cups of the stays but hadn't inquired. Instead, her eyes kept bouncing back to the bandage around my upper arm. It had come loose in the struggle, dipping low enough to show off the yellow bloom of the healing bruise, the red escarpment of scar tissue.

"Oh, nice, you packed my real clothes," I crowed when Susan opened the valise for us. I slid on my purple Chucks and my hat, to hide the tragedy of my hair. I longed to don my jeans, but discretion was wiser. I yanked out the black gown and cranberry-colored spencer. Susan had done a remarkable job of getting all the back-alley grime off of them.

"There's a much nicer tawny cotton—" Susan trailed off and stopped as I also pulled my button-down, jeans, and jacket out of the bag.

"Best not to leave with anything that's not actually mine," I explained.

"Leave?" Susan asked, even as she helped me re-dress.

Daisy resumed her post at the window.

"That is—" I began.

Daisy neatly cut through my prevaricating: "The judge has been jilted."

"I see," Susan said, going very still.

"I know I promised I'd protect you," I told her. "I can find a way to—if this will endanger you, I mean, we can—"

"He'll never know I helped you," she said. "What's more, he'll also never hear of it from me."

"Thank you," I told her sincerely, and sealed my gratitude with a kiss on her cheek. She blinked in surprise but otherwise didn't seem to find it weird. Okay, so maybe the Georgians weren't as prim and hands-off as I'd worried.

"Give me those clothes," Susan said, stripping off her apron to fold my remaining modern clothing into an easy-to-carry bundle while Daisy packed the wedding clothes into the valise. Then Susan was back out the servant's door with the bag and a hasty but heartfelt, "Good luck, Miss Franklin."

"Same to you," I said earnestly.

"No time to linger. It appears that Finch has secured us a carriage. I see my mother haranguing the driver," Daisy said, then headed for the other door.

She paused to check the hallway.

All clear.

"Will we fit?" I asked, then followed her down a rickety flight of stairs, around a corner, and down another, definitely less grand corridor. It seemed the rooms Lewis had secured for his would-be bride's family hadn't been quite so nice as his own.

"Finch can ride. I presume he meant to do so anyway, he has a penchant for escaping onto horseback when the conversation becomes too feminine for him. Or he can—"

"I can do what, sister?" Fenton interrupted, coming up behind her with a mischievous air.

He's the younger brother, I decided on the spot. *He's gotta be.*

And then he got an eyeful of me.

"Dear lord, Samantha," Fenton blurted. "What are you—" He clocked my clothing. "*Why* are you—" He looked behind me. "Where is—"

"There has been a change of plans," I said, echoing his words to Lewis from last night.

Fenton understood immediately. "You have not . . . ?"

"No," Daisy said. "And she never will."

"Thank god!" Fenton shimmied around Daisy to close me in an embrace that even I knew was too intimate to be proper. "He received my payment and released you from the contract?"

"Weeell," I hedged, giving him a squeeze and backing out of his arms. He was an engaged man. I had to remember that. "More like I left him at the altar? You didn't happen to get that annulment of the special license, did you?"

All the color drained from Fenton's face. "The archbishop was not in. Miss Franklin, what will you—"

"Miss Franklin has agreed to become our lodger, has she not?" Daisy said, with all the calm authority of someone who was lying through her teeth.

"Forgive my vulgarity, but with what *money*, Miss Franklin? I have sold your watch—and what a fascinating piece it was, the watchmaker was *enchanted*—but the whole of that has gone to satisfy my debt to Sir Lewis in the stead of your marriage."

"Miss Lewis has an education," Daisy said, proving that she did listen keenly indeed. "The little school that Marigold runs out of our back parlor is proving more popular than she can manage—we had discussed the possibility that I would take on some tutoring duties, but it would be better still if Miss Franklin were to step into the role, for my management of the household would have quite divided my attention. Marigold can take on more pupils that way, and Miss Franklin has already agreed that rather than request wages she will be content with her share contributing to her upkeep."

"That certainly does solve the problem of how to stretch both Marigold's and Mother's widow's portions while freeing you up to resume pursuing a suitable marriage," Fenton said, with no little relief.

Daisy grimaced at the mention of marriage but didn't contradict him.

"Well, with *that* settled," I said, deciding it was neither the time nor the place to bring up the fact that Daisy and I'd had no such conversation, "should we shake a leg?" Both Goodenoughs shot me identical looks of confused bemusement. "Get going, I mean."

"Mother has ordered a lunch."

Daisy was off with a quick, "I'll chivvy our mother along, shall I?"

"Tell her to get it to go!" I shouted after her.

And then I was alone, in a half-lit hallway, with the man who had sold me to a qualified domestic abuser.

The punch was both well deserved and cleanly landed. Mostly because Fenton wasn't expecting it. He reeled back into the wood-paneled wall, holding his jaw and staring at me with wide, hurt eyes.

"I can't believe you did that to me!" I snarled, shaking out my hand. "I can't believe you were going to do that to your own *sister*. And your mother ordered lunch? Which means she didn't *know* there would be a wedding breakfast? Weren't your family *aware* that they'd come to London for Daisy's wedding?" Fenton was too much the gentleman to squirm, but the shame was clear on his face. "You disliked selling Daisy to Lewis *so much* that you didn't even *tell* your mother? *Jesus Christ on a piece of melba toast*, Fenton."

"It was badly done," Fenton agreed, working his jaw.

"It was *cowardly*," I corrected. I stepped closer and he flinched. Good. "And on top of that, you turned me into your *side chick*."

"I do not know what that means—"

"It means," I said, poking a sharp finger into his sternum, "that you've been a fuckboi. A douche canoe. A *rake*."

That last term hit home. "I am *not*."

"No? 'Cause I sure as hell wasn't the one to flirt with the mermaid when I knew I was already engaged. Just saying."

He folded his arms over his chest and scowled. "I find you irresistibly fascinating," he said, uncomfortable with his own feelings, and making it my problem.

"And that's flattering," I said. "But it's time to be grown-ups about this. I refuse to be a stereotypical greedy bi slut, and you have a fiancé. I'm going to have to stop relying on you and figure out my own path in this shithole era. So we're drawing a line under this."

Fenton fidgeted. "If I'm to have the reputation of a fashionable libertine, I don't see why we shouldn't—"

"Who's calling you that?"

"Sailors talk, as well you know, and it escaped no one's notice I squired you around Gibraltar—"

"If you think"—I pushed him back against the wall with the force of my poking—"for a *second* that you're getting your dick wet ever again, after *everything* that's happened, you can jump off a cliff."

"But you—" Fenton sputtered, confused. "You want—"

"To be loved. Not *used*."

Fenton took a moment to digest this, then deflated. "I am being uncouth."

"Hey, I get it, the wanting to be in control when you've spent so long feeling like you're not, trust me," I said. "But fucking around only to feel like a big man again? It's a dick move."

Chastened, Fenton tugged on his earlobe.

"Lewis is not a man to be crossed," he said at length. "He will not take lightly to what has happened. He will come after you. If nothing else, he will sue me for breach of promise."

As changes of topic go, it wasn't subtle.

"How can he? Either it gets around that I jilted him, in which case his reputation takes a hit, or, as per the breathtakingly arrogant move with the newspaper, he goes on acting like the wedding actually happened and there's nothing to sue you *for*. Either way, if he makes a stink, he'll look like an even bigger idiot. *And*, with your debts paid, going after you will look like a vendetta. I'm sure that's something we can take to his bosses. No one wants a dirty judge, right?"

"I suppose," Fenton allowed. "I personally delivered the money to honor my debts to Lewis's bank, so there is no question of it being outstanding. Moreover, I have no ship with which to do his dirty business." His whole demeanor brightened. "I am free of his control."

"Hold up, how do you mean, no ship?"

Fenton not-squirmed again. "The *Salacia* is being sent out with a different man at her helm for this tour."

I took a moment to process that. "Is this your boss punishing you? For what?"

"I was *late* to the battle."

"Because you *rescued* me."

"I was still late," Fenton said. "And Lord Nelson is still dead."

"That's not *your* fault."

He shook his head grimly, just once. "The *Salacia* was not with the fleet."

"Are you fired?"

"No, but I am on shore leave with no prize money, which means that I cannot . . ." This time he fidgeted. "It's the least of what I deserve for my pusillanimity."

Then he turned on his heel, the conversation over in his mind. I grabbed his wrist.

"Hey, Fenton," I said softly. "*Why* did you do it? If you knew it was wrong, if you knew Lewis would grab you by the soul and smear you through the tar, use it to glue you to his side, *why*? Why gamble with him, why smuggle, why agree to what he tried to do to Daisy, what he *did* do to me, why *witness* it, and still walk away?"

His lips trembled, water like mercury lining his bottom lashes. "Have you . . . have you ever been so in love that it makes you *puerile*?" he whispered. "That it takes away any sense of longitude or latitude, for your sextant points only to them? That they become your magnetized north? That sense abandons you and propriety flees, and you would do every vile, despicable thing demanded of you if only it meant they would *smile* at you?"

The question hit me like an arrow through the heart, driving the air out of my lungs in a pained grunt.

"Yeah," I gasped. "Yes."

"Who was he?"

"Her name was Dahlia," I said, voice thick with emotion.

Fenton took a moment to wrap his head around my confession, and the full scope of its meaning. "And this is permissible, in your wild land of shorn hair and fist-sized blackflies?"

I snuffled hard. The bundle of my modern clothes still dangled from my wrist, and I dug through it to find the handkerchief Fenton had given me back on the ship. I mopped my nose. "Yeah."

"In your far-flung year of two thousand and twenty four?"

I jerked my gaze up to search his face. "You believe me?"

"I have seen the inside of that watch. It was both a marvelous and terrifying thing to behold."

"*Thank* you." I wanted to hug him, so I did. "And yours? What's her name?"

"Eliza," he said, exhaling her name like it was the first breath of spring. "Miss Elizabeth Gale."

His whole face lit up just *thinking* of her. It was clear that he loved Eliza Gale with everything he was. And maybe she loved him the same.

Maybe she didn't, and was only hooking up with him because she had no other choice too. But that didn't matter. She would wear his ring, not me. She would bear his children. She would keep his house. She would be entitled to his presence and presents, paychecks and affection. She needed him, and if I got in the way . . .

Then she would end up like me. Abandoned, alone, with nothing.

And honestly, if Fenton wouldn't pledge himself to me, then I hoped that he could at least take what I'd shown him over the last few weeks and use it on her to good effect. I mean, *somebody* better be getting orgasms out of this whole thing.

Wow, I suck at this jealous girlfriend schtick, huh?

"But?" I asked. "There's a but, right there, on the tip of your tongue."

Fenton dimpled. "Your idioms do baffle me, Miss Franklin."

"The future is a far-flung country, Captain Goodenough," I teased. "You'll learn the language eventually. What's the 'but'?"

"But," he said slowly, "the *Salacia* captured no enemy ships during the battle, and so we earned no prize money. Without it, I am unable to marry Eliza. I have not mentioned this before, as I had hoped that selling what we'd salvaged from your craft would have made up the shortfall. It was not enough."

"Oh." I felt like an asshole. I'd thrown suitcases, cameras, clothes, bottles of pills overboard. Things that meant nothing to me, and I'd just chucked them. I'd made him kill some of his own men in my defense, waste good medicine on my arm and money on two dresses that I'd immediately ruined. I'd refused to wed the man he'd found to take care of me (though not even my guilt could make Lewis any less of an asshole) and now I was about to become a financial burden on his family. "I'm sorry."

"I am now living only on my wages, and even those are throttled, for I will not be at sea again for six months at the earliest. Yet I am expected to arrive in her father's house ready to wed—we had agreed that it would be after this last tour. We are anticipated. Tell me, how can I take my sisters, my mother there, and prostrate myself at the feet of her father and beg him not to call it off, when he has every reason to do so?"

"Does he hate you?"

"No—he approves the match most strongly. Yet it would not be sensible to proceed when I cannot provide for his daughter."

I rucked up my skirts and dug up the side of my corset.

"Miss Franklin!" Fenton gasped.

"Oh, don't be such a prude," I scolded. "You've seen it all anyway. Here, stick your hand up—"

"Absolutely not!"

"—the side of my stays, you dork. It's slid around the back, and I can't get—there's a hard, rectangular thing—"

"Oh, lord forgive me," Fenton groaned heartily. He pulled out my phone. "Do you mean this?"

"Yeah, that. I don't know what it's made of—plastic and metal, but I'm sure there must be some quantity of copper and gold in it. The battery is garbage but the little circuit boards, I don't know. Surely you can sell this too?"

"You cannot simply give me *everything* you own worth pawning." But he was already entranced by the smooth face, the acid-eaten, bloated backing.

"Why not?" I asked. "You heard your sister. I have bed, board, and a job now. What use to me is a smartphone that doesn't work? *Make* it worth something. Marry her." I closed his hands around it.

"Samantha."

"You saved my life. Twice. Three times, if you count helping me get away from Lewis, though technically I don't know if that actually does count if you're the reason I was in danger in the first place." He huffed and touched the swelling spot on his jaw where I'd socked him. "Take it."

"I will need to get it appraised, immediately, *before* I can join you at Swangale House. I am meant to escort the ladies, though—"

"I have trousers, and short hair, and I'm a pushy bitch. I can play brother for a few days," I told him. He wavered. "I'll take care of them for you. Good luck, Captain Goodenough."

I stuck out my hand. He shook it.

"Fair winds, young Master Franklin." He chuckled.

And then he was gone, back up the passage in the direction we had come.

I turned to track down Daisy, and jumped when I damn near ran into her. This close, I realized my eyes were exactly level with her pretty, pink little flower bud of a mouth. A mouth that was twisted in an unimpressed moue.

"Hi," I breathed, entranced by the bald fascination in her moonstone eyes. "How much of that did you hear?"

"Nothing of note," she said, cold and swift. "The carriage waits only for you, *brother*."

"Then let's be off," I said, with a playful bow.

~

"What is *she* doing here?" Marigold spluttered, then quickly regained her decorum as Daisy shoved over on the bench to make room for me opposite their mother. "Where's Finch?"

"He's a last-minute errand," Daisy said blandly. "He'll be along after us, and will likely catch up before Swangale if he pushes that poor sweet mare he's borrowed off his first officer."

"Yeah, not to make this sound too much like a Hollywood car chase, but can we *go*?" I asked, pulling the door closed behind me.

Daisy rapped on the ceiling, and the carriage lurched into motion. I caught sight of Susan by the judge's carriage, watching our escape anxiously, fingers twisting in her skirts. Then we were out in the bustling streets of London, just another nondescript vehicle in just another inner-city traffic jam.

We wriggled out of our hats and coats and cloaks, the air of the carriage already stuffy with the windows closed tight against the January cold. The interior wasn't luxurious, the padding worn flat, the fabric on the wall crushed, the curtains dusty. But the one thing it was good at was keeping in the body heat from four adult women.

As soon as Daisy had bundled up her own cloak behind her in a makeshift pillow and hung her bonnet from the door handle by its ribbon, Iris plopped the basket of foodstuffs into Daisy's lap.

"Be a dear and manage that for me," she said, settling back opposite under a lap rug. "I'll help myself to a pie."

"Can the basket not sit on the floor, Mama?" Daisy protested.

"It's cramped," Iris said, and held out a mittened hand imperiously.

Daisy sighed—the put-upon sigh of a daughter indulging her mother hadn't changed in the ensuing two hundred years—and rooted through the basket for still-warm pastries for each of us.

"Aren't you meant to be wed this morning?" Marigold asked me as we did our best to keep the crumbs off our fronts.

"Mary, leave off," Daisy warned.

"Mary?" I asked.

"My Christian name is no more Marigold than my brother's is Finch," Marigold said.

I turned to my seatmate. "Are you really Daisy, then?"

Daisy only smirked at me like butter wouldn't melt.

"Your *marriage*," Marigold prompted sniffily.

"I allowed the horse to lead me to water," I answered. "But I didn't like the look of his teeth, so I decided not to buy."

The attempted levity had the opposite of the intended effect on

Marigold, whose scowl grew deeper. "The judge is a very finely established man who has a great deal of comfort to offer any woman. Marriage is a fine and noble institution, not to be undertaken—"

"—lightly. I agree, Mrs. Kempel. Which is why I've elected not to enter into it at all."

Marigold had little to say to rebut that, so fell back on belligerent chewing.

The pies lasted us until we passed the disappointingly diminutive Tower of London, and Daisy was quick to hand out further victuals to keep our mouths occupied more with peacekeeping endeavors than sniping. Wrinkled winter apples, candied nuts, and a glass bottle of lemonade were shared. Luckily, the meal had a soporific effect on Iris and Marigold.

Outside the carriage, the warehouses, docks, and riverside taverns of Limehouse slowly made way for meadows dotted with cattle. Inside the carriage, Marigold and Iris slumped toward one another like tired old barns in an abandoned pasture.

Daisy waited until the first snuffling snort from Iris, and then wedged the luncheon basket between her fine leather boots and the door.

"I thought she'd never drop off," Daisy lamented in a low voice.

"Why did she make you hold it?" I asked.

"So I could not retreat into a novel," Daisy said. "Mother says I shall ruin my eyes."

"She's not wrong," I pointed out. "Especially in this light."

"Then I shall procure spectacles," Daisy said, with the same imperious air as her mother had used asking for the pie. "I think I should look rather well in them."

"They'd be cute, yeah," I agreed.

The compliment, like my attempt at a joke, landed wrong. Daisy stiffened and turned her face away.

"Okay, *now* what have I done?"

"Nothing," Daisy said, frost hanging from every consonant.

"Then why is everyone in this carriage giving me grief?"

I dared to rest my hand on the round of her shoulder. Daisy unthawed under my touch by inches. Finally, she slumped as much as her stays would allow and rested her back against the window to face me. This meant I lost contact, but she pressed her feet between mine, and that was just as nice.

"My sister is not fond of change," she said after another indeterminable few moments of studying me. I wished I knew what she was looking for. I'd gladly give it to her. "After the loss of Mr. Kempel, she was heaved up like a dinghy dashed upon the stones of the Cobb."

"How awful." I had no idea what the Cobb was, but I could still picture a driftwood-gray boat smashing on a rocky shore.

"Mary relies on me most heavily," Daisy confessed. "I am happy to be her support in such griefs, but of late the weight of her sorrow has grown too much for me to bear alone."

"Can't your mom—"

Daisy shot me a sardonic look.

"I sometimes feel as if I am *their* mother," she said. It was the closest thing to a complaint I'd heard out of her. "It is *terribly* selfish of me, Samantha, but having just one other intelligent, resourceful female in the house will free me up to pursue other pastimes, ones I have missed fiercely."

"So, I'm to tutor *and* be a caregiver in return for my bread and butter?"

"I'd be so grateful if you could find it in yourself to do so." Daisy clasped my hands between hers, and then immediately released me at my wince. "Does it hurt much?"

"Less than it used to," I said. "Do you want to see it?"

"Is it *too* gruesome?" Daisy asked, sitting forward, fascination lighting her eyes from within.

"Why, Miss Goodenough," I joked as I worked the sleeve of my dress up. "Are you *excited* to see a disgusting, gaping wound?"

"Mother says the novels I read have addled me, filled as they are with ghouls, and curses, and all manner of thrillingly horrid tales," Daisy confessed, a delicate flush skipping over her aristocratic cheekbones.

"They sound like fun books."

"Your wound is not . . . " She hesitated. "Not *properly* disgusting, I hope?"

"Not disgusting at all." I presented my arm with a flourish.

The wound had closed over into a lumpy knot of angry scar tissue. It was slowly hardening, getting shiner and whiter by the day. It was a proper divot in my flesh now, like a jagged bite taken out of a pear, and the last of the bone-bruise clung to my skin like sickly yellow pollen.

I thought I'd hate it. Looking at it now in broad daylight, for the first time in weeks, I thought I would despise the way it marred my skin, resent it for the weakness and pain it forced on me. But I could only be proud of it. This scar was proof that I had saved someone I admired and spared everyone in this carriage from the pain of his loss. No matter how it ached, here was an eternal reminder of my bravery—and a reminder that silence could, in certain circumstances, actually be a virtue.

"Oh, the wound is closed," Daisy said. Her nose wrinkled as she studied it, but it was in concentration, not revulsion. "May I?"

"Yeah."

Her hands were warm, the callouses on the tips strange. Were they from needlework? Or some other pastime or device I was unfamiliar with?

The press of travel-chapped lips against the top of the scar startled me out of my contemplation, and I came back to myself to find Daisy's sweet blond head bent over the sensitive skin of my inner elbow. I clamped down hard on a shivering surge of desire.

Down, girl.

I was doing the baby duckling thing again; the first person to treat me with any compassion after yet another trauma had become the new object of my fantasies.

Daisy was *not* my Fenton rebound.

"There," Daisy said, smoothing my sleeve back down. "Surely now it will not pain you, for I have kissed it better, and my littlest cousins find there to be great medicine in such a poultice."

"Oh . . ." I said stupidly, then swallowed hard. "Thanks."

"Samantha," Daisy said, straightening up. "If you are to join our household, if you are to be our companion and, I do hope, friend, then trust that you never feel that you need to hide or feel shame for who you are." She tapped the side of my arm gently, but she was looking at me so steadily that . . .

Christ. I really needed to stop reading into things so deeply. Especially with Marigold and Iris sleeping *right there*.

"Yeah, okay," I croaked.

"Do you enjoy novels?" Daisy said, clocking my discomfort and changing the subject with all the subtlety of a sledgehammer.

"I haven't had much time for fiction lately."

"Oh?" Daisy asked. "And why is that?"

"My studies," I said, thinking that sounded suitably vague.

"Yes! You went to *university*," she said, that breathless wonder back. "For which subject did you read?"

"Social history. Not battles and big historical figures. More like stories and clothes and everyday people, you know? But I don't want to bore you. What's the most recent thing you read?"

"Oh! Miss Edgeworth's latest tale is *quite* engaging," Daisy said, immediately engrossed with recounting the fate of lamentable Griselda and the unspeakable sacrifice her husband the Marquis of Saluzzo demands of her when each of her children are born. He commands her to give them up to be killed—while secretly sending them away to be raised with fine educations.

Her retelling of that story, then several more of her recent favorites, lasted until the driver stopped the coach at the side of the road for a comfort break a few hours later. It was both exciting and scary to realize that my brain was filled with pop culture, films, TV shows, and memes that I could never hope to explain to Daisy. And yet, at the same time, there she sat with her own brain stuffed with an equal number of stories, poems, and pamphlets that I, in turn, had never heard of.

Daisy woke Iris and Marigold, and together we donned our wooly armor and ventured behind our own individual trees to see to the needs of our bladders. Figuring out how to pee in skirts and a cloak without hitting my shoes was an *experience*. Our bend in the forest path proved a popular spot. As I scooped up some snow to clean my hands, another carriage pulled up behind ours, and a gaggle of giggling preteens tumbled out to find their own relief among the brambles.

"*What* a palaver!" one of them called to the other, and I leaned back against the tree to eavesdrop, amused by the fact that women shouting back and forth over bathroom stalls seemed to be a time-honored tradition. "I had it from my sister, who was walking outside the church, that the bride declared that she would not have him! But then the coachmen went off on foot after her, and my brother-in-law says he must have returned her the back way, because before he knew it, the vicar and the groom were out on the front steps shaking hands, and the coach drove up on the walk so the bride could exit without being gawked at, and now the judge and his 'adventurous' lady are halfway to Lincolnshire for their honeymoon, to be sure!"

A shiver of recognition crawled up my spine.

"You were right," Daisy said, from over my shoulder.

I hadn't heard her creep up, and her deep, thoughtful voice was right beside my ear. I may have jumped. But only a little.

"Daisy! Hi! Warn a girl. Right about what?"

"Lewis. His reputation is of more concern to him than the actual location of his bride. This story must be all over town by now. You are wed. He shall not pursue."

"And let's hope it stays that way."

Chapter Twelve

IN WHICH SAM REFLECTS

> *It is not time or opportunity that is to determine intimacy;—it is disposition alone. Seven years would be insufficient to make some people acquainted with each other, and seven days are more than enough for others.*
>
> —Jane Austen, *Sense and Sensibility*

Swangale House was located just outside of the village of Whitstable. The village was in the Canterbury district of Kent, between Seasalter and Upper Harbledown, and I swear to god, those are real places. Sometimes it felt like the British named towns via games of Boggle. We were about halfway there by the time the sun set at an appallingly early four thirty, according to the clock attached to the coaching inn when we stopped for the night.

Our comfort break had given me the opportunity to have the carriage to myself long enough to wriggle into my modern clothing. Daisy had caught me at it and helped me with the stays. Mama Goodenough and Mrs. Kempel didn't have the time to disapprove of my new look, though, because by the time they had come back Daisy was wearing my abandoned cranberry spencer, and I was wrapped in her gray wool cloak. Iris and Marigold had not nodded off again, so I'd spent the remainder of the afternoon fielding Marigold's questions about my education and what subjects I was versed in, determining what I could teach. Iris interjected frequently with blunt to the point of rude musings about Daisy's marriage prospects and the suitable bachelors she might set her cap for in Seasalter.

It wasn't until we pulled into the coaching inn in Rochester that they were privy to my trousers, when I shucked the wool cloak so I could stretch, and by then it was too late. I tumbled out of the carriage, butt sore from the lack of shock absorbers, and Daisy followed, eager to be out of the presence of the rest of her family.

"You look a rough sort," Daisy commented as we struck off for the common room to track down the landlord and bargain for our beds. "Why are your trouser hems turned up? Are your ankles not cold?"

"Promised you a brother, didn't I?" I teased.

I turned then, and caught her staring at me. No, not staring at me, exactly, but staring at my *ass*.

That's pretty awesome, I decided, smirking.

She didn't look into my face to catch it, just back down at her reticule. But her ears had turned pink.

"A brother would have this," Daisy said, and dropped a plain knit pouch with a coin purse mouth into my hand. It clinked.

"I don't know what to do with this," I confessed stupidly. "I mean, I don't know how much—"

That inscrutable look was back, the one that made me feel a bit like she was planning to mount me on a corkboard with a hatpin.

"A sixpence upon meeting the chambermaid and the ostler," she said as we hustled inside. "Two for the landlord, and one for the groom's lad."

"Which one is the sixpence? This one?" I asked, pulling out the smallest silver coin from the pouch.

"Yes. Do you honestly not know this, Samantha?"

"Currency is different where I'm from," I told her. "And so is tipping culture, apparently, if we have to tip *before* we get the service."

"You must tip to get any service at all," Daisy corrected. "Be sure to ask for only two beds, for Mary and I are well accustomed to sharing, and the driver may sleep in the coach if there is no room above the stables for him."

"You expect me to share with your mom?"

Daisy halted unexpectedly, expression going through a series of complicated gymnastics before landing on chagrin. "No, you are correct. Marigold and Mother shall share."

It was only after the business was done and we were halfway through our strained dinner of beer, cold cheese and meats, fresh bread, and more boiled-to-death vegetables, that it occurred to me that Iris and Marigold sharing meant that Daisy would be in the second bed with me.

I gulped down my beer to hide my sudden blush.

Fun fact! Dad's memory crowed, laughing at me. *For the great majority of human history, bed-sharing was the norm. Beds were the most expensive piece of furniture to make and dress, so sometimes whole families co-slept.*

Jesus wept.

Despite their naps, Iris and Marigold proclaimed their tiredness first and headed to bed a few hours after our arrival. Daisy, safely chaperoned by her "brother" (a fiction that I *knew* no one was buying, but were also, strangely, not challenging), was able to haggle for a bottle of Madeira from the landlord's wife. We moved from the dining parlor to a quieter common room populated by sagging, mismatched furniture and sagging old men reading sagging newspapers while their sagging wives went through the motions of passionless games with sagging playing cards.

We tucked into two such chairs before the hearth, and Daisy divvied the wine. This time the cups were earthenware, and what I would call a proper pour. The wine itself was sweeter than I liked. It reminded me far too much of last night's sherry. And the way it had tasted coming back up.

Had that only been yesterday? So much had happened, I was in danger of starting to cry if I tried to process any of it right then.

"Is it not to your preference?" Daisy asked.

"It's fine, it's just . . . I'm feeling homesick." I disguised my trembling bottom lip with a healthy slug of the awful wine.

"Of course," she conceded. And then, as if testing the ice on a newly frozen pond, she asked: "Will you tell me about your home?"

"What's to tell?" I asked with a shrug. "I live in a coral condo complex with in-shell cleaning service and a parking spot for my seahorse."

She grinned slyly. "Fine then, keep your secrets."

We drank some more. The fire crackled. The newspapers whispered and the cards shuffled.

"It is nice to have some silence," Daisy hummed at length, interrupting said quiet. "The carriage ride is proving to be quite the trial by fire. I do apologize for my mother—"

"No need. I get it."

Daisy leaned back in her chair, reassured, her prim posture melting somewhat in the cozy warmth of companionship. But her expression grew more and more hound doggy until finally I asked: "What is it, sourpuss?"

She blinked, jerking her head up from her contemplation.

"Sour? I beg pardon?"

"You look like someone just told you Father Christmas isn't real."

Her jaw dropped. "Father Christmas does not truly exist?" she gasped. For all of three seconds, she actually had me. Then I cracked a grin, and so did she. It was still sad looking, but it was there, at least.

"C'mon," I said. "Something's churning in your head. I can see you thinking."

Daisy scoffed playfully. "You cannot."

"I can. Besides, isn't this the part of those novels you like so much where the womenfolk, finally alone together, confess their terrible secrets?"

Daisy turned that thoughtful, probing look on me again. "Dialogue written in a novel hardly mirrors true spontaneous conversation."

"Oh, yeah." I quashed the stupid affection for her polysyllabic speech patterns. "Totally." I shifted in my seat and refused to let myself get awkward, even as the air between us thickened.

She gave that little amused headshake at my turn of phrase, then grew serious. "I must confess, I was thinking of your flight, and the determination it must have taken. I admire your ability to simply make a decision and see it through, as well as your *ambition* to do what you set your heart to, with no reservation. I envy that."

"I dunno." I picked at my cuticles nervously. "Leaping before I look can backfire." I pointed to my hidden scar.

Daisy dimpled. "To be frank, it *also* concerns and confuses me greatly that you seem to have no understanding of, nor regard for, propriety and etiquette. You set your mind on an action and then you complete it, consequences be damned."

"Time and tide wait for no man." I saluted her with my cup. "And neither does Samantha Franklin."

"What does Samantha Franklin wait for, then?" Daisy asked, intrigued.

There was *no way* she could have meant it like *that*. Still, raised as I was in the queer bars of Toronto, I nearly pitched out a soft opener. I only kept it behind my teeth by taking another gulp of the fortified wine. Eugh.

"I want to save the world," I said at length, when I was sure the urge to flirt had passed. "Or leave it better than I found it, at any rate."

Daisy's eyebrows climbed. "That is a lofty aspiration." Her slim fingers stroked up and down her cup thoughtfully.

Christ, I wanted to take her hand, to encourage her restless touches to stroke up and down my thigh instead. My fondness and admiration for Daisy had grown with every new topic of conversation we'd shared today, with how she took my eccentricities in stride and found them fascinating instead of mortifying, with every searching gaze she turned my way when she thought I couldn't see.

It was torture.

My love language was Physical Affection. Dahl had made me do an online quiz. (Hers was Quality Time, but we had to be totally chaste when we weren't alone, so no wonder we were at such odds). It was *killing* me that nobody touched each other in this stupid era unless they were a servant or a spouse. I was *starved* for contact, clingy bastard that I was.

And we were going to share a bed.

I gulped more wine.

Daisy would be warm, and soft, and pliant with sleep. Actual sex was the *furthest* thing from my mind after the last twenty-four hours, but *cuddling*, just tender, platonic hugging, I missed that *so much*, and she was going to be *right there* and—

I wonder what Daisy's love language is?

"But *how* one is to improve the world, that is the question," Daisy murmured, diverting my attention from my mounting panic.

"I suppose it's a matter of what you want to change, and what's in your power to affect," I offered, welcoming the distraction. "My education focused on the social history of rights movements. That's what I want to do—improve people's lot in life, ensure that the downtrodden, or ignored, or colonized, or discriminated-against are lifted up, given their own self-determination."

"Ah," Daisy said, warming to the topic. "Like a missionary brings enlightenment to the savage peoples of the new world?"

I winced. "More like directly opposing the missionaries imposing their own foreign norms on violently suppressed strangers, then doing what I can as the descendant of settlers myself to help those indigenous people regain their ancestral homes and lands and advocate for their right to speak their own languages and worship in their own way?"

Daisy stared at me as if I'd grown another head. "Are you opposed to the Church of England?"

"I'm opposed to *any* institution from *any* nation that strips innocent people of their cultures, families, or way of life." I leaned forward and lowered my voice. Daisy leaned in, too, close enough that a stray curl tickled my forehead. "How would *you* feel if suddenly an army from China invaded, burned all the churches and Bibles, demanded you speak Mandarin and beat you if you didn't, stole all the farmland, and force marched everyone who looks like you to camps and far-flung colonies where there's nothing to eat and no arable land to cultivate?"

"But that is not what a missionary does," Daisy protested.

"They're the first wave, though," I explained, getting into the rhythm of my lecture. Dahl always said I talked in essays when someone was foolish enough to let me ramble about my passions. "It starts with kindly benefactors and it ends with federally mandated genocide. Did you know that historically, being queer was *celebrated* in more cultures than it was reviled in, and it's only through colonization that homophobia has spread—oh." I stopped myself abruptly.

Daisy was staring again, but this time her moonstone eyes were trained solidly on my mouth. I licked my lips, partially because I needed to wet them after my monologue and partially to see how she'd react. She straightened as if she'd been electrocuted, rearing back and blinking. A dark, mottled flush spread up her face from her neck.

"My apologies, I got distracted by your . . . your *zeal*," Daisy said, scrambling for the wine bottle and refilling our cups to cover her discomposure.

The needle on my BiFi shivered in the red zone.

"You are going to vex Marigold with your lessons," Daisy said, after a healthy gulp of vino. "Your opinions are *certainly* not in line with what is preached from the pulpit."

I took a more moderate sip of my drink. Yup. Still awful. "I don't know. 'Love thy neighbor' and 'do unto others' seem pretty clear to me."

Daisy's dimples pulled down into a moue of thoughtful disappointment. "Then perhaps what I mean is that it is not what is preached from the Parliament."

"There you are," I agreed.

Daisy grew thoughtful again, and I left her to her musings.

Eventually, when the wine bottle was empty and the fire was low, the day caught up with me. I must have nodded off in my chair, because the next thing I knew Daisy was shaking me awake. She helped me stumble up the stairs to our room. I flopped out of my jeans and jacket, peeling them into an inside-out ball and tangling myself up in my sleep-muzzled haze while I tried to get my bra off without first taking off my button-down. Daisy was far more elegant in disrobing, laying out her clothing neatly on the back of the room's sole chair.

The bed was barely wider than a twin. I crawled up from the foot and dropped onto the mattress in just my shirt and undies. Daisy knelt primly by the head in her nightgown and folded her hands in prayer.

From anyone else, I would have assumed she was doing it to make a point. But nothing about Daisy's vibe gave me the impression she was doing this to be bitchy. She *believed* in this stuff. As much as Dahlia had been serious about her devotion to Islam. As much as I was devoted to my own pantheon of revolutionary feminists.

Though, after everything that had happened, maybe I should be considering converting to the C of E myself. If divine intervention hadn't put Fenton's ship directly under my plane, then what was it?

Daisy finished her supplication and quietly climbed under the covers with her back to me. Out of courtesy, I faced the wall.

Please, I prayed, figuring it couldn't hurt. *Please, don't let Lewis hurt anyone else. Um. Amen. Oh. And if you, you know, have any more good will left after that, think you could see fit to make sure I don't octopus all over Daisy in the middle of night?*

~

I had no idea if my prayer had worked, because by the time a nightmare jerked me back into the waking world, Daisy had already risen and left the room. It can't have been too terribly late, as the sky was just beginning to lighten. I hoped it hadn't been my fault she was awake.

My brain felt like it was wrapped in barbed wire. I was strained and disoriented, panting, swallowing against nothing, tangled in the sheets and clutching at my throat. The nightmare dissipated into the ether even as I tried to grasp it, to remember what had frightened me so much.

The dark of the deep ocean rose up behind my eyes, the flash of a knife coming at my face, the phantom squeeze of hateful hands on the back of my neck—I gasped against a burble of something stuck in my throat; a cry, a scream, a sob, I didn't know, it was all the things, and I—

Delayed reaction, I thought. *Shock.*

I sat there, unable to get my breathing under control, eyes watering, chin on knees, hands wrapped around my ankles, telling myself: *it's over, it's over, you're safe, you're on dry land, Fenton killed the man with the knife, Lewis doesn't know where you are, you're safe, you're safe, you're safe.*

Collapsing like a loose-limbed doll, I rolled into the empty space beside me—sheets still warm with body heat but devoid of the person I wanted to comfort me—and stuck my nose in Daisy's abandoned pillow. I inhaled. Violet hair tonic, harsh soap, feather stuffing, a molecule of last night's sweet wine.

Pathetic.

I could feel the post-traumatic depression gouging its talons into the flesh of my back. I rolled over to stifle it, pillow clamped against my chest, trying to push the foul mood away. I was going to shake apart. Every nerve was electrified, my skin crawling, even my hair aching. I wanted to scream, punch, fight, scream, kick, *scream—*

Pranayama, breathe, I told myself. *Inhale, two, three, four, five, six, hold, that's it, hold, exhale in a hum, come on, Sammie. Just focus on your breath, there's nothing else, there's nothing—breathe.*

It wasn't enough.

I slid onto the dusty rug and knelt into Balasana, forehead down, hands stretched out, knees spread wide to push my pelvis as close to the floor as possible. But the itch in my bones wouldn't let me be still, and I pressed up into Bhujangasana, cobra pose, legs straight out behind me, back bent in a deep arch, shaking with exhaustion and pain as I forced my scarred arm to hold my weight. I stretched my chin up, tilted my head back, and was startled by the tickle of tears sliding into the hair beside my ears.

Of course I was crying.

I was *so tired.*

I didn't want to hurt any longer, didn't want to be scared, or confused, or out of place, or condescended to, or—I pushed up, into Downward Dog, sobbing as my underarm throbbed, then tipped over, my hip hitting the ground hard, as I caught sight of Daisy from between my legs.

"Shit!" I said. "How long have you been standing there?"

Daisy, frozen on the threshold of the door with two cups of tea in her hands, needed a second to catch up. She blinked, pupils dilating, and only seemed to realize she was holding hot beverages when she moved to help me up. She dithered instead, looking around for somewhere to put the tea, but there was no table in our narrow room.

"Hold on." I minced upright and collapsed on the edge of the bed. "I'm a wreck, sorry, I'm not fit for polite company, I should put on some—"

"Nonsense," Daisy said. "We are none of us at our most attractive in the morning. And you passed a most distressing night, which of course would excuse all manner of sartorial sins."

Daisy passed me one of the teas, making sure I had a good grip on the saucer before letting go. Then she sat beside me and inhaled her own tea, eyes darting around the room before being drawn, as if magnetized, to my naked thighs. Then her gaze shot away again.

No.

No.

Yes?

"Good morning," I finally said, to cut through the weirdness. "Thanks for the tea."

It was milky. I hated it.

I drank it because Daisy had fetched it for me.

"Good morning," Daisy parroted back, out of knee-jerk politeness. "That was, ah, certainly . . . what *was* that? A form of gymnastics?"

"Kinda? It's sort of stretching and strength training mixed with meditation, uh, mindful breathing. It's from India."

Daisy dimpled, relieved to understand that at least. "Ah, like the best muslins and coffee, you undertake only the finest form of physical activity imported from the farthest corners of our trade routes."

A soft flush of attraction filled my stomach, warmer by far than the tea, and I wondered at how just the sound of Daisy's voice could drive all the panic out of my pores. What magic did she possess, that just sitting beside her made the terrible evils of the world seem surmountable? By what power was she able to banish my waking nightmares with a single smile?

"My friend, I have a question about a word you used last night. I wrote it down." She swigged her tea and set her empty cup on the bed. She retrieved a little book from her reticule, which hung from the chair. "What is *homophobia*?"

Oh, hon, I thought. If my BiFi was right, this was going to break her heart.

"From the Latin, I assume?" Daisy pressed, when I didn't answer right away. "A fear of sameness?"

"Where I come from," I began, fidgeting with the handle of the cup, "things are . . . different. The etiquette. The rules. The clothes."

"That much is *quite* obvious," Daisy says.

"Things that are frowned on here, things that are *illegal* here, are not there." I set down my own cup and saucer and screwed up my courage. "Daisy, do you know what a molly house is?"

Daisy gasped.

"You know that a molly is a man who performs a particular *act*. Here, that *act* is illegal. Where I'm from it was the *man*, not the act, that was considered wrong. His homosexuality—his same love—was the issue. Until it wasn't."

"Homo-phobia," Daisy said slowly, with dawning understanding. "A fear of those who love samely. If I am understanding what you said last evening correctly, you seek to make the world better by punishing those who hate any unfortunate person who is born . . . molly."

"Less 'punishing,' more 'helping them realize that the hatred is pointless,' with a side helping of 'celebrating the incredible diversity of human nature.' Also, being queer, molly, *other*, being *that*, it's not . . . Daisy, it's not *unfortunate*."

Daisy's hands, which had been fidgeting with her little notebook, went still.

"It's not *shameful*," I pressed, allowing myself to scooch closer, to take her hands between mine. "Sometimes it can be beautiful."

Daisy let out a shivering sigh, laden with a sort of hopeful anticipation that blindsided me.

Something was happening.

Something was *about* to happen.

"Samantha, I begin to think perhaps I—" She stopped and made that fluttering tremor of sound again.

My insides quivered deliciously. *Maybe*, just maybe Daisy understood what *else* I had been saying, what I really meant—

"Sister!" Marigold called from the hall, coming around the doorframe without knocking.

Daisy had left it *open*, and here I was, staring at her sweet mouth, rosy with the heat of the tea, where anyone could walk in on us. You'd think two years of having to look over my shoulder every time I wanted to PDA with Dahl would have taught me better instincts.

Idiot.

Homophobia, though the word didn't exist in this time, still existed in and of itself.

"I've brought you the lavender half-mourning dress from our trunk as you requested," Marigold barged on. "But I do not understand why—"

Daisy and I sprang apart, and she was immediately on her feet to hide her tiny book in her skirts. I think she was more worried about Marigold scolding her for that than for the way we had been leaning toward one another. But then, would Marigold even understand it as something sexual? Something forbidden?

Did Daisy?

"Why are neither of you dressed?" Marigold gawped. "If we had shared the room as we always do you would not be dawdling so! We will be late for supper at Swangale House if you don't make haste."

"I thank you for the dress, Marigold," Daisy said swiftly, plucking the gown from Marigold's arms, ignoring her frustration. "It is very kind of you to lend it to Miss Franklin."

"Miss Franklin!" Marigold said, and I don't know which nerve of Marigold's it was, only that Daisy's blasé announcement struck one of them. "You never *said*—"

"Do you not think Miss Franklin ought to arrive at Swangale in something less dour than full mourning? I do not think it proper she wear all black. *She* was not married to Lord Nelson."

"No, of course not," Marigold agreed, through gritted teeth. "Only have a care of it. It was remade from my late mother-in-law's own mourning attire. I am fond of it."

Daisy laughed. "You are a terrible fibber, Mary. You strongly disliked that the only dresses you had to make over for your own half-mourning gowns were those of that 'wretched old witch.' Those are the words that fell directly from your lips."

Marigold seemed more hurt by Daisy's laughing at her in front of me than the sharp reminder of her dislike of her late husband's mother. "I do sometimes *greatly* dislike that little trick of yours, sister, where you manage to recall everything one has ever said. Have a care how you speak,

Miss Franklin, for she will carve every word you utter into the immortal edifice of her memory, kind or no."

Before Daisy could apologize, Marigold fled the room, slamming the door behind her.

"Dash it," Daisy huffed. "That was unkind of me, I should—"

"After," I pressed, standing to rummage through my apron-bundle for my chemise, stockings, gloves, and stays. "We should get downstairs. I appreciate you thinking of this, by the way. I don't think the fancy-pantsy Gales would appreciate it if I showed up in jeans."

"I do not believe Sir Gale would give two figs," Daisy said, setting the lavender dress aside to help wrestle me into my underthings. "However, I do believe Marigold, who will not *say* so, sees this marriage as her ticket back into the circles she used to travel with Mr. Kempel. It is she, therefore, who would skin you alive."

Chapter Thirteen

IN WHICH SAM REALIZES

I think I may boast myself to be, with all possible vanity, the most unlearned and uninformed female who ever dared to be an authoress.

—Jane Austen, *Personal Letters*

We hit Whitstable in the early evening, and my sore ass rejoiced. I missed cars, trains, public transportation that moved at speeds faster than a horse, damn it. It didn't help that the road was a muddy mire with all the snow melt. As we pulled up the final stretch of the drive, Iris assured me that Swangale House was actually quite pretty when the orchards were in bloom and the gardens flourished, and that it was a shame that I was seeing it for the first time in winter.

The winter wasn't even remotely close to finished this time of year back in Canada. But the British Isles were surrounded by ocean, benefitted from the Gulf Stream, and didn't yet suffer from the global climate change that had made summers hotter and winters harsher. Instead of the winter wonderland I was used to in early January, it was all just brown.

We came to a stop by the front steps of a glaringly symmetrical house. It was rectangular, three stories tall, made of beige stone, and featured an even number of stingy-looking windows on either side of the door. We dismounted, and the carriage was taken away by a stable boy directly after our trunks and hat cases had been disgorged onto the gravel. The bags didn't stay there long, as nimble servants had seen our approach and were already waiting to whisk us inside.

The interior of the house was just as down-to-earth grandiose as the outside. The furnishings were a bit dowdy but looked comfortable. More importantly, every scuff on the floor, mark on the wallpaper, or little tear in the cushions told me that this was a *home*. This was a place where life happened. It wasn't showy and sparkling like Lewis's gilded prison.

We were met in a small dining room by an early supper and a silver tea service—for the first time, I looked forward to tea! I was frozen to the bone. It was also the first time I had arrived in a place and sat down to a meal without first being whisked off to fix my appearance, which I appreciated. Even though I wouldn't have said no to a bath and power nap.

Marigold took it upon herself to pour the tea with an imperious air, as if *she* was the mistress of Swangale.

Maybe that's what she was angling for, based on the way she looked at our host when he joined us a few moments later. Sir Charles Gale was a man comfortable in his skin, and approaching silver fox territory. He was introduced to me as the Honorable, and Daisy whispered to me that this meant he was the youngest son of a baron, unlikely to inherit unless a dozen other members of his family kicked it first. Apparently he did very tidily for himself by being a hands-on gentleman landlord, loyal and good to his tenants, and parsimonious with his late wife's dowry.

A fine catch for any widow, I assumed. I could see the appeal. But it would mean Marigold would become her own brother's mother-in-law and . . . yeah, no.

Sir Gale greeted the Goodenough ladies warmly, asked after Fenton's absence, and was mollified by the excuse that he had some last-minute business in town and was only a day or so behind us, then inquired how a third sister had suddenly sprouted.

The look he tossed me when Iris recounted the horrors I had suffered, in such great melodramatic detail it was as if she was the one who had been rescued from the ocean, was a calculating one. He didn't seem to fear for his daughter's prospects, but he was curious about this strange woman who had traveled openly with Eliza's fiancé.

"Sorry for the inconvenience," I said. "It's one more person pushing in where you didn't expect."

"Nonsense," he said. "It will be grand to have a friend of Finch's at the wedding."

"Oh yes, a friend!" I agreed, quickly. I made a point of exclaiming over how cheering it had been to be in the presence of a young man so in love, how I admired that he was so devoted to his partner, and how much I loved happily ever afters.

If the words choked coming out, no one knew but me.

Sir Gale looked appeased (it was a good show; I nearly believed it myself), and the topic turned to matters of wedding preparations, how ghastly the funeral had been, and the state of inns and roads. Iris held court on each topic, speaking with an authority that was as hollow as it was hilarious. Marigold did her best to get a word in edgewise, always one in praise of herself, while Daisy sat simply at her meal and took it all in.

I now recognized that her inscrutable, fascinated expression, thanks to Marigold's accusation, meant that Daisy was "recording" everything being said. I occupied myself with discreetly watching her reactions to the conversation, rather than trying to participate in it myself.

And, of course, I tried not to think too much about Eliza Gale. Did Fenton think she was the most beautiful woman in the world? Had my time with him changed his opinion? I couldn't decide if that was a good or bad thing, and so I chose not to make my mind up at all.

At least I didn't have to brace for Eliza's entrance. She had walked to town with her lady's maid, gone to Gale's sister's house for dinner as they hadn't been sure if the Goodenoughs would arrive today or later in the week. There was no fear of her being home before everyone was settled.

"I'll show you up. The travel must have wearied you, and I understand if you are longing for your beds. However, if you want for anything, do not hesitate to ring. Just this way, you remember, Mrs. Kempel? Finch will be put up in his usual room of course," Gale said as he accompanied us upstairs and down the hall. "Though I'm afraid this unexpected presence of a fourth flower in the bouquet puts rather a crimp on the usual arrangements for you ladies."

Marigold simpered at the compliment. Daisy and I exchanged a *look*.

"Daisy and I are very used to sharing," Marigold said before either of us could make an offer. "It will not be a hardship, we assure you."

"I, uh, I guess it's you and me, roomie," I said to Iris, who looked as enthused about it as I felt.

"Nonsense," Daisy cut in. "Mary is eternally irritated by my staying up late to read. Why put yourself out, sister, when Miss Franklin has already professed to not mind?"

Marigold's smile flaked away like cheap paint.

"Oh, do share with me, Marigold," Iris said, clinging to her eldest daughter's arm. "Let the young ladies stay up to gossip. Us widows may retire at a sensible hour."

Railroaded into accepting the arrangement out of politeness, Marigold nonetheless shot a glare loaded with a whole armory at me over her shoulder, while Iris chivvied her to their room.

Daisy and I were left to stifle our giggles in the second guest room. Her luggage—my cloth bundle had been packed in her trunk—was already stacked neatly by the wardrobe, the contents refreshed and hung inside it. Clearly the staff figured we'd be sharing too.

Awkward.

The toilette stand had been stocked with an ewer of warm water and a basin, fresh perfume and tooth chalk, hair serums, and a changing screen to hide behind. Daisy had packed a quilted dressing gown among her things, and rang the maids to borrow a second one, along with a nightdress, from the household. I ducked behind the screen and took the first turn, and half the water, to wipe away the road grime. I was nearly dry by the time the servant returned, and we swapped places so I could dress and she could clean up. While she did that, I emptied the pockets and lapels of my jacket, and bundled together our dirty laundry. I was sure my jeans wouldn't be too unfamiliar to the laundress, based on what I'd seen other laborers wearing in London. But I bet they would gossip downstairs about why I had them at all.

"Let me dress your hair," Daisy said, when we were both seated on the end of the bed in our clouds of lace and cotton.

"Nuh-uh," I said. "You've seen frizzilla. But you can show me how to do yours."

It was a selfish request.

Her hair was long, golden, and glossy.

And I was weak.

I used to do this for Dahlia. I relished the silky slip and zing of the brush, the soft cloud of strawberry-matcha scented hair products, the quiet intimacy of her trust.

As Daisy fetched her hair care items from her trunk, I contemplated the fact that this was the first I had thought of Dahl in days. And it hadn't stung. It was, instead, a comfort to remember that we'd been good together once.

But that was lost now behind a haze of bereavement and acceptance, like my brain had dropped a gauzy curtain between memories of my past life and this one. I could see them, vaguely, but they couldn't affect me anymore. Couldn't *pain* me.

Hell of a coping mechanism, I thought.

I accepted a soft-bristled brush, a fine-toothed comb, a bundle of paper slips, and a little stoppered bottle labeled ROSEMARY TEA from Daisy.

This is the first time I've seen her handwriting, I realized, inspecting the little bottle. *It's so fine and even. It looks like a computer font.*

Around talking me through the process of putting her damp hair up into what she laughingly called "paper shackles," Daisy gleefully filled me in on the gossip surrounding Swangale House. Her incredible memory meant she could recount entire conversations verbatim, and she did so in charming funny voices. Apparently the Gales were upright and long-standing members of the community, and Finch and Eliza had met at a ball held by Eliza's uncle in Chatham. The *Salacia* had been docked at the navy yard for restocking, and as the late and genteel Mr. Kempel had been in Rochester to oversee his company's accounts for said restocking—he'd been a merchant supplier to the king's ships—he'd invited his brother-in-law along to the party. Apparently, all it had taken was a single turn on the dance floor, and Eliza Gale had been smitten.

Remembering the joyful abandon with which Fenton had danced in Gibraltar, I could easily believe it.

Daisy's hair clumsily wrapped, she settled it under a sleep cap and took her turn with mine. She combed detangling oil through my moisture-starved locks, and finished it in a stubby braid. This was the longest my hair had been since ninth grade, when I'd cut it into a choppy pixie cut because my then-celebrity crush had done the same.

Then Daisy pulled the shutters tight, closed the curtains, and set a finely wrought metal screen before the fire to keep any popping sparks from leaping onto the carpets while we slept. We settled into the bed, back-to-back. As I lay there, willing the giddy swirling in my stomach not to flare up at the gentle warmth of her body heat, I wondered how I was supposed to handle more of these sweet, domestic evenings without expiring of a lust-induced heart attack.

~

I was accidentally woken up by a maid trying to sneak a fresh tea tray and our clean and pressed clothes into the room.

This maid was robust and apple cheeked, nothing like cowed and miserable Susan. She chattered about how fine the day was and how late the dashing captain had arrived last night while opening the windows, putting my modern clothes in Daisy's trunk, and laying out my Georgian underthings.

I also woke, once again, to no Daisy. As far as I remembered, I'd had no nightmares to drive her out of bed.

I'd never had a partner complain about snoring or talking in my sleep, or anything else that might drive someone from the room in the middle of the night. Which could only mean one thing.

Daisy was one of those disgusting *morning* people.

For my part, I decided one day without yoga wouldn't kill me, and rose to clean my teeth with the foul concoction on the vanity. I mourned my electric toothbrush and minty paste.

The maid hadn't made up a cup of tea for me, and I found the tray bedecked with lemon as well as the other usual accouterments. I decided to try something different, and found the tea far more palatable garnished with lemon than contaminated with milk.

The maid kept on about her sister's new position in the Smithson's house as a governess to their little boy, and the baker's new baby, and the pianoforte that the reverend's wife had just purchased and let the village girls play for their lessons, if they hadn't one of their own. Honestly, it was kind of nice, letting the mundane joys of people who were healthy and happy wash over me.

"Do you play the pianoforte, miss?" the maid asked. "Or the harp? I'm told accomplished ladies play something."

"I'm not accomplished," I conceded, enjoying my tea from the vanity, where I was out of her way as she went through the laborious process of stripping back the bedding to air the thin mattresses. "Captain Goodenough's already established that I'm a piss-poor dancer, and I couldn't fuddle out a note on the piano to save my life. I can sing a bit, though. Got a little French, though that's mostly just the back of shampoo bottles. My only specialty is ethnosociology and narrative inquiry."

The maid mulled that admission over, then apparently dismissed it for the gibberish it must have sounded like. "I'm sure your husband will be delighted with whatever you excel in."

Instead of telling her that I had kept my own apartment in downtown Toronto, that I had a job, friends, and a habitual queer bar, and was in no big hurry to find a husband of any sort, I just drank my tea.

See? I *was* learning when to keep my yap buttoned.

The maid helped me back into the lavender dress, as the black one was too heavy to wear around the house. She offered to help with my hair, too, but I just let it out of the stubby braid, patted down the flyaways, and called the sow's ear a silk purse.

Breakfast had been laid out, I was told, so I was given a convulted set of directions, then left to find my way downstairs alone.

With the interior doors closed, it was still quite dark in the house. I had no candle to guide me, and there were no electric lights. I walked slowly, wondering how Daisy had made her way in the pitch dark. She was probably already in the breakfast room. It occurred to me, halfway down the stairs, that Eliza Gale might be too.

I was way over Fenton, I told myself. There was no reason to be jealous or spiteful or anything else toward Eliza. I could smile and breeze through this visit and never drop a hint that I'd already had what was going to be hers.

I was arrested on the bottom stair by a soft murmuring laugh coming from a room off the foyer. The door was slightly ajar, so I didn't feel too bad for spying when Fenton's familiar voice rumbled through it.

A peek told me that the room was probably a parlor, where the ladies usually did things like knit, or paint, or read, or take tea and talk about boys. There were no lights here, either, save for a low fire in the hearth on the far wall. It threw the furniture, and the two inhabitants of the sofa, into cozy-warm relief.

Their backs were to the door. Fenton's temple rested on the side of a young woman's neck, a posture so intimate, so tender, that something inside me shivered. Certainly they were seated far too close for what was proper. But then, I'd already been proven mistaken when it came to thinking I knew the mores of this place.

Was it me who taught Fenton to forget propriety, or had he always been like this? He'd always made a point of keeping a gap between *our* bodies.

But his temple was on her shoulder and he was looking up at her adoringly, and she brushed a gentle hand across his cheek. He captured it and kissed her fingers and . . .

He loved Eliza. He *loved* her. And she loved him back. It was plain as spots on a ladybug.

Witnessing it hurt more than I thought it would, which in turn surprised me with a slap of self-anger. The truth was, I didn't want Fenton particularly, but what he *had*. I wanted the affection I saw between them. I wanted to pull that away like sticky toffee, and wrap it around my own shoulders.

They were so *privileged*, so lucky that the people around them approved and supported their relationship, and they didn't even know it. Or that I had tried to ruin it. I had been so pathetically desperate for affection that I had been willing to steal it from someone whose father had opened his home to me.

I backed away quietly. It was the least of what I owed Eliza.

After a few false starts in the mazelike gloom, found the breakfast room, which apparently was completely different from the dining room because it looked out on the gardens with the best southern light. The maid had been serious when she had explained that the point of the room was the view, for the shutters and curtains were flung wide open, showcasing the fresh snow that had fallen overnight, while the rest of the room remained unilluminated. Dark shadows clung to the corners, partially obscuring furniture.

The long oval table centered on the picture window was pristinely laid with a fine white cloth and serviceable pots of butter, salt cellars, and other accouterments whose purpose I would have to investigate. The sideboard was already filled with apples and fruit spreads, cheese and boiled eggs, cold toast, sausages, and some kind of icky fish. Otherwise the room was empty and silent. On the off chance that Daisy had gone back upstairs, I decided to hunker down next to the source of caffeine.

Wrung out by my emotional revelation, I plopped gracelessly into the first chair I literally stumbled against once I'd fixed my cup and plate.

A feminine grumble came from the heap of shadows in the corner, and one of them detached itself. Sunlight sparked off golden hair peeking out from under a rumpled cap, and moonstone-gray eyes narrowed peevishly at me. There was ink smudged up the side of her hand and a glower on her face.

"Daisy!" I said. "I didn't see you. You really will ruin your eyes if you write letters in the dark."

"I had thought you would be later coming down," Daisy said. "Did your gymnastics not appeal today?"

"I'll do them later," I said. "The maid woke me, and I thought I'd come looking for you, when I realized you weren't—oh. *Oh*, I'm a dummy. You wanted time alone for your—" I pointed at the little table I could now make out before her.

"It is of no concern now," Daisy said, rising to collect her own breakfast. "My concentration is broken and I shan't be able to recapture it."

"What are you working on?" I asked.

A page was propped up on a sloped, wedge-shaped case on the tabletop. I slid around her to peer at the paper while she was occupied, wondering if it was a letter, and if so, whom for.

I took a bite of the apple in my hand as I read:

Jane Tremble had met Death once.

Maybe it was twice. She didn't get a good look at the man at the end of the pier before he grabbed her by the scruff of her dress and held her back from the edge of the water. It could have been Death, then.

If it was, then Death had saved her life.

But the first time, the person who'd slid close to her father, tucking in beside him on that festering bunk with the tender intimacy of a lover, Jane remembered him. As her father's straining breath rattled through the belly of the ship taking them to the Old World, Death had kissed her father's poxy mouth.

For all that she had been six years old at the time, she had seen that face clearly.

She had known Death for what he was.

The funeral had happened at sea, if such a thing could be called a funeral. Jane Tremble recalled that the water had been gray. The sky had also been gray. They had blended together in a single, mist-washed hue, horizonless and damp as misery. Death had been gray too; hair like smoke, clothes like crumbling ash, flesh as gray as her father's lips.

There had been no casket, only her father's body wrapped in stained sailcloth, tied in frayed rope no longer fit for the rigging. His face had been visible, sheened with sickly sweat, red with fever, and spotted over with the hard lesions that had made their way out of his mouth and over his cheeks, down under his matted beard to spread across his chest to clutch for his heart.

It was only in the years that followed, as she dissected her last memory of him, that Jane had understood that when they had sent him overboard, her father had still been alive.

The apple dropped to the carpet, rolling out of fingers numbed by shock.

And recognition.

"This is . . ." I said, unable to finish the sentence as every hair I possessed prickled upright. Instead, I pointed at the page, terrified of what my voice might do.

Daisy lunged to the table, shuffled the pages back into the box, set aside the open inkpot, and snicked the rest closed into a neat, rectangular carrying case.

"You should not have *looked*," she snapped. "I will not have you judge it, Samantha Franklin, especially when it is not complete, and—"

"It's really good," I said quietly.

But it was more than really good.

I had the opening narration of Dahl's comfort-watch show practically memorized. And this was it. Word for word.

I'm a fucking idiot, I realized.

"Is it truly?" Daisy asked, pausing in her frantic packing to stare at me, hope sparking in her gaze. It felt like it weighed a million pounds, crushing the air out of my lungs. "You must tell me at once if you are simply sparing my pride—"

"It's not, you don't have to worry, I'm not . . . this book is going to be a masterpiece, it's going to change the goddamn world, I know that, only I just realized, silly me, you never answered me when I asked what your—" I took a breath. "Finch is Fenton, Marigold is Mary, and you, you're *Daisy*, but your real name is—" I couldn't finish the sentence. Couldn't make myself say it.

"It's from the French," Daisy said, as if I should already know. As if it was obvious.

It was.

"A daisy. La marguerite," I translated. "You're *Margaret*."

Chapter Fourteen

IN WHICH SAM YEARNS

There could have been no two hearts so open, no tastes so similar, no feelings so in unison . . .

—Jane Austen, *Persuasion*

The deep thud of furniture toppling alerted me to the fact that I was now sitting on the carpet, legs splayed out in front of me like a rag doll. For a wavering moment, I felt like I was under water again, out of breath, unsure which way was up, too saturated with my epiphany to bubble to the surface.

Beside me, the small table rocked back and forth as it settled on its side, bumping gently into my hip. Daisy had rescued her portable writing desk at least, and was clutching it to her chest.

"What just . . . ?"

"You swooned," she said, with wary amusement, unsure if I was in the mood to laugh about it or not. "It was not at all as artful as I've read about. Nevertheless, I swear I shall not tell a soul that you were overcome by the magnificence of my prose."

She set her case on the dining table. She reached down to help me up, and to my shame, I flinched.

Flinched, because that was *Margaret Goodenough's* hand, *Margaret Goodenough's* wordless offer of help, *Margaret Goodenough's* teasing, and I was stupidly, moronically, speechlessly starstruck.

Margaret jerked back, confused by the rejection.

Well, *yes*, Margaret. And not Margaret. This was Daisy. This was my friend. This was my stupid little crush, with her kissable mouth and her mischievous dimples.

Daisy.

"Are you hurt?"

"No." I gasped, lungs spasming with the shock of both the tumble and the revelation. "I'm fine."

"You are very much not fine," Margaret-freaking-Goodenough said. "Please, let me help you up."

"I—" I licked my lips, nerves flaring. "Yeah? Yes. Please."

As she was hauling me upright, Finch and Eliza blew into the room.

So not the first impression I had wanted to make.

"We heard a noise," Finch announced, one hand hovering over his hip, though he was not wearing his sword or pistol just now. The other was entangled with Eliza's.

Miss Gale had a pleasantly sweet face, plump curves, and unaffected black ringlets that made her English rose complexion all the more delicate. She had laugh lines around her hazel eyes, and a sort of fluttering calmness to her, like a butterfly who could flit away at any moment but had chosen to rest nearby, opening and closing its wings slowly.

"My fault," I said, feeling utterly stupid. "I was too busy, uh, enjoying the view—" I gestured at the sunlight sparkling on the fresh snow in the garden. "Wasn't watching where I was walking, smashed right into the table, what a klutz! Ha-ha!"

Daisy regarded my fibs with open curiosity but didn't deny them.

"I am very glad that you are well, then, Miss Franklin," Eliza said, detangling herself from Fenton. "As I was just on my way to make your acquaintance. Oh, your *dress*—"

I looked down. The inkpot, which Daisy had left open, had spilled down my front.

"Aw, shit." I dove for the salt cellar. "Someone, sorry, help—just pour it on the stain—"

Eliza applied herself to the task as I held the front of my dress out. That "recording" look was back in Daisy's gaze while she watched the crystals soak up the ink.

"Wherever did you learn this?" she asked.

"It's how you get wine stains up. Figured it'd work for ink."

"Come, let me hold that for you while you clean your hands. You should not like the stain to spread," Daisy offered as Eliza worked, and crowded close. "Quick now, so we can get this to the laundry before my sister is the wiser."

"That is Marigold's dress?" Fenton asked, gawping with mischievous glee. "Oh, Miss Franklin, you are in *trouble*—"

"If you cannot help, dearest, then *hush*," Eliza scolded, and Finch immediately backed away with an apologetic pout.

Oh, I liked Eliza Gale.

"Right—" I fumbled with a napkin as Daisy and Eliza bent to their tasks, tongue-tied all over again because *Margaret Goodenough* had her hands resting on my thighs and I just, I *just*—

"I heard a crash, is all—Miss Franklin!" Marigold shrilled from the door, and we froze guiltily. "I specifically requested that you have a care with that dress!"

"I'm sorry. It was an accident. I'll clean it myself, I'll—"

"How selfish of you!" Marigold went on, pushing Fenton off when he tried to soothe her. "How thoughtless! It is ruined."

"The stain will lift, sister," Finch pleaded. "Peace, please."

"It was an accident," I repeated.

The twist of Marigold's mouth made it clear she didn't believe me. She turned on her heel and stomped away. Instead of cursing, I bit the inside of my cheek.

If Marigold didn't have reason enough to hate me before, she absolutely did now.

~

As soon as we were upstairs Daisy took the time to get herself up to the bare minimum standard of polite dress: hair in a knot, piled under a frilly muslin day cap, and a dress of serviceable fabric in a light gray that did glorious things for her eyes. Then she went to soothe Marigold's temper and scrounge up another dress—her own clothes were just too slim cut to fit me—while Eliza helped me strip, then bustled away to the laundress. I was standing by the fire in my borrowed dressing gown—the ink had gone through to the chemise and stockings and they had been whisked away too—when Eliza returned with a soft rap on the doorframe.

"Miss Franklin?" she said. She held a small basket between her hands and was accompanied by this morning's maid. "Miss Goodenough mentioned that you swooned. I thought, perhaps, if you're feeling unwell, we could spend the morning here instead of in the parlor? I brought some embroidery." She proffered the basket.

"That's kind of you," I said. "I don't embroider, but don't let that stop you."

"Ah," she said, with that same delicate yet calm gravitas I'd seen downstairs. "Something else, then. Do you play whist, Miss Franklin? Betty, leave the tea and bring the playing cards, please? And some breakfast, I don't believe Miss Franklin had the opportunity to finish hers."

Betty bobbed, left the tray on the chest at the foot of the bed, took away Eliza's basket, and bustled out the door. Eliza picked up the small table by the fire—amateurishly but enthusiastically painted with vines, roses, and a wonky cherub—and placed it beside the rumpled bed. I slumped over and sat. She pulled up the vanity chair and with a deft hand poured the tea. I added a slice of lemon to mine.

"Are you fatigued from travel?" Eliza asked kindly. "Or, Finch tells me you had a terrible ordeal with an unsavory fellow in town. I imagine that would be quite taxing."

"You imagine right. But it's not that, it's only stupidity," I confessed, feeling the corners of my mouth pull down, my chin tremble, the heat build behind my eyes. Had I ever cried as much in my previous life? I didn't think so. But then, I'd also had less to cry over. "I'm an *idiot*."

"Please don't berate yourself. Such accidents happen frequently, and I am certain that we are more than equipped to lift the stain."

"I just keep messing up. I thought being here would be *easy*, and I—" I cut myself off with a sniffle and decided it would be best not to continue. I cast about for a handkerchief.

Eliza anticipated my need and handed me hers from her sleeve, gently embroidered in one corner with a stylized *EG*. I wondered if this was one of her feminine accomplishments. If so, it was a more elegant effort than the table.

"Worry not, Miss Franklin," Eliza said. "You are a friend of the family I am about to join. That makes you my friend now. I shall endeavor to do all I can to ease your way."

She was so *nice*. I was struck with a sudden, viscous desire to say sorry for fucking her fiancé. But it was cruel. It was *unnecessary*. What would Eliza do with the information, anyway? How would she react, but to assume my apology was instead a deliberate attempt to hurt her feelings? And what would happen to her if she jilted Fenton as a result?

And it wouldn't make *my* life any easier. Fenton wouldn't forgive me if I ruined his upcoming marriage, and he certainly wouldn't return to me. And I'd be out on my ear faster than Marigold could snap her fingers.

An earlier version of me might have done it for the sheer pettiness, but there was something about Eliza Gale that made me want to take her under my wing and shelter her. I'd known her for a half a day and I already knew I'd keep her in the divorce if she and Fenton split up.

When Betty delivered the cards, Eliza laid them out and explained the game. I sipped and let her talk to cover the silence, grateful for her presence and the distraction it brought. She didn't push or press, just let me *be*. It was refreshing.

When I was feeling warm from the tea, full from the nibbles, and settled from the easy companionship, I said, "Thank you."

Eliza smiled calmly. "You're very welcome."

"Fenton is lucky to have you. I imagine having a partner so good at putting people at ease would be useful in the navy. All I ever did was make a scene, and I wasn't even trying."

I saw it there, in her eyes. Quick and repressed easily: envy that I had spent time out in the world on Fenton's arm. And she'd had to stay here. My first impression had pegged Miss Eliza Gale as timid and sweet, but the more time I spent with her the more I saw a steel core under that corset. I could easily see her as one of those shockingly modern wives who joined her husband aboard ship.

"Not that I think that playing hostess is the only thing you'll bring to the table, but perhaps he leaps before he thinks." *We both do*, I thought. *We'd have made each other worse if I'd managed to marry him.* "I can tell, the way you play cards, you're thinking ten steps ahead. He needs that balance. He needs *you*."

The vaguely hostile hurt in her eyes didn't fade but the lines around them relaxed, her expression still carefully neutral. She took the white-flag waving for what it was.

"Of course," she said. "The men think they are the ones who decide whom to marry, but you and I know, Miss Franklin, that it really is us women who arrange it to their best advantage. Finch is in want of a steady hand."

"You're marrying into a loud and headstrong family," I agreed.

"I am nothing if not patient, and even-keeled," she said, and with a triumphant grin, collected the final trick of the whist match.

Good girl, I thought, matching her grin with a proud one of my own. *You take what you deserve.*

~

Fenton interrupted us to convey an invitation to Eliza from his mother, who was now awake and ready for visitors. Iris had brought the bride a gift of lace for her trousseau and wanted to discuss the best use of it.

As I was still in my pj's, Fenton stood carefully outside the door. Eliza bid me adieu, and kissed him sweetly on her way past. Fenton lingered just long enough to tell me that he'd managed to sell my old smartphone for an obscene amount to some fascinated science kook in London.

"It was far more than I ever would have earned in prizes," he said. "More than enough for my needs. I think perhaps you are very proud, Samantha, but I beg you to take this along with my deepest thanks."

He held out a leather pouch that clinked softly when I accepted it.

"You know that I don't know what this is worth," I told him.

"It's enough to purchase some clothing of your own, to pay for your share of the meals and carriages until the wedding, and for several months of your lodging with my sisters and mother. It will tide you over comfortably. I could give you more, if you desire."

"This is enough. As soon as I start teaching, I'll be self-sufficient."

"It was your little device, after all."

"It was a gift, Fenton. Shut up and accept it."

He dimpled at me. "I do so enjoy your turns of phrase."

I snorted. "Right. Now get out. I'm practically naked."

"Lucky, then, that I have managed to winkle a spare dress out of Miss Gale's lady's maid," Daisy said, appearing over Fenton's shoulder. "You are dismissed, little bird."

"Aye-aye, Commodore," Fenton said, tossing off a rigid salute and marching away like a toy soldier.

"Our room has turned into a town square." I stepped aside so Daisy could come in. "Feels like everyone's dropped by today."

"Nearly everyone," Daisy said with a sarcastic twist. "The linendraper is downstairs; I could invite him up if you so desired."

"I'll pass," I said, as I skimmed out of my dressing gown. "What's a linendraper?"

Daisy gave me another one of those pinning-me-to-a-corkboard looks before shaking her head a little in disbelief. "A seller of cloth. Here is a chemise for you, quick now, turn and I shall tie off your stays and dress."

The dress itself was taupe, made of a serviceable cotton and printed with a repeating pattern of dark-brown and mustard-yellow daffodils. She lingered at the nape of my neck, the soft skin inside my elbow, the vulnerable tops of my feet as she checked the length. I tensed to suppress a shiver.

She didn't mean it like that.

No matter how much I wanted her to mean it like that.

"Are you much recovered from your queer turn?"

At *some* point I was going to have to stop finding people using the word *queer* that way funny. Today wasn't that day, though, and I snorted.

Taking it to mean something deeper, Daisy gave the ties at the back of my dress one final tug and stepped away. When I turned to face her, she was staring out the window, stiff backed and pouting.

"Marg—Daisy? Are you okay?"

"Have I done something amiss?"

"What?"

Daisy gestured at her writing desk, which she had closed up into a case and tucked beside her trunk. "You have spent all morning behaving oddly around me, and I suspect it is due to that."

"No!" I said. "I mean, yes, but *no*, no, there's nothing *wrong*—"

She whirled to face me, fists clenched and fire in her eyes. "Then *what*, pray tell me, do you find so distasteful? You call my writing 'good,' and yet you are overcome with nerves from just a few paragraphs. I know it is not a ladylike pastime, and you say that you eschew such rigid roles in society, yet you behave as if my hobby offends you. You call me friend, but share secrets with my brother that you will not disclose to me. You find my proximity uncomfortable. You shrink from my touch. You disdain to share a bed with me, sleeping against the wall or on the farthest edge. Yet you stare at me when I speak as if I am a greater orator than any who yet lived. You *bewilder* me, Samantha Franklin!"

I confused *her*? Ha!

"Daisy, I don't. Honestly, I don't know how to explain it." I scrubbed my hands through my hair, frustration and confusion sparking along the underside of my skin, an itch I didn't know how to soothe.

"Please try," Daisy begged, and the way she said it curled around my heart like a lover's fingers. "I want . . . I do not know what I want, only that I cannot bear to lose your regard over my scribbling."

"I swear you haven't," I promised. I held out my hands and she gripped them immediately. "It's *amazing*, what you do. I know how fiercely you have to carve out and defend your time, your *right* to do it"—*because I read it in a book two hundred years from now*—"and I think it's incredible."

"Then why do you recoil?"

"Because I . . . because . . ."

Oh.

Oh *fuck*.

I was going to do it.

I was going to kiss Margaret Goodenough.

Daisy.

I slid my hands up her arms, cupped her shoulders, rolled up onto my tiptoes. Daisy's mouth parted in confusion, then in surprise as I leaned closer and tilted my head, then in anticipation as she understood what I meant to do. Her tongue was a pink, wet flash against her bottom lip, her spun-gold lashes fluttered as we—

"Daisy!" Marigold called from the hall, harsh and sudden.

We startled apart, like cats doused with a surprise bucket of cold water. Though with less yowling.

"Make haste!" Marigold added when Daisy's only reply was a frustrated grumble. "Miss Eliza seeks your opinion on the twill stuff!"

I threw my head back and laughed, because of *course*. Daisy's annoyance broke like a wave upon the shore. She huffed a chuckle, more amused with *my* amusement than the interruption, but made for the door.

Okay, so we weren't talking about it.

Cool, cool, cool.

I could do not talking about it.

Shit.

~

The draper, a skinny man with a wisp of gray hair like cotton fluff and arms that never stopped flapping, was well into a song-and-dance routine about the virtues of locally made machine loomed muslin when we entered the parlor. The group of ladies had multiplied and now also comprised Eliza's two younger sisters and their governess, as well as her lady's maid and a pair of lollygagging chambermaids who weren't shooed out.

I decided that if I was going to spend the rest of my life around these people doing this sort of thing, maybe I should try to learn something useful. I sat amid the youngest Gales and amused them greatly by allowing them to educate me on the virtues of different fabrics and dyes, nodded over swatches, and learned that young ladies wore pastels while married women were privileged to the deeper, jewel-tone shades.

Which made me side-eye Marigold, as she was definitely sporting a pale-yellow dress today. Trying to look more marriageable for Sir Gale? Maybe.

It also explained the bolt of fabric Eliza chose for her wedding gown: a soft blush with an in-woven pattern of light-pink morning glories.

Fun fact, my dad chirruped. *White wedding gowns were popularized by Queen Victoria.* A woman whose parents weren't even married yet.

The ladies were already discussing what sleeve design would flatter, how low the neckline could be for church, and how the dress could be altered again after the wedding for evening wear.

Right, yeah, that was a thing, apparently—there was no buying a five-figure princess poof then preserving it in a box for the next thirty years. Not even the minor gentry could afford to buy something and never wear it again. Environmentally crippling fast fashion hadn't been invented yet.

"What do *you* think, Miss Samantha?" Eliza asked, looking at me deliberately but not unkindly. "You have been the lone companion of Fenton for these long months. Will he like it?"

I smiled, and gestured at the bolt unraveled on her lap.

"Miss Eliza, you could wear a burlap sack and he would still think you were an angel fallen from heaven." The women around me tittered. "Having said that, your silk would be a lot more comfortable."

Eliza's smile grew into a more generous, more genuine version of itself.

"What is the wedding fashion where you come from, Miss Samantha?" one of the younger Miss Gales asked.

"Not all that different," I confessed. "Usually less lace, a bit of a sleeker cut. Oh." I took in the piles of ribbons and buttons and swatches. "Where's your blue?"

"Blue?" Eliza echoed. "I do not wear blue. It does not flatter."

"You can't get married without blue," I said. "It's tradition."

Daisy, who had been sat as far away as the cozy parlor allowed with her "recording" face on, leaned forward. "Whose?"

"Ours," I said with a shrug. "I thought it would be yours, too, but I guess not. It's for luck. The bride is supposed to wear 'Something old, something new, something borrowed, something blue.'"

"I see," Daisy said, one finger on the handle of her teacup, pushing it in a circle around her saucer. "The dress will be new."

"You may borrow the amber crucifix that Fenton gave me," Marigold offered magnanimously, clutching Eliza's hand in a sisterly way.

Now everyone was grinning, thinking hard.

"Something old," Eliza said tentatively. "What of the veil that was my mother's?"

"That'll do," I said. "And blue?"

Eliza protested softly. "It is still not flattering."

"That's easy, then," I said. "Put one little blue flower in the middle of your bouquet. A spray of forget-me-nots, if you have them. It's what my mother did."

"Tell us?" Daisy implored, and I realized with a heart-shuddering jolt that if I really was to live with the Goodenoughs, that this was probably going to be a refrain I heard often from the authoress.

"It was in my mom's bouquet," I said. "A silk flower from her own mother's bouquet, surrounded by the new, fresh, real flowers, a pretty silver stickpin borrowed from her sister, and a blue ribbon to hold it together. She, uh,"—I had to pause to clear my throat, which had grown tight again—"she saved her mom's silk flower and dried some flowers from her bouquet for when it was my turn."

Don't think about how they'll never walk you down an aisle.

Eliza sighed. "How romantic."

"Yeah." I brushed at the corner of my eyes, disguising the maneuver by pushing back a piece of hair that had fallen forward. My parents had been stupid-face in love, too, the same way Eliza and Fenton were.

Conversation moved on from me, so I made an excuse out of fetching myself a cup of fizzy mineral water from the ever-present sideboard of snacks to compose myself. (*How* did these people stay hydrated? I'd sworn off plain water, but I'd yet to *find* any either.)

I helped myself to the only other seat in Daisy's corner, and she offered me a wry smile. We watched the rest of the fabric-choosing session in silence, the crackling tension of what had nearly happened upstairs thick between us, like taffy filled with Pop Rocks.

As the draper finalized Eliza's order and began to pack his samples away, and the other ladies' conversation surged excitedly, Daisy murmured: "I expect that the process of ordering clothes is unfamiliar to you?"

"Yeah." I did a double take. "Why would you expect that?"

Daisy offered me another of those inscrutable looks. "You are often confused about the value of coinage, you do not know how to order up a room or a meal, nor are you versed in bargaining for goods. I suspect that you did not engage with commerce often."

"I did my own shopping," I protested. "I just didn't do it like this."

"How did you do it?"

By delivery app.

"Order sheets," I said. "You make a list of what you want, the list is delivered to the merchant, a delivery person provides your order, and then you pay off your credits at the end of the month in one big lump sum."

"That sounds incautious," Daisy said. "I imagine it lands those not scrupulous with their accounts to debtor's prison."

"Collections agencies are a special kind of hell, yeah," I agreed.

What happens to student loans when someone dies? Will my parents have to pay them off? That's cruel, making parents pay for their dead child's education.

"This guy goes away with the order, then what?"

"He will deliver the fabric to Miss Eliza's dressmaker and Sir Gale will settle the account. Then a visit will be paid to the modiste to decide upon the style, based on the fashion plates. The wedding shall be a month from this coming Sunday, so the visit will need to happen in the next day or two."

"A *month*," I repeated. "We'll be here for a month?"

Daisy gave me the side-eye. "The announcement must be read each week in church for a minimum of three weeks, to allow those who may object to the union to speak up. All weddings must have the banns read."

"Mine didn't."

Daisy grimaced. "A special license allows for more immediacy."

"Can't they get one of those, then?"

"They are granted only by favor of the archbishop himself, and only to those who are of the correct rank." She rubbed her thumb and finger together in the timeless gesture for *loaded*. "Besides that, the full month gives the dressmaker, as well as us here, enough time to complete Miss Eliza's trousseau, and for my brother and Sir Gale to finalize the marriage contract."

"Just saying now, I will *not* be doing any of the sewing. Not if it's something that Eliza actually wants to wear."

Daisy found this confession charming.

"But we should go to town *today*," one of the younger Gale daughters complained loudly enough to interrupt our tête-à-tête. "The new ribbons came in yesterday and the shop will be picked over!"

"Honestly, Olive," Eliza scolded, but she was smiling. "A single day won't make a difference."

"I will confess I am quite stiff from the carriage ride, and those awful beds at the inn," Iris said, with no indication of said confessed stiffness. "A visit to town sounds just the thing, and the day is bright! Marigold, Daisy?"

"Of course, Mother," Marigold said, standing and brushing down her dress.

Daisy shot me a meaningful look that made it clear that she intended to dawdle well behind the clucking younger women.

And so it was that the whole of the female host donned thick stockings and spencer jackets, winter bonnets, scarves, and muffs, and ventured out into the freshly fallen snow. A big open sleigh with skis instead of wheels, drawn by two massive farm horses, was pulled around to the front door, and we piled in. Hidden under the lap blanket, bold as brass, Daisy laid her gloved fingers over mine and didn't move them until we reached town twenty minutes later.

I don't think I exhaled once the entire trip.

~

The town, when we arrived, was far quainter than I had expected. Frankly, I wasn't sure what I'd hoped for—towering Victorian brownstones? Tumbledown medieval cottages? A combination of both? But the town was paved, and the buildings of the high street aligned in a military procession toward a church on one end and a square with shops on the other.

We dismounted in front of the church, and Iris bustled importantly to the dressmaker's at the far end from where she'd had the driver drop us off. She spent the whole walk loudly and excitedly discussing the upcoming nuptials. Less for our benefit and more to rub it in with the other folks about town on their own errands.

I adored Iris's vicious enthusiasm.

I kept falling to the back of the group on purpose, hoping Daisy would linger with me, but one or another of our companions kept her wrapped up in conversation the whole walk down the high street.

Finally, the youngest girls broke off, herded by their governess, to stop by the grocer's for boiled candies. Eliza, Marigold, and Iris headed directly into the dressmaker's, which was thankfully too tight to contain all of us. Daisy and I peeled away to keep walking.

Thinking I'd finally have my chance, Daisy took one look at me once we were alone, turned bright red, and ducked into a consignment store. The proprietress was too attentive to give us the privacy I longed for, so I busied myself with selecting a sleep shirt, a dowdy men's dressing gown in dark green, and three secondhand dresses, all to be delivered to the house. One was a day dress in a cream and dusty-rose roller-pattern of sweet pea blossoms on a fabric Daisy called calico, which complimented my cranberry spencer. One was pale-blue muslin, good for informal evenings. And the last was something darn near slinky, in the closest thing to a deep purple that Daisy would let me get away with, intended for proper dinner parties.

They were each stripped of their expensive lace and ribbon, which would have been kept back by the original owners to use on new dresses, but I didn't mind. Lace always made me feel like a two-year-old being dressed up for a pageant. I also picked up a rectangle of plain white muslin for a fichu—one of those neck scarf things that was superficially supposed to make the deliberate plunge of the Regency-era neckline more modest.

From there Daisy hustled us to the trim store, which was crowded with massive chests made up of hundreds of little drawers of buttons, lace, flounces, silk flowers, feathers, and anything else a lady might need to bedeck herself. I marveled at the intensity of some of the colors, not at all the insipid sepias or watercolors I'd expected. The cloth was just as vibrant in 1806 as in 2024. Considerably less neon, though.

After checking in with her sister in the shop next door, Daisy found me staring at the ribbons lined up on their spools on the shelf.

"It's funny," I said, instead of asking the questions that felt like they were burning my tongue the longer they went unspoken. "I've never been a girlie girl."

Daisy snorted, a distinctly indelicate yet endearing mode of conveying disbelief that I was pretty sure she had picked up from me. "Oh?"

"One of those girls who spends all their money on lipsticks, curls their hair, and has a collection of perfumes. But standing here, now, I can't help but covet all the pretty things. It's freaking me out a little."

"Women are naturally competitive creatures," Daisy allowed. "Your field of competition has changed, but not the game, Samantha. We regard each other as potential rivals for our livings and for our husbands. Even those who have no desire to play."

"Doesn't matter, I don't know the rules anyway," I said, and heroically did not add a quip about cheating. That felt a little *too* on the nose.

Daisy sighed, and began inspecting the spool in front of her with a studiously expressionless face.

"Nor I," she confessed, voice deep with sorrowful yearning. "I fear I never have."

Chapter Fifteen

IN WHICH SAM CONFESSES

I am half agony, half hope.

—Jane Austen, *Persuasion*

I longed for just five minutes alone with Daisy, but Marigold seemed to have decided it was her personal freaking mission to get between us. On the ride back she squeezed in between me and her sister. Once we reached the house, Marigold swept Daisy away to the breakfast room for the cold luncheon that had been laid out for our return, even though Daisy protested that she wasn't hungry yet, and boxed her in at the end of the table. After, Marigold pestered Daisy into a walk around the garden and they were out the door before I'd had the chance to finish my own lunch.

Right. I could take a hint.

Part of me couldn't blame Marigold. She was used to having Daisy's attention all to herself. It must have been terribly lonely to be stuck with their mother, unable to have the intimate, sisterly conversations that I was sure they were used to.

The rest of me hated her guts for being just so bloody *inconvenient*.

I retreated to our bedroom and busied myself with hanging up my new clothes, which had arrived in brown paper parcels while we'd been eating, and sending my borrowed clothes to the laundry. I distracted myself by reading the book Daisy had left on her nightstand: William Henry Ireland's *Gondez the Monk*, a libidinous, lush, and vulgar tale about a perverted abbot, consort demons, and the people he trapped in his sex labyrinth with necromancy.

Yikes.

These Georgians were certainly *a lot* hornier than the staid romances of Austen and Goodenough had led me to believe.

Wait.

Except that I *knew* Margaret Goodenough. The work *and* the woman.

And I knew Daisy was enthralled by the grotesque, delighted by a good bon mot, and aware of the social issues and injustices of her time. That she read lurid novels, and was fascinated by true-crime news stories, if her exclamations over the morning papers were anything to go by. That she put on an air of dignified detachment in public but in private reveled in wine and gossip. That she was vital and *present* in a way that her mother and sister were not.

That she had been on the verge of letting me kiss her.

Beside the wardrobe, Daisy's travel desk sang to me like a siren. I had very little idea what, if anything, from Margaret Goodenough's life had survived to be displayed in museums in my time.

But this case had.

It would.

Dahlia had said so.

Feeling bold, and guilty, and a little foolish, I crept across the room and knelt beside the clever case. Reverently, I ran my fingertips across the scuffed corners, the honey-colored polished wood, the cracked leather handle.

Had anyone else touched the case since she'd received it?

Would I be the only other person to touch it until after her death?

I pressed one thumb into the wood beside the filigreed latch. I imagined my fingerprints sinking into the lacquer, somehow visible two hundred years from now, under blacklight, puzzled over by experts and literature lovers for the rest of time. Maybe, one day, Dahlia would stare at it in some overlit white-and-chrome exhibit while a curator explained the puzzle of the one incorrect and mysterious fingerprint to a gaggle of tourists.

When I lifted my thumb away, there was no mark.

I did not exist in Margaret Goodenough's world.

Only Daisy's.

I was desperate to open it and read the early draft of *The Welshman's Daughters*. Was it really as subversive and subtextual as the introduction of the book had purported? *Was* something hidden under the hand kissing and yearning glances—which I now understood *intimately* could be just as lascivious as grinding on a strobe-riddled dance floor.

I would never violate Daisy's privacy like that, of course. Especially after the dressing down she'd given me for just glancing over her pages that morning. But I *wanted* to.

As soon as I'd returned to the bed and picked up *Gondez the Monk* again, Daisy tumbled in the door. She was breathless with laughter and flushed from the cold. My intense desire to read her book was replaced whiplash fast with a desire to pounce on her.

Because here was the thing: Daisy was Margaret. And Margaret, according to history, was at least a little queer, if not all the way.

I knew, the way a bird knows how to fly south for winter, that Margaret Goodenough would welcome my attention. My kisses. My touch. My tongue in wonderful, secret places. But I also knew, with that same south-facing surety, that this was not the way to woo *Daisy*.

Daisy, who read about sex but wrote about romance. Daisy, who'd probably never met another woman who felt like she did in her life, at least not knowingly. Daisy, who liked to be thrilled but not grossed out or frightened.

Instead I made myself close the book.

"Good walk?" I asked.

"Yes!" Daisy enthused. "Though I am sorry we outpaced you. I did not see you following."

"I decided to stay in," I said. "Give you some sister time."

"How kind," Daisy said, and the best part was that she genuinely thought so.

Damn it, I had it bad.

"I think—" I stood. "I think we need to talk about what we nearly—"

"Sister!" Marigold called from the next room. "Do wear the silver dress tonight, and I shall wear my umber with the gold thread!"

"Oh Christ," I muttered.

"Daisy! Do come help me with my hair!" Iris added.

I covered my face and laughed. "I've never been clam jammed by the universe so hard in my life."

Daisy offered up one of those uncanny Margaret Is Paying Attention looks at the phrase.

"No, no, I'm not explaining that one," I said. "Please, go dress with them, I'll struggle along. I need to figure out how to do this by myself anyway."

Daisy's gaze softened. "You ought not need to."

"Yeah, well, that's me. Little Miss Hyperindependent as a Trauma Response."

"What do you mean by—"

"Shoo," I said gently.

Daisy fetched her silver evening dress and its accouterments and went next door. Biting my lip to keep from laughing, or crying, or any of the other of five thousand feelings that were tangling up under my lungs, I began the laborious process of dressing alone.

~

Eliza caught me halfway down to the dining room, declared me close but not quite, and relaced the back of my purple evening dress in the dark lee of the grand staircase. I'd left my hair loose in wavy tendrils brushing my shoulders, so she also pulled one of the ribbons from her own hair to fashion a quick headband for me. To keep my hair out of my soup, she said.

Dinner was served in the formal room. I found it hilarious that it was improper for me to walk in all by myself. Marigold, by virtue of her late husband's position in society, and Sir Gale, as the two highest ranking folks, walked in together. They were followed by Fenton and Eliza, Iris, then me and Daisy, then the remaining gaggle of children, which was where the parade of precedence fell apart.

Sir Gale took the head seat, with Marigold to his right, Iris to his left, then Eliza and Fenton opposite one another. I assumed there was a rule about who sat where and waited until Daisy glanced pointedly at me, then at a chair, before sitting. We were among the daughters and yet another sibling—this time a young boy who was just edging toward being a pimply, sullen teenager. He clearly would much rather have been upstairs with whatever the equivalent of a video game was.

Over the meal—a dozen dishes served in courses of soup and game, jellies and salads, cheeses and yet more overboiled veg—Sir Gale and Fenton spoke animatedly about the capture of Buenos Aires, and how the Batavian Republic was now the Kingdom of Holland, and what that may mean for gin trade. Fenton's manners were open and easy, his hair still a windblown mess and his cheeks red from sea salt and exposure. He really looked like a "Finch" now.

He looked unburdened.

Happy.

I had little to add to the general conversation of weddings, the war with France, or the growing abolitionist movement, save to strongly and heartily put forth that enslaving other human beings was *hello, extremely ethically and morally wrong and maybe that issue should be a bigger concern than the economic hardship it would bring on the enslavers if they have to start paying for labor* when it seemed everyone was being too polite to take a firm stance.

As for Marigold, she was flirting with Sir Gale so hard that even Fenton and Eliza were cringing from secondhand embarrassment. Where I might have laughed behind my sleeve at her before, by virtue of my recent education on how girls in this time and class were raised very specifically to be one thing, and one thing only, I now had sympathy for her.

She'd done her duty and married, and married up. But she'd lost him, and the entirety of her extended family, in what Daisy had called a horrid and unexpected sweep of cholera through the household while Marigold had been in Bath visiting Iris and Daisy. And if that wasn't nightmarish enough, Marigold had then also lost her husband's business to debts that she could not repay with all the funerals to cover. After which the house was given away to a distant male cousin of her late husband.

After a triumphant match and the realization of the girlhood ambition to secure her safety and future, she had been forced to return home childless, husbandless, positionless, and brokenhearted.

If it was me, I would be just as desperate as Marigold was to get back out of my mother's house again, to be in charge of my own fate and my own finances. And as the youngest son of a landed baron, comfortable without being obnoxiously rich, with no need to pester his second wife for more children on top of the half dozen he already had, and no expectations to inherit his father's title, Sir Gale was a big step up from a hardworking merchant provisioner to His Majesty's navy.

That didn't make it any easier to watch.

As for Sir Gale, he was far more patient and kind about it than I might have been in his position. It was obvious where Eliza got her compassionate and generous nature. He never rebuffed Marigold outright, but the more he failed to engage with her in the manner she desired, the more desperate for his attention she grew, until Iris finally murmured, "Marigold, dear, do please allow Sir Gale to take his turn in conversation with the rest of his guests."

Marigold turned a mottled, mortified red and kept her head down for the rest of the meal. Shit, if my mom had called me out like that in front of my crush's family, I would have lain down face-first on the carpet and expired on the spot.

After dinner, the good ole boys peeled off to their brandy, cigars, billiards, and whatever else they did in a cramped, overcrowded country house like this. We women retreated back to the parlor with sherry and cards, books and embroidery hoops, and, in Daisy's case, her portable writing desk. It had been set up on the little table in the back corner, and I wondered how she planned to get any work done with everyone chattering. One of the Gale girls whisked the cover off the skinniest piano I'd ever seen—I hadn't even known it was there—and began practicing a truly agonizing lullaby.

I found myself sitting at another tiny table with Marigold, who was pointedly laying out a game of solitaire. Fine. I didn't want to play anyway.

She concentrated on her cards and I . . . okay, I was staring at Daisy.

Stop mooning, I scolded myself. *Stop it, stop it, stop it.*

Daisy, preoccupied by what was on the page and sipping her own digestif, set down her glass and then licked her bottom lip to chase a stray droplet. I felt my stomach get warm, my eyelids heavy, and *Christ—no—bad idea. Now is not the time.*

"Though my sister's preoccupation with the written word may seem odd to you," Marigold ventured at length, without looking up. I snapped my attention back to her, a blush rising on my face at being caught. "She has great aspirations. I am her sister and therefore inclined to tease, but even I admit that Daisy is also possessed of no small amount of talent." She leveled a hard look at me, daring me to call her little sister a weirdo.

"I have great respect for any artist who works hard at their craft," I said, because first, it was true, and second, if I was going to be employed by these folks in the near future, I wasn't dumb enough to piss off my boss.

Marigold blinked at me, clearly not expecting that answer.

"Yes. Well. Good," she said, and dealt out another round of cards for herself.

I forced my attention back to safer ground. When Marigold's sherry glass was empty, I made a point of fetching the decanter and walking around the room refilling everyone's glasses, with Daisy's last.

"You are an abysmal spy, Samantha," Daisy murmured as I paused beside her.

"Pardon?"

"One is not meant to look directly at the object one is attempting to study surreptitiously. It's rather against the point of being *surreptitious*."

"Ha-ha," I said, deadpan. "So funny. Hilarious. I'm gonna bust a gut."

Daisy squinted up at me. "Curious idiom, but I take your meaning."

"I'll just leave you to . . . " I felt like a sweaty teenager bothering the cool high-school sportsball star.

"No, sit with me," Daisy said, seizing an opportunity for us to talk without Marigold in the way. "This will keep." She lifted the page so I could see what she'd written. "Although I'll admit that some days it feels as if I never will finish it. As if the whole of the world conspires against my ability to simply take the time to . . . why do you look so perplexed?"

"Is this . . . this is dialogue. I remember this, Olive said it in the carriage this morning. And that's what her governess replied." I set down the decanter. "Is this why you record everything? You're content mining for dialogue?"

"Yes, this is a record of some of the choicest things said today."

"Ah, no, I mean that look in your eye, like you're, um . . ." *Taking a video*. "Mentally transcribing it."

"I did not realize I had a 'look,'" Daisy said, shooting a guilty glance at Marigold.

Sometimes I despise your little trick, Marigold had said. Now I wondered if Daisy had even known she was doing it. Maybe she had perfect recall. Or an eidetic memory. I could imagine how helpful that would be as a writer.

I leaned forward, lowering my voice. "I've been trying to get some time with you all day. Can we go upstairs or—?"

"Miss Franklin, it's uncouth to hoard the sherry," Marigold said from the far side of the room, in a snotty enough tone that everyone else stopped what they were doing to stare at me.

"Sorry," I said, at a matching volume, and rolled my eyes to the cruel heavens.

Marigold's interruptions were starting to grate.

Or maybe it's fate, I thought, all of a sudden. *Margaret Goodenough had a lover. A wealthy widow. That's not you, Sammie-bear. Maybe the universe is blocking us for a reason.*

My stomach plummeted. I stood shakily to return the crystal decanter to the credenza. I was half afraid I would drop it, I was trembling so hard.

Margaret Goodenough was the staid and steady patron saint of closeted queer longing, as fine and unapproachable as a marble statue in a temple. I was a chipped dollar-store bowl of mismatched rainbow buttons and gremlin lusts masquerading as a functioning human being, a messy scholar, loud, brash, and more get-up-and-go than sit-down-and-think. There was no *way* history, or fate, or time, or whatever it was that was responsible for me being here was going to let me . . . *let* me . . .

There would be no cute little cottage-core happily ever after for me.

This wasn't the first time I had thought this, but surrounded by the judgmental stares of the complete strangers I'd entrusted my life to, it felt *substantial* in a way it hadn't before.

"Why, Miss Franklin, you look positively *ghastly*," Marigold said as I passed, with no little glee.

"Yup," I agreed, not in the mood for a scrap anymore. "I'm just gonna hit the hay. Long day."

"I imagine," Marigold sneered. "All that intellectual conversation at dinner must have been quite taxing."

"Not that intellectual," I said, before my brains caught up with my mouth, "otherwise *you* wouldn't have been able to follow it."

The youngest Gale sisters hissed something that sounded like the

Georgian version of *oh snap*. Marigold stood, hurt crossing her face before she quashed it. Eliza gestured sharply for the girls to stop giggling, and Iris set aside her glass and sat forward, going into mama-bear mode.

And Daisy . . .

Daisy flushed red with mortification. But not at Marigold.

It was *me* she turned her face away from, shamed.

Oh, no, totally, insult the older sister of the woman you're crushing on, that's a surefire way to convince the universe that you should be together. Idiot.

I, of course, immediately regretted it.

Crocodile tears dotted Marigold's lower lashes, and I was at a loss for what the appropriate response would be. All the same, I stuttered, "Marigold, I'm sorry, that wasn't kind of me."

"I know what I am," Marigold hissed. "I am not clever like Daisy or gregarious like Fenton, but you needn't be cruel, Miss Franklin."

"I'm sorry."

"Ever since you arrived I've been looked over and ignored, and I won't be, not by you, not by the esteemed gentleman in there—"

I cut a quick glance at Eliza, who looked like she had something to say about that, and none of it pleasant.

"Listen, Marigold," I said, dropping my voice and stepping closer so only she could hear. "You may not like me, but as an outsider, I have the privilege of perspective and, I dunno, maybe rethink throwing yourself at Sir Gale? It's making things awkward with Eliza and Fenton, and I just don't think he's that into you."

Marigold reared back, real hurt replacing the theatrical mask.

"Why must you ruin *everything* you touch?" Marigold blubbered, before fleeing the room. Iris was hot on her heels.

"Good question," I said, hating myself.

~

"You have behaved abominably," Daisy said shortly thereafter. We were standing opposite one another in our nightclothes, the bed between us, neither of us willing to be the first to broach the no-man's-land of shared space. "My family has been nothing but generous to you. While my sister was being very silly tonight, what you said to Mary was unkind."

"But it was true."

"It matters not whether it was true or not, it was hurtful! And deliberately cruel," Daisy snapped back, crossing her arms mulishly. "I was ashamed to call you my friend in that moment."

You always have to be right! Dahlia's voice rang through my head. One of the many times that we'd fought about my stupid inability to shut my damn mouth and let things slide. *Just because it's true doesn't mean you have to say it!*

"I didn't mean to embarrass you," I said.

Daisy scowled harder. "*That* is not an apology."

"I'm *sorry* I embarrassed you," I amended. "And I'll apologize to Marigold in the morning. I'll do better."

Daisy huffed, but dropped her combative posture. "I believe you will *try*."

"This is hard for me, too, you see that right?" I bit my lower lip, trying hard not to make this about me. I was supposed to be making amends. "I can't seem to keep from screwing up. I keep saying things I shouldn't, *doing* things I shouldn't. Being here is so—" I stopped myself.

"A-ha!" Daisy said, pointing at me in both irritation and elation. "There! You seem always on the verge of revelation, and then you bridle yourself. It is maddening, Samantha. *Maddening*. Do you have any idea how you fascinate and frustrate me by turns?"

"What?" I said dumbly, trying to play it. "I don't know what you're—"

"Do not lie," Daisy begged. She knelt on the bed, crawling halfway across to implore me from her knees.

"I haven't lied to you," I hedged.

"You omit truths, which is as much the same as a lie as to be indecipherable from one. Your *obfuscate*. Why?"

She wasn't playing coy or being sweet for the sake of luring me into outing myself in a lie. She was desperate for an answer, and after how I'd behaved downstairs, I felt I owed her one.

No, that was unfair. I *wanted* to tell her because I wanted her to know. I wanted a *connection* to a degree that even Finch and I hadn't shared. Something soft and intimate, for just us two.

Sap, I scolded myself. *And selfish. If you tell her, she can never unknow it.*

My head said to keep my secrets.

My heart screamed the opposite.

"Daisy—"

"Sam," she replied, without the honorific, using my first name the way I was using hers. On purpose. With devotion. "We are here, now. Us two. The family is downstairs. The servants are elsewhere. We are utterly alone, finally. Do you not think that this is the opportune time? Shall we not be completely open with one another, at last?"

She reached out to me, and as helpless as an iron filing under command of a magnet, I let her draw me onto my knees before her.

I tangled her fingers harder in mine, tempted, so *tempted* . . .

"Why not tell me the truth?" Daisy swayed closer, warm and soft, and smelling enticingly of violets. "There is some secret that you keep from me. One that you have already shared with Finch. Why my brother, and not I? Am I not your friend, Samantha?"

"You are."

"Then explain to me what you meant when you told Finch you had a beau named Dahlia, when he marveled at your timepiece and the small rectangle you asked him to retrieve from your stays, when he spoke of your being from the far-flung future and you did not take the statement as a jest."

"Shit," I gasped. "You heard all that?"

"I heard *everything*," Daisy said, thrusting her chin out mulishly. "Including that you and my brother had *participated* in intimacies while you were at sea."

"It was in an alleyway," I corrected with a sly smirk, just for the fun of watching her eyes widen and her face turn blotchy. "But, yeah."

"You are attempting to redirect the conversation again, Samantha," Daisy said with a frustrated swat to my shoulder.

"You're the one who brought up *intimacies*."

"I am not a fool, Samantha Franklin," Daisy said softly, and it sounded like a confession in a church, low and serious. "I doubted at first, but I am a teller of stories and I know when someone is spinning them. You confess more than you think you do when you speak, and your conversations with Finch are quite unguarded when you presume privacy. So where—"

She paused, blinked rapidly, and licked her lips, breath heaving in her breast, and for a second I didn't get it. She looked scared. What had she to be scared of?

Ah.

It was the question.

She didn't know how to ask.

"Two thousand and twenty-four," I said, so she wouldn't have to. "I crashed on October fourth, 2024."

"And were rescued on October fifth, 1805. You . . . you are . . . you have . . ."

"I traveled through time."

There.

I'd said it.

"How? How could one possibly—"

"I don't know," I said. Her nose wrinkled, unimpressed. "Honestly, that's the truth. One minute I was thirty-thousand feet up, soaring over the Atlantic on my way to Barcelona. The next, Fenton was fishing me out of the drink."

"Soaring over the Atlantic?" Daisy asked, eyes glittering with wonder and fierce curiosity.

I explained planes. Then I told her about university, and celebratory graduation trips, and burning oxygen, and yellow life jackets, and PTSD. I explained that same-sex acts had been decriminalized, that we had laws enshrining the protection of rainbow folk, about marriages and divorces, because even queer relationships weren't perfect. I told her about Dahlia leaving me on the sidewalk with my heart cracked in half, and about how maybe I had deserved it.

I talked until my voice was hoarse and the little clock on the mantle chimed midnight. The fire had burned down, and we had drunk our way through the pitcher of fresh water that had been left on the bedside table. For Daisy, I would do even that, because she had asked it of me.

"And this is why you are so free with your affections," Daisy whispered into the warm space between us. We'd migrated onto our sides, facing one another across a shared pillow, the hems of our nightgowns overlapping across our feet. "Relations before marriage are common, and expected?"

"Only if you want to," I said. "Some people don't. Some people *never* want to, and that's okay too."

Daisy's whole body jerked with surprise. "It is?"

"Why do you ask?" I propped my head up, leaning on one elbow, and decided to be bold. I ran the tips of my finger along her arm, stopping to pet them through the whisp of blond curls escaping her braid, below her ear. "Do you find intimacy repulsive? It's fine if you do. Being asexual is very normal too."

Daisy shivered and leaned into my touch instead of away from it. "I am not some priggish society miss, Sam," Daisy said with warm fondness. "I have no illusions about the nature of marital relations, nor does the thought of them disgust me."

"Okay."

"Though," she said softly, moonstone eyes dropping to my mouth briefly before she licked her own lips, leaving them pink and slick and tantalizing. She yanked her gaze back to safer territory, suddenly shy. "I will confess that I have had no *experience*. My knowledge is wholly theoretical."

"No experiments for research?" I teased gently, trying to lighten the mood.

"I found the tutors on offer unappealing," she admitted, pleased by her own wit. "And those I wanted, I could not approach. I wanted . . . dash it." Her face grew pink. "How mortifying, to pride myself on my wordcraft and to now find myself with none of the correct ones.

"Use the incorrect ones then," I said, brushing my fingers down her arm to her hip.

"I am *wrong*," she blurted, the mortified flush deepening.

I paused the sweep of my hand along her side and sat up. This felt like the kind of confession that deserved the whole of my attention. "How do you mean?"

Daisy turned her face away, hiding in the pillow even as her confession tumbled out. "I have vowed to myself that I shall not marry, for I refuse to do so without love. Though I have tried vainly to fall in love with a man, I am simply unable to do so. Whatever mechanism it is by which the gentler sex germinates an attachment to a man, it does not function in me. Perhaps our Creator made me with a fault, for I esteem *women* as a man ought. I thought it better to love not at all than to love *wrong*." Her voice wobbled and she sniffed hard, pressing her face farther into the pillow.

"Hey, no, babe, you're not broken, you're fine," I said, wrapping a comforting arm across her shoulders.

"Oh, Sam." Daisy hiccupped. "And now you tell me that I may love as I like, only that I must worry about cultural offenses and *homo-phobia*, that I am both natural and reviled—"

"Fuck, no, Daisy, that's not what I—"

"Please, Samantha," she moaned. "I feel such an attachment to you. Yet I am conflicted. You understand me, and my *wants* in ways that I can barely fathom *myself*. You see something . . . and you look at me like . . . like I *matter*."

She leaned forward, close enough to— Did she know? Was she doing this on purpose? She licked her lower lip again, and *Jesus fucking Christ*, no, she didn't; she couldn't possibly.

"You are. You're meaningful," I admitted, not able to tear my eyes off of that now-slick lip, its soft pink plumpness.

I swallowed hard. *Tread carefully*, I warned myself. *This is important*. Her eyes were iridescent with an unexpected sheen of tears, glittering like true moonstones in her determination. "Tell me, Samantha Franklin, am I at least as *meaningful* to you as Finch?"

Oh god.

"More," I said, strangled.

"More?" she challenged, stubborn now, determined. Her breath smelled of sherry. Would her mouth taste of it?

"So much more," I babbled. "Daisy, you—"

I didn't have the chance to tell her what I thought of her; of how admirable I found her, how easy her friendship was, how warm our companionship. How I liked laughing and teasing with her, how I appreciated her glitteringly vicious observations of the people around us. How she had so easily offered me a place in her life. How Fenton had tried to push me into a mold that didn't fit, tried to rectify his confusion about my past, my vocabulary, my life by making me into what he thought I should be: a simperingly grateful maid. But how Daisy took me at face value and evaluated each new part of me that she didn't understand as it came, redefining her understanding of the whole instead of blindly forcing it into a predetermined space.

I didn't say any of this.

I couldn't.

Because Daisy was kissing me.

Guess I wasn't the only one who had been preoccupied by what had nearly happened this morning.

And just as I realized it—her pretty little cupid's bow mouth on mine, her hand gripping my forearm, everything pressing just a bit too hard, squeezing a bit too much—she pulled back. A shocked, worried expression scurried over her features.

"Holy shit." I pressed my fingers to my tingling lips.

"Was that not correct?" Daisy asked. "Oh, I knew that I would be abominable at it."

"Nobody's perfect at anything on the first try."

"I was not meant for this, I think, this sort of gentle courtship, I *am* created wrong—"

Before she could finish her self-recrimination, I had both of my hands on her face, tilting my own to slot our mouths together. I sucked her upper lip between my own, darted my tongue out for a taste, then repeated it on her lower lip. She gasped, and I took the opportunity to touch my tongue, very gently, to the tip of hers.

"My goodness!" Daisy said, pulling back, cheeks flaming. "Was that—?"

"I won't do it again if you didn't like it," I said, but she paused, anylizing my own mouth like she was trying to figure out the best way to attack it.

"I should like to try," Daisy said. She tilted her head, considered the angle of our noses, and licked my bottom lip like a kitten.

I couldn't help the snort of laughter and she pulled back again, indignant.

I took the hand on my shoulder, scooted forward so we were pressed together from knee to nose, and placed it on the back of my head. "Go on. Dig in."

She curled her fingers into my hair, pressing against my scalp.

"Tilt, like this, yeah," I said, pressing light fingers to her jaw. "Just do what feels nice. If I do something to you, and you like it, do it back. We won't do anything but kiss, I promise. I won't move my hands below your shoulders, but you can put yours anywhere you want. Ready?"

Daisy took a deep breath. "Proceed."

Swallowing a giggle at the ridiculousness of it all, I kissed her again. Small light pecks, then longer presses on her lips, in the corners, on her nose and chin and cheeks. Kissing her was ecstatic, simple and intimate. It was in the taste of her, the soft noises she made. The delicate way she panted against my mouth whenever we paused for air. She gasped and laughed when I kissed her neck, nipped at the tendon. When she was more relaxed, sagging against me and bold with her own kisses, I opened my mouth, teased and tempted her inside sweetly.

After a beautiful eternity, she pulled back, mouth wet and swollen, pupils blown and eyes glazed.

"My goodness," she murmured again.

"Good?"

"Most definitely. Quite a skill you possess, Miss Franklin."

"I'll take that as a compliment, Miss Goodenough," I replied, cheeky in my delight.

"And this is how . . . how women love one another where you are from?" she asked gently, reaching up to push a piece of hair back off my face.

"This is how everyone kisses. Even here."

"Does Finch kiss like this?" Daisy asked, jealousy and smug victory in her voice in equal parts.

I groaned, flopping onto my back. "Don't do that to yourself."

"Do what?"

"Compare yourself to him. I'm not sorry I slept with your brother," I said. "I hadn't met you yet. But I am sorry that it's made you feel like an also-ran. I promise, you're not second best to him. You're not second best to *anyone*. To be honest, it was a desperation move. I do *like* Fenton, but I thought if I could lock him down, I'd be, you know, safe."

"It is the way of the world for women to throw themselves into the power of menfolk for their own security," Daisy said, both condemning said world and forgiving me. "That you did what you felt you had to does not lessen you in my esteem."

"It won't always be that way, though," I said, with perhaps a bit more viciousness than the bedroom called for. "I've *never* had to. Before I ended up here, I've only ever made love to someone because I *wanted* to."

Daisy wound herself around me, arms squeezing my waist, feet shyly tangled between mine. I turned my face to hers, watching intently as she settled her head on my shoulder. It was cute.

Smitten, that's what I was.

Fucked too. Utterly fucked and totally fine with it.

I grinned and pushed a gentle kiss against her mouth. Oh yes. This is what I'd missed—the softness of her kiss with no beard prickles, the beautiful view down her cleavage, the press of breasts against mine. Perfect.

"You are refreshingly forthright for all of your secrecy, Sam. Qualities, along with your intoxicating kisses, that I suspect made my brother doubt his attachment to Miss Eliza Gale."

"But he does love her," I pressed. "He really does."

"He really does," Daisy agreed.

"He's a good man," I said, relieved. "You really don't mind that he and I, er, rendezvoused?"

Daisy's smile turned sly. "If that is what you'd care to call it."

"Is it weird?" I groaned, hiding my face in her hair.

"It rather intrigued me more than I care to admit," she said, kissing the shell of my ear. "Not because he is my brother, but because of the self-assured way he spoke of you taking your pleasure. And giving him his own."

"Competence kink?"

"I do not know what that means," Daisy admitted, twisting to meet my eyes. They were a bit sad, though, a bit hurt. "I don't mind you dallying with him, so long as it brought you to me. But, Sam, why would you tell Finch but not me? Have I not earned your trust? Am I not your *very* good friend? Do you not . . . do you not feel for me as I am beginning to feel for you?"

"You have no idea."

"I believe I have some," Daisy said, smirking.

I sighed happily. "As much as I'd like to spend the rest of the night proving it to you, we should go to sleep."

Daisy cupped my face, leaned in for a nearly chaste kiss before pulling back to sweep the pad of her thumb back and forth along my bottom lip.

She leveled the cutest, clumsiest attempt at bedroom eyes at me that I'd ever seen. It made her breasts push up against her arm, soft and unrestrained, the nipples sweetly dusky through the thin nightgown. I wanted, very, *very* much to suck one into my mouth, make the linen transparent with my saliva, see if she was one of those lucky women who could achieve orgasm from that stimulation alone.

Instead I prodded her until she was facing away from me so I could snug up behind her as the big spoon. She melted back, skinny bum warm against my thighs, hair floral and sweat musky against my nose.

"Just sleep tonight," I said again.

"I've had no lover but you," Daisy husked. "And I dare say, I have no desire to have another. I could spend my whole life with you and never grow bored, Samantha Jayne Franklin."

"Because I'm an unwilling time traveler filled with weird social mores and bizarre juxtapositions to unpick, and you'll never get sick of winkling out my secrets?" I asked. I was going for light, but the real worry that this might be the only reason Daisy wanted me around must have leaked into the question.

"Rather, because you are a kind person, and a learned one," she said, lifting my hand from its splay over her belly to kiss the back of it. "Because you make me strive to be worthy of your attention and your admiration." Here, she glanced meaningfully at the writing case. "Because you understand and accept my predilections and judge me not." Daisy threw that wry smile over her shoulder at me, which I was beginning to really, *really* love. "And because I find you very handsome," she finished, with the single most delectable blush I had ever seen.

"Damn," I said, because what else can you do when a great classic literary mind basically calls you a smokeshow? I grasped her chin, leaned over her shoulder, and kissed her again, slow and lingering.

Screw the universe and its comedic timing. We're doing this.

Please, just let me live, I had begged, when the air had felt too far above my head, when Lewis's hand had been around my throat, when the society around me had felt stifling and choking.

Now, between sweet slow kisses, I prayed: please, let me just live forever like *this*.

Chapter Sixteen

IN WHICH SAM RELISHES

> *My idea of good company [. . .] is the company of clever, well-informed people, who have a great deal of conversation.*
>
> —Jane Austen, *Persuasion*

I apologized to Marigold first thing at breakfast, and she accepted it with grudging good grace in front of the audience of Finch, Eliza, and a scattering of younger Gales. She could hardly do otherwise with them watching. Things remained tense between us, and I spent the rest of the morning ingratiating myself to her, flattering her and being helpful, until her stiff-backed hurt melted away around dinner. Daisy rewarded me with more kisses that night.

And so the next few weeks passed.

There was something wonderful about a cozy, well-appointed life: not so luxurious that there were social responsibilities, not so close to poverty that there was scrabbling; with just enough servants to make anything happen when you wanted it to but not so many that it felt invasive.

Which left time for all the other lovely, domestic things—like taking tea or going on walks—that wove two lives into one. Kissing was as far as either Daisy or I were ready to go while still sharing a wall with her soon-to-be sister-in-law on one side and her mother and actual sister on the other. Honestly, I was in no rush. We had literally the rest of our lives together. What did it matter, then, when we got around to sex? Not that I didn't want it—but I was content to let Daisy dictate our pace.

That didn't mean Daisy and I didn't take great comfort in retiring after dinner. Not so early, though, that I cut her off from the company of the other ladies. I'd learned my lesson and made a point of not sticking too close to Daisy's side during the day. The more time she spent in her sister's company, the less Marigold seemed likely to snap at me.

Where possible, Daisy and I spent the evenings mapping the inside of each other's mouths, tasting and testing. I showed Daisy where to touch, where to tickle, where to pinch. She became more confident in pursuing her own pleasure, and giving me mine. I felt full to bursting that she trusted me enough, wanted this enough that she let me teach her, day by day, slowly.

I had fallen fast, and hard.

And we spoke. *Oh*, how we spoke.

We filled the air between us with the secrets, the confessions, the truths that we could never tell anyone else. I accepted Daisy for who she was, and did not condemn her for it, did not urge her instead to get married and stop being a burden on her family, the way everyone else in her life did. Daisy returned the favor by never calling me mad, never disbelieving my fantastical stories, never questioning my origin; letting me just be *me*.

I'd never been so honest about my fears and desires with anyone in my life. There were no stakes here, no ego, no one to judge me for what I did or did not want, for my yearnings and my frustrations, because here they meant *nothing*. It was freeing to be able to let go of societal expectations about life goals and milestones that I hadn't even *realized* had been burdening me. Of course, the life I had now came freighted with new expectations, but somehow these seemed lighter to carry, because I hadn't internalized them, didn't wear them hooked into my bones.

Daisy told me about her family, her best friend in Marigold, about the loss of her father three years prior and their domino-like move from their father's house in a middling-good part of Bath to less elegant accommodations, and how it had negatively affected Fenton's marriage prospects until the ball where he'd met Eliza. About the devastating loss of Mr. Kempel and his family's support. And how, without their father's income, the Goodenoughs had crammed into a very small row house, living as cheaply as possible on the two elder women's widow's portions and Fenton's modest inheritance. His naval wage did go in part to his family, but now that he was to be a married man, his first financial priority would have to be his own wife and children. Which was why Daisy's family was keen for her to put herself out there on the marriage market, and to rent Finch's former room to a lodger.

We did not speak of the book she was writing because she'd asked me to reveal nothing and I, to my shame, didn't know enough to reveal anyway. But Daisy did ask me all about the people I knew from home. She was particularly interested in their general characters and verbal twitches, which she in turn recorded in the notebook pages she never shared with anyone.

I never dared to sneak a peek again, out of both respect and genuine fear that she would stab any hand that touched her pages with the little knife she used to sharpen her pencils and quills.

Three Sundays in a row the household tromped off to the nearby church to experience the thrill of hearing Eliza and Finch's upcoming nuptials announced, with no impediment voiced from anyone in the congregation.

In between services, Eliza's fabrics and trims began to come in. The gaggle of ladies at Swangale, sometimes joined by married women from the town, devoted ourselves to patterning, chalking, sewing, and trimming the soon-to-be Mrs. Goodenough's linens, lingerie, and honeymoon wardrobe. Well. *They* sewed. I poured tea, fetched needles, handed out custard and fruit tarts, and generally made myself as useful and unobtrusive as possible.

The majority of the sewing circle conversation was held up by

Marigold and Mrs. Goodenough relaying the gossip of Bath. So-and-so had broken their engagement to Mr. Two Thousand Pounds a Year, and someone's son had joined the reserves, and someone else had commissioned a new dress in the Paris fashion, which was deemed terribly unpatriotic.

In between, I devoured all the history and society books I could get my hands on in preparation for my upcoming role in the little Goodenough school. While Marigold and I may have had a tense relationship, the prospect of being able to take on twice as many students and therefore bring in twice as much income was one that Marigold couldn't afford to recant.

My button-down became sleepwear, with the jeans and jacket destined to be forever hidden in the back of a drawer in case anyone was in need of a brother again in the future. My Converse remained my footwear of choice, the purple canvas and signature white rubber toe peeking out from under my hems when we went outdoors, and I wouldn't give up my wool Basque hat for anything. The lapel pins and my wallet remained wrapped in the pink gingham handkerchief, zipped into the jacket pocket, relegated to the place of repressed memory.

Breakfast became my favorite part of the day. Breakfast was when everyone else was too hungover to be up early or had already headed out on morning visits, walks, or rides. Breakfast was when Daisy sat at the end of the table farthest from the door with her writing case, disheveled and cranky, just barely decent and loath to be disturbed by any except me, so long as I kept her teacup full and my mouth shut.

Freed for just four precious weeks from the social and domestic responsibilities that would have been a constant interruption in Bath by virtue of Sir Gale's staff, Daisy hoarded every spare moment, working ravenously.

Daisy was rarely disturbed while she was *writing*. The word was spoken by everyone in the household with such a deliberate, almost spiritual hush I wondered if they somehow knew; if they all had precognition of what Daisy would someday become. As if they could touch the future as surely as I had touched the past.

This was the real authoress—the real Margaret Goodenough scrunched up paper, talked to herself, paced the room acting out scenes or hunched over her desk, nose smudged with pencil, muttered and cribbed dialogue from actual conversations, scribbled oblivious to anything else. She wrote, and wrote, and wrote. She *worked* for her genius. She suffered. She *cared*.

And it was my privilege alone to witness and support this Margaret Goodenough. I now knew she preferred wild berry preserves over clotted cream and just a very small dash of milk in her tea, that she wore more dark olive and plum than an unmarried woman ought, and stuck to muslin caps indoors to avoid having to brush out and style her hair every morning. She wrote between dawn and when the second person in the household woke, and always sat to breakfast with a wild grin and flushed cheeks.

It felt like I'd finally found my place in this world.

It was by her side.

And it was *grand*.

~

March came in like a lion, and we piled into the church first thing on a Saturday morning to hide from the weather and pay witness to a wedding exactly like every one I'd ever seen in every historical drama. Outside afterward, the breeze was brisk as we waved off the happy couple, the first promise of spring not quite strong enough to push off the lingering, tattered clouds of winter. The furled buds on the trees along the walk seemed to be shivering in their little verdant coats. Everyone hustled into the carriage to return to Swangale, hands punched into their coat pockets or muffs, shoulders hunched to protect their necks. The world smelled of approaching rain, tender new-growth grass, and the promise of renewal.

During my time with the Gales I had discovered that Daisy and I were the same age—twenty-four. She was two years older than Fenton, three years younger than Mary, and seven months my senior. But out under the clear sky, cheeks red with nip of the wind and her careless attempt at securing her hair up causing mischievous little tendrils to wriggle out of the back of her bonnet to dance in the wind, she looked ageless as a goddess. I wanted to kiss her on the steps of that little church, as well-wishers from the parish threw rice at the happy couple, and pretend it was for us.

I twined my hands behind my back and stayed out of the way.

The bride and groom left in Sir Gale's open-aired carriage (the name for which I still hadn't mastered; barouches, phaetons, traps, ugh, too many terms!) and took themselves off to Southampton, where Finch had rented a house. They'd live there in the months before his return to sea, on the hope that when he returned he'd be able to buy one of their own. Iris had also expressed a hope that it would soon be filled with the pitter-patter of little feet, and had promised Daisy to them as a nursemaid, if she hadn't done her daughterly duty and been married herself by that time.

"Do you even like kids?" I whispered to Daisy later, after the elaborate wedding breakfast.

"I like them well enough, for they are fascinating storytellers, and I am apt to believe that I will adore nieces and nephews of my own quite well indeed." Then her nose wrinkled. "What I *do not* like is my mother promising Finch my help by setting forth an ultimatum—marry or be the nursemaid. Neither of which am I prepared, nor willing, to undertake."

"Not to mention how much it would cut into your writing time, which you already get precious little of."

"Precisely!"

The morning after the wedding, while I did yoga in my nightdress (sweating off the decadent wines and gout-inducing foods we'd been indulging in at Sir Gale's expense), Daisy packed for us. Or rather, *re*packed for me. Apparently rolling things into balls and jamming them into the bottom of the trunk was the incorrect way to do it. Daisy's horror had been so palpable when she'd seen what I'd done that she had tipped out the whole trunk to start again. She was currently folding and laying our dresses into the bottom, and using gloves and stockings to cushion our accessories, bottles, books, and all the other feminine detritus that we had accumulated during our stay.

It was sensual, this intimate entwining of our lives; her bottles cushioned in my jeans, her hairbrush nestled against my pink gingham bundle. I secretly hoped her phial of perfume cracked midjourney, so it would seep into my clothes and I would get a burst of violets every time I dressed.

As soon as breakfast was had, we were on our way. Marigold was wistful about returning to Bath instead of staying in Seasalter, but was also pragmatic about the parting. She'd given up on Sir Gale, but had flirted with nearly every other single man of acceptable fortune in the intervening weeks, to no avail.

As we traveled, Marigold distracted herself by regaling me with the history of Bath, its start as a pagan place of worship, the health benefits of the spa, and the social circles that it drew. Bath was a fashionable place to be ill, and I quietly resolved not to go anywhere near the swirling cesspools of brewing disease that had to be the public bathing rooms. I knew for a fact that there would be no chlorine, no water filters, and no bleach. As *if* I was going to sit in the same water as someone with open sores, or syphilis, or consumption. Perhaps the spring *was* magical, like the ancient Romans believed, after all; it would be the only explanation for why people who came to Bath didn't get *worse*.

Kent and Bath were basically on opposite sides of the country. England wasn't that wide when you took into account that the whole of the United Kingdom would be dwarfed in Ontario, my home province. Yet by carriage it took us the better part of the week, resting at inns when we came to them and sleeping crunched together in a single room to save money.

The world got greener the farther west we drove, and by the time we arrived, the forest climbing up the hills that cradled Bath was casting bright emerald shadows over the honey-yellow stone buildings. Bath was a marvel of uniformity, all long clean lines and straight thoroughfares. They all led up to the top of a hill to the Circus, a roundel where the most important homes faced one another across a circular park and through the branches of an ancient oak tree.

The driver turned away from that avenue, affording me just one quick glance of the mighty tree, and down to Shaftesbury Road. The house we stopped at was an end unit, just two stories high, with a tiny back garden enclosed by a thigh-high stone fence, dutifully scrubbed bow windows, and a cute pointed dormer above the second story. The whole row of houses was constructed of the same honey-yellow stone, each door painted a different color. Ours was a cheery, welcoming red.

A letter had been sent before we had hit the road, and so a serving man and a maid were prepared to meet us.

I was introduced to Miss Brown, who took care of the household chores like cleaning, laundry, and some of the more arduous food preparation like making preserves, baking the daily bread, going to the shops, and maintaining the little kitchen garden out back. Next was Mr. Stewart, the manservant who ran errands, hauled around heavy things like firewood, served at the table, and did the sorts of repairs and business that women couldn't—or weren't allowed—to do for themselves.

That was the entirety of the Goodenough household.

Daisy and Marigold split the remaining chores, such as managing the finances, repairing clothing, arranging the social calendar, and whatever else popped up during the day. Their mother concerned herself solely with the business of getting her children married, and according to Daisy, she did it with a gusto that kept her out at engagements, teas, salons, and shops at all hours. What free time Daisy had around her mother's schemes she devoted to her writing, with the secret hope that her works might one day contribute to the household accounts. Marigold, as a widow herself, was less the target of her mother's plans (though not wholly free of them), and thus had devoted her afternoons to tutoring to shore up their purses.

And now that I was here, the little schoolroom carved out of the formal back parlor could be filled in both the mornings and the afternoons.

As I helped Miss Brown lug the trunks up to the family bedrooms, I took in the sparse and shoddy furnishings, the cramped and narrow hallways, the rooms so tiny and so filled with cupboards and cases that they could only be described as "tight." All the money they had, it seemed, went to keeping their wardrobes up to the level of outside expectations. I imagined they entertained very little, wanting as few people as possible to see the truth of their financial disgrace so plainly.

The lower floor comprised a study-slash-sitting room, which was the family's main living space, a dining room, the back parlor, which had been converted into the schoolroom, and a kitchen with a tiny closet off the pantry for Miss Brown to sleep in. The upper floor was divided into four narrow bedrooms for the family, and a little suite in the attic for Mr. Stewart. The room I was renting was only large enough for a twin bed with a side table, a wardrobe, a small desk, and a triangular tiered washstand.

And the toilet? That was an outhouse attached to the wall out back, accessible only by going outside, or a chamber pot stored under the bed with a tight lid to keep down smells.

On our first night in Bath, to show that I planned to contribute to the household as much as possible, I scrounged together enough leftover beef, mustard, cheese, and bread to completely screw with the timeline and introduce the Goodenoughs to open-faced sandwich melts (which required careful use of the bread oven and a steady hand with the paddle).

I'd yet to have a good bowl of spaghetti anywhere, and my realization was followed by an immediate craving. Crap. I would have to learn how to make pasta.

After dinner the Goodenoughs went their separate ways, sick of each other's company after being crammed together for so long, and Daisy and I had the minuscule study to ourselves.

Daisy crossed the room in three quick strides, threw her arms around my neck, and kissed me soundly.

"I've missed you too," I said.

"How torturous! To be so close to you for days, to sleep in the same bed, and to be unable to touch you!"

"Hard agree," I said, falling into her hungry mouth, kneading her waist. Then I groaned, and pushed her back a few steps, gently. "I can't believe I'm the one saying this, we gotta put on the brakes."

"Mr. Stewart could look in on us at any moment," Daisy agreed with a rueful smile.

"Uh-huh. And I really want a wipe down before we start any hanky-panky. I feel gross from all those communal beds."

"Hanky-panky," Daisy said with a giggle. "What a delightful word!"

I couldn't stop the stupid grin that spread across my face.

"Brandy, then," Daisy decided, moving to a cracked and mismatched set on the sideboard, which in itself was out of place among the rest of the room's decor. Wrong color wood. Family heirloom from the old house?

While she poured us each a tot, I perused the book-lined shelves of the study—a mix of what I assumed were Fenton's naval texts, their father's books on philosophy and Latin, finance and import law, Marigold's and Iris's etiquette books and fashion sketches, and Daisy's gorgeously trashy novels.

There was a small, battered piano—not a grand, but not a full upright—against the wall opposite the fireplace. I wondered who among the Goodenoughs was the pianist. Maybe it was Fenton. Maybe it had been their father and no one had touched the dusty, miserable-looking thing since he'd died, and they were only holding on to it for sentiment.

"It is not, perhaps, what you expected?" Daisy asked softly, handing me a glass.

"No," I admitted. I leaned back against the shelf, adoring the messy jumble of papers and tomes. "But I get it. Money's tight and none of you are making any."

"It is not embarrassing, but perhaps slightly uncomfortable, knowing how we used to live, which circles we have in the past been acquainted with. Never the Ton, but we were very respectable for a merchant's family." Daisy made a disparaging sound. "We should have moved house sooner but my mother would not hear of it. It ate into a great deal more of our savings than was wise."

"Don't be embarrassed, darling," I said. "I really do understand."

The student ghetto hadn't been my favorite place to live either.

Daisy downed her brandy, set aside the glass for Miss Brown to deal with in the morning, and twined her fingers in mine.

"Come, Sam," she said. "My mother and sister ought to be asleep by now. I desire that you take me upstairs and teach me how to hanky-panky."

~

Winsome, watercolor spring gave way to verdant, ripe summer and life settled into a comfortable routine.

Days were filled with Iris's friends dropping by for details of Finch's nuptials, Marigold's tromping around town to inform her pupils' families that she was back, bickering over the syllabus (*yes*, Marigold, I *would* be taking the time to discuss the horrors of colonialism and genocide when we discussed empires, whether you liked it or not), dedication to my morning yoga, my terrible attempts at making pasta (I wished I could pull up those video tutorials I'd only half paid attention to a lifetime ago), visits to the circulating library and the free art galleries, and walks through the town to browse shops in which none of us could afford to buy a thing in order to take in the latest fads and gossip.

Marigold and I traded off three-hour classes with rotating groups of children. They came and went based on their parent's schedules, finances, and what subjects would best suit their future careers. These weren't the boys going to Eton then onto Parliament, and these weren't the girls destined for finishing schools and grand ballrooms. No, our little backroom school catered to the children of butchers, bakers, and candlestick makers. Marigold taught the littles their letters, and the girls their needlework, deportment, and household management. I taught the littles their numbers, and the boys enough history and geography to keep them from getting lost when they turned sixteen and headed off to give Napoleon what-for.

It was nice to have a *job* again, to have a purpose, a schedule, and meaning.

And it was so radically different from the previous high-stress, must-get-commission work I had hawking cell phones at a mall stand that it barely felt like work at all. I just got to ramble about things I found fascinating and quiz them on lakes and mountains. When Daisy wasn't being dragged on the visiting rounds with her mother or escaping to take long walks along the leafy green avenues around town with me, she dutifully did her share of the household management: reviewing the accounts, adjusting the budget, working in the kitchen garden alongside Miss Brown, mending tears and lifting fallen hems, reworking old garments, making ink and poultices, and maintaining the never-ending mountain of letters that were business, pleasure, and family.

Where Marigold and Iris thrived on social interaction and were always flitting off in the evenings, Daisy and I preferred to stay in. Still, they managed to wheedle us into going out to common entertainments fairly often. We visited the Pump Room (no, thank you, I do not in fact want to drink water that smells like farts), went out for tea and Sally Lunn's Bath buns, patronized the Assembly Rooms for music recitals, and once to a very crowded, very sweaty public ball where I hugged the wall and drank too much ratafia (sweet, herby, and dangerous), followed by my first experience with a monstrous Georgian-era hangover.

One particularly fine evening, we made our way to the Sydney Pleasure Gardens, which were opened just once a summer for non-member lookie-loos like us. Daisy had a wonderful time dropping witty remarks in my ear about the petting zoo, little theme park rides, and the rumored lewd behavior of the toffs who used the grounds regularly for their scandalous liaisons.

On Sundays I went to church and tried not to fall asleep in the pew, because it made Daisy happy to go, and I liked making Daisy happy. After church I practiced my baking for tea time. Daisy carefully licked pastry crumbs off the fork tines, and I tried not to be a total pervert while watching her do it. We gossiped, played whist, and suffered Iris's jovial attempts to play matchmaker at every turn. I began a needlepoint that had to be constantly picked apart and repaired by Marigold.

On days when there were no plans, the four of us ladies crammed into the study. Marigold would plink on the dowdy, slightly out of tune piano while Iris amused herself with cards, or embroidery, or her correspondence, and Daisy hunched over her writing desk and edited what she'd written that morning. I devoted myself to my campaign of immersive study, devouring as many day-old newspapers as Mr. Stewart could beg from the neighbors.

Sometimes, feeling brave, Daisy would share some of her writing by reading it aloud. Marigold and Iris laughed or gasped in all the right places, and critiqued it gamely. Daisy looked to me, but I recused myself from commenting beyond a very basic "it's great" or pointing out a continuity error. Daisy thought it was because I didn't want to influence her as she wrote. Really, it was because, to my shame, I didn't want to admit that I'd never read it. I couldn't tell her that she was going to be published, do well, be famous enough that even two hundred years later everyone knew her name, and in the same breath confess that I had never seen the appeal of her work. (I was wrong; it was *so* appealing. I regretted never having picked it up. She was engaging as she read and lively when she explained plot snags. I loved the story all the more for hearing it from her own lips.)

Sometimes, when we were all getting along exceptionally well, we ladies just talked. Recent topics included Iris's determination to refinish the dining room, the same way that Mrs. So-and-So had last month. Both Daisy and Marigold tried to be polite every time it was brought up, but I could see the discomfort. It wasn't that they were embarrassed by their financial situation or that Mrs. Goodenough was obviously spending every penny they had to keep up appearances, but from trying to figure out how to say "absolutely not" to their own mother. Especially when she was used to quite a bit more luxury.

Whenever this happened, Iris switched topics and resumed the perennial questions about which play we would see next, when was best to promenade that week and what we would wear, and when I was going to Take The Waters™. *Everyone* in Bath was obsessed with discussing when *everyone else* in Bath would be Taking The Waters™. I would have given anything to soak away knotty muscles from hunching over students' work and kitchen counters. But no power on earth was going to get me into The Waters. Let alone *drink* them. I gagged every time someone mentioned the healing power of drinking unfiltered water straight from a spring where sick people lounged around mostly naked.

And after bedtime, there were other preoccupations to fill our time. Soft, sweet lessons that stopped before they went too far, conscious as we both were of the many other people under this same roof, as Daisy slowly became used to listening to her body, and exploring mine.

And in every spare microsecond she could scrabble together, Daisy wrote, and wrote, and *wrote*.

~

I couldn't use Daisy as my social crutch for the rest of my life, so one sunny morning when my entire class of rough and tumble boys decided adventure in the forests outside of town called louder than my lessons, I offered to do the daily shop for Miss Brown.

She handed over a purse and instructions to pick up a half dozen items, then pointed me to the shops with an admonishment not to linger in the rougher areas. I was pretty sure I could kick a street thug in the nuts and run if need be, but I appreciated her concern.

I took my time walking to the market, enjoying the scenery and memorizing the street names. I found the shops Miss Brown had indicated, a small dairy and cheese mongers where I got the milk, and then, next door to it, a cramped general store filled with barrels of wheats and grains, flours, powders, sugars, bundles of herbs, and little glass bottles of flavoring. The selection was overwhelming. I stood in the middle of the shop feeling ridiculously out of my league.

"Good morning . . ." a guy, maybe a few years younger than me, said with a quick glance at my bare left hand. ". . . miss. Is there anything in particular that you're wanting?"

He was broad in the way of people who hauled things around for a living. He had a curling flop of ginger-blond hair and wore a white jacket buttoned tightly across his chest, with white stockings that covered part of his shoes and went up to his knees, disappearing behind the long hem of his coat. *Practical outfit for this place,* I decided, noting the powder that had gotten all over him.

"Flour."

"Of course. What sort, miss?"

"Um?" I raised my eyebrows, feeling ridiculous. "The kind you make bread with, I guess?"

He laughed and said, "How much, miss?"

That I knew. "A pound."

"Good then. Follow me, miss."

He led me to the corner where barrels sat with the lids half on. He filled a paper bag expertly from a barrel he seemingly picked at random. I couldn't tell the difference between the types of flours, but apparently he could.

"Anything else?"

I recited the remainder of the list, and he flitted around the shop twisting bags shut with a showy flourish, hopping up stepladders to fetch down tins, and handing me little samples to approve where possible. He checked the weight of each package, pronounced a price that meant nothing to me, and took the proper coins from my hand when I held the lot out to him to pick through.

"That was impressive." I collected my bottles and packages in my arms. It wasn't a lot, but it was awkward. I had assumed I'd get a shopping tote when I cashed out, more fool me.

"What is?" the guy asked.

"Weighing out a perfect pound on the first scoop. Good day." I bobbed one of those ridiculous curtsies, and then stared at the door in dismay. How was I supposed to turn the knob with my hands full? Where was an automatic door when you needed one?

"I'm about to lock up for lunch." He came around the counter. "Let me escort you home."

"I don't need help," I snapped, embarrassed, and then mad at myself for being embarrassed.

He stopped and crossed his hands over his chest. "Then by all means, miss, please do open the door," he challenged, but his tone was light, his smile soft. He wasn't making fun, just pointing out the flaw in my logic.

Damn it.

"Okay." I sighed, then I added, "Yes, all right," when I remembered he didn't know what that meant.

He arched a confused eyebrow at me, but took the acquiescence in the spirit it was offered. I waited as he locked the cash drawer and lowered the curtains, stripped off his powder-covered jacket to reveal a white shirt and breeches. He put on a black jacket from a back room, worn and made of common material, but tidy. Then he was opening the door, locking it behind us, and taking half the shopping from me, balancing it easily under his left arm. The right, he offered to me.

I wound my left hand obligingly around his elbow.

We walked, and he let me direct our path with nothing more than an easy tug.

"I've not seen you before, miss," he said. "Are you newly arrived?"

I delayed my answer, taking the time to peruse the hats on display at a milliner's. It was too warm to wear my beret, but I hadn't yet acquired a bonnet.

I considered the coins jingling in my purse, then put the thought away. They weren't mine to spend on a stupid hat, even if I did buy only the most basic and tried to trim it myself. The money belonged to the Goodenoughs, meant for groceries. And while I did still have a few coins left from Fenton's sale of my phone, spending them on a hat seemed frivolous, no matter how much I hated the way people stared at me for the lack.

Look at me, being socially conscious and trying to fit in.

"I am," I answered as we moved on. "I'm still not quite acclimated to running errands, as you can see." *There, that sounded like a suitably Regencyish sentence*, I thought, proud of myself.

"From where do you come? Only, you've an accent."

"No I don't," I said, immediately and with perfect deadpan.

He stopped walking, studied my mock-serious face, and burst into laughter.

"I was born a mermaid, you know," I said. "But I gave up that life for the chance to be a wench on a pirate barge. I had a parrot and I used to tell Blackbeard to scrub behind his ears. I was the most adept swordsman on the seven seas." He howled louder. "But then the dastardly Stede Bonnet bested me in a sword fight. So I was sent to land to learn how to be a lady."

Further embellishments to my ridiculous tale carried us all the way to the Goodenough's servant's entrance, and the guy didn't stop laughing the whole way.

"Thank you. For, you know, your help."

"You are very much welcome, Miss . . . ?"

"Franklin."

"Thomas Cooper, at your service." He bowed low and handed me my packages. "Welcome to land, Miss Franklin. As a note, here we generally use baskets to carry our shopping, for our purchases cannot float in dry air." He knocked on the door for me, bowed again, and was gone back down the hill.

~

When I returned, Daisy was still hunched over the desk, scribbling. I intercepted Miss Brown on her way to serve tea, trading my booty for her tray. I doctored Daisy's cup the way she liked it and placed it gently beside her elbow. The clink of the saucer startled her enough to look up, and she smiled brightly to see me.

"Is it that time already?" she asked, stretching her arms above her head and shrugging. I heard the telltale crack and winced. Her setup was definitely not ergonomic.

After a quick glance to make sure we were alone, I bent down and pressed a quick kiss against her mouth. "Welcome back," I whispered.

"I did not go anywhere."

"You fell into the page. It's adorable, the way you scrunch up when you're absorbed."

"I am serious, consumed, *transported* by my prose. Not scrunched and adorable," Daisy whinged playfully.

"You should get a higher chair," I said. "It would be easier on your back."

Daisy only sipped her tea. We both knew it was a ridiculous suggestion; the *with what money?* was left unsaid.

"Let me, then." I circled behind her.

God help me, I found little curls escaping at the nape of her neck endearing.

I pushed in hard along her trapezius with my thumb and Daisy let forth a groan so low and genuine that I snorted. Adjusting my grip, I did it again and was rewarded this time with a sigh.

"What *have* you been doing to yourself?"

I worked my way across her shoulder, down the side of the shoulder blade, across to the opposite side and up again, finishing with her neck and then a quick, light kiss to that sweet little curl that was teasing me.

By the time I'd finished, Daisy was slumped forward with the most blissed-out face I'd ever seen. Her cheek was pillowed on her arm, eyes closed and lacking that little downward curve in the center of her eyebrows. She opened her eyes when I tapped her nose lightly.

"Feel better?" I asked.

"Infinitely. Your time is filled with wondrous magics, to be sure," she teased quietly.

"That's an *old* technique. Ancient Egyptians old. It's just that you people don't *touch* each other."

Daisy floated to the sofa. I sat in the plush chair to the side of it.

"I hold my sister's hand when we walk," Daisy said at length, but it wasn't really a protest. "I hold the arms of the gentlemen with whom I promenade. I dance."

"Oh, dancing," I teased. "Where we touch fingertip to fingertip and nothing else. Through *gloves*."

Daisy sat forward, intrigued now. "What else ought to touch? Dancing is merely a form of allowing a couple to converse privately while still in public."

"Dancing is sex," I said with a bounce of my eyebrows, deliberately crude. Daisy reacted exactly as I hoped she would, a delicious red flush climbing up her neck to settle like a flag on her nose. "Two bodies moving in rhythm."

"I do not know what sort of dancing you're referring to," Daisy said, part haughty, part horrified, but mostly intrigued.

"Waltzing." I drew out the vowel, remembering how scandalized Fenton had been. "Chest to chest, swaying in time, close enough to whisper. Or the tango—whipping around in circles, legs getting tangled up as the aggressor chases their prey with their hips."

Daisy went redder.

"The world will become very . . . free," Daisy said, and there was a hint of a question in the observation, and perhaps also a hint of disapproval.

"That's the point." I shrugged. "So long as everyone involved is a consenting adult, who cares what happens behind closed doors?"

Daisy regarded me with that thoughtful "recording" face, and gestured for me to go on.

"I don't need my father's approval to get married, and I don't have to marry someone if I don't want to. If I would rather just have intercourse instead, I can."

"And the resultant children?"

"Prophylactics," I said. "Sheaths that go over the penis so men can't impregnate a woman. Or medicines that block pregnancy until you decide to go off them. I'm sure you have similar teas, and sheaths, and potions now."

"One does not *talk* of it, but yes." Daisy chewed on her bottom lip. "And what does the church say?"

"Some faiths are against it, some don't care." I shrugged. "I'm not a church person, so it doesn't really have any bearing on my choices."

"Not a . . . ?" Daisy asked, startled. "Well."

"C'mon," I groaned. "You can't tell me there aren't people who would rather sleep in on Sunday, even in 1806."

That wry smile crawled into the corner of Daisy's mouth, and I leaned forward and pecked it. She was smiling genuinely when I pulled back, fingers curled happily in her skirts.

"The church is not so respected then? Not so powerful?" Daisy asked.

"A much larger group of people don't take religion as seriously as now," I said, "including me. There's been a lot of atrocities carried out in the name of a supposed perpetually forgiving God. It makes it hard to invest your trust in an institution when humans use it as an excuse to harm each other for being different."

"Different . . ." she asked, picking at her nails, suddenly shy. Or thoughtful. I wasn't sure which.

"Let me ask you this, then: If God loves all his children, why do humans kill each other for worshiping him differently? Why are Africans enslaved and indigenous people put on display in circuses? If God made everyone in his image, then why are sodomites evil instead of just accepted as being one more variation on the theme? Where I come from—"

Daisy rose to her feet. "Enough," she hissed. She was shaking with sudden, surprising anger.

"Whoa, wait—" I stood too. "What's happening here?"

"Sam, I am quite attached to you, fascinated by what you have told me of the days yet to come," she said, genuinely agitated. "But your smug superiority is exasperating."

"Sorry," I said, hands up, *don't shoot*. "Religion is just not a big deal to me."

"Well, it is a 'big deal' in this household," Daisy snapped. "So mind your tongue."

"Mind my . . . ?" I echoed, something behind my sternum going hot and squirmy. I wasn't sure if it was shame, or anger, or what. But I didn't like it. I didn't like being told what to do, how to think, how to *behave*. Never had. And, yeah, I knew there were things I would have to bend on in order to get along in life here, but I wasn't going to shut up, sit down, turn off my brain, and be a good little girl. Not by a long shot. "I'm not gonna stop being who I am. I suppress enough, I won't let this tragedy *rewrite* me."

"Tragedy?" Daisy gasped. She rocked back on her heels, like I'd slapped her. "You think—?"

But that hot squirmy thing flared into a full-sized rage.

"What, *you* think I fucking *asked* for this?" I snarled. "You think I don't miss my home, my culture, my friends and family? You think I'm *happy*?"

Daisy sucked in a horrified breath, opened her mouth to snap back, then closed it with a huff. She stalked out of the room so stiffly that I wondered at how quickly those knots in her back had returned.

She didn't slam the door behind her, but only because she was too well raised to do so.

I waited a beat.

Two.

She didn't come back.

Fuck.

"Stop being a mouthy know-it-all," I scolded myself.

I wasn't in 2024 anymore, and my way wasn't the only way; it wasn't the *right*er way simply because it was *mine*.

Unsure where Daisy had gone, I decided a peace offering tea tray would be in order either way, and set the kettle to boil. Miss Brown had clearly heard the shouting but refrained from commenting, keeping her attention on peeling potatoes. While I waited I popped into the back garden with the kitchen scissors and snipped the sweetest, most voluptuous dusty-pink rose blossom I could find amid the ornamental hedges.

A thump and a clack from upstairs gave me a direction to follow once the tray was laid with cups, the pot, milk, lemon, and last week's wonky attempt at baking chocolate chip cookies two centuries too early.

I found Daisy in her bedroom, furiously throwing open wardrobe doors and trunk lids, slapping piles of notes and papers onto the top of her travel desk.

Slipping inside and without a word, I set the tray down on the chest at the foot of her bed. She stared at it, fury giving way to tenderness, then plucked the bloom from the tiny empty flavoring bottle I'd recycled to stand in for a bud vase. She pressed the petals to her chin, thoughtful, then raised her eyes to me.

"I didn't mean to—" I started at the same time she said, "I am ashamed of—"

We both stopped, and Daisy tugged me down to sit on the mattress next to her. We kept a good inch of space between us because the door was open. But she laid her hands on the blanket and I copied, touching her pinkie with mine in apology.

"I *was* being a self-righteous bitch," I said.

"And I an intolerant and selfish friend," Daisy said. She looked down at our hands, biting her lip, and I was startled to see her eyelashes spiking with tears again.

"Daisy—"

"Of *course* you miss your homeland," she blurted hastily. "How callous of me to not consider—"

"You don't have to—"

"But I *must* apologize, my dear heart," she said desperately, turning to face me so we were nose to nose. She leaned forward just enough to catch herself doing it, then back hastily. "How awful to answer each of my childish demands to hear more of your life and to never be able to express how much you have lost.

And yup, now I was crying too.

"Shit," I sniffled, pressing my arm across my eyes, hiding my face in my elbow.

"Is there no way to go back?" Daisy asked, resting a gentle hand on my arm, not pushing it away, not grasping, only filled with tender understanding. It made me cry harder.

"No," I forced out. "Not—not that I can—I don't know. I don't *know*. I don't think so."

With a glance at the door to make sure we weren't in danger, Daisy wrapped me in a firm hug. "I am here for you," she whispered into my ear. "You may tell me anything and I will strive to be understanding and accepting. You are, of course, free to form your own opinions."

"Without condemning yours," I added, shamed. I risked pressing a kiss under her ear. "And, Daisy, I don't regret being here. With *you*. It is *terrifyingly* easy to love you."

"Though not perhaps so bluntly, I was thinking the same about you, in this moment," Daisy confessed, face flushing a sweet pink. "How easily all the small, wounded parts of me were filled with the balm of your affection when I had never intended on allowing myself any form of attachment at all."

"I get what you mean. It's like we're puzzle pieces that just clicked together." I risked running my palm up her neck, across the side of her cheek. "It's weird but like . . . I have never fallen so quickly before. So *effortlessly*. Like I was made for you."

"You *were* made for me, Samantha Franklin," Daisy said simply. "The Lord God our Creator has fashioned you specifically for me. Whether you believe in Him or not, I do, and I have begun to believe that He made you for me. The Lilith to my Eve."

"Now who's being blasphemous?" I snorted. "Don't I get a say in it?"

"No," Daisy said playfully, kissing the tip of my nose. "You shall just have to lump it."

"Oh nooo," I said, with woo-woo hand flaps. "The most important queer writer in history is in love with me. Whatever will I do?"

Daisy's expression switched over to her "recording" face so fast I nearly missed it.

Oh, shit, Sammie-bear. Watch your mouth, don't go destroying the space-time continuum with your sarcasm, I thought.

"What? What did I say?" I hedged.

But she dismissed it with a little headshake.

Whew, crisis averted.

"On the topic of your dolor, please do believe me when I tell you that I was not cognizant of it," she said slowly, separating to wind the rose into the ribbon of her cap. I didn't think twice about leaning close to secure it for her. "I did not *think* of how difficult it must be for you, to have been forced to leave everything that defined you behind, to lose everyone you loved through no choice of your own, and end up in a place where the unspoken rules of society do not match your own. Where you are restrained by practices that you find barbaric."

"*Barbaric* is a bit harsh," I said, and I was surprised to have to stop and clear my throat. "*Antiquated*, maybe."

I grinned with theatrical self-depreciation and was relieved to see Daisy match it.

"You are in a new place where everyone means well but does not understand," she said softly. "So I will endeavor to remember that your upbringing did not match mine."

"Thanks. And I'll do my best not to pass judgment on things that are different. I just . . . I think this would be easier if I could have, you know, said good-bye. Made it final." I huffed. "I couldn't if I wanted to, anyway."

Daisy fetched her writing case.

"You dictate, I will transcribe," she said.

"There's no way to deliver this letter," I protested.

"There are two hundred and eighteen years to devise a way," she rejoined. "I'm sure it can be done. Come."

"I guess that if nothing else, it could end up in a museum." I had the sudden premonition that I would spend the rest of my life being bossed around by Daisy. I was totally okay with that. "With a gold plaque that reads: A LETTER ADDRESSED TO MR. AND MRS. FRANKLIN OF TORONTO, IN THE YEAR 2024; MARGARET GOODENOUGH'S ONLY ATTEMPT AT SCIENCE FICTION."

Daisy looked up at me sharply, decided I was joking, and laughed.

Chapter Seventeen

IN WHICH SAM AVOWS

You must allow me to tell you how ardently I admire and love you.

—Jane Austen, *Pride and Prejudice*

"You have to try at least once," Marigold prodded. "You cannot call yourself a resident of Bath without Taking The Waters™ at least once."

Fun fact! Humans are persistence hunters. That means we catch our prey by wearing them down.

"Fine!" I finally said, throwing my hands up over breakfast the next day. "You win. I'll sit in the plague water."

"Oh excellent!" Iris said. "We shall go as soon as you finish lessons today, before the time slot for the gentlemen bathers opens. I shall need to have Miss Brown put my hair up, for I shouldn't like to wet it before supper, which of course we will order up in the Pump Room—"

"You've made Mother happier than she's been in some time," Daisy whispered to me. "She's had an urge to gossip."

"She's got an urge to spend money, you mean," I replied, while Iris listed off the luxuries she intended to indulge in at the bathhouse: at least three cups of the fizzy mineral water (gag), the rental of a floating tea tray on which, of course, we were to take our afternoon repast, a bottle of liquor, a new lemon-scented soap shaped like a seashell, and perhaps even the rental of a fine Turkish towel.

Daisy offered up that wry smile instead of an answer.

"Will we be naked?"

"Of course not." Marigold cut across her mother's shopping list, and I sat back from Daisy, doing my best to not look mortified that she'd been paying such close attention to our whispers. "We will wear bathing costumes."

"Don't have one," I said. "I'll have to skinny-dip."

"They are *rented*," Marigold huffed, flushing and storming upstairs.

"Samantha," Daisy scolded me. "Cease tormenting my sister."

"But it's so *easy*," I said.

"Mark my words," Daisy said, taking to her own feet, "you'll make a proper enemy of her one day if you're not careful, and I shan't forgive you for it."

Right, yes, the golden rule of being a good girlfriend: don't piss off the bestie.

I spent the school day trying to find time to make peace with Marigold, but she avoided me like the opposite end of a magnet after classes were finished. She seized Daisy's arm the moment we were out of the house, walking along the river to the historic Roman Baths and the sumptuous Palladian palace that contemporary architects had constructed around its ruins, leaving me to trudge with voluble Iris.

She really was a sweet woman, with a deep pride in and affection for her children, even if her topics of conversation were repetitive and depthless. While nodding along to her shocked whispers about this affair, or that hairstyle, or Miss This-and-That's new gown, I'd gleaned a treasure trove of information about the morals and fashions of the time. Iris had helped me to blend in even more than Daisy, just by virtue of being herself.

Marigold ignored me to the point of awkwardness. We shuffled through the process of disrobing and putting on our rented yellow canvas shifts and bloomers, which would nonetheless leave exactly nothing to the imagination once they were wet.

The bathing chamber was made of Bath's famous honey-colored

limestone, and open to the elements. Wide steps led down to a narrow trough of water, separated from the pool at large by a row of columns in the pool itself, and a grandiose set of double doors made of rust-stained wood. The columns supported an open-air gallery with geometric stone balustrades, from which people coming to dine in the Pump Room could peer down on us.

Dark tiles hugged the narrow rim of the rectangular pool, filled shoulder-deep with water that was such a vivid toxic-teal color that it looked like it should give you superpowers if it splashed you. Heavy, faintly sulfurous mist fogged the air, making it hard to see the people just on the other side of the pool. Frizzilla immediately made an appearance as the humidity grabbed hold of my hair under my muslin cap.

Iris was the first to walk down the shallow steps and push open the door, with Marigold and the copper floating tray not far behind, and Daisy in tow. I froze on the edge, twisting my hands in my stupid bathing costume as the married Goodenoughs bobbed over to a flotilla of chatty ladies. They all had their hair piled up under cloth caps and bonnets, and some were even wearing their *stays*.

The water threw back and amplified every whisper, every splash, every sharp bark of laughter at a wince-inducing volume.

Daisy turned back to regard me where I stood at the top of the stairs, dithering.

The ancient Romans were acknowledged geniuses when it came to plumbing and water transportation. They singlehandedly revolutionized bathing habits in the Europe of their time, laying the foundation for pretty much every modern Western hygiene custom, even in the twenty-first century.

What they were not so clever about was the use of lead in their piping.

Which isn't entirely fair of me. It's not as if they *knew* that lead was poisonous, only that the alloy was easy to manipulate for plumbing.

Water poured over a plain fountain and into the pool, still steaming, flowing without end from a pipe hidden under the floor, and I swear my paranoia meant I could see the microbeads of the stuff in it.

"Miss Franklin, do get in," Daisy teased, grinning up at me with sparkling mirth. "I have yet to take sick from taking waters that are legendary for *healing*."

I didn't move.

Daisy came back to the side, her breasts floating to the surface, enticing and so not the point right now. "Miss Franklin, you *do* know how to swim, do you not?" she asked worriedly.

"Of course I do! I don't know if I . . . I *can*."

Okay, fine, I'll admit it. The water scared the shit out of me. I hadn't been fully submerged since the accident, and while nobody was putting their heads under, the idea that I would be surrounded by water made my heart try to crawl out of my mouth and run away screaming.

This was just like immersion therapy, right? That kind where you faced your fears and did the thing to help you get over the terror of the thing. And Daisy was here. Daisy wouldn't let me drown.

"If I die, I'm blaming you," I quipped shakily, hiding my nerves behind my bravado.

The water closed over my feet. I forced myself to stop, take a few deep egg-farty breaths, and keep going. My hands balled up reflexively, knuckles white, as the water rose to my hips, closed over my back, soaking the flimsy cloth of my costume.

Pause. Keep breathing. Go.

My lungs seized and stuttered as I reached the bottom of the pool. I was short enough that the steaming water touched the bottom of my chin. It curled around my throat like a pair of hands, squeezing, crushing with wet, closed in on all sides, infiltrating, getting *inside me*, no escape—

The bottom of the pool was slipperier than I expected.

My feet went out from under me.

I screamed as the water closed over my head.

I pushed up, flailing, splashing, choking on air and the fumes of the natural spring.

Around me, the bathers screeched and gasped.

"Sam!" Daisy yelled, forgetting to use my full name in public.

I flailed blindly for the steps, hauled myself out as fast as I could.

"I—" I said, standing beside the pool, shaking, and feeling like I was about three seconds away from vomiting. Dozens of faces turned to me, delighted and horrified in turns at my outburst.

"Samantha . . ."

"I *can't*," I sobbed, and fled for the change room.

Daisy found me there a few minutes later, sitting on a bench alone, shivering from both evaporation and the memory of the crushing cold of the mid-Atlantic.

She retrieved one of the big, thin towels and draped it over my shoulders, scrubbing my hair with one corner. She sat behind me, pulled me against her chest, grounding me in an embrace. Her costume was still wet but her body was hot, so I didn't care. I crumbled into her, pressed my face against her shoulder, inhaled the scent of minerals and ink and Daisy.

"I'm sorry," I said. Something inside caught and tore, and I was sobbing, ripping and hot, and I couldn't *stop*, I couldn't stop. I clutched at her shift, wrapped the wet fabric in my fists, holding on for dearness and life.

"All is well," she said softly. "Shhh. I should have considered the accident. I am foolish for hectoring you. My deepest apologies."

"I can't," I repeated, over and over. "I thought I could, I thought I was over it, but I can't. I'm sorry."

Daisy kissed the side of my head, the only place she could reach with my limpet-like grasp on her thighs. She kissed the shell of my ear, the tender spot where the jaw met the neck, my favorite place for a hickey, and I shivered, delicious frisson climbing up my back.

This.

I wanted *this*, this heat, this proof of *life*.

I pulled away, offering up my face. She kissed my nose, each eyelid, my cheeks, and my forehead, and I made a frustrated sound, waiting, impatient for her lips to touch mine. But we were in public.

Shaking, miserable, and damp, we dressed and made our way back to the house in silence.

Miss Brown took one look at us and sent Mr. Stewart out to fetch a fresh bottle of brandy. She hastened us upstairs with as much hot water as we could carry before taking herself to the back garden to gather chamomile for a soothing drink. Daisy hounded me through a warm rinse to rid my hair of the old-iron reek, and into my nightdress and dressing gown. She pushed me onto the bed so she could straddle my hips and wash the tear tracks from my face.

Feeling a thousand times more settled from the warmth of her touch and the lovely animal weight of her body, I reached up and tugged the ties out of her hair. It fell down her back, golden, curling slightly, and glossy.

Daisy moaned.

I sat and scooted up to the headboard. "Turn around. Lean back on my knees."

I tucked my feet under her bum and she leaned back, hair spreading across the intimate triangle of my thighs and into my lap. I ran my fingers through her locks, combing down any knots I found, setting aside the pins, finding my center again. Daisy hummed contentedly, let her head fall back, and closed her eyes. I gave in to the temptation to dig my fingers in, scratch the nails lightly across her scalp, rub at the tension lingering by her temples, across her eyebrows.

She started panting, cheeks flushing red, and I grinned, leaning down to lick and nibble on the shell of her ear.

"Really?" I whispered. "Just from this? Kinky."

She chuckled, reached back with one hand to curl her fingers around the nape of my neck, redirected my head so she could arch, thrusting her very pretty breasts into the air, tilting so our noses wouldn't bump. Her mouth was hungry.

Slowly, sensually, I pulled her dress up her calves, fingers brushing her stockings, teasing. She wriggled and made a high sweet sound that made me want to bite her shoulder, so I did. She squeaked, then pressed her own hands to her mouth to stifle any louder sounds.

"That's it, shhh." I tongued the bite mark. She'd need to wear a fichu tonight to cover it, perhaps a full shawl. I liked the thought of watching her over the dinner table, knowing that she was wearing my mark in a room full of people and being forced to keep it secret. Keep it safe.

"Do that again," I said. "I liked the view. I'll—"

The door opened.

The *unlocked* door.

"Daisy? Mother is humiliated, how could you think it proper to just *leave* without—"

"I'm coming back!" Daisy shouted, springing across the room, catching the door before it could open all the way.

Fuck, that was *too* close.

"You must," Marigold said, craning her head to peer at me over Daisy's arm. "Are you already abed, Miss Franklin? Your queer turn was quite alarming."

I spread my hands, mea culpa. "And now you know why I didn't want to go."

"You could have just *said* that you could not swim," Marigold said, pushing Daisy aside to stand at the foot of the bed in all her disappointed, dramatic glory. "There was no need to cause a *scene*."

"I didn't mean to," I said. "I apologize. I really thought I might be able to deal with it—"

"I do not forgive you!" Marigold hissed.

"Mary—"

"Hush, Margaret," Marigold snapped. "Already there is talk! Mr. Gibson's aunt was in the pool and quite unimpressed." Mr. Gibson was Marigold's matrimony target of the week. "Now she'll never recommend me to him. Once again, Miss Franklin ruins *everything*."

The accusation thudded between my ribs like a well-aimed arrow.

"Samantha," Daisy said, turning wide guilty eyes to me. I was hoping that her next words would be to defend me and my very-justified PTSD triggered freak-out to Marigold, but instead she just folded her hands in front of her and shook her head sadly.

I understood, all at once, that Daisy wouldn't dispute her sister's accusation.

"Go back," I croaked. "Both of you. I'm fine. Thank you for walking me back, Miss Goodenough. Please, Mrs. Kempel has gone to the trouble of arranging supper for you—you shouldn't miss it."

"Oh, *Sam*," Daisy started, taking a step toward me. But Marigold cut her off.

"Come, sister. Leave Miss Franklin to her *nerves*, and let us see if we cannot salvage what little standing I still have with Mrs. Gibson."

She flounced out of the room and Daisy followed, as docile as a lamb.

And the worst part was I couldn't blame her for it.

~

The next morning was Saturday. I'd passed a bad night, wrestling with nightmares of sirens digging their claws into my throat and dragging me into the crushing abyss of time.

Iris and Marigold were a-visiting, and both servants were enjoying their half day off, so for the first time in weeks Daisy and I had the whole house to ourselves.

The study windows were open, letting the breeze in to ruffle our hair and the corners of Daisy's pages, banishing yesterday's panic and fear. I finally had hair long enough to pile it up like the other women around me, and the air felt good on the naked skin of my neck as I dozed on the sofa.

Daisy was fidgeting more than she was writing. She had a habit of tapping her teeth and nibbling when she was working—on her cuticles, on the tip of her pencil, on the corner of her lip. The fidgeting was distracting. But not in a bad way. Her hand reached for her teacup, paused midair, and rerouted for her pencil. She scribbled, tapped, nibbled, reached for her cup, found it empty, set it down, and started the cycle over again.

I'd heard about artists getting distracted while creating but I'd never witnessed it firsthand. Writing my own essays in university had been a painfully slow and deliberate process. I'd never looked down to write one instant and looked up the next with thirty pages completed and six hours lost, like some of my classmates had. Like Daisy did.

About midmorning, Daisy sat back from her perpetual hunch. The long, lean lines of her were gloriously tempting as she stretched, and my mouth went dry.

"Break time?" I asked, hoping Daisy would say yes.

We'd been making a survey of the broad green walks around town, and there was a gated one by the river only for posh people. We'd been talking about sneaking over the fence. It seemed like a good day to flout a few laws.

"Decidedly," Daisy agreed, rising and shuffling the pages she'd spread out to dry into order then tucking them into the leather folder that held the rest of the manuscript. "And I shan't write tomorrow either."

"No?" I asked, setting aside my schoolwork.

"No," she echoed, crossing to the decanters. She poured two small glasses of sherry, sank onto the sofa with no small amount of relief, and handed me mine.

I held my glass up and she obligingly clinked. "What's the occasion?"

Daisy flushed prettily as we sipped. "I have finished my book."

"Babe!" I gasped, yanked her glass out of her hand and set them both on the floor. Then I pulled her into a hug. Daisy giggled as I wrapped my legs around her waist, making it a proper squish. "I'm so proud of you!"

Daisy chuckled and, with one hand firmly on my left breast, pushed me back down on the sofa, which gave me just the right alignment to get a beautiful handful of her skinny bum. She rocked the full weight of her body into the cradle of my thighs, her breasts pillowed warm and soft against mine, and plundered my mouth for a truly filthy kiss.

"Will you read it?" she gasped against my lips, voice trembling. "You will be honest with me, won't you? Tell me if I—"

"Yes," I said, biting at her lower lip, digging my fingers into her hair.

"You must understand, no one has read the full thing," Daisy said breathlessly, as she scrabbled to push up my skirts, skimming her palms along my thighs where they laid against her hips. "I would very much treasure your opinion of it, if you will forgive that I have only just finished it and not had the opportunity to go back and rewrite."

"I understand."

"I lay myself bare before you, beloved," Daisy said earnestly. "My soul is on those pages. My heart also. I give them to you."

She framed my face in her hands and kissed me like it was her last day on earth, like it was the first kiss ever invented, like it was every kiss we'd ever had, and ever would have, rolled into one. It felt permanent and permeable; thin as gossamer and strong as steel cabling. It was a kiss written in ink that bleeds through all the layers of paper, from the first page of a tome to the last—visible on every leaf, overwriting everything that came before it, drying light enough that it could be overwritten with the next kiss, and the next, and the next, spooling out golden and vivid for the rest of forever. A palimpsest of kisses.

Daisy sat up, pressed one hand into the sofa beside my head, stroking my cheek with the other, and looked down at me like I was something wondrous. And how lucky was I, that I was the first person she has offered this trust? That she was willing to carve out a facet of her heart and *hand* it to me.

"I'll read it." I leaned up to chase her mouth with mine. "Tonight. I promise."

"Now that I am no longer preoccupied by the novel, there is something else I should like to do. Something I have been *dwelling* on, quite ardently."

"Yeah? What's that?"

"Sam," she breathed, petting my head and shoulders. "I want. But I do not know what it is that I want."

"I'll teach you. Lay back." I gently navigated her into the corner of the sofa, head up on the arm so she could watch. Daisy made that delightful little frustrated sound again and tugged at me until I lifted my face to hers. Her kisses were demanding and her body under mine surged like the tide, up and down, pelvis and spine rolling, uncertain what it was exactly she was striving for but trusting her instincts and my knowledge to guide her.

She was quite literally putting herself in my hands. It was humbling.

"Daisy, *ah*," I gasped, nosing at her chest until I could get her dress yanked down, my teeth and tongue on her nipples. She arched and shook. "Have you ever—ah!—um, there is literally no way to say this without sounding like a bad porno, *Jesus* . . . explored yourself?"

Daisy laughed and bit the shell of my ear before laving it with her tongue, then whispered into it: "I know what a cunt is, and I know what to do with mine."

"Oh good," I said with a shiver and a smirk. "So you have no issue with me doing this?"

I slid my hand from ankle to knee, slow and delicious, then knee to hip, keeping her gaze locked on mine so I would see the look on her face when I brushed the pad of my thumb across her clit. Daisy jerked, her eyelids fluttering and the corners of her lips curling up in possessive satisfaction.

"Only should you stop," she said breathily, daring me on.

I sank back and dropped a kiss on the side of her knee, then ran my thumb up from the very bottom of her folds, pressing just hard enough to feel them part, to the top, ending with another little circle. "And this?" I asked, biting her wiry thigh softly.

Daisy's head dropped back and she made a breathy sound. Deciding that humping her leg was maybe not the classiest way to get myself off during our first time together, I flipped my own skirts up as high as I could so Daisy could watch.

"How about this?" I asked, stroking her folds again, letting my humid breath blow over her skin.

"Lord almighty, Sam, your quim is wet," Daisy moaned, curving over my shoulder, eyes drawn downward. "Don't . . . please, do not stop."

"Yours too," I said. Then I purposely leaned close and blew a light stream of cool air against her entrance.

Daisy bucked so hard she bashed me in the chin with her pelvis, her thighs slamming closed. I got one hand up in time, but she kneed me in the neck with the leg she'd had braced on the floor.

"Darling! Apologies!" she said, trying to sit up, but I only laughed, and slung her knee over my shoulder. I pushed her back down, trailing licking kisses around her hip bones and thighs, working my way inward.

"I've had worse. It can get dangerous down here," I teased.

"Dangerous?" Daisy asked, and then nearly jackknifed off the sofa when I ran my tongue up the same path my thumb had taken. I was prepared for it this time, and braced an arm across her hips, my own thighs splayed to pin her legs in place, my other hand working industriously between my own legs. "Good lord!"

"Should I stop?" I asked, switching to kiss her labia, nibble at the skin, brush my nose through her moist bush.

"Samantha Jayne Franklin," Daisy growled. "If you do not continue—"

Her threat turned into a high trailing squeak when I pressed an open-mouthed kiss right on the lips in front of me, rubbing the tip of my nose on her clit, flicking my tongue inside just a bit. God, I had missed this taste. I'd thought I might have to spend the rest of my life without it.

"Can I put my fingers in?" I asked her, panting and delighted.

Daisy shimmied up a bit, and obligingly, I shifted into a bastardized yoga pose and tilted my hips forward so everything was on display. Ignoring the strain on my neck, I kissed her again, and that yanked her attention back to her own body.

"Whatever you like," Daisy gasped, kneading her breasts. "Whatever you want. But please, don't stop. Ah, my love, *don't stop*—"

The L-word tipped me straight over the edge. As I pressed my tongue hard against her clit, my orgasm ripped through me swift and hard. I resisted the urge to bite down, mark her, make it clear whom Daisy belonged to.

My orgasm surged up again as Daisy reached down to slip one of her fingers inside me alongside my own. She twisted her finger, relishing, I think, the moans her touch plucked from my chest.

"You're so warm," she whispered, a delicious, delightful pink flush spreading down her neck, over her breasts and her cheeks. I snarled against her skin, pushed her back quick and hard, spread her thighs wide and buried my face between them.

I returned the favor, slipping one finger in, pressing down on the floor of her pelvis, rocking back and forth gently. My limbs were still shaking from the comedown even as I slipped in a second finger, crooked my fingers and, yes, *there*.

Daisy hooked her hands in my hair hard enough to scratch my scalp. I didn't care, just kept at my task, letting her ride my face to her own completion. Daisy, steady and statuesque, came with her eyes screwed shut and her mouth dropped open; the only noise she made was a lovely, breathy grunt.

It was devastating.

It was *incandescent*.

We collapsed on the abused sofa, out of breath and damp. My chin was wet, and her fingers were in her mouth, curious. We settled in a messy tangle of loosened curls, wrinkled fabric, and slouched stockings, then immediately started giggling. I didn't know what was so funny. Nothing was funny. It was . . . relief was what it was. Relief and joy and an afterglow that bubbled like golden champagne.

I crawled up Daisy's body, flopped onto her bare breasts, kissed the nearest swell of the mound, and snuggled into the lovely creamy pillows, pleased with myself and the whole world in general.

"That was worth the wait." I sighed blissfully.

"Agreed."

"Now what?"

"Now we should wash and change, for I feel myself much energized, and if we stay indoors I fear I will rip the manuscript out of your hands and begin my revisions immediately."

I sat up and helped Daisy get herself properly tucked back into her stays.

"I meant with the book, sweetheart," I said, twirling a winsome curl around my finger before tucking it back up under her cap for her. "After I read it, and you make your revisions, then what? Do you just make a copy and send it to a publisher?"

Daisy made a face. "Yes. But I fear that it will not be considered. I am no Ann Radcliffe, with her Italians and Udolphos. I am very proud of what I have written, but what if no publisher wishes to take it on commission? I may be forced to sell the manuscript entire, and never see another shilling from it."

"That doesn't sound awesome."

Daisy slumped against my shoulder. "Failing that, I may have to *pay* the publisher to print the book myself, though I have no concept of how I may afford to do so." She chewed her thumbnail for a moment before the bitter taste of the ink stains made her wrinkle her nose. "I suppose I could open a subscription, but who would pay a penny for a chapter a week when I have published nothing else, and none know of me?"

I suddenly wished I still had something of value left to hock. My cell phone and watch had both gone to Fenton to buy my freedom, and his bride. I had nothing to give Daisy except my assurances.

"Trust me," I said. "Someone will buy this book."

She laughed, and it was such an ugly little self-deprecating sound that I was actually startled. "Nobody will wish to read the romantic nonsense of a silly woman."

Fuck it. Tell her your last secret.

"Daisy . . . Margaret. They will. I know this."

She sat back and her eyes went wide. "You *know* it?" she repeated, that clever brain of hers putting the pieces together like lighting. "My god. You *know* it. That explains the expression you wear when I read. You are familiar with it already!"

"Yes," I admitted, intimate, whispering this final truth into the sex-perfumed air. "Do you want me to tell you what happens to it?"

"No," she said immediately. "No, pray, tell me nothing of its reception. I dare not know if it is published, or brings me acclaim, or financial comfort, or, god forbid, fame. I only need to know that it is not in vain. That my hard work is rewarded."

"It's rewarded," I reassured her.

"Oh, Sam!" she said, wriggling in delight, clutching me close and kissing me hard and fast. "I believe you! You have read my book in the *future*!"

"To be honest with you, it wasn't me who was the fan. It was my ex. She would read me passages while I did the dishes, or we would watch dramatic adaptations." I shook my head, smiled wryly, shrugged with one shoulder. "Besides, I always confused the plots of your books."

"Books," she repeated, filled with awe. "Plural?"

"Oh fuck." I covered my face. "I'm a terrible, terrible time traveler."

"I have more ideas," Daisy enthused, and in a flash she was up and pacing, manic with glee. "But I have not done more than jot down notes. But now I'm uncertain. What if they are the wrong ones?" She stopped and turned to me, lip between her teeth, shy. "Which . . . ? Which book is *your* favorite?"

Of all the questions Daisy could ask about the future, about how well known she was, about any awards she'd earned or how many novels she'd published, this wasn't one I was expecting. Still, I could answer that one without hesitation.

"*The Welshman's Daughters*," I said. "That's *everyone's* favorite."

"*The Welshman's Daughters*," Daisy murmured. "Which one is that?"

I reached over to her writing desk, and, grinning, tapped the leather folder.

~

The rest of our morning free, we washed quickly and changed into clothes suitable for walking—me in my cream-and-rose calico, purple Chucks peeking out the bottom, and Daisy in pale olive with coral trim, with a sparingly decorated bonnet that Iris continually despaired of. Daisy looped my hand through her elbow as we passed the milliner's and I peered through the glass at the hats.

"What's this?" I asked, shaking our linked elbows gently.

"Me, *touching* you," Daisy said smugly.

Our walk took us directly past Coopers, so I waved hello at young Thomas. He was behind the counter with an older man who couldn't be anyone else but his father, counting out a handful of change for a serving girl. He caught my wave, grinned fit to break his face in half, and tried to return it, forgetting of course that he had a handful of coins. They went flying like a shower of sequins and I laughed, covering my face with my hand and wondering if this was the sort of instance where one needed a fan.

"Who is that?" Daisy asked as she tried to hide her own smile.

"That is Mr. Cooper. I buy our flour from him. Or, I guess it's young Master Cooper, if that's his dad, there. He says we're friends."

"And are you?"

"Sure, why not?" I shrugged.

"You seem pleased with yourself," she said as we walked on.

"Oh, I am," I said. "Do you know how long I've been cooped up while people did things *to* me? *For* me? I actually *missed* going grocery shopping, if you can believe it."

"You were very independent?"

"I lived alone, yeah. No servants. Just me."

"That must have been . . . " Daisy sighed and squeezed my arm.

"What? Expensive? Nerve-racking? Busy? Hard?"

"Freeing."

I laughed. "Yeah, it kinda was. I could leave my dishes in the sink if I wanted to or lounge around naked after a bath. There would be no new mess when I walked into the apartment besides the one I had left behind."

We stopped at the top of a street, one of the many hilly protrusions that dotted Bath, and I gestured to the river below us, the rows of houses, the fiercely green fields and woods beyond. "But this? This is great. We don't have anything like this."

"No trees?" Daisy teased.

"The human animal is inclined to reproduce and sprawl," I said with a shrug. "People generally don't start building upward until they crash against their neighbors and have to. A little garden like yours is worth a pretty penny nowadays." I frowned. "Then-a-days."

Daisy frowned too. "I do not think I would like to visit your time, Miss Franklin," she said, mirth evaporated. "I like open skies and leafy laneways far too much."

"There's still lots of green left. Just not in the cities. Not unless there's a park carved out of the concrete. So little of it is untouched." I waved at the forest encroaching on the edge of town.

Instead of breaking the law today, my talk of trees had Daisy longing for them. We made our way to Daisy's favorite walk. It was covered with the arching branches of sturdy thick vines, giving it the feel of an arcade covered with emerald stained glass. The sun shone through gaps like arrow shafts, and, aside from the faint tweet of some sweet little bird or other, all the sounds of the world vanished, muted by the foliage.

Halfway through, I pulled Daisy aside to sit on a decorative rock so we wouldn't stain our bums. I suddenly remembered Margaret Goodenough's "green gowns," and then tried very hard *not* to. We were too exposed, more's the pity.

Daisy pinched a loose fold of my calico dress thoughtfully. "Daisies and sweet peas are both April flowers, you know. The month of rebirth and new beginnings. They are often illustrated *entwined*."

She bit the tip of her tongue between her teeth and shot me a smoldering look.

Egad, I'd created a monster.

"Poetical," I said. "You should be a writer or something."

"Har-har," Daisy quipped, in perfect imitation of my own flat dead-pan delivery that it sent me into a flurry of giggles.

Maybe this was private enough, after all? I nosed at Daisy's cheek and she turned obligingly to let me at her mouth. That sweet bud, indeed.

We jerked apart at the sound of someone calling Daisy's name, and a breathless young woman who couldn't have been more than twenty, with a dark complexion and hair, skidded to a stop beside us.

"Well, Miss Margaret!" the interloper scolded us. "I swear, you are an impossibly deaf old woman!"

"Not that old," I butted in, and the teenager rolled her eyes, but kept grinning.

Daisy stood. "Miss Wilhelmina Donaldson, may I introduce you to my companion, Miss Samantha Franklin?" Daisy cut a look at me, humored but already weary. "Miss Donaldson is the youngest sister of my brother's friend Richard. What brings you to Bath, Miss Donaldson?"

"Well! Papa got a house for the season, *finally*—it's taken him ages to see sense and that Bath is where one must be to catch a husband, now that I'm out!" I jolted at the phrasing, and had to remind myself that *out* meant "marriageable" and not "of the closet." A shame we could never convince your father to host us when he was still with us."

"Indeed," Daisy agreed, and meant clearly the opposite. I could imagine how infuriating this chatterbox would be to Daisy as she tried to write, and how badly she would clash with Marigold, who preferred to be the sole arbiter of conversation.

"And you, Miss Franklin? Are you here to net yourself a lord? Perhaps even a duke? Then we will see a great wedding!" Wilhelmina enthused. "Well, Miss Margaret, you must have a new dress made for the occasion!" She turned to me. "She always dresses like such a fuddy-duddy."

Daisy curled her mouth in a way that looked like a smile but that both of us knew very well was not.

"I'm content with what I have." I tugged sweetly on the dangling ribbons of Daisy's coral sash, where Wilhelmina couldn't see.

"Well, then! Are you engaged?" Wilhelmina squealed. "Please, show me the ring, Miss Franklin! I'm ever so fond of the rings!"

"I . . . er," I said, begging for help from Daisy with a pleading glance.

"What Miss Franklin means is that she is currently attached to our household, and is in no rush to establish her own," Daisy said tactfully.

Wilhelmina snorted. "Well, then you have been spending too much time with Miss Margaret," she told me. "The woman behaves as if she is a spinster already, doomed to a life with no romance, when she could have had Mr. Vaughn as easily as that." She snapped her gloved fingers neatly.

"Mr. Vaughn?" I repeated, curious.

"No one," Daisy assured me.

"A 'no one' Margaret was engaged to for a whole four months!"

Wilhelmina pressed with another laugh, utterly failing to clock the sour look on Daisy's face. Yeah, there was definitely a story there that I was going to ask for later, if Daisy was in the mood to share it. "Well, perhaps your brother will have other friends for you, now that Richard is engaged to Miss Worthing, and Judge Lewis is married."

His name sent a jolt of long-forgotten terror up my spine. I must have made a noise because Daisy grabbed my hand hard, to keep me from bolting.

"Oh, and did you hear!" Miss Donaldson went on, oblivious to the change in our moods. "They had quite the falling out when your brother returned to London for his orders last week. 'A bloody great row in the square,' is how Richard tells it, for he was with the captain when Sir Lewis confronted him over 'that woman'! Goodness, do you know who he meant? Not a mistress surely, what a scandal that would be, so soon after the judge's marriage to . . . well, now what was the name of Lewis's bride, again? It was ever so cleverly put in the papers—the adventuresome colonial."

"No idea!" I cut in before Daisy could answer. "Probably best not to spread gossip, though."

"I suppose. Marriages all around." Wilhelmina pouted, the wind gone from her sails, twiddling her fan and fighting back an unhappy expression. "Well. For all but me, it seems."

"You'll find someone." I cupped her shoulder sincerely. "I know you will. Someone who appreciates your enthusiasm and loves your, ah, verbosity. But trust me when I say, woman to woman, don't say yes to just anyone simply because you're afraid to be alone. That never ends happily."

As I gave my little speech, Wilhelmina's eyes grew rounder and rounder, until a spark of understanding was struck behind them.

"I see. Well!" she said again, smoothing down her gown. "Please pass my felicitations on to your brother, Miss Margaret. We long to meet the new Mrs. Goodenough when she visits you. We are staying on

Avon Street, should you like to drop by for tea. I would very much like to further our acquaintance, Miss Franklin."

"Same," I said, surprised to realize I meant it.

Wilhelmina blinked at me, like most people did when I replied in a way they understood but didn't expect, then curtseyed and scampered away, calling to another passing victim: "Miss Jemima! Oh, Miss Jemima, I say! Your new reticule is an absolute delight!"

"You really wish to deepen *that* acquaintance?" Daisy asked, as we resumed walking.

"She's talkative, so what? She's clearly down on herself. She's probably been told her whole life that the entirety of her worth is tied up in her face and how rich the dude she bags is. Don't *you* feel sorry for her?"

"I suppose I did not consider that."

"I bet she's a romantic," I said. "Maybe she desperately wants to be in love. Wanting to have someone special, someone they can grow old with and—"

I was struck by a weird niggle of something I couldn't quite name.

"And?" Daisy asked.

"I . . . sorry, I lost my thoughts there for a second. What was I saying?"

Daisy smiled, the genuine one that crinkled up the sides of her eyes, and I was slammed with that weird swoopy feeling again.

"You were expressing the understanding that marriage can be genuinely desirable for those who have a life partner they cherish."

"Yeah. That." Why was I suddenly all sweaty? "I mean, this Mr. Vaughn, you don't regret . . . I mean, of course not, or you would have married him but, I—man, I don't know what I'm trying to say."

Daisy raised a curious eyebrow. "You're not the only one who has had past chances," she said. "Simply because I'd never been kissed before, please do not assume I was unwanted."

"Of course not."

The nebulous swoopy thing swirled as she regaled me with the story of meeting him at a house party and how interesting and kind she had found him. But how, ultimately, she had realized she would never be able to love him the way he deserved, the way she *wanted* to care for her life partner, and had released him.

The swoop resolved itself into a soft-edged cloud of jealousy. I rested my forehead briefly against the back of her shoulder when she paused to inspect a flower hanging at eye level, swallowing back the *feelings* clogging my throat.

"What is wrong, Miss Franklin?"

"Nothing," I lied. "I'm just being a jealous bitch, honestly."

Daisy laughed and it made something in me soar.

"Do not be," she said softly. She pulled my hand up to her mouth and kissed my palm sweetly. It still made my blood fizz. "You are far more wonderful than any fellow who only sought to marry me to inherit my father's living. I am also content with what I have."

I'm in love, I realized, like the smack of a wet fish between the eyes. *Like, honest to god, get down on one knee love. Holy shit. No wonder the marriage talk is making me squirmy.*

I turned her quickly and grabbed her shoulders. "I wish—" I began, and then stopped. Because it wasn't true.

No, I did *not* wish I had met Daisy in the future, in Barcelona, because I wouldn't have cared. I would have shared a bottle of wine, a fuck, maybe a few days of smiles and tours, and then I would have left her. And missed out on *this*. The careful comfort, the ability to mean something to her, to be of use to her. The slow intimacies and the easy burn of her kisses. I wanted so badly to *mean* something to Daisy. To be irreplaceable. To make her mine and be hers forever and I couldn't. I *couldn't*.

"Daisy, I lo— I . . . *I* . . ."

Daisy waited, patient as granite and twice as supportive, for me to finish my sentence. I didn't.

Her own eyes widened, cheeks pinking, reading my epiphany in my gaze like in one of her own fucking books.

My heart lurched toward hers.

"Oh," she breathed. "Oh, Sam. *Yes*."

I wanted to kiss her, and get down on one knee and tell her how much I adored her, and that I wanted to marry the hell out of her.

And how *selfish* was I, when I knew that this wasn't how history was supposed to go?

Knew, and didn't care.

"Let's go home," I said, trying to keep the smolder out of my voice. *"Now."*

~

Miss Brown had returned early, and thwarted my salacious plans. Disappointed but energized by the day's successes, Daisy threw herself into her own chores while I was given the shopping purse, the list, and a wicker basket with a handle large enough to loop over my arm. I lingered at the errands, reliving the phantom brush of Daisy against my arm, the taste of her, the humidity of her breath on my cheek, the way the hems of our skirts had flirted with one another as we walked, the little noise she'd made when she'd climaxed.

I love her, I love her, I love her, my heart thundered, so loud that I was surprised that passersby didn't remark on it.

First I stopped outside of the milliner's, to smile at the hats I could never have, feeling a bit like a kid staring at the kittens that Mom had already said no to in the pet shop window. Then I moved on to a stand filled with vegetables in season and shriveled little fruits out of it, the butcher's, the dairy, and, lastly, Cooper's general store.

"Miss Franklin!" he said as I entered, as he had every time I'd arrived, with his megawatt grin. I wondered if he ever turned down the voltage, or only used it on his female customers to charm them into buying more than what they came for. He finished serving a man in a footman's uniform, and when we were alone added: "I saw you with your pretty friend today."

"That was Miss Goodenough. I need many supplies." I read the list of ingredients off of the paper, and he moved around the store like a choreographed dance to fill my order, stretching up to reach the tops of shelves, crouching low to reach others. I let my interest wander to a collection of bottles by the window, each label proclaiming them to be "Essence of" some herb or flower. I was learning every day in the kitchen with Miss Brown that what I considered delicious, the people here might not. And vice versa.

Eventually Mr. Cooper returned to the counter with my assembled packages, I paid, and he began to close up. I loaded the basket, careful to shift the veggies so the heavy flours and powders would not bruise them; it cut into my elbow but it was still manageable.

"Have a good evening," I said to Mr. Cooper and walked out the door.

He caught up to me a few shops later, red cheeked and grinning foolishly, in such a rush that he hadn't even changed. His white coat was practically phosphorescent against the twilight. "Please allow me to escort you again. Your basket looks heavy."

"I'm fine," I said. I was.

"Miss Franklin—"

"Mr. Cooper, I'm female, not feeble."

He stuttered to a halt. "I did not mean . . . I apologize, Miss Franklin, if you thought that I . . . ah . . . I just want to accompany you. If I may."

I stopped and looked into his face. It was wide and open everywhere Daisy's was sharp and pouting. He was generically handsome. Ordinary. In another life I would have called him a himbo, bought him a drink, and asked him if he'd ever thought about getting pegged.

"Why?" I asked.

"Why what, Miss Franklin?" he asked.

"Why do you want to walk me home?"

"It is . . ." He floundered, confused by the forthright inquiry. "It is merely polite. When one's acquaintances are far away, and I do understand the bottom of the sea to be quite far indeed, it always benefits to make new friends. And friends walk each other home."

I sighed and held out the basket. He grinned like a golden retriever, took it, and offered his arm again. I accepted it and we resumed. "When is it my turn to walk you home?"

The impertinence of the question startled that sweet belly laugh out of him. "But that would defeat the purpose, Miss Franklin, as I would have to promptly turn around to return the favor."

"What, I can't walk home alone in the dark?"

"No, Miss Franklin. It is not wise to do so, not even in Bath."

"Plus ça change," I huffed.

All the same, it was nice to have a friend outside of the house, and I liked hearing about all the dramas of his shop just as much as Mr. Cooper the Younger liked hearing about the upstairs/downstairs life of the Goodenough household.

As we passed the milliner, also closing for the day, Cooper excused himself to run a quick errand inside. He returned carrying one unfinished poke bonnet by the slash of blue ribbon sewn across the point where straw brim met the raw fabric tuft at the back.

"Mr. Cooper," I said. "I'm not entirely certain that those ribbons are your color."

"No, no," he said, fumbling with the bonnet, looking at it, then me, then back down at it. He tucked it, shamefaced, behind his back, then blushed furiously and held it back out. "They are yours, though."

"My . . . what now?"

"Your color, Miss Franklin," Cooper said, but with none of the lightness his teasing usually came with. "The blue is the same shade as your eyes."

"I suppose it is," I admitted.

And then, of course, I understood.

Shit.

He flushed again and said, "Miss Franklin, I couldn't help but notice you often peruse the wares at the hatmaker's, and, well, I thought it would be an accurate token of my affection if I were to, uh, provide you with a bonnet. A lady ought to have a bonnet."

I winced, more out of embarrassment for his stuttering confession than out of discomfort over the fact that the dude that I bought flour from every other night seemed to think that our evening walks were leading somewhere they were not.

Idiot, I scolded myself.

Of course that was what he would think about our strolls. I was a woman interacting regularly with a man, both of us single and unchaperoned. Where I came from, Harry could meet Sally with no orgasms required, but this was 1806 and Mr. Cooper probably had every right to think that I was actively attempting to, as the phrase in the dramas went, "attach him."

No, no, no, abort, I thought frantically. I deliberately did not reach for the hat.

"Thank you, Mr. Cooper. But I fear I cannot accept your gift."

He opened his mouth to argue, I saw it flash in his eyes. Then he changed his mind. "All the same, I should still like to walk you home."

I wanted to say no.

"Mr. Cooper," I said instead, hesitating. *This is ridiculous*, I thought miserably. I hadn't resented being in this era so much as right in this moment, because I couldn't just tell him I had a girlfriend and put an end to it.

"Please," he said, and it was so sad that guilt bloomed in my lungs.

He offered me his elbow, then tucked the bonnet against his other side. I wouldn't let him take back the basket. The rest of the walk was silent.

When we reached the garden gate, he held the bonnet out to me. "I have no use for it besides as a gift for you," he said intensely. "No sisters, no mother. Please. Take it. As a friend."

"It's an extravagant gift, even for a friend."

He looked crestfallen. "Please?"

"All right," I croaked, plucking it from his hands. "Thank you, Mr. Cooper."

"It's my pleasure, Miss Franklin," he said. He leaned toward me—dear god, for a *kiss*—and I jerked out of range. He wrinkled his nose, looked away, and dropped a resentful little head bob.

"Good evening, Miss Franklin," he said, and turned away. He was halfway down the road before I could say anything in return. When I looked up, Daisy was already at the door, Miss Brown behind her to take the basket. I followed them inside, and Miss Brown said nothing about the skeletal bonnet dangling by its ribbons like a dead cat. Daisy fled into the parlor.

Piano music, halting and slightly out of tune, wafted into the kitchen.

I hung the bonnet on the peg beside the door, hesitated, then called myself a coward.

"Daisy?" I said, softly, knocking gently as I entered. "I'll help Miss Brown get dinner laid, do you want anything before I go?" She was silent for long enough that I thought perhaps she hadn't heard me. "Daisy?" I asked again.

"I find that I do not like your Mr. Cooper," Daisy replied, rising to glare out the window, down the street Cooper had gone down, winding the drapes between anxious fingers.

"Yeah. Look, sorry about that, I thought he was just a guy I hung out with, but it turns out he was girlfriend-zoning me this whole time."

"You offered him no discouragement, Sam," she hissed.

"I did," I protested. "As soon as I figured out what he was after."

Daisy chewed on her bottom lip, but after a moment, nodded and released the curtains to turn into me and press her face against my neck for a hug. "This is wretched. I dislike immensely that I must endure men swooping on you like *vultures*."

"Totally sucks," I agreed. "If it's any consolation, I hate it every time your mom sets you up on a date too."

Daisy groaned. "I long for a home for just us two. But I daren't hope that my writing will be sufficient to fund such a thing."

"It might. You never know."

She pulled back to narrow her eyes, bright with unshed tears, at me. "Do *you* know?"

"I actually don't," I reassured her. "But it'll never happen if you don't finish it, and you can't finish it until I read it, so I guess I better get on that, eh?"

"After your dinner," Daisy said, stepping back to lead me to the kitchen. "I would have you at your full strength before facing that challenge."

"How magnanimous," I murmured, pinching the end of her coral sash and following in her wake like the besotted duckling I was.

Chapter Eighteen

IN WHICH SAM READS

If I loved you less, I might be able to talk about it more.

—Jane Austen, Emma

Knowing that I would likely be up all night and not wanting to disturb anyone, after dinner I changed into my sleepwear and took the manuscript into the night-quiet schoolroom. Besides the cluster of the half dozen chairs we used for our lessons, there was also a wingback chair beside the hearth. It was worn, the leather cracked, but comfortable in the way that only old furniture that's been molded around the bodies of decades of readers can be. I stoked up the embers, lit the oil lamp on the mantle, put a kettle of water on the rail above the fire to keep the room from getting too dry, and tried to settle.

Excitement had me back out of the chair instantly, pacing between the desks, shaking out my hands as if I could throw off the sparks of gleeful, giggling excitement that tingled along my skin.

This is it, Sammie-bear! History! Being made right in front of you!

I forced myself to take deep breaths, to smooth out my dressing gown, to stop squealing under my breath, and sit again. I lifted back the leather cover and ran my fingers across the words inked on the first page in a bold, sure hand:

~~Letters Across the Sea~~

The Welshman's Daughters

I'd never actually made it to the first page of *The Welshman's Daughters* on the airplane, but even I knew that it opened at the end, with the protagonist sitting in a pool of blood in the divination-drenched family chapel in the house on the cliff, musing on her father's burial at sea and her metamorphosis from Jean Trembley of Montreal to Jane Tremble of Tŷ ar y Bryn Manor. This is what I had read, all those months ago, at Swangale House.

Much had been made in every adaptation of the symbolism of the blood—was it there to evoke transformation? Did it represent the moon, and women's pain, and the witchcraft of bleeding and yet never dying? Was it Jane's blood, was it Death's? Was it real at all? Or was it just simply blood, the thing that happens when a sharp silver knife meets living flesh?

Yet *these* pages were clean of gore.

They instead began with the correspondence of a brother—whom I recognized as a proto-Kendall ap Hywel, the dashing and tragic sailor with a poet's heart and Byronic figure that had all the twenty-first century girls, gays, and gentlethey's hearts a-flutter—and a milquetoast sister I supposed was meant to be Mariana, but who lacked the fierceness that stepping into her mother's role as head of the household had instilled in her.

In this version there were no other siblings—the dead baby brother was not a plot point, the ennui-laden middle brother entirely absent. In this version, Mariana's mother was both alive and a snide busybody not unlike Iris. More importantly, the book was entirely devoid of the damp, creeping menace that soaked every scene with roiling fog. Missing was the seductive warning of crashing waves, the easy slip of a smooth slipper on dew-wet rocks beside the deceptive lip of a waterfall, and windows rattling in gales that might actually be the murmur of ghosts.

The letters went on endlessly about the daily toil on a ship that carried mail and passengers between Cardiff, Wales, and St. John's, Newfoundland. For a gothic romance, the romance happened entirely offstage, as if it was instead a Greek drama. And it was utterly devoid of anything "gothic."

I read the first dozen pages with confusion, squinting hard, with rolled-in shoulders, mouth tight.

My excitement melted into slow-creeping dread.

It's just a first draft, I told myself, as I set the leather folder aside. *That's why I don't recognize it.*

Though I really wanted to raid the wine stash, instead, I set the manuscript aside and took my anxiety to the kitchen. Miss Brown hadn't yet settled in her little trundle bed, so I wasn't bothering her while I made myself a small pot of weak twice-brewed tea, with leftover squidges of lemon rind from that afternoon's cake. I walked in circles around the tight schoolroom as I waited for the tea to steep, crossing and uncrossing my arms, picking at a loose thread on my dressing gown, biting my lower lip.

It's not bad, I thought. *The word choices are good, the story is compelling. It's very well written. It's just . . . not what it's supposed to be.*

But then how would I know?

I'd only ever seen adaptations, and of course it would be boring if Mariana and Kendall just sat at desks and wrote at one another for a whole film, right? *Obviously* creative license had to be taken by directors.

It was fine.

It was *all* fine.

I nearly believed myself.

I returned to the chair, tea in hand, and applied myself to the novel.

The siblings shared stories about travels, romance, marriage, and woe. There was a section about a woman Kendall had met in port, who appeared so suddenly in the book I wondered if it was a new addition Daisy hadn't managed to go back and insert yet, or if it was meant to be a plot twist. In her return letter, Mariana was irrationally anxious about Kendall falling in love when Mariana wasn't there to caution him against it.

And then the sister, too, was in romantic danger: an overdressed, controlling terror of a man, only made buffoonish. I saw in him a parody of Lewis, his anger and threat reduced to pathetic self-flattery and childish, entitled ridiculousness instead of the dangerous spider spinning traps for Mariana that I was familiar with from Dahl's TV series.

Suddenly, at the midpoint of the book, the letters stopped. I flipped a page and the novel was written in the third person. Daisy changed tack, simply *telling* the story.

Like a clockwork music box, the gears tumbled and the story opened up and *sang*.

I heaved a sigh of relief, posture loosening.

This, I knew.

Here now were windswept coastlines and dark cottages, the whispered oaths and phantom shawls, scenes that I had watched unfold before, dialogue that I knew in the way that everyone knew famous, quotable lines.

Kendall became the man whose morals saw him refuse to participate in a mutiny and needing to flee his fellow murderous, greedy seamen. The catty Evangeline, Kendall's mysterious portside lover became vicious, secretive, lusting for power and doing all she could to bring him under her thrall—finally, she was the desperate selkie from the film, whom generations of ap Hywel men had abused, whose pelt lay buried in the foundations of Tŷ ar y Bryn Manor, and whose magic had soaked into the stones and wood, the very soul of the ill-fated house. The man hounding Mariana grew perilous, his desire to discover the secrets of Tŷ ar y Bryn's riches turned carnal and predatory.

And there, *finally*, appeared the narrator Jane Tremble.

Mariana's childhood playmate, orphaned and plain, and of no worth to anyone in the household save to keep the wealthy young miss entertained. Raised alongside Mariana by the now listless mother, who was grieving so strongly for her lost baby that she had abandoned her living children while they still breathed.

Jane, to whom Mariana cleaved. Jane, whose own arranged marriage to the hapless Mr. Cooper (*not very subtle, Daisy*) threatened to tear the two young women apart. Who, in his average, boring, casual misogyny, was the greatest threat to Mariana's happiness of all of them. Jane, who had looked Death in the face on the crossing and remembered its visage. Jane, whose compassion for the tortured Evangeline saw her free the creature instead of killing her in that final, piteous confrontation with Mariana's suitor in the blood-slicked chapel.

Jane, who embodied the best of Marigold.

And Mariana, who stood in for the worst of me.

This was, unmistakably, *The Welshman's Daughter*s.

But *this* wasn't right either.

It was shallow. Pretty, but feckless. It was nothing but page after page of descriptions of dresses, and sunsets, and petty rivalries, women who cried in every other scene and beastly men who ravished, blood that glittered, waves that wailed.

Where were the disguised but shockingly progressive themes that the book was known for? The push for abolition framed as Evangeline's magical captivity? Where was the feminism hidden in Mariana's reluctance to become chattel and breeding stock? Where was the discussion of toxic masculinity in the mundane horror of Cooper's blind faith and the railing against classist social structures that Jane's self-determination shattered?

All of it just so much sound and fury, all of it meaningless, all of it . . .

Wrong.

I reached the last page, where all the wrong people were punished for all the wrong things, and closed the leather cover carefully. I leaned back and stared up into the darkness that pooled in the corners of the ceiling, shoulders shaking and eyes watering with grief.

All those evenings spent in conversation with Daisy, her thorough and thoughtful questioning, her "recording face," her mornings coming to breakfast with ink splattered on her fingertips, graphite smudges on her hands and cheeks.

So much work, and for what?

Nothing.

The book wasn't at all what it was supposed to be.

And it was all my fault.

~

I woke, stiff backed and sore, when Miss Brown came into the schoolroom to start the fire the next morning. Shamefaced, I collected Daisy's papers—some of which had spilled off of my lap and onto the floor—and tried to put them back in order. Dread pulled at my sternum as my eyes caught on lines, lacerating as fishhooks.

By the time I'd returned the manuscript to Daisy's writing desk and gone upstairs to freshen up, Iris and Marigold had already had their breakfasts and were on their way to church. I lingered over my breakfast for once, loath to join them. Practically vibrating, Daisy slid into the empty chair beside me as soon as the door had shut on Marigold's skirts. She wasn't even trying to pretend that she hadn't been watching my face for a reaction all morning.

"I can see that you are desperate to speak, yet reluctant to broach the topic," Daisy said softly. "Was it that terrible?"

I shook my head, unsure what I could—or should—actually say.

"But you are behaving as if . . . you hold yourself stiffly—"

"I fell asleep in the chair. My neck hurts."

"It put you to sleep?" she asked, ever so slightly distraught.

I can't do it, I realized. *I can't lie to her. I respect her too much, I respect how much work she's put into it, I respect what it could be too much to . . .*

"Samantha?"

... let her keep thinking it's great. I'm the wrong muse, she shouldn't be writing about me, she needs the Wealthy Widow.

"Sweet Pea?"

But how on earth can I tell her without it sounding like I'm dictating what the book should be, and—wait, "What did you call me?"

"For the pattern on your dress," Daisy said, suddenly shy. "I thought ... a flowerbed of Goodenoughs, and you are one of us now, are you not? Sheltered from the gaze of the world by the garden wall, entwined with the other blooms. My Sweet Pea."

No, she doesn't mean it like that, I thought viciously. *Hidden, in the shadow, tucked away in the back ... closeted.* I swallowed hard, throat clicking, and downed the rest of my stone-cold tea with a shaking hand. The scar under my arm flared with deep heat, the pain making me gasp.

"Did you dislike it?" Daisy asked, eyes growing wet and worried.

"The pet name? I love it."

"And the book?

"The writing is *beautiful*, the setting is so evocative," I said at once, because that much was true. "But. Babe. The letters."

"Obviously," Daisy said, tapping her teeth in distress. "I must rewrite the start, the epistolary nature is too distant. It was too ... womanish, do you see? It was circuitous and coy and all the things that I thought a woman must be." Daisy wrung her hands harder, frustrated that she wasn't articulating herself the way she wanted. I waited her out. "You must understand, epistolary format is very traditional, but why may I not be direct in describing the action? Why must letter-novels be the providence of writers of the fair sex, couched in layers of hidden meaning? Why may I not simply and forthrightly relate the actions and emotions and, and, and feelings of my characters, as male writers may do. As *you* do."

"Yes," I agreed, grateful for the easy step into critique. Unable to sit still, I stood and paced to the windows and back. "But also it's ... "

"It is?" Daisy prompted, looking up at me with such naked, trusting hope.

And I was such a bitch.

But the way I saw it, either I spared her feelings . . . or I destroyed the most seminal work in queer literature to have ever existed.

I had a sudden sense-memory of Dahlia on that hot concrete outside of the airport, the smell of her strawberry-matcha shampoo and the baking garbage, the mascara running down her face, her arm shaking as she held out the book to me. Terrified to be who she was. Begging for connection the only way she knew how. Imploring me to read a tale of desire, lust, repression, fear, and of hiding one's true self, of having something as essential and vital as your own skin torn from you, and the things you must do to cover up your naked shame at being exposed. To understand Dahlia's struggles through the lens of Jane Tremble.

Instead, I'd thrown it back in her face.

Thrown it in the *trash.*

Your way is not the only way, simply because it's the most modern way, I reminded myself. *Dahlia needed this book in a way you'll never understand. History needs this book. You owe her that much. You owe them all.*

"Where's the heart?" I asked softly, voice crackling and heart stuttering under the fist of my own cruelty.

"The heart?" Daisy breathed.

"It's beautifully written." I hated myself for the way her lips flickered up into a relieved smile. "But that's *all* it is."

The smile died.

Murderer, I accused myself, but I went on. The knife was in my hand now, raised in the moonlight, glinting silver. Time to bring down my arm.

"You're not writing the right book," I explained, trying to phrase it as gently as possible.

Daisy gasped as if I'd pinched her all the same, eyes sparking with swelling hurt.

"It's all . . . the motivations are, well, wrong. Shallow, and look, here's an example," I leaned on the table so I could meet her gaze earnestly. I tried to take her hand but she sank back into her chair, jerking away from my touch. "Jane falls in *love* with Mariana because Mariana is clever and selfless, and will not let her father dictate their lives or marriages. Jane loves Mariana because she is sparkling and headstrong and generous. And Mariana loves Jane because—"

"*Loves,*" Daisy choked. Her eyes narrowed, heavy with unshed tears. "How is it that you *presume* to find truths in my story that I did not put there? They are *friends*, they don't *love*—"

"Like you and I are just 'friends'? Come on, Daisy, please—"

"You hated it," Daisy accused, voice thick now with sorrow and building anger.

"I promise I didn't. But I don't know how to explain it," I said, scrubbing my hands through my hair. "The story isn't what it becomes."

"I do not understand—"

I'd call the look on her face the "recording" expression, if it wasn't so fucking shattered.

"It's good, but stuff just *happens*, for no *reason*. There's no depth."

Daisy drew herself up haughtily. "Must every happening have a reason? Can a story simply not be entertaining?"

"It can," I allowed, too much of a coward to look her full in the face and take in the torment I was putting there. "It can, but *this* book—"

"Why are you so *singularly* devoted to this manuscript?" Daisy asks, breathless with confusion and passion. "Why has it become the whole of your focus?"

"No, Daisy, I'm sorry if I made you feel that all I care about is the book. Of course I *do* care about the book, but it's not my destiny, it's your—" I reached for her hands, to reassure, to apologize, but she took a step back, sudden and frightened. "Babe?"

"Do not . . . do *not*," Daisy choked, the color draining from her drawn face. "I cannot listen to this anymore."

I groaned, "It's just a book critique, I—"

"It is not about the book! It is about *this*." She cut her hand at me, vicious and sudden. "This legacy that you seek to crush me under! Your future *strangles* me, my darling. I am not some mythical creature, petrified already in the granite walls of history! I can be only myself, my book can only be what it is, newborn and caterwauling and begging the comfort which you now deny me!"

"I'm not—"

Daisy slapped the table so hard the dishes rattled. "You refuse to see me as anything but a symbol of everything you have lost!"

"That's not fair." I reeled back under the force of her hurt.

"You have been here for nearly a year but what have you to show for it?" she challenged through gritted teeth. "You ask much of me, my love, but have made no attempts to remedy your plight. Yet you demand that I bend to your will and fulfill your terrifying prophecies? That I simply *trust* that all you say is in good faith and to help me—"

"It is! I swear it is!"

"—become your 'most important queer writer in history'!"

"That's not fair!" I shouted again. "I'm trapped here, Daisy. Don't you understand, I am trapped. I can't bend the space-time continuum and magically transport back to 2024. I'm trying to survive!"

"And when do you plan on *living*?"

"I am!"

"You live for me, Samantha, but what have you to call your own? Have you acquaintances?"

"Marigold! Miss Brown tells me all the servant's gossip. I'm doing my best to create a life here. I have a job—a place for myself in this world."

"And beyond the little boundary of *my* world?"

"Thomas Cooper."

Daisy's nose scrunched up in disgust. "Oh *yes*, what a kind soul he is, too, giving you a bonnet."

"You don't get to tell me I need friends and scoff at the single one I have with the next breath. Baby, I know this is the first time you've been given constructive criticism, but you—"

"Constructive?" Daisy gasped, horror crawling over her face. "You think calling my book *wrong* is helpful? It is cruel!"

"Daisy—"

"Especially in light of my confession! I shared with you my deepest fear, that *I* was wrong, and now you call—"

"*Fuck*, I didn't think," I pleaded, horror crawling up my spine. How senselessly callous I'd been. "I'm sorry. Please don't overreact—"

"I am not overreacting, you are attacking—"

"I'm not! Don't you see?" I shouted back, the revelation striking in the same instant that the confession tumbled out. "I can't go burning the whole fucking patriarchy to the ground, because that doesn't happen yet! I hate living in this world but I don't *dare* change it in case I screw it all up and it *never* changes for the better. So you can't tell me that I have to go find a hobby or a meaning to life when everything I've ever wanted I *can't have*."

Like you.

Like Dahlia.

Daisy hurled her teacup at my head, and I ducked just in time. It sailed into the thick fall of drapery. Instead of shattering, it just thumped impotently to the carpet.

Surprise more than fear of her temper drove me back a few steps.

"I wish you'd said nothing!" Daisy snarled, advancing on me with one sharp finger raised at the level of my eyes. "Do you think I am not entirely aware that this time, this world, *me*, we are not what you want. But we are all that you have. You wish for me to be someone who exists only in the annals of history. But I am not! I am a living, breathing woman, and I am *here*."

As she backed me into the garish wallpaper, I started to wish I'd said nothing too.

"Do you understand how terrified I am? How the weight of a legacy I know nothing of save for the shape of its bulk *crushes* down upon me, how it is a more lethal gravity than any burden I have ever shouldered before?"

"No, I didn't, I—"

"It *frightens* me, Sam. I cannot write for second-guessing myself." She hiccupped. "I no longer trust my heart and hands. I hate it! I hate *you*, sometimes!"

"You don't mean that," I said.

"I ask you again—why this book? Why *me*?" she growled. She shook off my grip and leaned in close, framing my head with her bare forearms against the wall. She loomed over me, making my breath clench in my lungs and a heat flutter to life between my legs. She was flushed and panting with her anger, eyes dark, hair falling in a frazzled halo around her head.

She was magnificent.

"Because there's two hundred and eighteen years' worth of queers who *need* you," I whispered, voice a tremor, insides quivering.

The truth gripped at my guts like hoarfrost, spreading slow and insidious, through every cell of my body, leaving hollow understanding in its wake.

They *did* need Margaret.

They *needed* this book, the *right* version of this book, more than anyone or anything in history would ever need *me*.

I had been flippant about it up until now, jokey, too starstruck and lust addled to really *understand* but I . . .

I was *this close* to destroying *everything.*

"No, I need *you*," Daisy gasped. "I swore to myself that I would never . . . but you have broken apart my vow to remain unattached like it was no more substantial than spider-silk I *need* you."

"And for you to write, you *can't* need me. Don't you see that?"

"I'm wrong!" Daisy warbled. "Everything I create is wrong, the way I love is *wrong*, I cannot even please you in so small a thing as my book—"

No, it was *me* who was wrong, who was screwing everything up. Who was ruining everything.

Who had been wrong from the beginning.

It was *me.*

Am I at least as meaningful as Finch? she had once asked me.

Yes.

But more meaningful than *The Welshman's Daughters*?

Yes.

No.

I didn't know.

All I knew was that the book was wrong.

And so was I.

I've done it again. I've dragged someone else out of the closet before they're ready, forced them to live their life the way I wanted them to instead of listening to their wants, and fears, and needs. It's Dahlia all over again, getting out of that taxi, already crying because you've forced her into a showdown, you selfish, selfish, selfish—

"I can't. To be what you need me to be, *I* can't be what I need to be," I sobbed, tears cascading down my cheeks, flooding up from the deepest chambers of my shredded heart. "I can't suffocate myself like that. Even for you. I can't go back in the closet. And I'm starting to think that you can't thrive creatively outside of it. Marigold was right. I ruin everything I touch. Including you."

"Am I not the one who gets to decide that?"

"No," I keened.

"Then I hate you," Daisy snarled, shoving herself away, hands fisted and shaking like she wanted to punch something but had never been taught how. "I wish I'd never met you. I wish you'd never told me about what is to come, I wish I'd never listened to your tales. I wish you'd never *infected* me with your love!"

And then she stormed out, slamming the door behind her. Understanding careened into my sternum like a shooting star.

I can't stay here.

Chapter Nineteen

IN WHICH SAM WEDS

I am convinced that my chance of happiness with him is as fair as most people can boast on entering the marriage state.

—Jane Austen, *Pride and Prejudice*

It was cowardly. I knew that. But I did it anyway. I waited until the whole household was asleep then packed all my admittedly sparse possessions into the large shopping basket, left the last of the money I'd saved from the sale of my phone to cover my final expenses, and slipped into the predawn light.

When Thomas Cooper arrived at his shop that morning to open, I was dozing on the stoop, clutching the basket on my lap. And wearing his bonnet.

"Hey, little buddy," I greeted him, when he shook my shoulder kindly.

"Good morning, Miss Franklin," he said quietly. "I would call it a pleasure to see you so early in the day, only for fear that the reason is an unhappy one."

"Why do you say that?" I asked, even as I wiped at the dried tear tracks on my cheeks.

"Oh, Miss Franklin," he said softly, pity softening his gaze.

It made something in me bristle. I didn't want his pity. Or his softness.

"Hey, so, I was thinking," I said, accepting his help to stand, and wincing at the soreness in my back from crouching on the stoop. I dusted off my skirts instead of meeting his eyes. "Wanna get married?"

"I—" He turned red as a tomato and then blurted: "Yes!"

After I'd given him a brief song and dance about how my visit with the Goodenoughs had come to its natural conclusion and I'd decided to act on my infatuation with the grocer's son, we were on the next coach bound for London.

Thomas proposed to me in turn as soon as we arrived at the final stop—a tavern in Cheapside—three days later. He even went so far as to get down on one knee in the rushes covering the floor, stale beer soaking into his trousers, as he offered me a dinged-up ring he'd found in a pawn shop.

And I smiled, and tittered, and blushed, because Thomas Cooper was a good man and I was using him for my own security. The least he deserved in return was my enthusiasm.

It wasn't his fault that he wasn't Margaret Goodenough, love of my fucking life.

I had already resigned myself to a loveless security-marriage once—I figured I could do it again, and this time follow through. There were worse things to be than adored by one's husband, after all, and it wasn't like we wouldn't have a whole lifetime together for me to fall in love with him in return.

Because we were going to be married.

Married to Thomas, and not Daisy. Married for real, with a ring and a license.

It galled. But what else could I do? I couldn't stay in Bath, couldn't live in Southampton with Finch and Eliza, couldn't strike out on my own. As Lewis had once pointed out, with no character references and no papers, the only options available to me were to become a wife, or a sex worker, passed off from one person to another, never finding true friends, never being safe and self-sufficient, never being *known* to anyone.

No. Thom was the far more appealing choice.

The more—as Lewis had once put it—delicate route.

I could *do* this.

I could fucking do this.

It was only the third time I'd started over. I was a pro at it by this point. And the third time was supposed to be a charm, right?

Right.

Damn this century.

~

My fiancé and I were eventually bound for Mevagissey, on the southwestern tip of the island (on the English channel, triangulated between Tregony and Lanjeth. See? *Boggle*). There, Thom's father had a cousin with no sons and a thriving living as a baker that would be going spare as a result.

But first, we'd overwinter in London. Thom, to learn his new trade from his brother Joseph, who was also a baker, and me, to help his sister-in-law through the last trimester of her pregnancy.

(As if I had any effing clue about getting babies out of people.)

The first night we'd washed up on their stoop, Mrs. Anne Cooper, just pregnant enough that getting up from her chair was a challenge, had greeted the news of our engagement and our request to stay with her with gentle joy.

"Now, love," she had said, noticing the tightness around my eyes and misinterpreting it for post-engagement jitters. "Never mind you none about your wedding night." She patted her impressive belly and smirked knowingly. "There ain't nothing wrong with lovin' your husband all the way through the mattress."

I'd chuckled at Thomas's blushing protest of his sister-in-law's crude insinuations.

Thomas had been sent to sleep with the stable boy who served in the livery for this part of town, for there were no spare rooms at his brother's besides the one they put me in. And it wasn't the done thing to let an engaged couple sleep in the same room. The room I was given was already decorated as a nursery, sparse and cheap, but filled with affection for the child on its way. These Coopers were only slightly better off than their Bath relations, but I had no illusions that Mrs. Cooper didn't work just as hard as her husband in the bakery that made up the ground floor of the building.

From that day on, Thom and I worked just as hard: stoking fires, mixing dough, kneading bread, selling loaves. (Finally learned the value of the coinage, ha!) Dusk came and we slept; dawn came and we woke, and did it all again. Days passed. Then weeks.

And I hated London. Because, let's face it, I was a cranky introverted old mog, and my fiancé was a himbo extroverted husky. Where Thomas Cooper thrived in the sweaty, cramped bakeshop or the bustling, noisy, river-reeking city, I just wanted to be left alone in a cottage for the next decade or so.

I would get one, eventually. The old cousin had promised one, by the sea no less, but first Thom had to learn how to bake, and I had to learn how to wife.

But mostly I hated London because this was where Daisy wasn't.

And yet, it could be worse.

It nearly had been. I learned that the gossip pages in the ladies' magazines reported that Sir Lewis's blushing bride had returned to the Canadas soon after their honeymoon to care for a sick relative back home. How convenient for him. How fortuitous for me.

It took a month for us to settle with the City Coopers, another two weeks to get enough time off from bread-and-impending-baby duty to visit the courts and apply for a petition of marriage, a week again to arrange for the first reading of the banns, and then suddenly it was the last week of October.

I'd been in the Georgian era for a full year.

Helluva trick.

~

For the third Sunday in a row nobody stood up in the little church crammed onto the corner beside Cooper's bakeshop to declare that they saw an impediment to my forthcoming marriage. For the third time I found myself in a foul depression afterward, insides twisting viciously when my secret hope that Daisy would slam through the big doors at the back, throw herself down the aisle, collapse at my feet, kiss my hem, and beg me to come home again had failed to materialize.

But who was I kidding?

I had left *her*.

Already very familiar with my moods, Thomas suggested that we take in Hyde Park to clear our heads. It was free to the public, and as the day was bright and shining, I agreed. I wanted to wash London out of my nose, and a garden seemed like an ideal place to do that. We spent a few of Thom's precious shillings on a cab, and disembarked in front of a bookshop. I couldn't help but stop in and ask if the publication of Daisy's book had been announced yet. It hadn't. I wondered if she had even finished revising it yet, if she'd sent it out. And if she had sent it out, had she already received her offer letter, or if it was only rejection after rejection.

If I'd screwed everything up and no one wanted to take it.

Or worse, if Daisy had abandoned it.

The year 1807 was only three months away, and while I didn't know in what month *The Welshman's Daughter*s had been published, the date felt like it was rushing toward me along the tracks of history like a runaway train. Either the book would be a triumph or I would be smooshed on the rails.

Distracting me from my worry, Thom directed us through the wrought-iron fence that marked the entryway to the park and down a gravel path, where it seemed that most of the city had had a similar inclination to take advantage of the sunshine. The October breeze was temperate enough that I wore just a shawl, a gift from Anne, though we had to walk close to keep the wind from cutting away our words.

We admired the couples far more handsome than ourselves—wives who could afford to just visit each other all day and husbands who dined at clubs instead of on whatever their wives ordered from their cooks. Thomas grinned at me, sideways and sly, when the rich couples passed by, puffing out his chest to mimic their toffee-nosed self-important struts, and I laughed, not embarrassed by the roughness of my dress or my husband-to-be's calluses.

Thomas was honest, and so was his work. More than that, it brought him joy.

I could be proud of him for that.

And he made me laugh. I hadn't laughed in *weeks*.

I could do this.

I could *do* this.

"Are you nervous, almost-nearly Mrs. Cooper?" he asked as we strolled. "Faith, I think I'm near fit to burst with the idea of getting to sleep beside you this time next week. Just sleep, mind. The other things sound fun enough, but what I'm anticipating most is waking up beside you in the morning light. Doesn't that sound grand?"

"It does," I agreed, and I meant it.

He pushed a stray hair back behind my ear and smiled sweetly at me, then jerked his hand away and blushed. His innocence should have been endearing but instead it reminded me of just how young and inexperienced he was, how desperate he was to find love and win the heart of a good wife. Of the expectations riding upon both of us, of the restrictions of this time and place.

I tried to smile but it tangled up under my tongue. In my time this boy wouldn't be blushing from merely touching the woman he was about to marry. In my time we would have been lovers already. Where I had once found this prolonged courtship endearing, I now found it tedious.

If people would just stop being so goddamned invested in *manners* and start worrying about *feelings*, then maybe I wouldn't be here, trapped in a loveless engagement.

I was just contemplating whether it would be better to go back to the house and see how Anne was faring—she was taut as a blimp, ready to pop any day—when in my peripheral vision a figure approached.

I turned to greet the man, assuming the person was one of Joseph and Anne's friends, (or else why would he be approaching?) and blanched.

Holy shit.

It was George Lewis.

He was dressed for walking, sporty but no less cruel than the last time I'd laid eyes on the son of a bitch. A grin was stretched across his pink face, a vindictive rictus of savage pleasure.

I took a step back, away, and he kept coming. I couldn't run, not now, not with so many eyes on us, curious about the disparity of our obvious social situations, the way he tipped his hat at us as if we were friends. As if the last time I had seen him he hadn't been screaming obscenities down the nave of a church.

"Hello, mousie," he said.

"Fuck off," I snarled.

Thom, perplexed by the violence of my answer, stepped between us. Lewis raised his walking stick and prodded Thomas to the side indolently.

"Thom, move," I told him, worried that the next swing of the walking stick would be far less gentle if he didn't.

Lewis darted in and grabbed my hand to finish the ritual of greeting, kissing the back of my glove against my will.

"Miss Franklin," he said, his grin razor sharp, his eyes calculating. His voice still sounded like nails on a chalkboard.

I tugged my hand free and crossed my arms behind my back to keep any and all appendages out of grabbing range.

"My lord Jackwad," I replied.

Lewis sneered. "And that young man lingering like an orange shadow behind you would be your young Mr. Cooper, I presume?" His opinion of Thomas was abundantly clear by his moue of distaste.

"Screw you. What are you even doing here?"

"I was passing through Cheapside just now, and, to my amazement, I heard a *very* familiar name being called out in a pokey little church. Now, mousie, whose name do you think that was?"

"Fuck. You."

"Such language, mousie," Lewis sneered, amused by my grim determination. "Quite unbecoming in a lady."

"And also not your problem," I sneered.

"Actually, it is," Lewis replied. He doffed his hat and bowed ironically at us, but his eyes were darting all over the place. Still worried about his reputation. "I shan't have my wife cussing like a sailor."

"I'm not yours. I never said 'I do.' I never signed the registry."

"And who was at the wedding to say otherwise?" Lewis chuckled and leaned in as if sharing a delicious secret. "Who is familiar enough with your signature to prove the one on our certificate is a forgery?"

"Samantha is *my* betrothed," Thomas blustered, hand on my shoulder protectively, trying his damnedest to find some moment to dive in heroically, and finding himself woefully out of his depth. "And I'll thank you to—"

"The adults are talking, Cooper," Mr. Lewis cut across him, whipcrack sharp and commanding enough that Thomas actually cringed.

Oh, that poor boy, I thought. *He has no idea what I've stuck him in the middle of.*

"Samantha is with me," he tried again, screwing up his courage.

"Is she?" Lewis said with a cat who decapitated the canary grin. "And how can that be, I wonder, when she is already married to me? Unless he already knows how much you take *pleasure* in adultery, little mousie?"

It was a blow both deliberately and professionally executed.

Swift. Hard. Staggering.

Thomas stuttered back a step, color draining from his face, hands shaking. "Samantha . . . what is he— Surely, he's mistaken, you aren't—"

I considered denying it for about four seconds. At second five, I realized that there would be no point. No matter what I said, the rumor mill was already grinding at full speed. I could hear the whispers around us jumping from bystander to bystander like fleas. Joseph and Anne would likely hear of it before Thom even got home, and for the sake of their own reputation and business, convince him it was true.

And, if Thom hated me, jilted me, abandoned me here and now, then it would keep Lewis's target off his back.

If I walked into this trap now, I could spare Thom from being caught with me. Getting out of it later would be tricky, but not impossible.

Lewis read the decision to capitulate—for now—on my face even as I settled into it.

"It's true," I said. I didn't turn my face from Lewis, didn't dare put myself in such a vulnerable position. But I was speaking to Thom.

"You're *married*," Thom burbled.

"No."

"But you're . . . you've . . ."

I thrust out my chin, determined to remain unashamed. "I have."

"Miss Franklin—" Thom wobbled. "I—I . . . I—"

And then he turned on his heel and left.

Lewis didn't even bother watching him go.

The Coopers would be safe.

The Goodenoughs were out of his debt.

Good.

But me? Not so much.

"I warned you I'd make your life miserable," Lewis purred smugly as soon as Thom was out of earshot.

"And I told you, I'll give as good as I get."

Lewis stepped into my personal space and wound a tendril of hair hanging in front of my ear around his finger. From the outside it appeared to be an affectionate gesture. Then he tugged it, hard enough to hurt but not so much that anyone else could tell.

"I do not appreciate being made a nine day's wonder, Miss Franklin."

I thought of Miss Donaldson, and of how much my leaving him at the altar must have been spread if she'd heard about it all the way out in Bath.

"And now we will correct it. I will have you under my thumb, precisely where Fen promised you'd be."

"Fenton paid off his debt to you," I said, squaring up. "And you can't blackmail him, not if you don't want me screaming your secrets from the second floor windows. You're not owed a bride anymore."

"And yet I find that I still require one," Lewis said. "And an heir. I cannot very well marry anyone else while the whole country thinks I'm still married to you." He pouted theatrically. "I was thinking of killing you. In the papers, I mean, don't look so alarmed, mousie. I would let it slip that your ship sank on your return crossing, then pick a wife from the mourners come to comfort me. But then, miraculously, *here you are*." He tugged again, and this time I whimpered. "Alive and well, and just standing here like a complete *dolt* in the most crowded thoroughfare in London, where everyone can *see* that you're alive and well, you petty *bitch*."

"A shame," I hissed. "I would have preferred to have died."

Lewis loomed so low that our noses practically touched. "That can be *arranged*."

He grabbed my upper arm, digging his thumb hard into my scar. I cried out, the pain dancing stars in the side of my vision, which gave Lewis an opening to shout, "Oh dear, my wife is swooning! I shall bring her to some shade!"

He wrenched me back into a copse of trees. I tried to kick but my

Chucks were no match for his tall boots. He clapped a beefy hand over my mouth, hauling me along the path in the opposite direction, until we disappeared from view.

And not a single person cried out or raised an alarm. They all goddamn bought it. *Assholes.* Or maybe they were all as scared of Judge Lewis as I was.

On the far side of the copse was a path and a conveniently placed carriage with a stylized *L* on the side—black, like Fenton's crates. I was shoved inside. Lewis crowded in behind. And, before the door was properly shut, it lurched into motion and we raced recklessly through the streets to god knew where.

~

The first person I clapped eyes on in the Russell Square townhouse was Susan. She was waiting at the door, timid and still, not daring to look up at us, but she was *there.* I was filled with such an overwhelming flood of relief to see her hale and whole that I nearly hugged her. I didn't, of course, because Lewis was already dragging me past her, fingers sunk cruelly into my screaming scar. I was thrown into that same horrible parlor, tripping on my dress and sprawling on the rug.

"Miss Franklin!" someone said, bending to offer me a hand. "Really now, my lord, there's no need to be quite so coarse."

"Marigold?" I gasped, as she levered me upright.

"Oh yes, the whole bumpkin garden is in town, you know," Lewis chuckled. "Come to chase you down like the mangy little rabbit you are."

"No."

Daisy was here?

Not in this house, I hoped. *Please, not here.*

Lewis closed the door behind him, locking it with a portentous finality. "Who do you think told me where I'd find you?"

I pushed Marigold off, steadying myself on the arm of the sofa. "Jesus fucking Christ on a pogo stick," I growled at her. "Do you really hate me *that* much? What have I done to—"

"You ruin all that you touch, Miss Franklin," Marigold said, cutting me off with such venom that I actually took a step back. "But I will not let you ruin Daisy. She means the world to me. Her wit and kindness brought me back from the precipice of my unending grief when I was widowed, soothed my every sorrow, brightened my every pleasure. She made my life worth living again. Until *you*."

"Marigold, I—"

"She forgot I existed when you entered the room!" Marigold wailed, cheeks flushed and eyes swimming. "You became her favored sister."

"No, I . . . she loves me differently than that, we—"

"You pushed her to forgo every bit of society, to chain herself to that wretched desk."

"I thought you were proud of her writing—"

"There is a hobby and then there is *obsession*. She does not eat, she does not sleep! You left and she has done nothing but scratch, and scribble, and push me away. Even in your absence you *ruin* her. Well, no more—I have found a solution."

"By selling me out to *that*?" I threw a rude gesture at Lewis.

"If I must," Marigold said, prim and grim faced. "Do not be ungrateful."

"Wasted effort," I said, struggling to get the world back under me. "I was marrying Thomas."

Marigold sneered. "A boy you can easily abandon? Oh no, Miss Franklin. I would see you unable to crawl back."

"Hah," I said. "You two are so good at colluding, maybe *you* should be marrying Georgie here. You're both conniving, masochistic *fucks*."

Marigold raised thoughtful eyes to Lewis. He leaned against the sideboard, a drink already in hand, terribly smug and amused.

Oh no, girl, I didn't mean it. Run, I thought. *He's a red flag on legs.*

"Perhaps I will," she said, mostly just to spite me.

"Perhaps I will ask you," he replied. "There is no harm in planning for a third wife while the second is in decline, is there?"

"Decline?" Marigold echoed, startled.

I pointed to the welt he'd left on my cheek. "I know that we haven't been friends, but for the sake of the woman we both love, you have to get out of here, and you have to get the police. Right now. Or I promise you'll regret this."

It wasn't a threat. It was true—and not just because of the misery she was putting me through with this farce. Daisy and Finch would make Marigold regret her bargain.

I hoped.

God, I hoped.

"The constabulary are of no help to you, Mrs. Lewis," Lewis said. "You are my wife. Well." He paused for dramatic effect. "Almost. We have yet to enjoy the pleasure of consummation."

"That's *not* happening." I took a deliberate step away.

"It is," he said casually. "Or I shall suppress *The Welshman's Daughters* in perpetuity."

Of all the threats I expected him to make, that one wasn't even on the list. It was so far out of left field that it took me several rounds of confused blinking to even parse what he'd said.

"You what?"

"When Mrs. Kempel sought to rid you from her life, she had such *interesting* things to say about your time with them in Bath. Your single-minded focus, your obsession with Daisy and her writing. It was singular, Samantha. It was *odd*." He pulled a thick bundle of papers from his inner coat pocket, creased like he had been carrying it around for weeks. He likely had. "And so, when I heard from one of my editors that a rather engaging little novel by a M. Goodenough had crossed his desk, I just *had* to acquire it."

"She finished it?" I gasped, the words torn from my throat like vomiting seawater. I whirled on Marigold. "It's done?"

"It is done, for all the good it will bring to the world!" Marigold spat. "Daisy has wasted *reams* of paper copying it out in fair hand and sending it off to every publisher in Christendom. She turned down entertainments, and dinners, and concerts. She had promised to choose a husband and be settled this season, and instead she has done nothing but waste her time on this! We cannot afford for her to throw herself away. Mother *needs* her to wed."

She promised to find a husband this season.

The words rattled between my ears, thundered in my blood.

Daisy had promised.

And she'd found *me*.

I didn't know what hurt more, that Marigold would never know, never *accept* that Daisy had found the love and commitment that her family had been pushing her to seek, or that Daisy had been submitting the book and I hadn't been there for it. Grief surged hard against my larynx, a burning, angry thing that was too large to swallow. I had missed *everything*—the anticipation, the joy, the giddy nerves. I hadn't been there to comfort her during the rejections, and I hadn't been there to celebrate the sale.

I didn't think I could resent Marigold any more than I already did, but in that moment, knowing that it was in part her intolerance that had robbed me of those moments with Daisy, I loathed the woman.

Almost as much as I loathed myself for leaving. Even though, clearly, it had been the right choice.

Daisy had finished the book!

"And you—" I turned back to Lewis, still unclear on how he even *knew* about it, let alone have the power to acquire or suppress the manuscript.

"Oh, did you not know, my darling mousie? I am the black sheep of the family. While I practiced the law, my father and elder brother were in the business of *books*."

"No," I gasped.

"Our mother was a Pickering, and my father married into the firm. My brother became sole director on the passing of our father. Sadly, my elder brother succumbed to consumption only three months ago. Leaving me, fortuitously, with the controlling share."

Smirking in triumph, Lewis shook open the bundle of papers. My eyes caught on the words *Margaret Goodenough*, and *print run*, and *debut edition*, and my heart jumped up and caught in my throat. This was the publishing contract for *The Welshman's Daughters*, with an indication that the licensing rights had been purchased *outright*, with no royalties, by Pickering & Sons Publishers. With Daisy, no, *Margaret's* neat little signature already on the bottom.

"Bastard!" I breathed, flattened. "You don't understand. You *have* to publish it."

"And I will," he said with all the condescension he could muster. "*After* you provide me with an heir."

"Oh god," I moaned.

"*After.*"

What was more important here, really? Me? And a kid that, honestly, I didn't want but would love and protect from this *monster*? Or the most important, most seminal work of classic queer literature and every good thing it would engender? Of the eyes it would open, the lives it would save, the laws it would help change, the hearts it would lead to one another?

Without it, where would the lesbian romance literature renaissance begin? What would young queer girls have to point to, to show their parents to help them come out, or to read for the first time and recognize their own impulses and desires?

Cold dread shivered down my spine as insight took hold.

This whole time I'd been assuming that because I remembered

The Welshman's Daughters, just because I'd seen the films, its existence was ensured.

But what if it wasn't?

What if I was the fly in the ointment? What if Daisy was supposed to have met her companion already, and run away with her? What if I had gotten in the way? What if the book was never published now? What if she never wrote her follow-ups, never had her hard work rewarded?

Never changed the world for the better?

Fuck.

My hands shook and I couldn't get a breath . . . I couldn't . . . I *couldn't . . .*

This book was important. To thousands of people. Millions. To history. To society. To the queer community.

To *me*.

Would I have ever had the strength and safety to live my authentic life if two centuries' worth of people before me hadn't found their strength in Jane and Mariana and that beautiful, meaningful, goddamn *history-changing* kiss before I was even born?

The choice, when put it like that, seemed easy.

"Okay. After," I agreed, trembling.

"A *boy*," Lewis growled, as if the genetic code for biological sex wasn't stored in the sperm, and he could threaten me into it. As if I'd deliver him a girl just for spite.

I'm not delivering him jack shit.

I would find a way to publish then escape before it came to that. I knew I would.

I just didn't know how yet. But that was okay.

I would figure it out.

I always did.

I just had to ensure Pickering & Sons honored their contract with Daisy. Or find a way to help Daisy to buy rights back. With the

Goodenough's finances and Lewis's scheming little brain being what they were, I could imagine that the only price that Lewis would be willing to accept was Fenton's return to subservience.

Something that I, in turn, would never allow if I could help it. This son of a bitch had us all in a neat little circle trap, where each one of us was both the insurance and bait for the other.

"A boy," I agreed.

Distraught, Marigold stumbled toward us, hands out for the contract.

"You *cur*," she spat. "You *rascal*."

He simply laughed and held the contract above his head, out of her reach, like the bully he was.

But Marigold was apoplectic. "You said you would be leaving us out of this. You said you were a man of your *word*. Oh, Miss Franklin, I did not mean for this! I did not!"

Lewis just laughed harder. "Do shut up! Women. You are all so fickle. She asks me to take you in hand, then quails when I do."

"Just promise me you'll publish it," I said to Lewis. "Promise me, and I'll go upstairs with you."

"Miss Franklin!" Marigold implored, and her face was so white from the shock of this nasty business that I thought she might faint. It served her right.

Lewis chuckled darkly, replacing the contract in his coat pocket. "You have decided to trust me?"

"I have to," I hissed back. "And I have to trust that whatever you do to me, you'll leave the Goodenoughs alone."

"Even her?" Lewis flicked his eyes at Marigold, who was trembling and teary and so, so angry. "No desire for revenge, my mousie?"

"Plenty," I seethed, outraged with myself and trying so hard to stay still that it was like a full-body tremble, skin flushed and jaw clamped. "But not against her."

"Then you are dismissed," Lewis said, gesturing magnanimously at

Marigold. Shaking with regret, Marigold fled into the hall. "Now, kiss me, wife."

Lewis mashed his mouth so hard against mine I actually stumbled.

"Get off me." I shoved him back, or tried to.

"Let us pick up where we left off, Mrs. Lewis," he said, and went so far as to actually lick his upper lip. He crowded me against the wall, and I shoved at his shoulders, but his bulk was immovable. "I keep what is mine."

"I'm not an object to be possessed!" I said. "I am a woman."

"They are one and the same."

I would have snapped something back, but his mouth was on mine again, breath-sucking and crushing. I reeled away when he stepped back, lungs burning and lightheaded.

He swung me around and tugged me out of the parlor into the foyer, toward the stairs and the bedroom at the top of them.

"Wait, slow down."

"Obey your husband!"

"Wait, wait!" I dug my heels into the rug. "Give Marigold the contract first!"

He paused, having gained the first step of the staircase and extra looming height over me, and turned to stare down at me with a grin.

"No," he said, then jerked me up about six more.

"Mr. Lewis!" Marigold cried from the foyer, scandalized. The tears were in her lashes, and her eyes cut between us, dawning realization and horror on her face.

"Get her out of here," Lewis said to the butler, who had popped into the hallway at Marigold's shout.

Lewis pulled me up steps seven, eight, nine, closer and closer to *that*.

The butler dragged Marigold to the door. She snatched at the banister, clinging hard, and I thought, *There's some damn passion, at last!*

"You gave your word you would be honorable!" Marigold shouted. "Let me have the contract. For safekeeping. You swore!"

"I did no such thing," Mr. Lewis snarled, turning to gloat, already preparing to step back down to get in her face.

Now . . .

Here's the thing with split-second decisions.

They happen fast.

So fast.

And yet, at the same time, so brain-meltingly slow.

It was all spur of the moment.

And entirely inevitable.

A choice is made in the time it takes to inhale, for a heart to pump once, for a blink to flicker shut and open again. It's a flap of a hummingbird's wings, a crack of lighting, the leap of light across a room to an eye.

And yet it feels like all the space in the world exists between their start and stop. Universes, galaxies, eons pass in the time it takes to assess a situation, consider all the angles, and arrive at a conclusion.

To make a choice.

Like grabbing hold of a yellow life jacket. Like putting your own flesh between a knife and a friend's face. Like finally, *finally* closing the gap between your lips and those of someone you had loved for so long, and so completely, that you couldn't remember a time when you hadn't.

Like stretching, ever so carefully, up on your toes, balance perfect, core tight, in tune with breath and body. Like extending one leg. Like sliding into Svarga Dvijasana, bird of paradise pose, one foot flat on the ground, extending your root into the earth, immoveable, while the other comes up slowly, knee bent, then . . .

Interrupted by the weight and momentum of another body.

Like tripping someone who is running down the stairs.

Like sending them into an unstoppable, inevitable, headlong fall.

Fun fact, the illusion of time stretching is because your brain is laying down extra sets of memories due to the high-stress situation.

Gravity carried Lewis down and down. First into the newel, face forward, then into the tread.

Crack.

Lewis flopped onto the foyer floor.

Marigold yelped and backed up against the front door, face white, eyelids fluttering and breath coming fast.

The butler froze, just to the side of the bottom stair, eyes like saucers and hands spread open in shock and indecision. Then he straightened to his full height. He took a deliberate step back, and I saw for the first time that the fall of his hair had been hiding what looked like a cigarette burn on his temple.

I thought maybe I should be flooded with panic. Instead I felt reassured, safe, *calm*. My hands shook with the adrenaline still rushing through my system, but the need to fight or flee ebbed. My face cooled as the flush of anger drained away. I straightened my spine, thrust out my chin, closed my eyes for just long enough to take a deep, cleansing, slow breath, and let it out again.

I set down my extended foot.

From rooms all over the house heads poked into the hall, followed by shoulders, bodies; a dozen in all, and all of them shuffling like beaten dogs. Slowly, the serving staff collected, ashen faced and grim, to bear final witness. At the forefront of the phalanx, Susan stood with her chin raised, a small smile playing around determination-bruised eyes.

Blood pooled on the final step, where Lewis's head had struck the ornamental molding, splitting his skull like an egg.

He was still alive.

More's the pity.

He was twitching, jerking, eyelids fluttering, throat working, and no one, not a single person under that roof lifted a hand to help him. Not *one*.

Slowly, quietly, I descended the stairs, lifting the train of my calico dress away from the gore he had scattered in his wake.

"Su-sur-surgeon . . ." Lewis begged as I crouched on the final tread.

Blood bloomed around him in a gory, glossy halo. I reached into his breast pocket and withdrew the publishing contract. I tucked it against my heart, safe between my chemise and stays.

Then I leaned down and pressed my face against the side of his. His eyes widened, mouth working, lungs laboring, body shaking.

And I'm not ashamed to admit that I smiled when I hissed just one word into his ear:

"No."

By the time I had straightened, the Right Honorable George Henry Lewis was dead.

Chapter Twenty

IN WHICH SAM INHERITS

There is nothing I would not do for those who are really my friends. I have no notion of loving people by halves, it is not my nature.

—Jane Austen, *Northanger Abbey*

For a long, silent moment, nobody moved.

I didn't fool myself into thinking it was out of respect for the dead. They were all holding their breath, waiting to see if he'd ever take another. After a few moments of staring, I addressed the collected household:

"What a horror," I said, loud, and slow, and clear. I had no idea where this plan of mine had come from, only that it'd arrived, fully formed, in the instant Lewis's eyes had rolled up in his head. "What a tragedy, for my dearest Georgie and I to have returned from our walk, only to find a burglar in my bedroom. What screaming there was when the man set upon me, when he beat my darling husband back into the hall, when he fled down the stairs, tripping Georgie on his way. Such a repugnant coward, absconding with half my jewels and stealing my Georgie's life along with them. How I wailed. How we mourned. And how *quickly* it was all over. There was *nothing* we could have done."

I met the eyes of each and every servant, and one by one, each nodded their agreement to my story. In the front of the crowd, Marigold wrung her hands at her breast and shook, silent tears falling down sunken cheeks, her dark eyes rimmed red. But even she nodded when I turned my eyes to her.

To the nearest maid, I said, "Take Mrs. Kempel into the kitchen, get her some sugary tea. In fact, take everyone in the kitchen, crack a bottle of wine, soothe your nerves. Wait, not you—" I nabbed one of the hall boys by the arm. "You are not old enough to drink, boyo."

"Am so!" he protested, as everyone shuffled off.

"All the same, off to the police with you. I need to report a crime."

"Police?"

"The, um, the Bow Street Runners," I said, dredging up the name from a misty memory of a historical mystery I'd once watched.

"Yes, my lady." He shot off.

My next instructions were for Susan, who had remained by my side, out of the way of the pool of blood. "My bedroom, the jewels—pick pieces that are easy to break down and pawn."

"Yes, my lady," she said, skirting the vile *thing* on the ground to race upstairs.

"And you," I said to the only servant who hadn't met my eyes, hadn't fled with the others, hadn't nodded. The butler. I remembered him from my first visit to the house. I remembered his obedience. His collusion. Time to see if it was loyalty or something else. "Where did he keep his legal papers? Contracts, deeds, wills, things like that?"

"There is a strongbox in his study, my lady."

"Can you open it?"

"I have the spare key."

"Good. Leave it where it is for now, but I want you to go through his office and make me a list of everyone in his pocket. There had to have been more than just Captain Goodenough. I want everything he had on them, and if he had personal items or revealing documents, I want those too. And their addresses, so I can send it all back with letters ending their indenture."

The butler, who until then had regarded me with resentful wariness, blinked three times, sucked in a lungful of air, and then burst into tears.

"All of us?" he sobbed.

Oh fuck, he'd been controlling the servants too? Well, of course he had, how else would he have been able to keep staff?

"All of you," I promised. "And if you want, you'll be released to find other positions with hefty bonuses and only the most glowing of character references."

Before he could say more, there was a knock on the door.

He let in the hall boy and a huffing constable, red faced from running. The constable's complexion promptly turned greenish as he came face to face with the gruesome tableau. With a shaking cry, I collapsed on the steps behind me, hands covering my face, and burst into tears that were only partially faked.

I'd had a traumatic day, okay?

Susan came barreling back down the stairs, all "My poor mistress," and "Yes, ma'am," and "Let me get you some brandy, Mrs. Lewis!"

And I clung to her, and buried my face in her neck, and wailed.

Okay, yeah, so maybe I was laying it on thick. But the shock and the realization had finally set in.

I had, effectively, committed murder.

I mean, was it premeditated?

No.

Did I mean to hurt Lewis?

Yes.

Did I regret it?

I didn't know.

Susan got me up and into the bedroom, which certainly looked like it had been rifled—chair toppled, vanity ransacked, jewelry box overturned. I couldn't have told the Runner whether or not anything was actually missing—I hadn't owned the stuff long enough to know the catalog of its contents by heart—but Susan could. Obviously.

I sat on the end of the bed and dabbed my face with a handkerchief while the constable asked me questions about the burglar and the mark on my face. Susan clucked over me, saying how awful it was to watch the ruffian to lay hand on her mistress, how dare a gentlewoman be struck so, which sent the Runner into tizzies of indignation and boy, was I glad that Sir Arthur Conan Doyle hadn't been born yet.

More Runners showed up, tailed by an enterprising undertaker who asked if we'd hired anyone to furnish the funeral yet (wow, talk about ambulance chasers), and the next few hours became a blur of tears and brandy.

By the time the Runners and the undertaker had cleared out, dusk had fallen. Someone had scrubbed the steps and removed the body. I was told it was customary for the dead to be washed, dressed, and laid out in their own home for final good-byes, but even the grim-faced butler didn't want the old bastard hanging around and stinking up the place. He had bid the undertaker remove the master, to spare the mistress's nerves.

Mistress.

Mistress of the house.

That was me now.

Never mind that we had never consummated the marriage, that I'd never said I do or signed the parish register, he'd made certain that in the eyes of society and the law I was his wife. And now I was his widow.

"Well, my lady," Susan said as we saw the last Runner out the door. "That was quite well done, indeed. Now, if you don't mind, you should eat something. Get up your strength for the trials to come."

"That's thoughtful of you, Susan," I said, and meant it. "I'll follow you to the kitchen, we can make sure everyone gets their fill there."

"Oh no, my lady," Susan said. "I mean, yes, I'll ensure the household is looked after. But what I mean, ma'am, is that I took the liberty of requesting a light supper for you and your guests, to be served in the formal parlor."

"Guests? What guests?"

"Mrs. Kempel's family has arrived. They're in the private dining room past the kitch—"

I was down the hall like a shot, skidding on the tiles still damp from cleaning, and through the crowded kitchen where the staff startled apart like a flock of pigeons, to the back parlor. Along with the corpse, it appeared that a handful of the servants had also vanished. I hoped they had thought to take as much portable wealth as they could stuff in their pockets. They bloody well deserved it.

I skidded over the threshold to the dining room and came to a sudden halt when just one person was there to greet me. She had her back to me but I knew the golden curl that tumbled out of her cap and danced along her nape as surely as I knew my own heartbeat. Then she turned around, and I was struck full force by the look of desperate relief in a beautiful pair of moonstone eyes.

"Daisy." My voice crackled, tight and dry. The world, which had been shifting like ship's decking under my feet since Lewis had appeared in the park, went still. Grounded. The vague burning ache that had lived behind my heart for months was quenched by the way her smile curled at the corner of her mouth.

"Sweet Pea," she whispered back. She threw herself against me, and enveloped me in an embrace so fierce I toppled into the door, slamming it shut behind us.

Daisy buried her face against my neck and breathed deep. I turned my own face into the side of her head, inhaling the lingering perfume of her rosemary hair treatment, clutching hard at her back.

Something inside me swelled, something hot and wet pooling low in my stomach, my heart fluttering against my rib cage. Daisy pulled back, lifted a gloved hand, and ran the palm over my cheek, her thumb along my bottom lip.

Then she pinched my bruised cheek hard.

"Ow!" I pushed her away and cradled my smarting face. "What was that for?"

"I thought you were lost!" Daisy hissed at me, lashes spiking with tears. I had hoped that the sparkle had been tears of relief, but maybe they were anger. "I thought you . . . come upon the town!"

"Come a what now?"

"For heaven's sake. You left with no money and I had no inclination of how you could have supported yourself if not for the, the *worst* of . . . my imagination ran rampant, Sam, and I was awake every night imagining horrible, wretched—"

"I'm already 'ruined,' Daisy," I said, unable to help the ridiculous goofy grin that just being back in presence brought out. "You made a pretty thorough job of that."

"I thought you a *prostitute*," she snapped, peevish with my attempt at lightness. "And not the well-kept kind! And when it came out that you had run away to London with the Cooper lad to be *married* . . . to believe that you had cast me aside with such speed!"

"I'm sorry." I cupped her face in my hands, gazing into her face with all the earnest emotion I could muster. "I didn't mean to make you worry."

"You *left*," Daisy said, chin wobbling, sweet rosebud mouth turning down, until she heaved a breath and broke into full-body sobs. "You *left* me. You left *me*."

"I'm sorry, I should have—"

"Why didn't you stay? Why didn't you stay and fight with me? Fight *for* me?"

"I didn't think you'd want me to," I admitted, running my thumbs over her cheeks as she kneaded my waist like a kitten. "I thought I was doing what was best for you."

"Who are you to decide that?"

"History says—"

"Oh *dash* your history!" Daisy cried, and mashed her mouth inelegantly but passionately against mine. She wept, and gasped, and kissed me over and over, fingers restless on my sides, my neck, gentle around the wound on my upper arm that still throbbed from Lewis's cruelty. "A pox on history! I care nothing for legacies, or futures, nor the opinions of others. All that matters is that you make me happy, and I would like to return the favor, for the rest of my life."

"I'm sorry. I want that too," I said, sliding the words between her lips. "But—"

"But?"

"Why?" I asked, running my fingers through her hair.

"You have the confounding habit of esteeming yourself quite highly in one moment and then expressing your certainty that you fall short of every mark of a good person and amiable friend in the next. I do wish you would do *me* the courtesy of *believing* me when I tell you that you are enough to make me happy. I'm beginning to be insulted by your lack of faith in my ability to know *my* mind and happiness."

I wiped my nose on my sleeve. "Yeah, okay, but you're still Margaret Goodenough and I'm . . . *not*."

"Not?"

"*Good* enough."

Daisy reared back, pushing hard against my chest to stare down at me, agog.

"You daft creature. Not good enough?"

"Repeating my question isn't an answer, babe," I murmured.

"Because you are as infuriating as you are fascinating. You were a puzzle at first, yes, I will admit that my first stirrings of attachment came from the thrill of unraveling your mysteries." She pecked a kiss off my lips and went on. "Then I suppose it was merely proximity and convenience—I'd never met another woman who desired her own sex before, and I wanted you simply because I might be able to have you. I thought I was not destined for love, yet you, you loved me so quickly and so fiercely that I came to understand that what I mistook for a divine flaw was instead a sublime blessing. But beyond that . . ."

"Yeah?"

"Samantha." She tipped herself forward, pressing me back into the door with the weight of her adoration. "You are clever, and kind, and encouraging. Your laughter fills a room and your anger at injustice causes my breast to surge with pride. You have rectified something within me which I thought irreparable. You cradled my broken heart in your tender hands and showed me that what I thought was shattered glass were, in truth, diamonds. You have *healed* me in a place where I did not know I was wounded. Oh, my love, don't weep—"

"M'not," I snuffled, literally moved to tears. Heat prickled along my cheeks. "I just . . . you've, uh, you've healed me too. I mean, with the . . . you really think I'm enough?"

"Yes."

"And that I'm not too much?" I burbled. "I know I can come on too strong, and I'm opinionated, and soapboxy, and—"

Obnoxious, the voice that was Dahlia's sneered.

"And my perfect match," Daisy chuckled, gentle and adoring, and cupped my face in her hands. She arched her thumbs gently across my wet cheeks, brushing away the tears. "Where I am cerebral, you shall draw me with your passion. Where you are ornery, I shall gentle you."

I wrapped my arms around her wrists, not to pull her hands away, but to keep them there. Forever, if I could. "Sounds nice," I said, the bland word not at all consuming enough for the blossoming nebula of hope flaring behind my breastbone. "If you're sure that's what you want."

"Oh, my Sweet Pea, how can you doubt that I love you when just being near you gives me breath, and fighting with you fills me with fire, and defending you grounds me, and loving you cradles me in the sweetest waters? When your face fills my imagination when I close my eyes, and I hear only your heartbeat in the pauses between my own?"

Shit. That's what I get for falling for a writer.

"I missed you, Daisy."

"I missed you so much, Samantha Franklin."

"Lewis," I corrected, and Daisy startled, eyes wide with understanding and despair. "Mrs. Lewis," I repeated, with a wry, self-deprecating thinning of my lips. "Widowed, of course."

"You are free of him!" Daisy said with slowly expanding delight. She stepped back to allow me space with a handkerchief she produced from her sleeve. It smelled wonderfully of violets. "Your new circumstances are to be envied. You are released by the expectations of society, just as you wished! You now wield all the liberty and power of a wealthy widow."

Her phrasing struck my insides like lightning. Every short hair stood at attention, goose bumps racing up my spine, my scalp shivering. I pushed her to arm's length, swallowed hard against my shock, and in a small voice, entreated her: "Say that again."

"Your circumstance is to be envied?"

"No, the bit at the end. The—"

"You are a wealthy widow."

"No," I breathed. My grin stretched so wide I thought it might split my heart in two. But that was okay—half of it was Daisy's anyway. It'd just make it easier to give it to her. "I'm *the* wealthy widow."

"I do not understand the significance of emphasizing the definitive article—"

I dragged her back in for a joyous, messy kiss.

"Sweet Pea." Daisy laughed, reeling away when we both came up for air. "What are you—"

"All this time!" I crowed, turning us in a circle, punching the air in glee. "All this time I thought I was standing between you and your destiny, and it turns out I *am* your destiny!"

"Your opinion of yourself is certainly high!" Daisy teased.

I reeled her back in. "Margaret Goodenough was supported for the entirety of her creative career by a patron known only as the Wealthy Widow.

All the history books say so. *Nobody* knew who she was, nobody could trace her origins, or family, or lineage. She just *appeared* in the authoress's life one day and made her publishing dreams come true."

"And how do you propose to do that?" Daisy asked, wonder spilling across her expression. "Mary told us everything about horrible Lewis, and my contract."

"Fun fact," I said, reaching into my stays to pull out a bundle of fold-worn papers. "Did you know that when a man with the controlling shares of a business dies with no issue and no heirs the shares pass into the trust of his widow for his future children?"

"But you're not pregnant," Daisy gasped, reaching for the contract. I let her take it, watching proudly as she unfolded it with trembling fingers.

"Something that no one else needs to know until I've figured out how to exert full control."

"Oh, Sam! My book—" She slipped the contract back into my stays, using the excuse to feel me up deliciously. "I've worked so dedicatedly on it, I've improved it immensely, everyone has said so. I wrote a new scene the night we fought. The night you—"

Left.

"I've carried it with me, the first draft of the scene I wrote for you, every day since," she said, turning away to where her reticule and bonnet sat on a chair. "Will you read it?"

"Of course."

She retrieved a folded square of paper and flicked it open for me.

I read it aloud: "'And, with infinite patience and tenderness, Jane reached for Mariana's hand, pressed between her palms the fingers of her very dear friend, and kissed her not on the cheek, but on the soft sweet bud of her . . .' Oh, Daisy, this is—" I cleared my suddenly tight throat, blinked back the heat prickling at the back of my eyes, giving this paragraph the dignity it deserved; the weight of the history it was about to make.

"Go on," Daisy urged, back ramrod straight, hands balled in her skirts, waiting. Hoping.

I swallowed hard, throat clicking, blood fizzing.

"'And kissed not her cheek, but the soft sweet bud of her mouth.'"

My heart flittered like a dove behind my ribs, my breath coming fast.

One of the most famous kisses in the history of English literature and here I was, someone who'd nearly failed grade twelve lit, reading it aloud for the first time.

Ever.

I didn't fuck it up, I thought, the realization rushing through me like a tidal wave, leaving me breathless with shock and nauseated with how quickly relief unspooled every tight-wound anxiety I clutched.

"Good news," I warbled around the mass of *feels* clogging my throat.

"Oh?"

"Your publisher loves it."

Daisy threw back her head and laughed, her whole body shaking with delight.

I folded up the page and slipped it into my stays beside the contract.

"I'm so proud of you," I told her, fair choking with it. "You finished it and you submitted it. I was afraid that I'd made you hate it. *Why* did you keep going?"

"Because I thought it would bring you back to me."

"What?"

"I thought that if I could finish my revisions, if I could find a publisher, if it was displayed in a bookshop window and you were to walk by it one day, you would see it, see my name on the cover, think of me, perhaps even miss me, perhaps even *return* to me."

I kissed her then, hoping she could read all the gratitude and pride I felt for her in it. I thought she might have, because when we parted she licked her kiss-swollen lips and sighed. "I love you."

"I love *you*," I replied, at once. My heart flipped over in my chest, beating like a jackrabbit behind my ribs. I was just ass-over-tits, disgustingly, inescapably in love. I was *fucked* with it. And I couldn't be happier.

"If I could," she said softly, words a choked croak, her palms sweating in my hands, "I would ask you something, my love."

"Ask me anyway," I dared her.

Apparently deciding to go the full nine yards, she dropped onto one knee.

"Marry me," she whispered. "Spend the rest of your life with me, Sweet Pea. Please."

I always thought it looked silly, the way people covered their mouths as soon as they were proposed to. Yet I caught myself clapping my palm across my face, mostly to keep back the squeal of surprise and delight.

My past was dead.

This past was all there was.

And I planned to grab it with both hands.

"Yes," I blurted, hiccupping the words. The room was shimmering, dancing, and I realized it was because I was looking down at Daisy through tears. "I love you," I said again.

"Then kiss me," Daisy growled, tugging herself up. The rough demand of it made my knees turn to jelly, but luckily she was there to catch me. "Kiss me."

I obliged.

"Shall we have a wedding night?" Daisy asked when we'd paused for breath, her gaze heated under the lace of her golden lashes. It staggered me, as if she'd hit me directly in the sternum.

"Heck, yeah. Now?"

Daisy laughed. "After supper. I'm not sure how much longer Marigold can delay Finch and Eliza in the garden."

"Tease," I accused.

"I am the one who proposed," she pointed out. "I am, as you are wont to say, 'a sure thing.'"

I lifted her left hand and pressed my mouth to her bare ring finger.

"My wife," she murmured. "I will buy you a ring with the sale of my first book."

A thumping on the door behind me interrupted what I was going to say next, and from the other side of the door, Finch bellowed, "Are you *quite* finished?"

"Finch, dear!" Eliza scolded him.

"What? I'm hungry, Edelweiss," he whined theatrically. "Our supper is locked in there with them—"

I wrenched the door open so quickly that Finch near tumbled into the room. He caught himself on the jamb and immediately looked me up and down. Ensuring I was unharmed. His gaze then lingered on my kiss-red mouth, my messy hair, and he smirked.

"Edelweiss?" I scoffed. "It's actually *longer* than Eliza, how is that a nickname? You Goodenoughs and your—oof."

Finch wrapped me in a hug tight enough that my feet came clear off the floor.

"Put her down, dearest," Eliza tutted, bustling past us to go straight for the buffet on the side table. "Come eat."

My eyes caught on the balloon of her belly under her dress, just barely noticeable when she was in profile to us, and she caught me looking. She smiled, and I offered her an impressed head-tip back. Girl knew what she wanted and didn't waste time. I could admire that about my new sister-in-law.

Marigold followed them in, drawn and shaken, and Daisy took her under an arm and fussed until we were seated at the small table with our plates and wine.

"I wanted to thank you, Samantha," Eliza said, laying her hand on Finch's. In the glint of the candlelight her wedding band winked gold.

"For?" I asked. Not to be obtuse or to fish for compliments, but because I wasn't sure what was known by whom.

"Exonerating Finch," Elizabeth said. "And for helping him settle his debts and escape Lewis when he had . . . had . . ."

"I rather threw you to the wolf," Finch said, staring down at his lap, shamed.

"But you pulled me back out of his jaws when it mattered," I pointed out. "So I forgive you."

He cleared his throat awkwardly, and smiled ruefully. "I am happy to see you well, and returned to us . . . Mrs. Lewis," he offered.

"I am happy to be returned, Captain Goodenough," I replied, smiling gently.

"Yes. Yes, of course, Mrs. Lewis. Only I am so confused about . . ." Marigold trailed off and slumped back into her chair, defeated by her own nerves and the dictates of polite society. She hiccupped a sob and turned her head away, pressing her palm to her mouth.

"Finch has told her everything," Daisy said, reaching around to rub her sister's back soothingly. "About the airplane, about the future . . ."

"Oh," I said. "That's fine. That's great, actually. I'm glad I don't have to hide that from you. Are we telling Iris too?"

"No!" both Finch and Daisy shouted in harmony.

Eliza and I laughed, but Marigold looked determined to say something. "Samantha—"

"I forgive you," I said quickly, saving her the mortification. "You were mad, you were protecting Daisy. I get it. I mean, it was a shitty thing to do, but I understand *why*."

"It was for her sake and hers alone I acted," Marigold sniffled. Then she sat up, firming her resolve. "And I want her to remain happy, Mrs. Lewis. By any means necessary."

"You don't have to make me sound like a terrorist." I couldn't help my smirk at her surprised gust of laughter.

"I will endeavor to do my best," Marigold said. "To behave as a sister, and friend, ought."

"Thank you. And," I added, with a glance at Daisy. She dipped her chin to give her consent. I laid my hand over hers on the tabletop, a mirror to Eliza and Finch. "You better get used to this. I'm not going anywhere. Not ever again."

With an expression that dared her siblings to comment, Daisy took up my hand, and kissed the back of it.

"It's true?" Eliza asked with compassionate curiosity.

"It is. Samantha is my wife, and I am hers," Daisy said determinately, despite the shake in her voice.

"I want there to be no tension between any of us," I entreated. "I love your sister, Marigold, Finch. I'd like to love you all like a sister-in-law."

"We are . . . what's that word you used, Sweet Pea? Ah, yes, sapphic. Lesbian. Of Lesbos," Daisy mused, chewing on the term. "How delightful, to be known by the pen of another authoress. Sappho of Lesbos."

"I guess that makes me Samantha of Toronto," I teased. "And you, Margaret of London?"

"Heavens no."

"Of Southampton?" Fenton asked, but with no real hope in his voice.

"No."

"And not of Bath?" Marigold added.

"Decidedly not. Perhaps Margaret and Samantha of Tintagel. I've heard life is calm there, the coast ruggedly picturesque, and the village quite without nosey, gossiping crowds."

"*Boggle,*" I laughed. At Daisy's raised eyebrow I said, "I'll explain later."

"And you will retire there, together . . . as wives?" Marigold said, struggling with it, but, I think, ultimately just happy to see Daisy happy. "As lesbians."

"Well, *Daisy's* a lesbian," I said, shooting them playful finger-guns. "I am, as someone once put it, obnoxiously bi."

Of course, then I had to explain what that meant.

Chapter Twenty-one

IN WHICH SAM LIVES

My characters shall have, after a little trouble, all that they desire.

—Jane Austen, *Personal Letters*

Marigold, Eliza, and Finch retired to their inn after supper, promising to look in on me again the next day. After that, the butler introduced himself as Mr. Graves and furnished me with the list I had requested, and Daisy and I worked until the wee hours of the morning making record of what was being returned or promised to whom. It was nearly dawn by the time we left the staggering pile of letters and packages to be hand delivered by Mr. Graves at an appropriate hour

Too exhausted for much more than a cuddle, Daisy and I poured ourselves into my bed around dawn, and I left a note pinned to the door for Susan to leave us alone until at least noon. On the bedside table sat that fucking copy of *The Singular Joys of Marriage for a Lady.* I took great "singular joy" in pitching it into the fire before rolling over to spoon my wife.

At three minutes past noon, Susan knocked to wake us, in order to usher me down to the morning parlor to meet my new solicitor. Daisy stayed behind, the slugabed, and purred promises to encourage me to return quickly while Susan helped me into a fine crepe gown of matte black and a sparkling set of jet jewelry likely worth ten times what Thom made in a year. And black leather boots. Not my purple Chucks, for once, because I was here. And I was staying. I was Margaret Goodenough's

Wealthy Widow, and it was time to start acting like it. Besides, purple wouldn't send the right message in this pageant of mourning.

As she dressed me, Susan explained that I was expected to keep to my widow's weeds for *at least* six months, out of respect. Only then could I start introducing purples and blues.

Lewis didn't *deserve* the respect of widow's weeds.

He didn't deserve the wake, or the paid mourners, or the lavish grand parade of a funeral that the undertaker had hinted at. And he wouldn't get it either. Lewis had no parents, no brothers, no children. No one to kick up a fuss if I shoved him in a cardboard box and a moldering hole, with the smallest grave marker a church would let me get away with.

I decided that I'd wear the plain wool dress Finch had bought me for Nelson's funeral to Lewis's. It felt appropriate that the first dress my late "husband" had seen me in would be the one I wore to bury the bastard.

Once I was downstairs in all my finery, the solicitor informed Mrs. Lewis that there would be no inquest to endure. The coroner had proclaimed the death accidental, and that "Mrs. Lewis" therefore had been declared legally a widow, and the official inheritor of the judge's estate.

"That was quick," I remarked as I sipped my coffee—*coffee! Finally coffee! Bless Susan!*

The solicitor tipped a nod to me and made noises about it being the least he could do for such a dear *friend* to him. And then he hinted that I could expect similar favors from many, many other well placed and grateful *friends* in the near future. It was only then that I recognized his name as one from the list that Mr. Graves had given me the night before.

How far in Lewis's pocket had this guy been, I wondered, *that he's this grateful to be given the means to climb out of it?*

Between us we hashed out the arrangements for the funeral (sadly, "throw him in the Thames" wasn't an option), the estate in Lincolnshire (sell it lock, stock, and barrel to the first lordling to come along with a good head on his shoulders and compassion for his new tenants in his heart—with the proviso that the new owners send Daisy and me a tithe of fresh veg from the farms every season), the fine carriages and horses (sell), the art (sell), my late husband's wardrobe (donate to a charitable institution for distribution among the poor), the furniture (we'd pick through it for what we wanted to keep and sell the rest), the Russell Square house (sell!), his shares in the publishing firm (keep!), and the staff (retain Susan, Mr. Graves, a chambermaid, and the cook, but only provided they were willing to move with us; gift the remainder with a shockingly handsome severance and glowing references).

The only exceptions were the family heirlooms—some pieces of furniture, some paintings, and some jewelry that Lewis had snatched up as his brother and father died. Apparently, Lewis had an estranged sister (good on her for going no-contact with him), and, at the solicitor's suggestion, I arranged for the family jewels and heirlooms to go to her, and *only* her. They were to be placed in trust for her as her widow's portion if she outlived her husband, and for her daughters if she didn't.

The solicitor told me to expect to have a sheaf of papers legalizing our decisions to sign by the end of week. Then the whole sorry business would be put to bed and I would have access to the accounts.

Thanks to Susan's industrious back-door conversations with the downstairs staff of the other houses on Russell Square, the morning paper, which I took back upstairs with me, reported the tragedy kindly. The household was exonerated of any wrongdoing, and the new widow Lewis's request for privacy to mourn, until such a time that she was ready to reenter society, would be honored. Of course, Mrs. Lewis was never going to apply to join Almack's or host balls, or do any of the things the other fabulously wealthy high-society dames did after their husbands had been dispatched, but the people of London didn't know that.

After Daisy and I had broken our fast on carraway-sprinkled Bath buns, I summoned the carriage. We dropped Daisy off at the inn to spend some time with her siblings. Coming out was hard, and I knew they'd need to talk, just the three of them, to ensure all was well. I had no doubt it would be, though. They loved each other too much to let it not be.

I continued on to Cheapside.

Anne, so pregnant now that it made me wince, answered the door. She waddled me into the little house and the receiving room with bitter manners. I'd broken Thom's heart, after all, so I was persona non grata. But she couldn't very well leave someone in as fine a dress as my matte crepe just standing on the doorstep, either, not with all her neighbors pressing their noses to the glass.

Joseph went to fetch Thomas from the bakery downstairs, and I took a few minutes to let them settle and to psych myself up for the conversation to come. I needn't have worried so much.

They'd read the paper that morning.

My shopping basket was already packed with all my things and sitting by the door.

When Thom slipped up the back steps, Anne and Joseph left us to speak alone.

"I'm not entirely sure I believe the story as it was laid out, wholecloth," Thom said, in lieu of a hello. "You were genuinely frightened of him."

"It's complicated," I admitted. I decided he deserved the truth. "He blackmailed me, Thomas. I didn't want him to hurt you too."

His eyebrows raised in shock. "You did it to protect me?"

"Among others."

He looked down at his callused hands again.

"I don't suppose you fancy having a baker for your second husband, then?" he asked as he straightened, aiming for a gentle humor that didn't quite hit the mark.

"I don't intend on having a second husband," I said, as kindly as I could manage.

"And yet, there has always been somebody you loved," he said softly.

"Somebody who meant more to you than me." Thomas hesitated, then leaned in to kiss my cheek gently. He quirked a sad smile. "I always had the feeling you were more attracted to my stability than me. I had hoped that you would have grown to love me."

"I'm sure I would have," I agreed gently. "And think of it this way: now you have the chance to meet someone who will genuinely love you for you."

"Suppose so," he said glumly.

I looked down at my hands, wound my fingers through my skirts as I searched for my words.

"I'm a selfish, selfish person, Thom. I'm not nice, I think. You deserve someone nice. I'll visit you in Mevagissey once you've found her, I promise. Have some tea and scones at the little café you were dreaming about adding to the bakery."

Thom huffed a laugh. "And how do you suppose I'll afford that?"

I pulled a roll of banknotes out of my reticule and pressed them into his palm.

There'd been dozens of them hoarded in the strongbox, and while I still struggled with translating the value of currency in a meaningful way, I knew that it was a criminally large stash.

Thom gasped at the sheer size of the roll. "Samantha, you can't buy my forgiveness—"

"This isn't me buying you off," I said. "This is a thank-you for your friendship when I needed a friend most." I added a second roll to the first. "And this is to thank your brother and his family for their hospitality. And, er, maybe to hire Anne a midwife. One who washes her hands, eh?"

Thom bit his lip, but nodded and closed his fingers around the money. I returned the kiss on his cheek, and picked up my basket on the way out.

It was funny—now that I was here, I knew that Margaret Goodenough had named the insidiously witless Cooper in *The Welshman's Daughters* after him. His name would for the rest of literary history stand in the company of the Wickhams and Willoughbys, Lintons and Lady Ashtons, Senator Palpatines, and Viktorias, and Prince Einons. It seemed a bit crap, but then, who except Daisy and me would know where the name came from?

By the time I returned to the house Susan had already begun the grim slog of sorting through the piles of letters and condolence cards that had begun to arrive, accepting the flowers sent our way, and reviewing the household accounts. I rolled up my sleeves and got to work alongside her.

As far as "first day of the rest of your life" could go, it had been a surprisingly good one.

~

Three months later, a widow named Mrs. Samantha Lewis moved to a quaint stone house in Tintagel, Cornwall, with just enough rooms for two grown women, four servants, the entirety of a townhouse library, and a ginger kitten with a surprisingly on-pitch yowl named Beyoncé. The house was backed by a large rambling garden, and fronted by the sea. She was in the company of her companion and very good friend Ms. Margaret Goodenough, and no one cared to comment about the change in her marital status and surname because no one in Tintagel knew any different. She was husbandless and melded into the trusting, sedate community of the village, never to be seen in London or Bath again, and that was all right by me.

I'd spent so much time wondering *why me*, and *what's the point?* and *if time travel exists for a reason, what's the reason?* and here it was.

This house, this place, this woman.

That book.

This life.

If Fenton Goodenough had never found reason to stand up to his blackmailer, he would have been sucked into a smuggling operation that would have ended his naval career. As a result, Margaret "Daisy" Goodenough would have married Judge George Lewis. In doing so, she would never have held a pen again, save to make up meal lists and send insipid society invitations. And with Lewis's violent predilections, it was entirely possible that she might never have lived long enough to do even that.

Margaret Goodenough would never have written *The Welshman's Daughters* nor become a queer icon, nor would her work have inspired baby queers and activists like me, nor romantics like Dahl. No movies, no television shows, no "green gown" costume balls, or "pulling practice" Pride floats. An entire way of recognizing, internalizing, and speaking about ourselves as sapphic women would never have existed, and *all of it*, all of it, came down to the fact that the crew of the HMS *Salacia* hadn't let me drown.

Fenton Goodenough had saved Samantha Jayne Franklin, and Mrs. Lewis had saved Margaret Goodenough. And hundreds of years later, Margaret Goodenough had saved Dahlia El Sayed, alongside thousands of other lonely, scared, closeted women who just needed to know that their love was valid.

Please, let me live, I had entreated, and I had. And because of that, so had 218 year's worth of queer love.

Once it was clarified that Daisy and I had no intentions of returning to it, Marigold and Iris had given up the Bath house, and were now ensconced in a house in Southampton that was large enough for all four adults, as well as any wee ones that were on their way. Finch and Eliza had chosen to prolong their stay in London, presumably to give their family a chance to settle and to allow Iris to make all the fuss she wanted about decorating her first grandchild's nursery as she pleased.

As I'd sold the Russell Square house (furniture, paintings of the wretched ancestors, and all), Finch and Eliza were taking advantage of my newly acquired, far less grand townhouse. I hadn't wanted one but my solicitor had recommended it, and so I'd found a sagging, dowdy thing in a mostly respectable part of town, where two old maids could visit the amusements of the capital without having to be in the crush of it all. I'd given Eliza, who was heavily in her nesting phase, a budget to furnish it for the family's use—including some rooms set aside for the children, in case any wee Goodenoughs wanted to come visit their aunties for the season, in a decade or two.

"Why did we stay in London so long?" I asked as the small carriage that my solicitor had also convinced me to keep approached Tintagel. "The air out here doesn't *smell*."

I pushed down the glass and stuck my nose out the window to prove my point.

"Of much more than the barnyard," Daisy teased, shooting me a fond, long suffering look, and rested her hand on the top of my thigh. One of the nice things of private travel was I could slum around in my jeans.

Susan and the chambermaid, Molly, had gone ahead of us to supervise the cleaning and furnishing of the house. They'd brought along with them Miss Lawrence, who was delighted to move from a kitchen maid in Lewis's oppressive house to head and only cook for two strange, joyful spinsters who called each other wife.

Daisy and I had agreed that if we had to be closeted in public, we refused to be in our own home. Lawrence had pinged my BiFi, so I figured she wouldn't have a problem with it.

Mr. Graves traveled with us, my forgiveness of his debts and my proclamation that I wouldn't pry into the reasons behind them having accidentally ensured his loyalty for life. It was like having our very own guard dog. He was traveling on the box with the driver and horses we'd leased for the journey, and jumped down to open the carriage door before we had even properly stopped at the garden gate.

"Welcome home, my lady," he said, as we alighted on the charming gravel walk.

"Glad to be here," I said, rubbing at the scar on my arm. Long travel made it ache, even now. "I am sick to death of inns."

Daisy and I each went up to our own bedrooms (joined by a door between them, but separate because as much as I loved my wife, I knew we would both need space for our stubborn tempers) to change and wash off the road dirt. My room had been supplied with those things I'd picked to keep from the detritus of Lewis's ostentatious and tasteless house—books and toiletries, the simpler gowns, furniture from the attic that looked well worn and well loved, the least ostentatious jewelry and hair things. I threw back the curtains and opened the windows to let in the crisp, early spring air.

Below me, the kitchen garden, already ringed with lavender and dotted with broccoli shoots, threw up scents of chlorophyll, herbs, and the good, clean earth. Past that, a wild tangle of neglected roses half obscured a bench set against the low stone wall that divided our garden from the rolling cliff-top meadows.

Soon enough there was a tap at the adjoining door. Daisy didn't even wait for confirmation that it was unlocked, just walked through and closed it behind her.

She came to stand beside me, golden hair loose and blowing gently around her shoulders. She held her chin high, and every line of her body was relaxed, content. I hooked an arm around her waist to draw her against my side.

"Happy?" I asked. "Do you like the house? The town?"

"*You* make me happy, Sweet Pea," Daisy said. "And, as you like to say, *fuck* the rest of it."

The word had existed for centuries, but Daisy rarely used it.

"That is way, way hotter than it has any right to be," I said.

I herded her in the vicinity of the bed.

"Say it again," I murmured into her mouth.

She fell backward on the bed, twisting at the same time so she landed on top. She straddled my thighs and ran her hands down my sides, dipped at the waist, reversed direction and skimmed them up to grasp my breasts, skimmed sweetly over the scar under my arm. She leaned down, dimpling smugly.

"Fuck," she whispered into my ear, her breath warm and shiver inducing.

We were very, very late for afternoon tea.

~

After supper Daisy and I retired to the deep leather chairs of the library with a bottle of wine, two earthenware cups, and a woolen pom-pom on a string to amuse the kitten. Candles flickered merrily in the mirrored sconces around the room and the fire had settled into glowing red embers in the grate.

"I have something for you," I said, as Daisy poured for us. "A house-warming gift."

Daisy handed me a cup with a sweet, chaste kiss. "That is kind, but I need nothing more than you, here. My truest friend. My confidant. My editor and my sounding board. My lover."

"Too bad," I replied, as she settled into her seat. "I've already wrapped it so you have to take it, now."

"Then I beg you allow me to present you with my gift first," Daisy said, digging into her stays to produce a small black box. "I promised you I would make this purchase with the money from my first book and, well . . ."

I took the box, hands shaking only a little as I flicked open the filigree lock and tipped open the top. There were two rings inside, identical save for the size. Thin gold bands carved with little curlicues resolved themselves into a design of interwoven stems and leaves. A cluster of small pearls with a yellow stone in the center was meant to be a daisy, and tucked in beside it, flat purple gems were arranged in the shape of a pea blossom.

"They're beautiful," I said, and fell in love with my wife all over again. "Put it on me?"

"Only if you put mine on me," Daisy said, sitting forward to do just that.

It felt like I should solemnize the moment she pushed the ring over the knuckle of my right ring finger, but I decided that everything Daisy was saying with her eyes were vows enough. I set the box aside, and Beyoncé immediately leaped onto the arm of my chair to bat it into a corner, and scampered after it.

From under my own chair, I retrieved a small, rectangular package wrapped in ocean-blue chintz fabric patterned with seashells. "Here."

"What is it?" Daisy said, sitting up.

"Just open it," I urged gently but firmly. "Trust me. You'll like this."

Glaring at me playfully, Daisy plucked at the knot. She pushed the fabric away, revealing a rich emerald-green leather cover embossed with a gilt frame of decorative waves.

"Sweet Pea?" Daisy said slowly, eyebrows climbing upward in her disbelief and slowly dawning comprehension. "What is . . . ?" Her words dried up and her eyes widened in awe when she turned the little book on its side to read the gold lettering on the spine.

"Oh!" Daisy breathed, and then suddenly she was trembling, face hidden in her hands, the book laying in her lap.

I crossed the hearth to snug up next to her in her chair, wrapping an arm around her waist, and resting my chin against her shoulder. Her hair tickled my cheek when I pressed my lips against her ear and whispered:

"Congratulations, babe. That's the very first copy of *The Welshman's Daughters* to come off the press."

Margaret picked up the book and reverently placed it on the side table. She threw herself at me, and made it very, very clear how overwhelmingly pleased with my gift she was. I definitely returned the favor.

An hour or so later, while we were lying on a plush blanket beside the hearth, admiring the way our rings glinted in the firelight, I surprised her with the other part of my gift—a handful of letters of congratulations signed by Fanny Burney, Anne Radcliffe, Jane Austen, and Mary Wollstonecraft.

What?

I was a rich, eccentric widow now.

I could establish a writer's circle to encourage the mutual celebration and support of a whole gaggle of female writers if I wanted to.

As a treat.

~

And that, more or less, was that. Daisy's book made a modest splash, but launched to no big fanfare. Sales of the book increased steadily as word of mouth made it popular, but it wasn't a big runaway bestseller straightaway. This suited Daisy well enough, as she had no use or desire for fame. It would get in the way of her ability to spend time at her writing desk.

It was out there, and that was all that mattered to both of us. Cult followings didn't appear overnight, anyway.

We spent our days much as we used to in Bath—writing and editing in the morning, spending our afternoons in the little town running errands, going to shops, meeting with our growing circle of casual friends, or visiting the amusements. Evenings were for entertaining, reading, and keeping up our correspondence with her secret writer's group.

PTSD nightmares would plague me occasionally, brought on by storms that drove the water against the cliffs below our cottage. Long walks in the fresh air always helped, and my trauma-induced depressions burned away like mist in the dawn of Daisy's smile.

As Daisy began work on what I knew was going to be her best-selling sophomore book, I took up my own bit of pencil to ham-fistedly record my own story.

"Are you trying to compete with me?" Daisy asked one morning from her writing slope by the window, overlooking the garden. I was on the sofa we'd put in her study, the small journal balanced on my knees. "Will you write something to best my own work?"

"Never." I stood to press a reassuring kiss to Daisy's temple. She had been teasing, yes, but there had also been a shaking thread of real concern in the question. Despite the good reviews, Daisy was still very unsure of her own talent. Imposter syndrome was a bitch.

"Then will you not tell me what you are writing?" she asked.

"When it's done, you can read it." I craned my head to look at her own papers, which she covered with a blank sheet. "What, you won't let me see either?"

"It is only fair."

It didn't take me long to write my tale. I was very familiar with the characters, after all, and knew the plot intimately. Three days later I laid the journal in Daisy's hands and said, "Let me know when you're finished."

Then I went to my room. I stirred up the embers in my fireplace, adding wood and blowing until there was a roaring blaze. It was nice to be warm, dry, on solid land. I didn't think I would ever take that for granted. Besides, the dry heat helped soothe the way the scar ached in the damp.

From my dresser drawer I fetched the pink gingham bundle. I dragged the settee as close to the fire as the protesting hairs on my calves would allow, to study my ID cards in the firelight, tilting them to make the holographic print chase back and forth across the surfaces. The sheen was the same shade of yellow as an airline life preserver.

Footsteps creaked along the landing and then Daisy entered quietly, closing the door behind her. She crossed the room in a swish of skirts and sat down as close to me as she could, thighs pressed against one another from knee to hip, warm and soft through the silky fabric of her nightgown.

"Thank you, Sweet Pea," she said. She had my journal in her hand, a bookmark already at the end. "For telling me about your childhood. For sharing your family and your life with me."

I kissed her, soft and sweet. "I wanted the truth to be somewhere. For it to be preserved in one last place before I—"

I looked down at the handkerchief bundle on my lap.

"What's this, then?" she asked, sliding a hand down my arm, tickling over the pulse point, then sliding along the back, over the knuckles, to tap what I was holding.

She stared at the cards for a moment. Then, without turning to me, laid her head against my shoulder and said, "These are from your time."

"Yeah," I said, the warmth from the fire and the warm bubble of lust and contentment from Daisy's proximity making me languorous. "Driver's license, right to universal health care card, student ID. These other two are money, believe it or not—debit and credit. Totally useless."

"They're beautiful," Daisy said.

"They're the last proof that I have that I'm not crazy," I confessed. "That I didn't make it up."

Daisy tilted her chin up, put her lips against the lobe of my ear and puffed, "I believe you. I would not have filled my stories with yours if I did not believe you."

"Then that's, excuse the pun, good enough for me."

I leaned forward slowly and fanned the cards out above the flames.

"Samantha." Daisy grabbed my wrist, but not hard. Steadying, not pulling. Making sure that I really wanted to do what I was about to do.

"It's okay."

I dropped the cards one by one onto the hottest part of the fire. They sat there for a second, the lamination glittering in the refraction of the flames. Then the clear plastic coverings curled up and blackened.

The student card was cheapest. It bubbled in the center, the corners withering like rose petals before it collapsed with a whizzing hiss into a puddle of white goo. The credit and debit cards joined the pool of molten plastic in an instant. The health card went next, sturdy government issue weight, bubbling green and yellow. Then the driver's license spat up smoke, and that horrendous picture where one pigtail had fallen out and the DMV photographer hadn't bothered to tell me imploded in a smear of greasy black.

I let the pink gingham handkerchief, stained and worn, flutter into the flame. It burned swiftly, and I made my silent and final good-bye and thank-you to Dahlia as it did.

"There." I was trying not to breathe too deeply as the plastic fumes curled around the mantle, before the colder air of the night sky sucked them up the chimney. "Now there is no more proof that Sam Franklin ever lived. There's just Samantha Lewis."

I cradled Daisy's face between my palms.

"Hello, Sweet Pea," Daisy whispered against my mouth.

"Hello, Daisy," I said, and kissed her.

I pulled away, just enough to take in the curling spray of flaxen hair, the laughing eyes, the reddened, swollen lips, the high flush on her cheekbones, obscene and beautiful.

And all for me.

"Now what?" Daisy asked, when our kisses had reached a natural pause, having turned slow and indulgent.

Please, let me live, I had once begged and now, joyfully, I could say that I had.

Happily ever after, even.

"We do this," I said. "Just like this. We live here, we raise a cat, we love each other."

Daisy smirked. “I write. You publish the rest of my books.”

“Yeah.”

“As ‘lifelong companions’?” Daisy teased. She dimpled, sunny faced and content as her namesake. “That sounds like a most excellent idea.”

“It does,” I agreed. “You know, I think I read about it in a book once.”

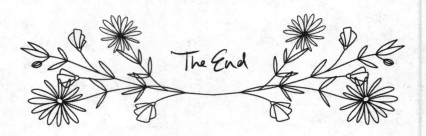

The End

Acknowledgments

My first thank you for this book goes to, as always, my family. Thank you, Mom and Dad, for believing in me, thank you to my big little brothers for not teasing me too much, with a second thank-you to Mom for being my skilled typo huntress.

We lost my beloved Granny, our matriarch and rock, while I was originally working on this novel in 2019. I am heartbroken that she won't be able to read this book. She read every single one before this. Even the one that I handed to her less than a month before her passing, rushing against the darkness, I think, to make sure that she said good-bye with each of my tales completed. I am so grateful to have been loved so honestly and so fully.

My next thank-you is extended to the Wattpad scouting and support team, and everyone working tirelessly to help bring new and wonderful stories to the readers who want them: Laura, Delaney, Rebecca, Robyn, Kimberly, Deanna, and my *incredibly* insightful editor, Margot. You are all a *joy* to collaborate with.

My most heartfelt thank-you goes to Steph. She has been through every moment of this beautiful, terrible, frustrating, incredible, uplifting, sorrow-making, and happiness-creating thing we call being a professional storyteller. I don't know what I'd do every time I hit chapter eighteen without you, Fefu.

Many thanks to Adrienne for encouraging me to lean into my hopeless romantic side. Writing is hard, publishing is harder, and finding friends who not only like your ideas but are willing to hold you when you are overwhelmed and emotional, and with whom you can cry, and rage, and laugh, and jump up and down in joy is rare and wonderful.

More scattered thanks to Sarah, for letting me borrow her freshly hatched son's nickname. Ruth, from Literature & Latte, who absolutely saved my bacon when I, like a complete numpty, corrupted my working version of the revisions file on Scrivener. My uncle Bruce, who is the king of the "fun fact." Rose, for coming up with the title while on a drizzly ramble. Rodney and Deb for holding my hand as I navigated the Wattpad community.

I feel like it's now just tradition that I thank Lucy Worsley for all of her spectacular books, documentaries, and edutainment series, which form the foundation of so much of my own domestic history research. I want to be just like you when I grow up.

And lastly, my thanks to the queer community: we are all hungry to be seen, to be loved as we deserve, and to see ourselves not only on the page, but in the happy endings. I hope this satisfies that craving.

About the Author

J.M. Frey is an author, voice actor, and lapsed academic. With a BA in Drama Lit and an MA in Communications and Culture, she's appeared in documentaries, and on podcasts, radio, and television to discuss all things geeky through the lens of academia.

Her debut novel garnered a place on the *Publishers Weekly*'s Best Books of the Year list, and subsequent works have been nominated for Passionate Plumes, CBC Bookies, Bi Book Awards, Prix Aurora Awards, Lambda Literary Awards, and named an Official Selection of a handful of international film festivals.

She lives in Toronto, surrounded by houseplants because she's allergic to anything with fur. She's also allergic to chocolate. But not wine. Her life's ambition is to one day set foot on every continent (three left!).

Book Club

QUESTIONS FOR DISCUSSION

1. What is the significance of the book title, and would you have chosen something different?

2. We all love Jane Austen, but have you read any of her contemporaries? What differences or similarities are there to her work?

3. Do you prefer books *written* in the Georgian and/or Regency eras, or contemporary books *set* in the Georgian and/or Regency eras? Why one over the other?

4. If this book was made into a miniseries, like *The Welshman's Daughters*, which scene do you think the fans would watch over and over? Is that scene *your* favorite, or just the one you think would be most popular?

5. What do *you* think *The Welshman's Daughters* is about? What about Daisy's other novels?

6. Sam begins the book as a selfish, mouthy, brash know-it-all. Discuss her arc and whether you believe she grew into a supportive, generous woman willing to focus on making her wife's dreams come true (as the author hopes she achieved!).

7. Sam learns that some traditions surrounding Western weddings are a lot less ancient than she assumed. What traditions or rituals are part of your daily life whose origins are different from what you thought they were?

8. Authors writing books set in what is for them a contemporary time period generally take for granted that their readership has a deep understanding of the cultural cues or present-day morals and issues the author sprinkles into the texts. In reading these novels centuries later, context and deeper meaning can be lost. Like the kiss between Mariana and Jane in *The Welshman's Daughters*, what moments are you aware of in classic novels that have been reinterpreted or whose meaning is not well known?

9. Sam finds her assumptions about what people believed and felt in the past challenged in this novel. What assumptions about the morals, ethics, hygiene, or technologies of other eras or cultures have you run up against, and how did it make you feel when you learned you were wrong or biased?

10. If you traveled in time, what code of ethics would you impose on yourself? If it was possible to do so, would you try to change the past or the future?